The Owls of Afrasiab

First English edition published in 2011 by Arktos Media Ltd.

Copyright © 2011 by Arktos Media Ltd. and Lars Holger Holm.

All rights reserved. No part of this book may be reproduced or utilised in any form or by any means (whether electronic or mechanical), including photocopying, recording or by any information storage and retrieval system, without permission in writing from the publisher.

Printed in the United Kingdom.

ISBN **978-1-907166-54-9**

BIC classification:
Historical fiction (FV)
Byzantine Empire (1QDAZ)

Editor: Michael J. Brooks
Cover Design: Andreas Nilsson
Layout: Daniel Friberg

ARKTOS MEDIA LTD
www.arktos.com

The Owls of Afrasiab

The Secret Story of Constantinople 1453

Lars Holger Holm

ARKTOS
MMXI

'Everywhere spiders weave their webs and seem to feed on nothing.'

– Statistics? Well I'm sure they have something to do with our current situation, so would you be so kind as to tell me more about it while we now together move down towards the Horn to make sure everything is under control there as well.

Said and done. As soon as Longo had made sure the guards had proper instructions, and that these would be passed on over the entire Theodosian wall, the imperial party, now including Longo and Francis, remounted their horses and rode off along the Marmara Sea wall. Towards noon they reached the Petrion Gate by the Phosphorion Harbour, where they met with Lucas Notaras, Grand Duke and Admiral of the Byzantine fleet. Scattered enemy ships still dotted the Bosporus, but most of them had already anchored beneath the Double Columns north of Pera. Other vessels patrolled the Sea of Marmora in search of potential weaknesses in the sea wall. Apparently they feared no counter-attack from the defenders as long as no ships could be seen moving inside the Golden Horn and the boom was down.

Apart from being a distinguished naval military officer, Lucas Notaras was also a gentleman and an experienced negotiator. He was now in his fifties, in full possession of himself, determined and easily recognisable from afar through his curly dark hair and characteristically noble profile. As trusted counsellor already to Constantine's brother and predecessor on the throne, John Palaeologus, he had earned a reputation for steadfastness *and* flexibility, characteristics not necessarily considered mutually exclusive. Much to Secretary Francis' dismay he also had the full support of Constantine.

As the party approached the Petrion tower they saw the Grand Duke waving at them. He had been alerted to their arrival. Like Constantine he appeared in full regalia. When they had all saluted each other, the Emperor proceeded to interrogate the admiral on his preparations. Notaras briefed him.

– As soon as we heard that the enemy fleet was approaching, and we were informed that the boom was properly down and secured, we immediately began to interlock some of the larger galleys to prevent any sudden attack or intrusion along its length. We likewise arranged the remaining ships in the harbour to form an unbroken chain. But our principal line of defence is right here, along the chain, where we have stationed ten of our largest ships, among them Doria, Gataloxa of Genoa, Filomatia, and Gura of Candia. We also have soldiers posted by the wall of Galata to ensure that the chain is safely attached also on their side. I just received a report from Alex Diedo, the harbour commander, that we have completed our work and now wait for your further instructions.

Constantine raised his right hand to his forehead to shield out the glaring sunlight as he focused on the wall of vessels constituting the first line of defence in the Horn. So far there was no movement to be seen on the hills opposite.

– What about Galata? he asked. When on our way down here we could not detect any Genoese activity whatsoever on its shores.

– Well, the Grand Duke sighed, they maintain their declaration of neutrality, and so they take pains not to be seen preparing for the defence of their town, obviously hoping that the Sultan shall ignore them.

– And how do we know that they won't just open their gates if and when the Sultan asks us to either surrender in peace or fight and perish to the last man? Constantine asked.

– We don't. Notaras said. The only thing we may count on is the common responsibility imposed on the Genoese here and in Galata. If word spreads that they have opened their city to the Sultan without even trying to defend it, I don't think they will be very popular with their folks at home. In reality, that's the only guarantee we have.

Constantine nodded. As he turned to Longo to ask for his evaluation of the situation, the two men, pointing out various points and strongholds on the coasts, moved closer to the battlements, momentarily leaving Francis out of hearing but face to face with Notaras.

– You seem very distressed by the fact that the Genoese have declared themselves neutral, Francis furtively said, a faint smile shading his lips.

– Yes, why shouldn't I? It would be a good deal better to know that they were on our side.

– *Our* side? Francis said, demonstratively widening his eyes. I didn't know you really had a side.

– What are you implying? Notaras said, his face darkening.

– Oh, considering that you, in this time of dire need for the Holy Mother of all Christian cities, have chosen to place most of your legendary fortune in Italian banks, and bought yourself not only Genoese but also Venetian citizenship, I thought that perhaps you had already begun to plan ahead for a life out of the Sultan's reach.

– How do you know about my citizenships? Notarias asked, taken by surprise.

– Oh, what and where would we poor state secretaries be if we didn't have our – informers? Well, where will you go, to Venice or to Genoa?

– This is insidious. In the service of the late Emperor, I have, with his full consent, been bestowed two honorary citizenships for my efforts to ensure the continued support of the Italians in our struggle to safe-guard the most holy seat of the true Christian church against the infidels. If it hadn't been for me and my contacts, we would not only be facing the Turks at this hour; we would also have the Genoese and Venetians against us in open insurrection!

– I see, Francis said. – I suppose that is also the reason why you have been heard saying that you'd rather see the Sultan's turban in Constantinople than the mitra of the Pope?

– I never said such a thing!

– Of course not. It is only an unsubstantiated rumour, but you know how these things are. If not immediately stamped out they spread like wildfire. Soon it becomes too late for truth to prevail; the lie, inevitably, rears its ugly head. Now, I suppose the simple fishermen in your part of town don't mind hearing that you have taken a firm stand against the union of the churches. I just thought that being a senior military officer you would not primarily count upon a miracle to save the city, but rather rely upon the strength of its walls and the skill, courage and tenacity of its defenders.

– Enough! Notaras exclaimed. – Who sat in on the entire church meeting last year, trying to reconcile the claims made by the Pope through his envoy Isidore of Kiev and those of our own ostriches, refusing to see that the Catholics of Italy are our only hope, at least for the time being? I did! I don't mind that nobody thanked me for it. In fact, I was distrusted and depreciated by both camps, and this just because I clearly realised the precariousness of the situation and acted accordingly. The only thing that matters to me, then and now, is that our holy city doesn't fall into enemy hands. This is what I am here to do, and so I shall. And as far as you, State Secretary George Francis, are concerned, I shall not even mention the disaster you have reserved for us by magnanimously and single-handedly recalling the Emperor's marriage proposal to the Doge. If you only knew how much money and effort I have put in to try to restore some of Foscari's confidence in us, you would be utterly ashamed of yourself speaking to me the way you do!

Francis was just about to answer but the Emperor and Longo returned to them whereby their amicable conversation was involuntarily brought to a halt. It was obvious that the two men held grudges against one another, but whether they liked the idea or not, they would now have to join forces to defend a city to which, everything considered, they both owed their existence and loyalty.

Chapter 4

It was a dark afternoon. All morning menacing clouds had been amassing to the north, and by early afternoon squalls rushed down southward through the narrow straits of the Bosporus, everywhere whipping up white foam.

– Captain, the Turk urges us to tack to shore. I'm afraid if we don't stop immediately he will unleash the bears of the Throat-Cutter! It was the helmsman expressing his alarm for the second time.

– Let him try to sink us as best he can, Captain Rizzi answered. If he possesses only the slightest sailing experience, he must realise that for us to try to reach the shores in these winds would be utterly dangerous, if not downright impossible. Besides, from what I've heard, his aim is as wide and puffy as his turban. With this wind in the rear we'll be in Constantinople in the blink of an eye. He won't even have the time to launch a vessel to come after us before we're…

…"there", he was about to say but the ship was literally cut in two by the fierce blast. Rizzi just had the time to see all the crew amidships colour the water red while their severed limbs began to spread in the strong current, before he and the helmsman found themselves up to the neck in cold water. Seconds later Turks from both sides of the Bosporus took to the sea and rapidly closed in on those remaining crew members who were unfortunate enough to be able to swim, fishing them out of the waters with hooks and nets. They were delivered to Rumeli Hisar more like a bunch of half drowned cats than like human beings. And for sure, the fate that awaited them was hardly preferable to being drowned as a cat.

The prisoners, wet and freezing, were rounded up on the inner court of the fortress. The question was asked if their captain was still among them. When no answer was given the Turkish soldiers, on order of the

Sultan who had now arrived with his retinue, began to pull one listless body after the other out of the human heap and drag them to a scaffold placed in one corner of the square. By then the crew members selected began to come to life as they realised what was going to happen to them, but it was unfortunately too late for some. So quickly had they been dragged to the execution block that they hardly had the time to express their agony before their heads rolled. As the crew now clearly understood what was soon going to befall all of them if they didn't give up their captain, they all looked at him in such a way that it was impossible for the Sultan not to recognise him. At this point Rizzi himself realised there was no way he would be able to escape his destiny and he stepped forth.

He was brought before the Sultan and thrown to the ground. Through an Italian interpreter the Sultan addressed him,

– What's your name and where do you come from, wretched Italian?

– I'm Captain Antonio Rizzi, of the Serene Republic of Venice, he answered.

– You have been found guilty of deliberately violating the regulations applying by ordinance of our Majesty to all ships navigating these straits to report their cargo, crew and destination to the local authorities, and, if this is found to be relevant, to pay appropriate taxes. Now, if there is anything you have to say in your defence of this flagrant offence before I decide your fate, this is the one and only time to do so.

Rizzi, realising that since two Venetian ships had already managed to slip through the Throat-Cutter and still hang on to their lives, the Sultan had no choice but to forcefully set an example once he finally got hold of someone who had openly defied his ordinance. In other words, since Rizzi suspected that no matter what he was going to hang for this, he seized the occasion to tell the Sultan what he really thought about him. Not only was this the mouse who roared, but one who on second thought would probably have preferred to just have had his neck broken in the trap. However, his voice was clear and without a trace of fear as he declared,

– Your Majesty, it was not my intention to try to escape without reporting to your harbour command, but the fact was that the wind was too strong to be negotiated while beating against it, so I felt I had no other choice than to spur the ship on to its destination.

Had Rizzi stopped right there, he might still have stood a chance of appeasing the Sultan, but alas his good judgment abandoned him just when he needed it the most. Death defying he therefore continued,

– I must also point out that Your Majesty has usurped land that according to the peace treaty concluded under your father Murad, endorsed by yourself at your accession to the throne, belongs to the Byzantine empire. Since Venice enjoys trading privileges with the Emperor, we are in everything that concerns our trade through the Bosporus subject to his jurisdiction. Your new ordinance is in direct violation of all previous agreements. We Venetians are unable to honour such breach of contract.

The apparent obstinacy of Rizzi in the face of hard facts flung Mehmet in a fury,

– The treaty is null and void! he shouted, and what you, whether you're Venetians, Catalans, Genoese or Greeks have to relate to is what I tell you to do, because I'm the master of these straits, and no one, do you hear, no one gets past me without my explicit permission! Now, since you're not even showing the slightest repentance for your criminal act, and since it matters to me a great deal that the message is hammered home once and for all among you merchants, as well as in Constantinople, I shall have you impaled in front of your own men.

The scene now taking place was so obscenely cruel that most of the crew couldn't even bare to watch it. In the blink of an eye, Captain Rizzi, who had stood up boldly in front of the Sultan himself, was again flung to the ground and stripped of his remaining clothes and then held to the ground while a sharpened wooden pole, about 5 foot long, was driven up his rectum with a sledge hammer, sending a stream of blood, bile, faecal matter and massacred entrails along his legs while he was helplessly put up on display in the square like a butchered hen ready to be roasted. The desperate cry, soaring towards the black, wind driven sky of November, from the commander as he received the lethal thrust through his belly was blood chilling. It was followed by an ominous silence. His forcibly stretched out arms and legs suffered spasms horrible to behold, and framed the picture of his drooping head where the eyes, shaded by wet, blood-stained wisps of hair, bare witness to the fact that he was still alive while suffering indescribable pain. Indeed, the executioners thrust had been perfect and ensured that the pole had stopped short of the heart. For what seemed an eternity to the crew – and there were even members of Mehmet's retinue who seemed on the verge of throwing up – he lingered on until he was finally bled white.

For good measure the Sultan then decided to have a few more crew members decapitated, but suddenly the afternoon seemed to grow too cold and damp even for him and his retinue. Apparently satisfied with what he had achieved, he put an end to the gruesome procedure. There were now in all no more than ten men still alive, but the Sultan apparently felt he needed some survivors to spread the news. Thus they were all released, save a young ship boy whom Mehmet had found so pleasing that on the spot he picked him out for his harem. Already that same evening the remaining crew, terrified at what they had experienced and hardly able to believe their luck, were huddled together on a small vessel and rapidly brought down the straits to be deposed beneath the walls of Galata. In this way it came to pass that during that same night, just as Mehmet had intended, the ghastly story of the unfortunate Antonio Rizzi and the majority of his crew was passed from tavern to tavern in Constantinople and Galata by the terror-stricken survivors themselves.

Another dark and cloudy day, this time in December, the news of the seamen's tragic fate finally arrived in Venice. Elenor, Rizzi's wife, was at home with her two daughters when a messenger arrived from the port, handing her a letter from the Governor of the Venetian colony on the island of Argos. In it the gruesome details of her husband's death were disclosed along with the formal regrets of the loss of a trusted captain and exemplary member of the Republic. Condolences to the deceased's family members were included.

The words struck her like thunder bolts and, numbed by the shock, she fell in a pile to the tiled floor. The sound was heard and alerted the chamber maid. Entering the room she found her mistress in a state of apathy. Elenor's brother Giovanni – visiting Venice partly to look after his sister while her husband was absent, partly in an attempt to convince the council of the Republic to supplement Genoese reinforcements to Constantinople – was in the house and immediately sent for. He found Elenor reclining on a canapé gazing motionlessly into the richly decorated ceiling. It was apparent that she was not actually watching it. Her mouth, half open, had frozen in the very image of agonising pain. Her left arm and hand hung limply down the side of the couch. Her entire body was listless and her face pale as ivory. Giovanni, seeing the letter that had fallen out of her hand, picked it up and glanced through it. He sat down beside her and caressed her hair. He caught her hand and placed it above his own heart. There was a long, long silence. Finally he could feel her hand regaining some life. She grabbed his shirt and held on to it like someone ship-wrecked to floating debris.

– Antonio … she whispered. Antonio … how could they do this to you … why are always the few good ones prematurely lost to the world … my hero and husband … and that Turkish animal … Oh, Lord Jesus!

– My dearest sister, Giovanni said. Your husband, though not by birth and blood a Genoese, was a brother to me. We fought two campaigns together against the French, and as you know, he once saved my life. I am indebted to him, and he was your husband. Now that he's dead, how can I repay him? By caring for you, for Lucia and Mariana? It goes without saying. But that it is still not enough. He merits even more. This is what I will do for him, for you, for all of us, and may God and Christ be my witnesses: I hereby solemnly swear, in the name of my sister Elenor Maria Isabella Rizzi and the Holy Mother, that I shall avenge her husband's ignoble death by killing the perpetrator of this crime, should it be at the expense of my own life!

At first Elenor remained motionless, then slowly caressed his hand,

– Dearest brother, it's enough that he's dead. If I were to lose you as well, despair would be complete. There is of course nothing you can do to stop this beast from freely roaming the earth. I know your pride, Giovanni, but you would only risk your life for nothing, and you'll end up the same way…

– Never, Giovanni replied. – Don't you worry about that. The Sultan, like the rest of us, is vulnerable too somewhere. It's only a matter of finding that point. Now, let us pray together.

Three days later, after having crossed Lombardy on horse back, Longo was back in his native Genoa. A week later he had mustered his force of four hundred seasoned mercenary fighters and was ready to set sails. In Rhodes and the Genoese island of Chios he recruited an additional 300 soldiers.

Had it not been for the brutal execution of Antonio Rizzi, it's very doubtful whether Constantine would ever have received the reinforcement of so many skilled Genoese soldiers under commander Giovanni Giustiniani Longo's leadership. Had Longo himself been older, it is probable that he, in spite of his rage and his solemn vow, would finally have come to renounce the idea of travelling to the very needle point in space where one could be absolutely certain that the Turk would strike next with overwhelming force. But he was thirty-five, at the height of his career and he felt invincible. No matter what scheme it would take, whatever the cost, he was going to challenge the Sultan and, in the name of the cross and family honour, personally liquidate him.

Chapter 5

The Sultan's army, amassed from all corners of the expanding empire, could be seen moving like a gigantic caterpillar over the undulating hills of Thrace. A hundred thousand troops composed of Turks, Tartars, Bosnians, Albanians, Serbs, Greeks, Hungarians, Italians, irregular bashibazouks, Anatolians advancing in impeccable Roman formation and, last but not least, the Sultan's pride, the elite fighters forming his personal guard and the army's backbone, the Janissary regiments, exclusively recruited among Christian boys of conquered territories; all these men, with all their horses, tents, women, children, weapons, ammunition, foundries and siege engines, slowly but relentlessly advanced towards their promised prize: Constantinople. The Sultan was impatient but knew he had to restrain himself; there was no way this enormous convoy could be made to move any faster. Because in its midst a strange, inflexible creature determined their pace.

Seventy oxen were harnessed in front of it and charged with the task of pulling it forward. It was placed on an enormous wooden cart to which two hundred men catered in order to prevent it from sliding or tipping over. On top of this wooden construction the creature itself rested in terrifying, sphinx-like majesty. It had a body and a trunk that made a trumpeting elephant seem like a delicate animal. It was at present silent, but its fierce roar and sharp breath could awaken the dead and its charge topple fortresses. It was a creature that was to haunt young Leonardo da Vinci in his dreams, a creature the command of which would have made Archimedes the founder of a new Rome, a paradoxical monster of the past with a future ahead. Its head alone, with its never closing wide open jaw, was a battering ram ten times more powerful than anything previously brought to bear upon a line of defenders. Indeed, it was the *instrumentum diabolicum*, the uncanny visitor from a future yet to come, the triumph of destruction over and against man's fragile creation. It had no mother. It had only been fathered, and its father was certainly not the one to whom the prayers in Hagia Sophia were unanimously directed. The creature, strange as it may sound, was the one and only son of a human progenitor. But its father was not content to remain unrecognised and unknowable in his seven heavens. On the contrary, he wanted his intentions to be clearly known to the world. As a matter of fact he had already visited Constantinople in person not very long ago.

During the summer of 1452, scarcely a year earlier, a stranger from the remote forests of Transylvania had been granted audience to the Emperor. In a heavily accented but nonetheless surprisingly fluent Greek he presented himself as a Hungarian of German descent, named Urban. Asked what he wanted, he answered he had in his possession the engineering designs and the mathematical calculations necessary to construct, to his Majesty's benefit and to the detriment of all his foes on land and at sea, a weapon of total destruction bigger and more devastating than anything the world had seen so far. All he needed was a large enough foundry, a fully equipped smithy and fifteen tons of the best bronze available. Within three months, Urban claimed, he could have his beast ready to be unleashed on his Majesty's enemies, blowing them to tiny bits. For this service he would only ask the modest sum of one hundred thousand ducats.

The Emperor, after having examined the details of the proposal with his ministers and chief engineers, answered that he was very interested in the idea, but he also said that he neither had at his disposal the raw material necessary nor the, surely not extortionate but for the sadly impoverished city, still considerable amount of money he wanted in recompense. On this Urban replied that during his stay in the city he had noticed that there were literally dozens of churches that were no longer in use, and that all of them seemed to have bells of various sizes cast in bronze. This is true Constantine retorted, but unfortunately it would not make much of a difference.

– Even though the bells of these churches are no longer tolling, my people would regard me as a traitor of the empire and the true faith if I gave the order that the holy bells, even if no longer in regular use, should be dismantled and used for the making of guns. Believe me, I wish it were different, and that popular opinion were willing to consider the dire need of sacrifices of this kind to reinforce the city's defence against an increasingly aggressive enemy. However, I do not think I can do much about it right now. You see, most generous gentleman, my position is precarious for the sole reason that I have not clearly spoken out *against* those who say that we must ratify and take concrete measures to manifest the union of the Western and the Eastern churches. We are bound to this union by a written agreement made under supervision of God himself. But my people, alas, are violently against it. I can't risk at this hazardous time to indirectly promote their insurrection. I need their support in every imaginable way, and so my hands are in this regard tied behind my back.

Urban, willing to arrange his remuneration in separate installments, still tried to convince Constantine that the plan was practicable by pointing out that the material could also be taken from vessels, statues, old gates and so forth. Still, the Emperor felt obliged to decline, in the final instance on the grounds that the prospective cannon was primarily a weapon of attack, and that the Empire, reduced in power and strength, was in no position to consider an attack on its enemies.

– Your Majesty. Understanding the nature of your dilemma, I nonetheless believe you are about to make perhaps the biggest mistake of your life, Urban replied, an ambiguous smile shading his face framed by vigorously shaped reddish hair and beard.

– Why do you say that?

– Your Imperial Majesty, please realise that I am a stranger around here, and that I shall have to try to put my talent to some good use in order to survive in this foreign land.

– Do you thereby intend that as soon as you are out of here you will take your proposal straight to the Turk?

– On my Christian honour, your Majesty, I would never contemplate doing such an abominable thing. It is however my duty, as an obedient warrior of Christian denomination and an engineer skilled in the latest technologies, to inform your Majesty that science knows of no borders and that progress in its name may have to be bought at the expense of human lives.

With a bow, a little bit too deep to seem altogether in keeping with the stern expertise he radiated, Urban bid farewell and left the Imperial council held in the audience chamber of the Blachernai palace. For some time afterwards he was known to linger on in Constantinople, trying to subsist on a small salary which the Emperor had granted him. As resources grew more and more scarce in the city, even this small allowance had a tendency to not be forthcoming. Urban eventually lost patience and left the city on a Cretan ship eager to get back to Heraklion. A few days later, Sultan Mehmet II, personally dispensing the finishing touches to his fortress Rumeli Hisar on the Western bank of the Bosporus, was told that a Hungarian engineer wished to meet with him in regard to an urgent matter. The Sultan, bored at the conversation of his ministers which he overheard from behind the anonymity of a screen, had them continue their debate while he himself, in secrecy, made himself ready to receive the strange guest, whom he intuitively felt had some quite vital services to offer. This assumption, in fact, proved to be an understatement.

– Can you make me a cannon capable of firing a stone-ball this wide?, the Sultan finally asked and stretched his arms wide to illustrate what calibre he had in mind.

– I can make you the cannon, Urban said, but I can't guarantee you its fire capacity and range.

– What if that matter could be solved, how much devastation could a weapon like that possibly inflict upon stonewalls thirty feet high and fifteen feet thick?

– A cannon like that would bring down even the walls of Babylon if your Majesty so wished.

Though it wasn't clear why Urban considered the once no doubt mighty walls of Babylon superior to those of Constantinople, the Sultan declared himself satisfied with the cross examination. He concluded a deal with Urban that would promise him four times the salary he had asked for at the Emperor's court in case he was to succeed, and a somewhat more uncertain future in case he wasn't. Meanwhile, all expenses would be covered and no efforts spared. Mehmet then issued an order that all the bronze bells still remaining in the Christian churches in Thrace should be taken down and without delay be brought to Adrianople.

Chapter 6

The news of Sultan Murad's death in 1451 had occasioned happy feelings at the court of the Black Sea empire of Trebizond. At the time George Francis was paying a visit to its Emperor, John IV Comnenus, on behalf of his own master, who, though long since a widower, had been incited by his mother and public opinion in Constantinople to remarry. To appease the strong anti-Latin sentiments among his citizens Constantine had concluded that a Christian bride of Orthodox origin would be the best choice. Francis, happy to oblige, suggested a Georgian princess of his knowledge. Tireless as ever, he was already on his way back from Georgia to Constantinople to inform the Emperor about the results of the negotiations when the news of the Sultan's death reached him. Unlike Emperor John at his Trapezunt court, Francis felt this was a bad omen. Better informed on the character of Murad's successor than his host was, it seemed obvious to Francis that the truce with Byzantium, which had been mutually respected during the reign of Mehmet's father, would sooner or later – and rather sooner *than* later – come to an end. In vain he had tried to explain the nature of the game to John. Summoned to a banquet at which toasts were even frivolously proposed in name of the new Sultan – still believed to be little more than a willful youngster – Francis daringly asked to speak to the assembly as the laughter accompanying the Emperor's latest jest abated. Suddenly there was silence and all attention in the festively-lit hall turned to the Greek envoy. Francis rose from his seat, which was to the right of the Emperor in honour of the visitor representing no less than the Byzantine Emperor, took a good sip from the wine cup to steady himself, and began his speech,

– Your Majesty. With all due respect. We should perhaps do well in reminding ourselves that for every head cut off from the Lernian hydra two new ones emerged. The new Sultan is such a hydra. Although hardly twenty years of age he has developed several heads. One is belligerent, another deviously diplomatic. A third loves hunting, a fourth one speaks Persian, Hebrew, Greek and Latin fluently. A fifth knows the entire Islamic jurisprudence by heart, a sixth is accurately informed about the fathers of our church. A seventh drinks copious amounts of wine while the yet another studies maps, siege engines and weapons of mass destruction. The scope of his general intelligence and single-minded ambition is matched only by the fierceness of his many passions. He already has children but is said to prefer hardly mature boys to satisfy his lusts. He is, as you can understand, a perfect monster, but one to whom the designation of neither intelligence nor discipline can be denied. Above all, he's the most formidable, the most ruthless and implacable opponent to our Christian world since Tamerlane. And he will never give up the ambition to conquer every area still within his reach in Christian hands. Therefore, most venerable Majesty of the glorious House of the Comneni, I dare to disagree with the optimism expressed among our many friends around this table. Instead we should all concentrate on how to best unite and counter this formidable new threat to our peace and prosperity.

For a moment the silence around the banquet table grew embarrassed, but then the Emperor, still in a genial mood and known to always have a ready answer , asked,

– Very well, but if this is the case, my dear Francis, how can the new Sultan's alleged hatred of Christians and Christianity be reconciled with the fact that, on his ascension to the throne, he allowed his father's widow, the radiant Mara of Serbia, to escape a long and mournful seclusion in the House of Sorrows. Instead, so we heard, she was sent been back to her father, the despot Brankovich of Serbia with all honours. How can this be if he's such a sworn enemy of Christendom?

Francis owed the Emperor and his guests an answer to that question, but just as he was reflecting on what to say, he was struck by a brilliant idea. Instead of continuing the debate, for which he as an inveterate courtier had both the knack and the patience, he declared that he needed some time to think about his answer and hastened to retire to his quarters. Francis made sure not to appear in any way offended by the apparent naïveté of his host, and with one or two rather dry jokes he prepared for an acceptable withdrawal. Soon afterwards the happy ambiance returned as a swarm of jugglers entered to entertain the guests. Francis, on the other hand, hastened through the sparsely lit galleries of the royal palace to reach his quarters located in one of the wings. Guided by two wax candles, overlooking the tranquil haven of Trapezunt, its ships flooded in moon light, he then penned the following letter to his master.

"*Your Majesty,*

By my arrival in Trapezunt I have been informed that the Sultan is dead, and that the Sultana most honourably and with full consent has returned to her home land and her parents. When I got to hear about this, I thought about the purpose of my journey and decided to make your Majesty aware that the two prospective marriages I have been sent out to investigate, by far seem less purposeful and desirable to me – and insofar this would please you – than it would be to direct all efforts towards gaining the above mentioned Sultana as a wife. As I am absolutely sure that the parents of the Sultana would happily agree to this union, I strongly recommend your Majesty to send a member of your court, or a monk, as your trusted envoy, so that the persons concerned could without delay bring this matter to a happy conclusion."

Francis put down his pen and remained transfixed by the magic of the full moon, creating a whole theatre of imaginary shapes and figures in the harbour. A few lanterns on the decks of the ships hovered like fire flies in the air. He heard a lute playing, and through the open window streamed the fragrance of oriental gardens. He was convinced. A union with Brankovich of Serbia would tie him in as a military ally. Simultaneously it might buy them time with the Sultan, who by this gesture would for the time being be invited to engage in diplomatic rather than war activities. It was a golden opportunity, and Francis was so eager to see his idea materialise that he couldn't even wait for a messenger to arrive at Blachernai palace. That same night he dreamed that he went to Constantinople to deliver the message to the Emperor in person. As he fell down to kiss his feet, Constantine raised him up and kissed his eyes. At this point Francis blissfully woke up, feeling not only the immense gratitude of his friend and master, but also the sweet smell of the Holy Spirit fill the room. It might just have been the moon still shining through the shutters, but Francis had the sensation of being embraced by a holy, supernatural light. As he looked at his arms and hands, he saw them glow in the darkness too. He decided to make a mental note of the exact date of this extraordinary revelation. It so happened that it came about in the early morning of May 29, 1451.

Chapter 7

Two years later and the time for teary-eyed wish-thinking on the part of trusted ministers had come and gone. By now Francis was only all too aware that all marriage plans would have to be postponed indefinitely. Meanwhile he hadn't just been content waiting for Mehmet to show up before the walls. On the contrary. Tirelessly he had used all his energy, intelligence, patience and cunning to father diplomatic epistles. On behalf of Constantine he then dispatched them to potentates all over the Mediterranean basin, on the Balkan peninsula, even as far as to the Hungarian, German, French and British kings.

However, at the time when the Turkish fleet had begun to gather at Gallipoli, to send letters by sea had become increasingly risky. Francis tried to compensate for this by having several copies made and sent by alternative routes. The problem was that the alternatives had been reduced to two very dangerous missions: one was to try to get past the steadily growing concentration of enemy troops in Thrace; the other was to try to out-sail Turkish ships in the Dardanelles. Even though Greek and Italian seaman-ship was still undoubtedly superior to Turkish naval skills, the latter had a fleet vastly superior in numbers to what any Greek and Italian convoy could ever hope to muster. And even though Francis had reason to believe that some of his letters must have reached their destined recipients, and even though they basically contained the same plea for man power and material help as the ones he had been sending one, two and three years earlier, he now began to doubt that any assistance would be forthcoming in time. For two months no clear and positive answer from the outside world had arrived by either land or sea. But there was a slight possibility, Francis believed, that the Venetians, encouraged by the Pope, would finally endorse their promise to send reinforcements.

In principle it was a well founded expectation save for one annoying detail. Francis himself knew that in the end he was perhaps the one to be principally blamed for the unduly prolonged absence of Venetian ships and supplies. Constantine had never spelled it out, but there were moments when his silence was eloquent. Sometimes, in Francis' presence and in connection with the dynastic question, the Emperor's gaze became clouded, as though he had suddenly been reminded of an embarrassment. Francis could not explain to himself why he felt awkward about it – his intentions in this matter had always been dictated by a genuine concern for the Palaeologi imperial dynasty – but over time he could not help suspecting that Constantine somehow actually regretted having granted him a free hand to find him a suitable bride. What had happened?

Some years earlier Francis had both drafted and sent a marriage proposal on behalf of Constantine to the Doge of Venice. The Emperor's ambassador was favourably received by Francesco Foscari who consented to give the hand of his beautiful daughter in marriage to what was still only the brother of the reigning Emperor, albeit simultaneously the despot of Morea on the Peloponnese (always of key interest as a trading post to the Venetians) and the heir-apparent to the Byzantine throne. When in 1448 Emperor John died, their mother intervened and made sure Constantine, her favourite son, was proclaimed new Emperor. At this time Foscari thought the time ripe to remind him of his marriage proposal. He received a curt answer from the Byzantine court that the prospect of an intimate liaison with the most noble house of the Republic was no longer of serious concern to the Emperor. Foscari correctly interpreted this to mean that Constantine at present considered himself too superior to be betrothed to his daughter. He was deeply offended, realising that Constantine regarded the possibility of a political, military and economic pact between Venice and Byzantium as a misalliance. What he didn't know was that it was not primarily the Emperor, but his childhood friend Francis, who now suddenly opposed the plan he had himself previously devised.

The Doge eventually recovered his bearings, but in his heart he never forgave the shrunken head of a non-existent political body, glorious only in memoriam, for not realising the obvious benefits that a beautiful young wife, a huge dowry, natural heirs and the continued financial as well as military support from the world's most powerful Republic could provide it with. Foscari felt that he had been reaching out far and generously to finally build a bridge between the people of Venice and those of Constantinople, a move which would not only help to hold the Turks at bay, but would also challenge the preponderance of Genoese merchants in the straits and the Black Sea.

In Foscari's view, a political union between Venice and Byzantium could even have ushered in a new golden era of commerce and prosperity which might one day enable Greeks and Venetians to find further allies for their cause to eventually force the Turk back to Asia Minor. It was not going to be easy, but it was, given proper alliances, an idea designed to integrate on a dynastic level the Greek-Orthodox and the Italian-Catholic worlds. In other words, where church men had visibly failed, princes and merchants could possibly succeed.

The Doge had been hopeful and ignored scattered protests among some members of the Grand Council. Undertaking to reorient his entire foreign policy to suit his new scheme, he pretended not to bother, but was in reality devastated when the news arrived that the Byzantine Emperor had recalled his proposal in favour of, first, some Portuguese lady affiliated to the royal house of Aragon and Naples, then, some obscure Princess from Asia, then, a fifty year old, infertile ex-wife to the late Turkish Sultan!

Francis, for all his efforts to save the empire, had in the end chosen to let religious prejudice and self-conceit prevail over a helping hand. Now, as the Turks were about to besiege the city, and the Emperor realised that he still hadn't done anything to secure his position by an adequate nuptial alliance, he couldn't help feeling that Francis had unnecessarily complicated things by frivolously turning down the Venetian offer. In retrospect it was perhaps not only a vain, but a downright naïve attempt to appease the Turkish predator, who couldn't care less about what eventually happened to one of his father's many Christian wives. Even if the negotiations had resulted in her consenting to remarry, it would have been a strike in empty air as far as the warding off of the Turkish threat was concerned. Francis had intended to offer the Sultan biscuits when the smell of blood was already in his nostrils. It was a serious political mistake, and only the kind of vanity which life-long loyalty instils in a civil servant prevented Francis from clearly realising how potentially disastrous the consequences might be.

In the last instance though, an Emperor can only blame himself for having listened too closely to the advice of one of his ministers, and it was not Francis but the Emperor in person who, when still an ambitious despot of Mistra, had well-nigh provoked the Venetians into war by ousting their governor of Vitrinitza on the Greek mainland. Foscari had eventually chosen to remain silent and try to forget, but to witness the now Emperor mend an insult by adding a fresh one to the score, was more than he was prepared to tolerate. The Doge, far-sighted in his political vision, instinctively knew that without active support of the many Venetians inside the city of Constantinople, of the Venetian colonies in the Greek archipelago and, last but not least, of Venice herself, the days of the Roman Empire were indeed numbered. For the time being he felt little inclination to provide the city with more reinforcements than were necessary to secure the escape, should it be necessary, of his own people from what he held to be a doomed city. Pre-emptively he also continued negotiations with the Sultan.

Chapter 8

Hadije, daughter of Ibrahim Bey, Lord of Sinope, had been both fortunate and unfortunate enough to be considered the Turkish wife of the late Sultan. In the wake of his death she had escaped the gloomy fate of joining his other wives, concubines and slave-girls in the twilight seraglio of deceased Sultans. Because of her intimate relationship to Murad she had instead, on Mehmet's ordinance, been most honourably remarried to the Second Vizier, Ishak Pasha, recently appointed Governor of Anatolia.

Ishak Pasha did everything he could to make his new wife happy. The palace they inhabited was situated on a hill with a commanding view of the surrounding plains and the nearby coast. She had an entire court attending to her needs and could devote her life to whatever activity she preferred. Mostly she was seen walking and resting in the garden of delectations bordering directly to her wing of the palace. It was a lovely place, a haven of exotic plants and flowers, birds, animals, fountains, statues, porticoes, alcoves and pilasters overgrown with vine. But although she, as opposed to many other harem ladies of the Ottoman Sultanate, was free to come and go at will both inside and outside the palace, she couldn't help feeling like a bird trapped in a golden cage. Often times she caught herself in the act, staring at the clouds as they slowly drifted across the sky, sailing out over the open sea. These were moments when she sought relief from the agonising pain and bitterness that haunted her heart.

In the theatre of her mind one and the same scene kept repeating itself. Sometimes she felt a distress so great that she cried out loud, sometimes she just wept silent rivers. At yet other times her tears burst forth like a sulphurous hot spring and she could be seen clenching her fists, shaking them against the sky as though she was cursing an invisible adversary or calling for a terrible vengeance by the Almighty. And the scene eternally re-enacted in her soul was the following.

In the gilded audience hall of the Sultan's palace in Adrianople, she was admitted to offer her condolences for her husband's death while simultaneously congratulating Mehmet on his succession. She respectfully fell to the floor as custom prescribed, but then the Sultan rose from his throne, went all the way up to her and helped her to rise to her feet. He accompanied her back to his throne and seated her next to him. Plates with glazed fruit and pastries were offered her; he personally poured wine into a cup and gave it to her – an exceptional gesture.

– I feel most honoured and touched by your presence here today, the young ruler began his speech. – In this deeply sad moment, when we are both grieving the tragic loss of our father and husband, it is a privilege to know that you, being one of the persons he cared most about, are here to help me endure the deep sorrow and prepare me for the daunting task of continuing his glorious work to bring the truth and law of Allah to bear on all the peoples of the earth. My father, may he be blessed in Paradise, has singled me out as his heir. I know he would not have done so without your consent, and I would like to thank you for having stood by his side and considered me worthy of such responsibility. I have taken measures to ensure that you are also forthwith shown all the respect and honour due to a Sultana and I beg you find peace in the ways of Allah, who now has decided to call upon my father and prepare him for eternal life.

While Mehmet finished the last phrase he gave a sign to one of his attendants. A servant brought a lavishly decorated box to him. He opened it and handed it over to his step-mother. It contained a necklace of precious stones on a gold chain. Beautiful Hadije became speechless and blushed.

– I have decided, Mehmet continued, that only the very best is good enough for you. My father's closest friend and advisor was always Ishak Pasha. I have asked him to take care of you as would my father had he still been alive. You will consequently marry Ishak Pasha and take up residency in Anatolia. You may consider this a wedding gift from someone you will always be able to regard as your affectionate son.

Since it was far from granted that the wives of departed Sultans were shown any more respect than his dogs and slaves, Hadije felt that her fate could have been a lot worse than the one Mehmet obviously held in store for her. She was about once again to bow to the floor, when the young Sultan reached out and closed her right hand in between his two palms and then moved his hand towards his own heart. It was a most unusual sign of respect and she felt exhilarated realising she was not going to spend the rest of her days in the House of Lamenting and Sorrows.

Upon all this the Sultan bid her farewell and she was escorted out from the audience hall by two Janissaries. Hadije, the gift box under her arm, joyfully made for the gate to the seraglio to prepare herself for her future life. It was a great relief for her to realise that she would no longer have to bother about the safety and upbringing of her baby son Ahmet. Knowing that it was the Sultan's offspring, Ishak Pasha would surely regard him as his own son and treat him accordingly.

As she arrived at the harem gate, she was received by the chief Eunuch, who at first curiously blocked her way. In between the folds of his swathing dress she nevertheless caught a glimpse of a disguised man, disappearing through one of the back doors. Only now did the Eunuch step aside. Bewildered Hadije advanced towards the pool where the harem ladies and their children were habitually taking their afternoon baths. When she came closer she saw a group of women bending over something on the side of the pool. They looked up at her. Their faces expressed terror but there were no tears in their eyes, since to cry in the harem was punishable by death. Hadije, however, reeled backwards, as though hit by a tremendous blow, when the blue body of her infant was brought to her. In a desperate embrace she wrapped her arms around the lifeless body. As she realised that any attempt to bring it back to life were in vain, she lowered her arms. Still holding onto the child she staggered a few steps ahead, met the baby's glazed stare and emitted a cry so heart rending that it could be heard beyond the palace walls. Around his thin neck ran a circular red rash, the trace after the cord the unknown man had used to strangle the baby with while still in the bath.

It was this second necklace that Hadije, wife of the late Sultan Murad, would always remember as her true wedding gift from Mehmet.

Mehmet himself, on the other hand, never admitted having arranged for the child to be murdered. Quite to the contrary. As chaos threatened to break loose inside the seraglio, he quickly issued an order for the capture of the disguised man, who by some ladies of the harem was identified as one of the darker household slaves. The man was apprehended and the next day brought before the Mehmet accused of murder. Having been told that he would eventually be secretly released and comfortably set up in Anatolia as a free man with a handsome pension, if only he admitted to be the sole instigator of this abominable crime, poor Özkök did not suspect what the Sultan held in store for him. He confessed to the murder, saying that he had acted solely on his own initiative and in order to prevent a future up-rising against his master, on account of the popularity which the baby's mother enjoyed as the late Sultan's wife.

Mehmet pretended to listen attentively to his confession and even had several other people interrogated. In the end, however, he had Özkök escorted to the middle of the outside court yard, where, still in sight of the entire assembly, he was brought down on his knees while the executioner approached him from behind. At this point Özkök understood that he had been betrayed and cried out that he had only done this because the Sultan had threatened him with death or worse if he did not comply with his order. Mehmet, however, had made sure that drums, cymbals and other loud instruments should accompany Özkök's execution, and so nobody in the council hall could actually hear what the poor man was yelling. In the next instance his head was half severed from his body, only to fall to the ground by the second blow into a pool of blood.

To the bereaved mother the entire show added even more despair and pain as she realised that Mehmet would stop short of nothing to ensure his enduring power. She also understood that her only chance to save her own life was to pretend to believe in the cruel comedy Mehmet had fancied to stage in order to gain unquestionable authority. There might have been others doubting Mehmet's innocence, but whoever held on to his or her life would take pains to conceal from him even the most fleeting regard. No one in the hall dared to watch anyone else for fear of retribution. Summoning all her remaining force Hadije fell to her knees, eyes on the marble floor, praising the Sultan for his passion for justice and declaring herself content that the villain responsible for murdering her beloved son and the Sultan's dear brother had received his well merited punishment.

But in her heart Hadije would never forgive Mehmet. Clearly seeing the danger she herself was exposed to she decided to bury her quest for revenge deep inside her until one day, perhaps, she could get to him. She would never let her new husband Ishak Pasha know how she felt, always pretending to accept her baby son's death as a tragic fatality. The only one who had an inkling of her real sentiments was another man who likewise knew for sure that Mehmet had been behind it all: Halil Pasha, Chief Vizier to Murad II and recently reinstated as such in Mehmet's government.

Chapter 9

In the palace of Menisa young Mehmet stood firmly footed on the cobbled stones of the inner court yard taking aim with his bow. One after the other the arrows hit the target. If only one of them landed outside it, he vociferously gave expression to his disappointment. The master archer and his teacher in this difficult art, Hasan, nodded slightly at each shot but did not comment upon his pupil's technique unless the latter expressly asked for advice. Suddenly, out of nowhere, a pigeon alighted on the frame of the target and remained immobile. It was a challenge Mehmet could not refuse. He intently raised his bow, hooked an arrow onto the string, pulled it back and aimed carefully. Then the tension was released. The bow squeaked while the arrow whizzed through the air and hit the unsuspecting bird through its chest. It fell dead on the spot.

Mehmet turned the bow over to the master and went up to inspect his kill. He picked up the arrow and the pigeon skewered on it and held it up to the light. It was a clean shot, probably straight through the bird's heart. A fine grey membrane of death already shaded the eye which moments earlier had been clear and vivid, but the body was still warm, and through the wound the blood had not yet stopped throbbing. The feathers, except where soaked in red, were a dazzling white. Unable to pull the arrow out of the bird without ripping it apart, he broke it in two pieces and then pulled out the remainder. Returning to Hasan, he gave him the bird and the broken arrow and said,

– This bird was sent to me by providence. I would like to have it served for dinner tonight and I want this arrow-head to be attached to a new arrow, the stabilizing feathers of which must be made from this same bird.

Hasan made a deep nod, showing he had understood. He then looked up, a smile shading his lips,

– With cranberry or ginger sauce, Sir?

– That is of no importance. Main thing is that it's served in its own blood.

Visibly satisfied with what he had achieved Mehmet decided to terminate his outdoor activity for the day. He was about to enter the interior of the palace when he heard the unmistakable sound of hooves from a horse approaching at great speed. Moments later he saw the man arriving before the sentinel and, visibly exhausted, dismount a grey horse frothing like one of Neptune's stallions. The guard holding the horse's reins duly announced the arrival of a messenger from the Sultan's palace in Adrianople. Mehmet turned round, hastened over the drawbridge and approached the courier, who could hardly stand up any longer. Judging from his appearance he was one of the Tartar horsemen who had came to reinforce the Ottoman cavalry in the wake of Tamerlane's conquests. They were known to be the best and most enduring messengers in the empire, rumoured to even be able to sleep straddling a galloping horse. But this man didn't seem to have rested much lately. His naturally darkly tanned face and Mongolian eyes were further blackened with dirt, his hair in stripes and his ripped clothes just barely still hanging on to his body. Receiving water from the guard, holding on to him to remain standing, he handed over a dispatch with the imperial seal to Mehmet, where-after he fell in a pile to the ground.

Mehmet feverishly opened the letter and glanced through it. Its message was short and succinct. And it was signed, not by his father, but by his Grand Vizier, Halil Pasha. It needed to contain no more words.

As soon as Mehmet had finished reading, he turned in the general direction of the Prophet's grave, fell to the ground and touched it with his forehead. He then made a sign to make sure the half-dead courier was properly taken care of and on the spot awarded him thirty gold ducats for apparently having made the entire journey from Adrianople to Menisa without interruption. Without a moment's hesitation he then ordered his Arabian saddled and released from the stables. The air electrified with expectation as more and more people now began to gather around Mehmet, pressing him for an answer as to what message the ominous letter might contain. But Mehmet would not answer until the horse was brought before him. When he had mounted it, he solemnly turned to his entourage saying,

– My father, may he blessed in heaven and graciously received by Allah, is dead. I am your new Sultan and I shall now ride to Adrianople to mourn my father, and thereafter, if it so pleases the Almighty, ascend the throne he has entrusted me. I'll wait here in the court yard for an hour only. Then I shall leave. Let those who love me follow me!

The news of Sultan Murad's death caused an immediate stir. Lamentations blended with the sounds of horses, shouting voices, clamour of weapons, hurrays and toasts mixing with the murmur of prayers. Like the eye of the storm, Mehmet himself remained calm and composed. In the now unexpected stillness of his mind it suddenly dawned upon him that the arrival of the messenger had coincided with his own killing of the bird. It had to be a sign, but of what? Mehmet, for a moment seized by fear that he might be the victim of a plot destined to have him killed like a sitting pigeon, once again called upon the always knowledgeable Hasan. But for all his many qualities, Hasan was not versed in the art of prophecy and he didn't dare to take it upon himself to express what this coincidence could possibly mean. Others around Mehmet were similarly at loss for an answer, but this only made Mehmet even more suspicious. Suddenly a voice was heard: "Send for the alchemist!"

The alchemist in question was an old man living in a small house along one of the narrow lanes next to the southern ramparts of the city. His name was Zacharias. Although of Greek descent he had been captured many years ago during the reign of Sultan Bayezid's while his army was raiding Serbia. Like so many other Christian boys he was sent to the Anatolian countryside to be brought up in the tradition of future Janissaries, all of whom were subject to the same education.

Until they reached the age of eighteen they had to share the life of hard working peasants, carpenters, masons and other craftsmen. In this way they were prepared for the manifold practical tasks incumbent on the Sultan's elite corps. But as Zacharias grew older his penchant and aptitude for science and learning became so obvious that he was singled out by the learned men around Bayezid and sent to pursue higher studies in the town of Üsküdar on the southern shores of Marmara. There he came into contact with a famous astrologer and fortune teller named Krhyseis, who claimed that he had found a method of turning metals such as pewter and lead into gold. This became a turning point for Zacharias, who subsequently was appointed soothsayer and astrologer at Bayezid's court. When Bayezid was captured by Tamerlane, Zacharias, who was with him, narrowly escaped just before they came to get him as well. After years of learned vagabondage he was finally washed up in Menisa, where he lived off a small pension granted to him by Bayezid's successor Murad, for the many services he had rendered the former. From time to time his services were still called upon, as he was known to have accurately predicted the outcome of a great many battles, the hour of death of the late Sultan as well as that of many of his enemies. Young Mehmet, knowing of his reputation and in deep awe of all men who seemed to be able to see beyond the visible, had sometimes asked for his advice. But those instances had been trivial compared to this, since Mehmet had never before had the same strong sensation of being presented with a veritable omen.

Zacharias, dressed like a Greek philosopher, his face adorned by a long, white beard, a wandering rod in his hand, arrived while Mehmet's men and horses had already begun to leave the court yard. Mehmet told him about the incident and asked him if he had an interpretation. At first Zacharias said nothing, but then he closed his eyes. Soon they could be seen rolling inside their sockets, as though he had been deeply in sleep and dreaming. Then, in a curiously muffled voice, he said,

– In the great church the dove shall make itself a living target. The Holy Spirit protecting that place shall thus give up its breath, and Allah will make there his abode. Many men shall perish in the struggle and in the end it will prove to have been all in vain. Thus the spider weaves the curtains in the palace of the Caesars and the owl calls the watches in the towers of Afrasiab.

Having uttered this last enigmatic phrase, Zacharias fell silent although his lips continued to move.

Mehmet eagerly seized him by the hand, but the old man once again opened his dim eyes, seemingly unaware of the words he had just spoken. Asked what and where the palace of Afrasiab was, Zacharias shook his head and said,

– Afrasiab, I don't know. I have never heard of such a place. You must ask Marco Polo.

– How can I, when the man has been dead for two hundred years? Mehmet exclaimed.

– So much better for him, Zacharias responded absent minded. He then turned round and went the same way he had come. Surrounded by agitated men all pressing him for a clearer answer, in the midst of weaponry and horses, he appeared to take notice of neither.

Mehmet and his followers were simply left to draw their own conclusions. But there was no time for meditation when the blood was boiling. The palace gates were pushed opened while guns fired a salute in honour of the new Sultan, who responded in kind by spurring his horse. Along the town walls curious citizens, alerted to the unexpected event, ran to the ramparts to behold some twenty-five heavily armed men set off at full speed to the north. Soon a cloud of dust, dissipating in the brisk evening air, was all there was left of them.

Like a flock of migrating birds Mehmet and his men swept over the hills and plains of ancient Phrygia, arriving in Gallipoli on the northern shore of the Dardanelles after only two days speedy travelling. A few days later they descended on Adrianople. The city knew of their arrival and Mehmet was met in the open landscape by a vast assembly of courtiers and a crowd of common people. When the silhouettes of Mehmet and his followers became visible through the fog on this unforgiving day of February, the whole party of officials dismounted their horses and began to walk towards them in utter silence. Suddenly they stopped and the age-old funeral litany, interspersed with outcries, cymbals, horns and drums, was unleashed in honour of the dead Sultan. Upon hearing this Mehmet and his men likewise dismounted and joined in the mourning ceremony.

For anyone not born a Turk, it would have been a strange clamour, as from a herd of animals in distress, rising from the ground and merging with the mist. These were ancestral sounds, drums, cymbals, pipes, trumpets, voices, recalling the immensity, loneliness and never ending horizons of the steppe. From out there, from the void, came the omniscient power of Allah. Now he had taken one of his sons back to his celestial garden. It was a moment of rejoicing in heaven, but on earth his departure had spread darkness and confusion, like the night itself descending on the herds surrounded by wolves. It was a lamentation in preparation for the restoration of the organised ring of guardians that would force the pack of predators to retreat, and to gather people like vast herds, spreading them all over the world to graze upon its lovely meadows under the dome of heaven.

For now the only thing that could be said with certainty, was that it was on this cold and impregnable day of February that the destiny of the future Ottoman empire hung in the balance. Although Mehmet had indeed been received in traditional fashion by what he had reason to believe were all the higher dignitaries of his father's government, he could not know what to expect once he set foot inside the city itself. To this end he had instructed his men to expect anything and be prepared to fight both for his and their own lives.

In his letter Halil Pasha had urged Mehmet not to waste time, which was sound and serious advice, since the deaths of Sultans would immediately attract scavenging throne pretenders eager to sniff out the smell of a decaying royal corpse. For this reason a Sultan's departure from his earthly dominions was traditionally kept secret for as long as possible, ideally until the heir, assigned as such by the deceased, had turned up on the scene. In this particular instance there was no heir-apparent to the throne other than Mehmet. Of his two older brothers one had died in mysterious circumstances several years earlier, while the other, more recently, had been strangled in his bed by an unknown murderer. The assassin had obviously had the nerve and leisure on the same occasion to also finish off his wife and their two young children.

There was, however, also prince Orhan, detained in Constantinople for the time being, but potentially very popular with the Turkish crowds. The Byzantine Emperors, well aware of the notorious confusion surrounding each succession to the Ottoman throne, had always in the past been keen on playing such wild cards.

To be sure, there was Little Ahmed too. As a toddler he represented no immediate threat, but his mother, Hadije, was known to be cunning and resourceful. None of this would have meant much though, if it weren't for the fact that Mehmet had never been much loved in Adrianople since the days when he had acted as a kind of vice-Sultan to his weary father. In particular, the Janissaries – who were the only ones to guarantee a new Sultan safety – had not been among the members of the reception committee. Thus the risk of an insurrection and a palace coup was not only impending. It would in fact happen here and now or never. To his great relief, Mehmet nowhere met with signs indicating that his arrival was not expected. On the contrary, he even felt welcome. And when the chief Janissary later that day presented first his condolences and then his best wishes for the new ruler by prostrating himself three times before him, Mehmet knew the battle had been won before it had even begun.

The next day, having been solemnly sworn in, Mehmet presided over the distribution of ministerial posts. He was seated on his throne surrounded by the trusted advisors he had brought with him from Minisa. The great question was of course what would happen to the late Sultan's ministers, in particular Halil Pasha, Murad's Chief Vizier and author of the urgent letter Mehmet had received some days earlier. Halil Pascha had on Murad's order acted as Mehmet's tutor when the boy had been first appointed as his the Sultan's heir, at this time expressing the wish to withdraw from his high office. One of Halil's main pre-occupations during the following years had been to try to convince the impetuous adolescent of the impracticability of his plans to one day conquer Constantinople. Now he no longer had the support of the young man's father. Instead the youngster could practically order his assassination by a secretive gesture; by all means he could force him to retire and to play no further role in politics.

Mehmet, entering the audience chamber in regalia and surveying the room, noticed that Halil kept himself in the background. But for the eagle-eyed new ruler, stooping slightly forward to enhance the clean-cut profile of his own aquiline nose and the dark fire of his eyes, Halil could not hide behind his long beard and fluffy turban. And he was not the only one to be nervous. It had happened before, on occasions like this, that heads would roll, and roll all the more quickly the closer they had been to the late imperial ear. Halil tried to compose himself, hoping that his speedily dispatched letter would in the end guarantee him safe-conduct. Only the ones who knew him well, and stood close enough on this occasion, noticed that his skin had turned just a shade more grey, his lips had become slightly paler and his knuckles all white. His jaw, framed and covered by the mighty beard, was tense too. So was the atmosphere, congealing as it were in an almost unbearably sustained silence. Mehmet took his time to inspect each and every face in front of him. Only after having done so

and whispered something in the ears of his attendants, did he finally choose to speak.
– Why are my father's viziers staying back?

There was some inner trembling in the pause that followed, but he cut the agony short by adding,
– Call them forward and tell Halil to take his usual place.

The confirmation did give reason for a sigh of relief among Halil's supporters, but Halil himself, attuned to the finest nuances of courtly diplomacy, knowing that the difference between life of death sometimes was only a matter of the Sultan's making use of one and the same word in a slightly different manner, immediately felt the smarting sting contained in the formulation "*tell him* to take his usual place". Had Mehmet addressed himself directly to him instead of passing the exhortation through his officials, it would have been an indication of continued respect. As stated, Halil knew that although he had for the time being saved his skin by immediately sending for Mehmet on the occasion of his father's death, there was no doubt the new Sultan resented his defensive attitude in the one and only question that really mattered to him: the conquest of Constantinople. Halil, saved for now by the mercy of Allah, decided to immediately make his quickly revised opinion on the possibility of Ottoman success in this regard known to both Mehmet and the public. But he also strongly felt that if, in the long run, he failed to convince the Sultan about his own sincerity, his only chance would be to discreetly arrange for the demise of his own former protégé. If not, Halil himself would surely one day have to exit from the scene in a way that didn't exactly promise to be pleasurable.

Chapter 10

The rumours of the Sultan's army's imminent arrival had been all but exaggerated. In the early hours of April 5 an immense mass of conic tents, helmets and spear heads began to refract the rays of the sun rising up behind Hagia Sophia. To reinforce the image of a glorious sun blinding its foes, Constantine persuaded the Venetian senior captain Trevisano to let the crews of the Venetian galleys parade along the land walls, harnessed in their characteristic western European armours, flying their lion emblazoned banners of Saint-Mark in the morning breeze. The display was meant to act as a token of the trust the Emperor put in his Christian allies. In a deeper sense it was also a prayer, a conjuration of benevolent spirits: if only one courier pigeon were to reach Venice, Genoa or Rome and, by its frailty as much as by its indomitable determination, convince these western potentates of the need of coming to the rescue of God's own city, then there was still hope.

Hour by hour one Turkish division after the other came into sight, taking up their positions in uncanny silence and with frightening expediency. The entire camp soon formed an embracing crescent along the entire length of the land wall. In the centre, near the Lycus river and opposite the Gate of Saint Romanus, the Sultan had pitched his reddish-golden, sumptuously decorated tent. Ahead of him a solid line of Janissaries set up their camp. On the Sultan's right flank down to the Golden Gate the Anatolians under Ishak Pasha moved in. On the left flank up to the Golden Horn the numerous European detachments under Karadja Pasha made themselves at home. Behind and on each side of the Sultan, as his rear guard and storm troopers, to be called forth when the command for assault was given, camped the wild and fearless irregulars, the bashibazouks. They were often neither Christian nor Moslem, but animals of prey in human disguise, prepared to fight and die at any reasonably bright prospect of booty, rape and murder. Across the Horn Zaganos Pasha's men began to spread out over the hills of Galata, and down in the Bosporus, at the height of the Double Columns, the entire Turkish fleet under its commander Baltoghlu lay in ambush.

From the walls of the city the entire camp looked like a field of giant mushrooms interspersed with stone marbles stacked in pyramids. Fire places and water cisterns were put in place, huge supplies of wood dragged forward by oxen yoked in pairs; there were barrels of gun powder and barrels of food; thousands of horses, even a large number of camels. Countless soldiers in ceaseless activity smoothly attended to this menagerie on a stretch of land so long that one could not even see its ends from the highest defence tower, and so wide that its rear guard disappeared beyond the horizon.

With the consent of Giustiani Longo, Constantine had taken the decision that the defenders, outnumbered by something in the region of ten to one, should concentrate their efforts on the outer walls. This strategy had been successfully adopted to fight off the Turks during the siege of 1422. The fact that the inner wall had never since been fully repaired increased the necessity of keeping the enemy at bay by the first line of defence. Constantine set up his head quarters close to the valley where the walls straddled the Lycus river. As soon as it became clear to Longo, stationed a bit further north at the Charisian Gate, that this was where the Sultan, quite predictably, intended to concentrate his artillery, he and his Genoese troops joined Constantine around the Gate of Saint Romanus. All along the battlements, facing land or sea, other Christian defenders took up their positions: Genoese, Venetians, Greeks, noblemen and commoners, priests and monks, all were called upon to stand watch. Constantine had taken pains to distribute his defending forces in such a way that the risk of conflict between members of the two republics and the Greeks could be held in check. But even though all officers had been told to repress any sign of internal strife, it was impossible to foresee where and when Italians and Greeks would suddenly begin to resent each other rather than stand united against the common enemy.

The position of the Genoese was, as always, particularly ambiguous in this regard. On the one hand they were emphatically represented by Longo and his mercenaries. On the other hand the professed Genoese neutrality in Galata across the Horn could just as well be interpreted as a silent rendering of intelligence and other services to the Turks. The attitude of the Galatians was bitterly resented by both Greeks and Venetians. But if, theoretically, there had to this very moment been a chance of the city's being spared the siege, whereby the animosity between fellow Christians living on opposite sides of a narrow bay could perhaps be suspended, the next events would exclude once and for all any such compromise.

In the afternoon the Sultan sent forth a group of standard bearing horsemen to present the customary formality. Against unconditional surrender the Emperor and his people were all invited to either leave the city in peace with their belongings, or to welcome Turkish settlers inside the walls, convert to Islam and become regular tax payers. The proposition, as old as Islam itself, had been made numerous times to the inhabitants of the city, and their answer had invariably been the same. The cavalry detachment returned to the Sultan to deliver him the news. He saw them approaching in impeccable formation and went out to interrogate its leader. As the answer was given, Mehmet raised his index finger. Seconds later the sound of fifty drums and twenty horns piercing the atmosphere unanimously announced his declaration of war.

Chapter 11

By sunset the following day the ferocious roar from a battery of smaller cannons pounding the walls abated. When the defenders began to take a closer look at their bulwark, they saw that a part of the wall near the Charisian Gate had been substantially damaged. Ceaseless bombardment the following day brought it down in ruins. Mehmet, confident that he was about to open a decisive breach, set his men to work on filling the moat so that they could follow up the crumbling of a portion of the outer wall with a sudden attack.

But as night fell, hundreds of silent shadows began to move all over the damaged walls. There were only scattered torches behind them so as to not invite the Sultan to start firing his guns again. In darkness, from hand to hand, from one whispering, crawling, digging, piling shadow to another, planks, barrels, sacks of earth, sand, gravel, animal hides and cloth were distributed along a chain. Meanwhile, in the dead of night, Longo and his men made a sudden sortie through the ramparts and fell upon the Turkish soldiers in the moat, killing them with spears, stones and arrows as if they had been snakes infesting a pit hole. The ones that managed to crawl out of the moat were either cut down or captured and conducted back inside the city. Once there the Greeks immediately began to torture them in the hope of extracting some information on the Sultan's next plans.

Hearing about his losses, Mehmet issued an order to counter attack, but it was too late for the Turks to inflict any real damage on the defenders, who had hastened to get behind their walls. There was little more for them to do than try to drag the corpses out of the moat and pile them on a funeral pyre. At dawn, as Mehmet impatiently waited for just enough daylight to survey the degree of destruction he had inflicted upon the city, he couldn't believe his eyes. There it was again, the entire wall, as if nothing had ever happened to it. Led and inspired by God himself, the defenders had managed to put it back again, stone by stone, brick by brick.

Frustrated Mehmet intensified his artillery. His fire capacity was steadily increasing, and after three days of intense work, Urban's weapons of mass destruction, including his *basilica*, "the super gun", had been hoisted into place, secured and aimed. Though it required so much attention and preparation that it could only be fired a few times a day, its irregular explosions, hurling gigantic stone balls enveloped in enormous flames and clouds of smoke through the air, heavily syncopated the sound of countless church bells desperately tolling against the sky. There was a moment at the end of the second day of bombardment when a huge stone ball hissed through the air above Longo and Constantine, separated by only a few steps, and splashed to a pulp, first, the body of an archer, then, the trunk of the tree he had been sitting on to finally crash into a defence tower. There both the projectile and the window it brought down splintered into a hail of needle-thin missiles putting three soldiers, caught in the inner chamber of the tower, to instantaneous death.

While the bombardment continued day and night along the Theodosian land wall, forcing the Emperor and Longo to constantly survey it and lead the nightly operations destined to make the ever more necessary repairs, there was also intense activity on the other side of the city. On April 18 around mid-day several lookouts on the sea walls and those of the Horn reported that the Turkish fleet, now reinforced by ships from all around the Black Sea, was approaching the Horn at full speed. Harbour commander Alex Diedo, however, was prepared to meet them. He had had ten of the largest merchant vessels lined up along the chain, in close array and with their bows and fire guns pointing in the direction of the enemy. Alongside these ships were stationed sturdy carracks, heavily armed and in excellent condition, charged with the responsibility to protect at any cost the many floats keeping the chain suspended. A few additional ships had been wrapped in wet cloth to reduce the risk of fire spreading between the tightly packed defending ships. In addition there were cannons posted along the sea line of the Cape of Saint Barbara. On the battlements Lucas Notaras stood ready with his men and further guns; on the shores of the Horn itself was Gabriel Trevisano and the Venetian guard.

It was like seeing the swarm of water born insects which Iannis had witnessed approaching from afar a week earlier, only now they were really humming loudly as they went on the attack. Many of the Turkish ships had guns mounted on their prows, and the men manning the ships were spurred on by wild battle cries. As the fleet came within the range of archers it slowed down and unleashed a hail of projectiles: arrows, just plainly lethal or flaming too, stone balls, metal bolts, threatening to wreak havoc among the Italian crews. After this initial cannonade, the Turkish ships clashed into the chain, trying by all means to slash anchor cables, to sink the floats, to attach hooks and ladders to the ships and board them. But as the Turkish soldiers tried to climb the high hauled carracks, they were in turn massacred by large stones, dumped on them from large cranes swinging out from elevated poops and sterns over their ships. Meanwhile smaller stones, arrows and javelins kept raining over them. The few individuals who actually made it up towards the deck of the ships saw themselves facing enormous Varangian axes, handled by the fierce descendants of Goths, Vikings and Anglo-Saxons, who in a steady torrent of blood ruthlessly severed arms, hands, knuckles, fingers, knees and feet from their owners as they appeared on the railings.

The Turks fired their cannons mounted on the prows at close range but the projectiles were either too small or could not reach sufficient elevation to pierce the thick hulls of the Italian ships. Both sides spat the infamous Greek fire on each other, which not only continued to burn as it hit the surface of the water, but would use almost anything – human flesh, clothes, skin, masts, hauls, oars, masts and sails – to feed on. But the Greeks had ample supplies of stored water to extinguish any fire beginning onboard.

The sound of mutilated, dying and scorched soldier, roaring from excruciating pain as they fell off the ships, hit by a spear, a sword, an axe, a stone, or consumed by fire, united in a ghastly clamour travelling the expanse of water. It could be heard as far off as Chrysopolis on the opposite side of the Bosporus. There, on the empty shore south of the town itself, her face covered so as to only leave a slit open for her eyes, dressed in a simple tunic to conceal her true identity, a lonely woman watched the scene. She remained there for just as many hours as it took the Turkish naval commander to realise that he would not in this engagement force his way beyond the chain, and that in order to avoid an even grander catastrophe he must order his ships to retreat over a sea now so littered with corpses that they seemed to form a single bridge over the inlet to the Horn.

Chapter 12

She drifted the beach to and fro as if in a state of trance. How she had ended up here she could hardly remember. Having meandered along the Marmora coast for many days she was now so starved and exhausted that she felt her legs give away and her mind swoon. It was a miracle that she had so far managed to pass unnoticed. True, she wore the dress of an Anatolian peasant woman or a fisher wife. Still there were myriads of guards and lookout posts all around her. By nightfall wolves and dogs howled at bats and crows swirling around the waxing moon while she curled up inside a ravaged house, a ruined church or a cave. At day break, numbed by cold and humidity, her body aching, she continued her journey. And now, when the last pieces of provisions she had brought in a small leather sack had long since been consumed, she stood all alone, singing a melody saturated with melancholy and desolation. The song, which she had learned as a child from Bulgarian shepherdesses, could easily be mistaken for a naked cry. But it did transform in secretive ways, recalling in her mind the profound stillness of her native Rhodopes mountains, bathing in serene purple as the sunlight ceded and the animals were herded for the night.

It was a cry, yet in essence that cry was only the outer clothing of an immense inner silence, gripping soul and heart like an eagle driving his talons into a running hare. She imagined the merciless and beautiful silence of the mountains, the distant barking of the shepherd dogs, the peaceful sound of sheep – oh, she would give anything to drink their milk now, taste a piece of moulded cheese and a morsel of dry bread. Above all these familiar ruminations, though, the eagle, soaring almost out of sight, had chosen his prey. As the call for home came, and the herd was rounded up by the dogs, one lamb had been temporarily separated from his mother. He did what he could to catch her attention, and she heard him. But she was surrounded by other sheep and could not turn around to guide him down the valley. He would have to follow the herd on his own accord. But the lamb was young and the herd moved fast to keep ahead of the dogs. Although he too moved as fast as his legs would allow him, he still lagged behind. He ran and ran and, yes, he saw them come to a halt. Somewhere inside the herd his mother was waiting for him; he was safe now, feeling he need not run so fast anymore. He felt proud that he had been able to cover this long distance without her help. Then, out of nowhere, a giant shadow appeared above him. In the very same instance he was pierced by razor sharp claws felling him to the ground. His heart was still desperately pounding as the huge raptor dug his sharp beak into his kidney and liver. No matter how agonising his cry for help, his mother could now do even less to save him. And so she sang, sang her heart out of her body, in memory of the lamb who had to be sacrificed for the others to live.

In the night that followed she could neither speak nor move. But she did see the shadow of the small boat washed up on the beach. Four or five men stepped out of it. When they drew nearer she heard them speaking in Italian. They almost stumbled upon her; maybe she even tried to crawl in their direction. Anyway, she had been discovered and would be instantly killed by the drawn sword, had not the wrapping around her face given away and exposed her face in the dark: – Ave Maria, it's a woman! the man next to the sword-holder hissed to the others. She still couldn't talk, but her eyes spoke a thousand words. Their choice was to kill her, to leave her behind as a living witness or take her along. – Madre Dio, kill her before she screams! It was clearly an order and the sword rapidly ascended menacingly into the darkness. She could only wait to hear it whizz through the air and mercifully end her miserable days and nights. Instead of coming down on her, however, a ray from the moon, suddenly emerging from underneath the heavy clouds while setting on the western horizon, vaguely illuminated her face: – Guarda! the low voice said, calmed down by its own astonishment, – Che bella bambina...

Before she lost consciousness she had the sensation that the sword in front of her changed into a wooden cross on which the god of the Christians was nailed. The crucified seemed to be in no pain, however, and looked at her in mild understanding. A purple halo surrounded his head. Otherwise the background was pitch black. The vision grew in intensity, the halo became golden, incandescent, and his deep blue eyes reflected the light around him like a pair of precious stones. When she felt she could no longer stand looking into his eyes, he gazed through and beyond her. In a wonderfully sonorous voice he spoke: "I also had a mother who mourned my death. But behold, I'm not dead, and all the children of the earth live in my kingdom."

Chapter 13

The Italian mariners returned to their mother ship with good news. There seemed to be no major batteries of guns or manned battlements on this stretch of coast. If, with God's help, the southern wind would continue to blow the next day, the fleet could manoeuvre close to the Anatolian shore, pick up speed and hopefully, in the rather rainy atmosphere still prevailing, not be sighted by the Turks until they reached the cape of Chalcedon. From there the southerly wind would come in just slightly from port side, enabling the ships to reach maximum speed, and thus being entirely in their favour for the last leg over to Constantinople. Any Turkish vessels trying to intercept them at this point would have to row or beat against choppy waves and a wind hopefully at its most vigorous. But it was now or never, because as soon as the element of surprise was lost, the Turks, possessing hundreds of ships of all kinds, could easily block the entrance to the city. The more ships they were able to send out before the fleet could reach the boom, the greater their chances of taking them.

Before arriving before the gates of Constantinople, the papal rescue fleet manned by Genoese soldiers had encountered stormy northern winds on the Aegean and been forced to seek refuge with the Genoese colony on the island of Chios, home to an important branch of Giustiniani's family. For days and days the sea had remained a witch's cauldron of heavy vapours and frothing grey waves. The cold rain hammering the ship decks lowered the sails just as much as the morale of the fighting men. The stalemate persisted over two whole weeks. As the fog eventually lifted a moderate southern breeze pushed in, bringing with it both warmer weather and favourable sailing conditions.

Still, the approach into the Dardanelles was surrounded by much apprehension, and the crews soon had to prepare for imminent battle. Just as the Genoese ships were about to enter the straits they caught sight of a large vessel menacingly approaching from the north-west. The three Genoese galleys went into formation, but the alert was blown off. The lookouts in the crow's nests had detected that the galley was in fact a heavy imperial cargo ship under the command of the Italian captain Francesco Lecanella, laden with corn and other much needed provisions which it had stocked in Sicily. The cargo ship had been storm ridden as well and forced to seek shelter. Now they could join forces. Together they entered the mouth of the straits, encountering no opposition.

Although the strait between Cannakale on the coast of Asia Minor and the Gallipoli peninsula in the Dardanelles was too wide to allow enemy gunners to aim at ships keeping to the middle of the inlet, it could indeed be heavily patrolled by Turkish vessels intent on cutting off at this crucial juncture any sea borne support for Constantinople from the Aegean Sea. To their surprise and relief the seamen detected no military activity whatsoever on either side of the strait and the horizon ahead remained open. But the absence of enemy ships here only indicated one thing, that all naval forces were already deployed around the boom at the Golden Horn. Just as much as there was no more time to lose, the captains now became distressingly aware of what awaited them. Conferring with one another they decided they had but one choice: to press on as fast as possible and use to the maximum the advantage of the southerly wind. Thus for the Genoese, sighting the immense dome of Hagia Sophia in the early morning of Friday April 20, avoiding a confrontation with the Turkish navy was no longer an option. Soon their ships were sighted by Turkish look-out posts who immediately alerted the Sultan. He straddled his horse and rode like the devil straight down to his naval commander Baltoghlu.

Chapter 14

Daniello was a ship boy of fifteen. As the sun rose over Constantinople he hid behind a barrel as to be out of the way while he witnessed how soldiers and sea men were making themselves ready. All around he could feel the tension mounting, he heard the rattling of armour, the clasps of helmets, the rolling into position of the guns; he smelt the sharp smell of gunpowder mixed with that of tar, petrol and resin, he heard the haul squeak as all ropes were tightened and the ship rolled heavily through the waves; he heard the Captain shout out orders and saw them carried out instantly. One sail after the other unfurled in the wind and at full speed the small armada, staying close together, approached the city. They were still too far out for him to spot the legendary boom behind the cape Acropolis. Instead he saw the adversary swarming out to meet them. There were no sails on the horizon, because the wind was still, thank God, too heavily against them. But there were biremes and triremes skimming the surface like water borne spears. He tried to count them but they kept multiplying and before he knew it, the horrifying sounds of drums, castanets and horns were all around him, fierce, guttural shrieks pierced the sky, gun shots hissed through the air, fire rained from heaven. Rapidly growing in intensity, hell broke lose upon them and Daniello, though still just a boy, his heart jumping to his throat, instinctively knew that there was no escape other than to somehow face death and fight through it. Though told to stay under deck, he grabbed a long stick with a hook at the end of it and threw himself into the turmoil. He found himself caught up in a desperate struggle to keep a Turkish vessel at bay. The trick was to prevent the enemy from being able to throw their ladders and landing bridges onto the railings. The hook he held was a very effective weapon at this stage, because he soon learned how to use it in order to free the railings of any enemy ropes. Meanwhile the shouting and the yelling accompanying fire, javelins and arrows was deafening, and the metallic smell of blood began to mix with that of gun smoke. He stood unprotected on deck and though shoved aside on numerous occasions and told to get lost, he always came back. At one time he received such a blow from one of the Italian soldiers who had found him to be in the way that blood began to rush from his mouth and nose. But that wouldn't stop him, and in the next moment he could be seen storming across the deck with his long hook and place it like a battering ram into the chest of a Turkish soldier about to enter the ship from a hanging ladder that no one seemed to have noticed coming. The Turk fell backwards and hit his head against the oars of the vessel beneath. He then fell into the water where he remained motionless. Daniello then quickly disengaged the ladder from the railing and sent it after the soldier into the sea. After this feat he was no longer chased off the deck.

The naval battle was eagerly followed both by the Turks on the shores and the defenders on the walls. Mehmet, wild with impatience, steered his horse into the shallow waters and tried to direct the course of fighting from there. Admiral Baltoghlu had insisted that it was meaningless to order the larger sailing vessels to put out to sea since the wind was so heavily against them. However, the longer the battle lasted it became clear that no matter how many fustaes, biremes and triremes Baltoghlu would throw at the convoy, the latter kept approaching the boom. The small Turkish cannons mounted on the prows of the large rowing boats turned out to be too close to the water surface and have insufficient elevation to inflict any real damage to either hauls or masts of the carracks. The Italian ships simply dragged the Turkish vessels along, unable to manoeuvre in the close interlock which they themselves had created as a result of the efforts to get close enough for boarding. Both Baltoghlu and Mehmet had underestimated the time it would require to neutralise the Italian ships, in fact they were still far from doing so. By now Turkish sailing ships, forced to make a vast round about manoeuvre to get to scene of action, would have been able to join in. But they were not there. They had not even been called to duty. To the fury of Mehmet and the euphoria of the defenders the convoy steadily headed for the boom. It was only a matter of time before the ships anchored along it would be able to open fire on the interlocked Turkish vessels, which would then be caught like mice in a trap. The miracle was about to happen in front of everybody when, suddenly, the wind, hitherto carrying the Christians gloriously towards their promised goal, dropped and the sails adorned with red crosses began to flap listlessly.

So close, yet still so far away. After the ships had turned around the point of the Acropolis – oh, they could already hear the cheers from friends and compatriots – they had to negotiate another quarter of a nautical mile to reach the safety of the chain. But as they came under land they also lost the benefit of the southern wind. Instead they fell victims to the treacherous and capricious currents known to haunt the inlet to the Horn. As if pulled by an invisible giant octopus the convoy and all the assailing Turkish ships were not only halted, but as far as Greek hopes were concerned, disastrously and helplessly dragged towards the shores of Galata, where Mehmet, his red robe eagerly licking the water, and the entire Turkish army stood ready to give them a warm welcome. Baltoghlu and his men, instantly filled with confidence, resumed the fighting with renewed strength.

For the Italians the setback was a disaster, but the captains, their crews and the soldiers were not inclined to give up. Baltoghlu himself concentrated all his efforts on getting his hands on the imperial galley, the largest ship in the fleet. But there was still plenty of ammunition for the dreaded Greek fire siphon placed on its deck to destroy the attackers. Burning like torches Turkish soldiers screamed in agony as they threw themselves into the sea where, among the jetsam and flotsam of sunken ships and dying men, severed arms, hands and heads made up the ingredients of a gruesome soup. A volley of missiles poured over the Turks from sterns, poops, yardarms, bowsprits and crows nests. In addition the Greek transport, though not the heaviest armed among the ships, had cranes which would normally be used to load and unload cargo. Now it was used to dump huge stones and filled water barrels onto the enemy vessels, sometimes instantly breaking them apart and sending them to the bottom of the sea. The carracks were equipped with stone laden catapults to the same effect. Occasionally the Italian ships themselves caught fire from the ceaseless bombardment of flaming spears and arrows, but since there were ample water supplies aboard they were quickly quenched.

As neither Baltoghlu nor Mehmet were much concerned about human losses as long as victory could be achieved, new boats with fresh warriors were constantly sent in to fill the empty spaces left behind by sunken ones. There was, however, knowledge also on the Italian side that sooner or later the imperial galley would run out of projectiles, whereby the Turkish superiority in number would eventually turn the tables in their favour. In order to forestall this fatal outcome, the captains of the remaining ships, shouting out orders from their poops, managed to coordinate their vessels so that they could be lashed together around the larger ship.

It was an astonishingly skillful manoeuvre, miraculous even considering that not a single waft of air came to their aid. To the spectators this unexpected turn of events gave the impression that the naval engagement had changed into a siege of a floating fortress dominated by four towers. Still, the Turkish flagship commanded by Baltoghlu himself held on to the imperial galley like a lion to the back of a giraffe, and though the long-necked animal would perhaps have been strong enough to eventually shake off its back a single deadly attacker, it could not in the long run withstand the concerted assault of a whole pack of lions. In the last instance the illusion of a besieged island was bound to dissolve as the whole of it drifted on to the shores of Pera. Fighting together with the valour of men knowing that they will go down together in an act of heroism, the Italians continued to inflict substantial damage on their relentless opponent. But now, as the sun was about to set beyond the walls and towers of the holy city, they knew that although they had been so close to their tantalizing goal as to almost being able to touch the great chain with their fingers, they would never reach it. God Almighty had not wanted the Christians to meet with success. Instead he had condemned them all to perish miserably. Knowing what their fate would be if they surrendered, they bravely fought on all the same.

But what about the southern wind which at first had smiled so promisingly in the face of mariners and defenders? It had been blowing steadily for a week and it just so happened that it had deserted them in the hour of destiny. But being a strategist older and more experienced than any man made admiral has ever been, the wind had not just disappeared without recompense. While the battle was fought it made a silent, circumspect move around the compass with its forces. In the clamour of death no one could either see or hear what was being prepared in the inscrutable and invisible, but in the very moment when the fate of the Italians seemed sealed, the gusts of Borea's trumpets rippled the water all the way from the enemy harbour to the melee of ships. Then came Neptune's horses down the hills of Galata to give the deserting sun a kick in the back. With their fiery breath they once again brought life and movement into dead sails, and the entire fortress, slowly but surely, began to move towards the Horn. The people on the walls held their breaths as their prayers soared to heaven. And yes, the maritime cavalry had come to their rescue and it stayed there for just as long as it took for the Turks to realise that, as darkness approached and the ships drifted towards the boom, it would not be bravery but suicide to wait for the Greeks to surround them inside the harbour and then tighten the noose.

Admiral Baltoghlu, who had fought furiously throughout the day, knew himself to be a doomed man as he reluctantly gave the signal of retreat. Mehmet, fuming with rage, tearing his clothes to pieces and, terrible to see, even the hair from his head, whipped up his horse from the water edge and returned to his retinue. When they saw his expression they all feared that he was either going to kill them all, kill himself, or just go plain mad.

Meanwhile the chain was lowered and in the darkness the crews of the ships inside it caused great clamour in order to make the Turks believe that they were going out with a huge fleet to meet their brethren. Escorted by Venetian, Genoese and Greek ships alike, they all made it to safety inside the harbour, whereafter the chain was again suspended. The day's work had cost some Italian lives, but the heavy losses were with the Turks, and the captains were heralded as heroes. So many were the questions, so ecstatic the gratitude and so riotous the joy, that captain Francesco Lecanella, who had untiringly spurred on his men to accomplish the impossible, almost forgot his human cargo. Suddenly he was reminded and accompanied by his officers he descended down the ship's ladder to the area where the woman had been held captive. When their torches hit upon her face they could see that she was in tears. When lowering their lights they understood why. In her bosom, his head unnaturally bent over her right arm, his legs over her left, the ship boy Daniello lay dead from the many wounds and flames he had sustained while, death defying and brave, helping the ship and its crew to finally reach Constantinople.

Chapter 15

When the tumult around the heroic convoy had somewhat subsided, the captains of the newly arrived ships made ready to report to Constantine in person. He had not been able to see for himself the eventual outcome of the naval battle as he and Longo had been forced to protect the land walls from any sudden follow-up attack. In the course of the late afternoon it had become increasingly obvious to them that a breach had really been made. If the Turks were now to launch a massive strike, there would probably be no means of stopping them. The Turks too saw the opening and began to amass one contingent of infantry after the other behind their guns. Before sunset the only thing the Turkish regiments waited for was the signal to attack. But it never came. Fear of the consequences of ordering an attack without Mehmet's orders kept the Turkish generals from releasing the trigger. By night fall it had become too late to strike and the troops were told to reassume their previous positions. Temporarily deprived of its high command the Turkish forces remained immobilised though their prey had been at closer range and more vulnerable than ever.

When darkness descended upon the defenders they were able to assess the damage done to the wall, and to conclude that not only had God worked a miracle for their ship crews by allowing them to finally and successfully reach inside the boom with their cargo unscathed; he had also protected the defenders on the walls from impending disaster. The Sultan on the other hand had been at Galata all day, spurring his horse into the water and the seamen to victory. Since his issuing of orders was all based on his exclusive experience of warfare on land, they made little or no sense to the mariners desperately trying to carry out Baltoghlu's original plan of attack. As time went on Mehmet's attempts to influence the course of the battle changed into furious cursing of his navy in general and its commander in particular. Even though news did reach him about the dilapidated state of the walls around the gate of Saint Romanus, he was now too eager trying to secure his victory at sea to pay proper attention to the details of these reports. Thus the discipline and centralisation of command within the Turkish camp for once stalled the effective deployment of forces when the decisive moment for a devastating strike had in fact arrived.

In a sense of awe at God's mercy the defenders once again undertook the Herculean task of repairing their crumbled outer wall, seeing that the Turks had withdrawn for the time being. The Emperor and Guistiniani led the operations, demanding hundreds of sacks filled with sand and gravel to be transported from inside the city to the most severely damaged sections of the wall. Masons did what they could to join stones together and civilians formed a never ending procession of curved backs loaded with whatever material could be spared and used to prop it up. It was an intensely tiring work following another day's ceaseless bombardment which, again, had cost some Christians' lives. But the relief which the news of the safe arrival of the ships brought the exhausted troops around the Romanus gate instantly invigorated them. Many a soldier simply fell to the ground and kissed it, only to subsequently raise his arms towards the dark sky in praise of God, Jesus Pantocrator and his most holy Mother.

While all this was going on, the captains of the ships and their senior officers steadily approached the Gate of St Romanus in a hieratic procession flanked by enthusiastic followers. Seeing them arrive, Constantine descended the stairs leading down to the peribolos, the area separating inner and outer walls from one another. Soldiers and civilians alike formed an audience on the walkways of the walls. Longo and the imperial guard followed the Emperor. At ten steps' distance from Constantine the delegation of captains stopped and bowed before him while touching the ground with one knee. Francesco Lecanella seized the word and said,

– Your Imperial Majesty. It is with deepest joy and gratitude to God and our valiant seamen and warriors that I have the pleasure to inform you that the ship you entrusted to my care to stock grains and other provisions in Sicily has now successfully returned. Three other ships, equipped for the purpose of reinforcing our defences by his Holiness the Pope, and manned with excellent mariners and warriors from the Republic of Genoa, have likewise braved the concerted attack of our enemies at sea, fended them off and securely entered the haven of the

Golden Horn. In this manner our goal has been reached and I kindly ask your Imperial Highness to relieve me from the duties specified in connection with this journey and to henceforth use my services in any way you may find appropriate. I, my crew, the worthy gentlemen and captains of Genoa, their crews and soldiery, hereby report mission completed and declare ourselves entirely at your command for any future action at land or by sea.

When captain Lecanella uttered these last words a roar of public acclaim echoed between the walls. Constantine, moved to tears by the return of a ship and a crew he had almost given up all hopes of ever seeing again, moved forward, raised Lecanella to his feet and solemnly kissed him four times on his cheeks. The crowd cheered and grew ever more joyous seeing their Emperor holding on to the arms of his captain, then kissing all the other captains in turn and blessing them. It seemed as though the public excitement would simply not cease, but Lecanella held out his hand, signalling with an ancient rhetorical gesture his will to speak once again.

– The cargo we bring is identical to what we were asked to bring back and is known by us to be in good order. However, as we approached Constantinople we stumbled upon a woman apparently sent out to cross our path by the enemy, whom we have consequently taken as a prisoner. We have questioned her but so far received no answer other than that she's Turkish and that she wants to help us to defeat Mehmet.

– She's lying! She's a spy! Hang her! The public outcry was unanimous at the mere sight of an infidel woman, and just as quickly as the crowd had turned into an ecstatic welcome committee for heroes, it now transformed into a mob ready to lynch the intruder. The Emperor waved his hand to stop rioters from rushing ahead in an attempt to tear her away from her military entourage, and as she suddenly emerged from the midst of the mariner delegation and was brought in front of Constantine, the cries abated. Though dressed in rags, her face darkened by dirt and her hair in wild array, it became apparent to the bystanders that this was not just a woman of the lower orders. She carried her noble head with great countenance, her limbs were slender and elegant, and the gaze of her inscrutable dark eyes was such that it could probably kill a man at ten paces, or, if choosing to do so, set his heart on fire. Commander Longo, being the first and last victim of the dark fire spurting from her eyes, felt both to be true as he succumbed to the regal command of her gaze, pinning him to the wall like a deadly arrow. A voice close to Constantine uttered,

– I know that woman. Five years ago I saw her in Adrianople, and I swear by the almighty God and his angels: that woman is the first wife of Sultan Murad.

Chapter 16

Sea commander Bathoghlu didn't experience any of his best days. The Turkish fleet had shown itself incapable of preventing the enemy from reaching its destination. Clearly somebody would have to be held responsible for the dismal failure, and if it wasn't the Sultan himself… in short, Baltoghlu knew his head must roll. Brought before the Sultan the following morning, he kneeled down in a plea for his life only to hear Mehmet order his immediate execution. As soldiers moved in to take him away and carry out the decapitation, some of Baltoghlu's officers bravely asked for the right to speak in his defence. All of them testified to his bravery. "Like a lion he had led the attack in one wave after the other, as indifferent to his own life and safety as to those of others. Unpredictable circumstances and sheer luck had finally allowed the enemy to escape. If it wouldn't have been for the wind suddenly rushing in from the north Turkish victory would have been certain, etc."

Although the Sultan was in no mood for ifs and buts, he was now seen letting mercy prevail over vengeance. He summarily recalled his previous death sentence. Baltoghlu was marched out in the open, surrounded by a ring of his own men and the Janissaries. Mehmet approached him and tore off all his regalia, stripped him of his sabre and had it broken in two halves. The executioner then ripped his shirt apart and he was stretched out on a wooden frame facing downwards. His hands and feet were tied to the frame with leather straps. A whip with seven knots was brought out. By the first sharp cracking Balthoglu could be heard moaning in pain, but he then endured the remaining twenty lashes without emitting a sound. When the flogging was over rivers of blood flowed down his back covered in blistering wounds. He was dismissed. His officers, fearing retribution from the Sultan were they to address a dishonourably discharged commander, did not dare to speak to him as he walked away in disgrace and humiliation.

A terrible silence and rows of glazed eyes accompanied his exit from the scene.

Having thus dealt with his admiral and passed him onto oblivion and obscurity, Mehmet issued an order to the effect of re-instating Hamsa Bey, his father's trusted naval commander, as admiral of the fleet. He then rode back to his tent in the Lycus valley. Here the generals had had the time to organise their moral defence, and it had been generally agreed that whatever Mehmet may come to hear from his Janissaries, general consensus was that the breach in the wall had not been sufficiently wide to allow for a killing blow. Instead the decision was taken to await further orders. The ploy worked. Mehmet could not be convinced that there had been negligence on the part of the commanders positioned with their troops along the land walls. He laconically ordered the bombardment to be continued against what, once again, proved to be a nearly miraculously restored piece of bulwark.

Meanwhile, in Constantinople, the revelation of the identity of the Turkish captive caused amazement and prompted Constantine to take action. That same evening Prince Orhan, the Turkish pretender to the throne whom the Greeks held hostage, was brought in to act as a translator between her and Constantine. Orhan verified her identity and then, at the Emperor's behest, began to question her as to her purpose.

Chapter 17

Pope Nicholas sat in the chair he always used when presiding over the cardinals. In front of him was an oblong table with intricate leaf-pattern inlays in mahogany, ivory and ebony, stretching towards the heraldic figures of the massive entrance door framed by pillars. The chairs, with their richly carved backs squarely set on lion feet, were all empty. The rays of the setting sun, passing through windows in Florentine mosaics, illuminated the slow dance of dust particles and cast a sharply defined luminous rectangle sideways over the table, igniting the passionate glow of mahogany, the sinister lustre of ebony, the dazzling white of ivory, and the noble ochre of oak.

In his hand he held an object of curious composition. It had been presented as a gift to him by a Dominican friar, who insisted it was an exact replica of the very wheel the venerable Ramon Lull had used in his days to meditate on the inscrutable wisdom of our Lord. In fact, the wheel was not one but two, concentrically arranged. Segmented into twelve compartments the outer wheel designated a number of *a priori* positive human characteristics such as Love, Prudence, Temperance, Fortitude, Justice, Generosity, Truthfulness, Faith, Hope, Charity, Kindness and Humility. In the inner circle twelve other segments indicated the seven deadly sins: Lust, Gluttony, Greed, Sloth, Wrath, Envy, Pride, and in addition, Hatred, Intolerance, Bigotry, Sodomy and Conceit. The two concentric circles could easily be moved around the centre so that any alignment of virtues and sins could be obtained. According to the Dominican friar this was exactly what Lull had done. He would for instance set the outer circle to show Faith in zenith, then position directly under it one of the deadly sins, for example Greed. Now, this would form the beginning, the point of departure for a meditation on the contradictions inherent in the human soul. What he would ask himself was simply: Is it possible for a man to be at the same time faithful and greedy? Depending on the qualities thus combined he would arrive at a positive, a negative or an indecisive response. In all cases though did he find it instructive to imagine human character as an outcome of what might at first, but not necessarily in the last instance, seem to be irreconcilable opposites.

The Catalan philosopher, so the Dominican said, had found inspiration to create this device in an astrological oracle found in Cordova, delivering ready answers to a great many typical questions that could be considered common to Jews, Moslems and Christians. Lull's idea had thus been to unite Christianity, Islam and Judaism into one divinely inspired consensus that would form the basis of a concerted resistance to the godforsaken Barbarian hordes that raided and laid waste large portions of Europe and the Holy Land in his day.

Nicholas turned the thing in his hand unable to decide whether it was the work of the devil or not. He was aware that his predecessors Gregory XI and Paul IV had condemned some of Lull's writings as heretic, among these the *ars generalis ultima*, of which the wheel he now held in his hand was no doubt a symbolic embodiment, and, perhaps even more strongly, the abominable views expressed in his *liber chaos*. Still, as he absent-mindedly fingered the device he suddenly came to align Prudence and Lust. Staring at the words, appearing like a celestial conjunction, he couldn't help asking himself if young Mehmet perhaps was precisely harbouring such contradictions in his character. Lustful to the point of terrifying cruelty no doubt, but then again apparently prudent and diligent in matters military. One needed only to think of the Rumeli Hisar, the fortress he had built as the first stepping stone to taking Constantinople, knowing that she was invincible as long as ships could still move freely in and out of her ports.

"Why had God wanted man to indulge in the, perhaps necessary but all the same undeniable, evil of warfare? Why had God created man such a rebellious creature, and why had he waited so long before sending his son to wash away the stains of men's innumerable sins? Why were the Greeks not upholding the union they had signed in Florence fifteen years earlier? Considering the power balance between the western and eastern churches – without the spiritual as well as material support of the Italians and the papal state Constantinople would long since have fallen to the Turks – it should by now have become indisputably obvious to Greeks, Armenians, Jacobites, Mesopotamians, Chaldeans, Maronites and Nestorians alike, that there was but one way for the church to travel, and that was the way leading to Rome!"

It had offended Nicholas to see the former Patriarch to Kiev, his trusted envoy Isidore, be imprisoned by the Russians on account of his insistence that the Muscovite princes must respect the union to which all clergy of the Orthodox church had agreed in ink and paper at a formally consecrated church council. Well, Isidore had now long since been released. Still.

It was all in vain. Nicholas rubbed his chin, apprehending the worst for the small military force he had finally consented to send out when, as a matter of fact, nothing less than the future of Christianity as such hung in the balance. Nicholas knew he had hardly done enough. Even so, Foscari in Venice had done even less. "Why," Nicholas finally asked himself, "when he has got everything to gain by keeping his colonies active throughout the Greek world? Or does he really think he'll be able to strike a lucrative deal with Anti-Christ in person?" Nicholas turned the circles aimlessly and then posed Lulls philosophical toy on the table. He marched towards the doors and alerted the Swiss guards on the outside. The doors swung open and then closed. The glow in the window had disappeared, but for anyone looking closely at the mechanical device in the abandoned room, the upper central column, aligned at twelve o' clock, would have read from top to bottom: Hope, Pride.

The darkly coloured message was there for any random bypasser to decipher. Dark indeed, and ominous, was the age-old wisdom saying that the road to Hell is paved with good intentions and that pride goes before fall. Not arriving in time to help the Greeks cast off the impending yoke of eternal humiliation would be a very high price to pay for knowing oneself to be in the right. Lull, put to eternal rest in his native Majorca, could only smile back ironically. He had known that since you can never persuade a mind scorched by the sun and forged by the desert to accept a world governed by anything else than one single blinding fire residing in heaven, you would have to make the one and only true God of love and forgiveness *seem* to be the same as his. The only way to obtain a degree of cooperation between Jews, Christians and Moslems, as the great Maimonides had so eloquently pointed out, was to emphasise the deeper concordance of ethical and moral precepts in all three creeds over and against theological subtleties, such as the 1000 year old debate on the true essence of the Holy Trinity or the number of rivers in Paradise. But then again, Ramon had been a heretic and a dabbler in dangerous sciences. There were even rumours that in his youth he had confessed himself a Cathar, and only accepted conversion to the one and only Catholic church at the point of the sword. Perhaps it was only right that this should be so, since what sin could in effect be greater than to try to identify God's intentions before He had chosen to make them known to the world?

Chapter 18

Although it had come to Francesco Foscari's knowledge that Pope Nicholas had sent aid to Constantinople, the Venetian rescue fleet still remained in port. To the members of the Council of Ten the delay, which could not longer be attributed to either political controversy or weather conditions, began to seem inexplicable. The ships, charged with supplies and man power, were ready to leave. Nonetheless days came and went without any of the ships putting to sea. If asked why they were not already under way, the captains answered evasively, saying they would all be leaving sometime tomorrow. However, as the new day dawned they were still there.

The decision to send help to Constantinople had been taken weeks earlier by the council and was signed by Foscari in person. Meanwhile idle seamen and soldiers spent most of their days quarrelling and gambling in the taverns. The city, having hired them to do a job abroad, now had to pay them for unsettling the streets at home. It not only meant a continuous strain on the city's finances, but a loss of prestige as well. In short, it was absolutely crucial to immediately dispatch the fleet – yet it didn't happen. Messages had repeatedly been sent to Foscari to inform him about the irregularity of the situation. When he didn't seem to care much about the daily complaints, brought to him by the harbour high commissioner, the general atmosphere grew dense as tensions increased on all sides and aggression spread throughout the city. Every man in the street knew Foscari to advocate war in almost any circumstance. During his long tenure as head of the Republic he had fought Milan in an almost interminable series of wars, some of which had been ill-fated. Lately Milan had concluded a truce with Venice's long standing main ally, Florence, leaving the Republic on the lagoon to drift in whatever direction she desired – except further inland.

On the day when the fleet finally heaved anchor and set sails under rainy skies, he called on his closest advisor and friend, Luciano Piombini, member of the supreme council and a experienced diplomat, for a confidential conversation. Foscari, dressed in a golden velvet coat and the ducal cap with elaborate leaf and flower patterns, received Piombini in his just recently completed palace in the Grand Canal. Piombini had not yet visited the Doge's family palace, and was much amazed by the sheer size and elegance of the eight arches crowning the loggia into which he first entered. Knowing the visit to be of importance he too had dressed up in full formal wear, a red dress, rich in folds with embroideries in gold, carrying around his waist a broad belt from which an ornate dagger was hanging. Although approaching his sixtieth year, Luciano Piombini still had no grey hair, making his middle stature, clean cut features and quick walk seem all the more youthful. A servant led him up the marble stairs and he entered a large reception room, the many richly carved and decorated windows of which all faced the canal. Seated, on a chair with a wooden back twice as high as his torso, clearly displaying his family's crest, with the winged lion in the upper left and red corner, was the Doge himself thoughtfully looking out over the misty canal.

The doors closed behind Piombini, and Foscari made a sign to him to move closer. As he approached Foscari rose, solemnly embraced him and bid him to sit down next to him.

– Don Francesco, let me first of all compliment you on your most extraordinary new abode, Piombini said, reverentially gesturing towards the many exquisite decorations and sumptuous works of art. You must be very happy with all this.

– Oh, my dear and trusted friend Luciano, it really isn't for me. My life is approaching its end, and I have little need for all these rooms myself. However when a man has lost almost his entire family – I had many daughters, as you know, all of them now in the custody of our Lord – he begins to fear the extinction of his entire lineage. All I have now is my son Jacopo.

Piombini reverentially nodded,

– For how long does he still have to remain banished to Crete? he asked.

– I hope not for very much longer. The judges were never able to squeeze a confession out of him.

– How hard did they try?

– Knowing him to be my son, they wouldn't physically torture him, if that's what you mean.

– That sometimes makes the whole difference. In practice it means that they were indeed lenient.

– Is that what they were? Foscari replied staring wearily at the dark gondolas moving around like ghostly specks beneath the windows.

– You still believe in his complete innocence?

It was a daring comment, but the nature of the relationship between the two men was such that Foscari could not afford to appear outraged. What he had to say in response was actually saturated with sincerity and emotion. He turned energetically to his interlocutor.

– Whatever the circumstances – and I can only say that to this day I believe him to be innocent of everything he has been accused of – I can not afford to lose my one and only heir. One day he must return from Candia and assume his rightful position among the leading families of our city. And to worthily represent the name of Foscari he needs a home that commands respect not only among his friends, but even more so among his foes. He who has nothing is nothing. I want my son to be someone, and if the will of the Forty, as well as the Council of Ten, will one day find him worthy of such position of trust, my greatest joy in life would be to know that he follows in my footsteps. I know, I have waged costly campaigns against Milan and her allies, but the day will come when people realise how necessary these sacrifices were, and still are, to protect Venice against the insatiable hunger for power of the Milanese. The late Philip Visconti made a fateful mistake as he, in return for manpower and arms, finally consented to marry off his daughter Bianca Maria with that condottiere Francesco Sforza, issued from the bosom of Venice herself! He's just as unscrupulous as the times ahead of him are, and mind my words, if he's not crushed before he gets the chance to overrun us, he will become the greatest military threat our Republic has ever faced. Whatever the apparent virtues of this man, his sons and grandsons will be dragon seed and the nemesis of our great city. The Viscontis are no more, it is now the Sforzas. I pray God to grant my son health and prosperity, and I hope for the tide to turn, so that he can return home, marry and have children. Dear friend, if you only knew how it grieves me to imagine myself the last member of the Foscaris. It simply can't happen. I must find a way to bring him back.

Luciano Piombini gave his friend and mentor a searching glance, wondering if and when he should utter what already lay at the tip of his tongue. He decided to take the risk to say it now, lest he one day be accused of having remained silent when he should have spoken.

– Dearest Don Francesco. You know I have always valued your great knowledge, your generosity, your experience, your military prowess and your political wisdom. I hear your words, and Sforza is indeed a dreadful threat. But suppose for the moment that the situation in Venice herself for the time being is a more imminent threat to our safety than any external enemy.

– Tell me dear friend, what are you hinting at? Foscari replied in a tired voice.

– Well, let me put it this way. If the rescue fleet bound for Constantinople would have remained another day in harbour, not only your political career but also your life as such would have been seriously at stake. Even now, as the ships have been seen departing, people keep asking many questions.

– What do they say?

– And your enemies here and now eagerly pick up on it and use whatever they can to denigrate you and scheme your downfall.

– Please, just tell me what they are saying. There was a cold gleam in Foscari's grey eyes. Piombini realised he could no longer circumnavigate the reef.

– They say that the reason why the fleet was delayed was that you, through your son on Crete, have already negotiated a deal with the new Sultan, and that you have declared yourself willing to silently sit back and let him take Constantinople at his ease in return for a large sum of money and other trading benefits for the Venetians. They say you are a traitor to Christianity, a foe of the Pope, some of your worst detractors even go as far as to claim that you will one day sell Venice herself to the Turks.

– That's infamous!

– And yet, it is only the beginning of the defamation. "Look at his new palace!", they say. "Where did a citizen, entrusted with the affairs of state and constantly spending all available resources on wars, get the kind of money from to build himself a palace like that? It's the Turk", they say. They call it "The Turkish Pavilion", yes, and there are even songs sung in the streets comparing you to one of the many wives in his harem.

– Is that all? Foscari asked, visibly bemused.

– Unfortunately Don Francesco, it isn't. What some of your enemies seem to know, and intend to use against you, is not that you delayed the entire fleet for three weeks because you have a deal with the Sultan – after all, we Venetians have always had a fateful tendency to throw Pope and Patriarch over board if only it will increase our gains. So a deal with the Turk is not really seen as the worst possible misfortune. What infuriates everyone is that your son is said to have expropriated these funds for himself, bribed everyone around him, and now intends to return to Venice with money provided by one of her most dangerous enemies.

– And that's not yet the end of the story. Your enemies, although they are cautious not to let the common people know this to be the case, also know that the real reason you delayed the fleet through secret orders, is that you still haven't forgiven the Byzantine Emperor for having refused to take your daughter's hand in marriage. They asked, and you said yes. Then they changed their minds, pretending your rich and beautiful daughter was not good enough to become the bride of a destitute ageing monarch, suddenly become "Emperor". An Emperor of what? Fifty decrepit churches and a hundred barrels of vinegar passing as wine! But you don't do that kind of thing to an Italian who, as it happens, is also the nominated leader of Italy's most noble republic, without incurring his hatred. I know it, and I know you know what I'm talking about… no, no, Don Francesco, please don't try to tell me it isn't true. Between the two of us it really doesn't matter. What matters, however, is that they know, that it's from personal vanity and hurt pride that you refuse to come to the aid of the Roman Emperor. As a consequence, the eastern city of God will, perhaps for all eternity, end up as the booty of a descendant of Attila, Djengis Khan and Tamerlane. Venetians by and large may not care too much about the future of conceited Greeks who run around expecting miracles and virgin epiphanies in stead of basing their happiness on reliable trading relations, but the thing that has infuriated people here is that even though we have a lot of our own people inside the walls of that wretched city, Venice herself has seemed utterly reluctant to answer their call for help. Don Francesco, to some people that is felt to be a downright betrayal of our kinsmen. Now, as the fleet is finally under way sentiments will perhaps be appeased for the time being, but I pray to God that it will not arrive too late to partake in the defence and liberation of the city.

– You need not worry about that, Foscari interjected, feeling that the innuendo of his trusted advisor had got the better of his friendly manners and diplomatic tact. – The ships are now sailing straight for Constantinople and they will engage the Turkish forces.

– I wish I could believe that, but something tells me that you don't really want them to get there. Now tell me, Don Francesco. Is this how you want to go down in history, as the man who set the future of his son's personal ambitions higher than the future of the Republic, who was content to see thousands of his own citizens massacred and eastern Christianity annihilated, just because he could not overcome his personal feelings of having suffered an insult in something that in the end was just another move in the eternal game of politics? Are you seriously trying to tell me that you allow yourself feelings of love and hate in regard to political allies and enemies? If, God forbid, that's the case, then I must urge you to do everything you can to regain your senses, because there is no passion more spectral and fateful than hate to lead a man astray from the path onto which he has been led by God.

Having listened impassively, Foscari now rose and put his hands on the shoulders of the other. – Luciano, he said, you have spoken like a true friend, not fearing to tell me what others would conceal and only hiss to one another like vipers in a dark pit. But you must trust me now that I'm not allowing vainglorious ambition to stand in the way of truth and justice. If God so wishes we shall indeed help the Greeks to liberate their city and free our own citizens, since to uphold

Christianity, in whatever despicable form, will always be preferable to succumbing to the hordes of the infidel. But there were urgent and confidential letters from the Pope, the French king and the Republic of Genoa to be carried to Constantinople on our ships. I had to wait for them to arrive before I could give the signal.

– Letters! Don Francesco, how are epistles and empty vows of friendship going to fortify their walls? You can't shoot anybody with a piece of paper! As we're speaking I can hear the roar of the guns. Meanwhile our fleet is, at best, several weeks away from its goal and I fear to say, that if they ever arrive there, it will be to see Turkish banners above the ramparts. Anyway, it can't be undone now, and let's hope that you are right about the impregnable strength of their walls.

– Sincerity may be humble but she cannot be servile. I appreciate the candour of your argument, Luciano, but as the elected leader of the people, I must do what I believe to be right for them. Times are indeed changing, the papacy has become an overt usurer, its sole aim to enrich itself at the expense of the people. Sforza is a godless man, and he's only the first in the train of many. Look here!

The Doge went over to the other side of the room, pulled out a drawer and came back with a leather portfolio which he opened on the table. Inside there was a series of small coloured drawings depicting all kinds of allegorical figures in the form of playing cards. Many cards contained images of either swords, wooden clubs, encircled pentacles or goblets. Others seemed more statuary or apocalyptic, some looked fiendish. Luciano looked at the pictures in amazement.

– I have never seen anything like this, he finally said. Is there some kind of meaning, some story told in these pictures?

– The whole set of pictures, and there are 78 of them in all, is called Tarot and they have some kind of hermetic significance. Apparently Francesco Sforza uses them as an oracle to predict the outcome of campaigns, sieges, battles and other important events.

– How is that?

– I don't really know, but look at this.

– Is it the same snake devouring a child that appears on his heraldic crest?

– Possibly. But look here. Underneath the snake the word "urobourous" has been written. I asked one of our learned men what that means and he said it is an image used by the ancients to express divine power at the service of man.

– Divine power given to man ... so it must be a sign of unlimited dominance. Does Jesus Christ appear?
– No.
– Virgin Mary?
– No, but there are many other figures, some similar to saints, but then again they look pagan in origin. Perhaps this was something that the Romans invented, or the Egyptians.
– How did you get hold of this collection?
– It is a copy of the 78 original drawings which Francesco Sforza himself commissioned from the artist, a certain Peter Bembo, to offer to the house of d'Este as a gift to obtain the favours of young Isabella in view of offering her his son's hand in marriage. Our spy at the Milan court found out about their plans, so we could ambush the courier and lay our hands on this strange deck of cards. Sforza doesn't even know we have them, and we still don't know how they are used. One idea is that it's actually some kind of cipher alphabet, and that certain constellations have definite albeit hidden meanings. Anyway, it goes to show how little the new prince of Milan cares about God and how much he relies on dark forces.
– Maybe so, Piombini said. In all events I do advise you to never appear in public without trusted men at your side.
– Don't you worry about that, I just raised the salary of my guard. Their loyalty is only to be had for money, and as long as they can see that I pay them well for staying in my service, they will. Meanwhile, I thank you for taking the time to come and see me. Would you care to take the cards with you? Why? Well, I would like you to bring them to the attention of the philosopher Battista. You know where he lives? Good. Say that I sent you and listen to what he has to say. Then report back to me. Goodbye my friend.
– Goodbye Foscari, may God be with you.
Piombini bowed reverentially. On his way out he couldn't help asking himself what would be worse: Foscari senior growing senile in his chair or his wayward son stepping into his shoes. Luckily it was not too late for alternatives.
Foscari on the other hand, seeing the back of his friend disappear through the distant doorway, slowly muttered to himself: "*Et tu Brute*".

Chapter 19

To Giovanni Giustiniani it seemed a supernatural déjà-vu. Was it in a dream that he had already seen her? Though he was sure they had never before met in real life, he felt as though she had entered his soul in a single glance. She was like a double of his own sister Elenor, yet different, and she was one of the enemy, he mustn't forget. All the more alarming that she kept haunting him like a phantom. They were all extremely tired after having spent several days in the direct line of fire and all the following nights rebuilding their fortifications. Giovanni himself, leading the work, couldn't even remember when he last had an hours uninterrupted sleep, and he was intensely longing to be able to just close his eyes. And just as he thought he could and would – the repair work seeming to proceed in good order under Luca's supervision and everybody's morale having been infinitely strengthened by the happy outcome of the naval engagement – he was unable to see anything but her under his heavy eyelids. Even when he eventually fell asleep, if only for moments, she was with him, and when he opened his eyes again he had the impression that she was talking to him, although it was only the night with its thousand hidden dangers infiltrating his over-active mind. He tried not to think too much of the responsibility he was carrying and just deal with challenges as they came. One by one, moment by moment. But precisely this kind of presence of mind demanded that he was not constantly distracted by a desire for a woman who wasn't even present in his field of vision. And yet she was, she had become the embodiment of that vision. It was definitely a dangerous situation, because if everything now concurred to prove that she really was a spy, then she would be tortured and put to death. For some reason this seemed absolutely unbearable to Giovanni who began to perspire in the cool of the night at the mere thought of it. He had just regained consciousness when Luca appeared in front of him, a torch in hand,

– Sorry to trouble you Sir, but the Emperor is asking for your assistance. No, no, there is no problem with the wall, we're putting it together as though no damage was ever done to it. Yes Sir, you can trust me, and believe me I didn't want to wake you up; looked like you needed a nap more than anything else. But the Emperor is adamant. It's about the Turkish woman. Yes Sir, she refuses to speak. More specifically Sir, she refuses to speak to anyone else but you, which is the reason the Emperor is now asking you to join him at the Blachernai.

Once again Giovanni felt that the border between being awake and being asleep had dissolved; had they not just spoken with each another? Didn't she just say she was there to see him in regard to a very urgent matter, a matter of life and death? And hadn't he just answered that there was not one single instance inside these walls that at present was not a matter of life and death?

– Well, Sir, I'm afraid I need your answer.

Luca's voice put an end to his reverie.

– Of course, I'll be there, just give me a minute to get myself together.

– Very well, Sir. I'll send the boy back with that message then?

– Yes, thank you, Luca.

– Thank you, Sir.

All evening there had been feverish activity in the Blachernai palace. The Turkish Prince Orhan, who had met with her in Murad's palace at Adrianople, had been called and could confirm that she had indeed been Murad's wife. It then became apparent that the woman, presenting herself as Hadije, spoke a fluent Greek almost without a trace of an accent. Although the prince and his Turkish, allegedly pro-Byzantine, entourage in the city had been assigned the defence of a portion of the sea walls that was unlikely to become a prime target, he was still Turkish and viewed with some suspicion. As soon as he had verified her identity, Constantine felt there was no need to further kindle the idea of a possible Turkish conspiracy, whatever its objective, within the city. Orhan was therefore dismissed and dutifully returned to his post. Meanwhile Hadije, who had been given some clean clothes to wear, was now also offered a jug of wine, bread, olives and a piece of goat cheese, which she thankfully received.

But even if she did speak Greek she now insisted she would not reveal her purpose for being there unless she could tell it directly to the Italian commander. Constantine scrutinized for her moment, then said,

– I suppose you're aware that I can have you put in chains, tortured and executed for refusing to speak to me?

– Please, I must talk to him. I have a message from his family. I will tell you everything you want if I can only speak with him first. Please...

Constantine was more surprised than offended. Surprised at her nerve and determination, dictating, as it were, conditions for her confidence. Realising he could always come back and continue the interrogation, he finally, and out of curiosity, decided to let her have her way. After all, it might be very interesting to hear what Giustiniani would have to say after having met with her. Clearly, though, the Emperor as well had to some degree succumbed to the compelling authority of her beauty.

Constantine met Giovanni outside the palace, briefing him about the prisoner's wish. – She says she knows you from before. Is that correct?

Giovanni energetically shook his head. – Never seen her in my life.

– Not even in your imagination? Constantine countered with a smile. Saving Giovanni the trouble of finding an answer, he turned round and fumbled in the dark for the reins to his horse.

– I'm going over to the walls to see how the reparations are coming along. Please let me know when you're done with her. I can't wait to hear her testimony.

Thus it came to pass that the room in which the meeting took place was the Emperor's bed chamber, recently converted into a military head quarter. The torches cast long shadows of both figures as they moved towards one another. Hadije spoke in a low voice to make sure nobody outside the room would be able to listen in on their conversation. A light breeze from a window ajar caused flames and lamps to create the impression of salamanders running criss-cross over the table and their faces.

– Why are you here? Giustiani asked.

– For the same reason as you are.

– What do you know about my reasons?

She paused, made sure her dark eyes had their target in focus and took a deep breath.

– The Emperor has no money. Why on earth didn't you take these men somewhere else, where they could really do something to increase your wealth and power? Instead, with personal courage as your guiding star you have led other Genoese men to follow your example. You should have seen these fighting men today. They wanted to get through, to save their own lives, of course, but most of all they wanted to show you that they too are men of your calibre.

– Don't be ridiculous, they didn't do it for me.

– I don't know what astounding feats you have accomplished, but these men venerate you as their hero. I even heard the captain say so. And I prayed for them throughout the entire battle, knowing what would happen to them and to me, if ever we were boarded, over-manned or sunk.

– God obviously heard you, but does that mean that your reason for being here is less unholy than mine?

– The purpose of my long journey is to meet with you and join you in your quest, because I know why you're here.

– You have absolutely no idea what brought me here, so cut the pretence will you! Giovanni exclaimed, annoyed by her self-assertive manners.

– You think I'm just talking, don't you? Let me tell you how and why I came to know everything about your mission to Constantinople. As I told you, I was the real first wife to Sultan Murad. Officially he also had that Serbian princess, but she was only for diplomatic reasons and he loved her just as little as she loved him. Besides she was getting too old and ugly to bear any child to him and he never demanded that she consummate the marriage. And why should he, with any beautiful woman ready to satisfy any of his whims at a blink of an eye? Anyway, with me he saw things differently. He made me the real first lady of the empire because he really wanted my son to become the future Sultan, but he knew that with Mehmet's coming of age and your Orhan waiting in the wings, the boy would stand little chance to survive into mature age. So he wanted to take the baby boy away from me and place him in secret custody until the day he could claim the throne for himself. There would then be documents of his hand proving my child's legitimacy.

– It was an ambitious plan, but I refused, fearing not only to lose my child but also that he would one day actually try to gain control over the Sultanate, and so make himself known and immediately call down upon himself his own destruction. At that time I didn't even consider what would happen to me. Then my husband died. The beast flew over the Bosporus and had my son murdered while he paternally embraced me, offering me his life-long pledge of loyalty. A betrayal in the coldest of cold blood, it was. Grief, desperation and hatred stirred in my blood and I swore to avenge myself, but of course I didn't show him. No, no, not as much as a tear did I shed in his presence. And I was married off again, this time to General Ishak Pasha. To make sure I was out of the way he told Ishak to move back to his palace in Anatolia, and this is where my journey started. Now I'm finally here, and my reason for this is that I, as much as you, want to see the tyrant and murderer dead. That's why I knew I must, at any cost, get inside the walls of Constantinople and meet with you.

While Giovanni listened to her, he was once again overcome by the irritating sensation that the woman in front of him was already under his skin. She spoke as though she knew everything there was to know about him, as though they had already had a an entire life together, united by a vow taken in the sign of an ominous secret. Still he couldn't figure out from where she came to possess all this information. To gain some time he said,

– And how do you know I so eagerly want to see the Sultan dead? Why wouldn't I be content to just see him and his troops retire? I mean there is absolutely no way of getting to him.

– Yes there is, and I'll tell you why. Just as everything was dark beyond hope and life itself seemed to abandon me on the shores opposite this water, God stretched out his hand to help me. I was saved an ignoble death and carried hither exactly as foretold in the prophecy.

– What prophecy?

– Well now, will you please listen you Great Commander? In the town of Menisa, in the western province of Anatolia, lives an old seer by the name of Zacharias. His outer eyes are almost of no use to him, but he sees the world and its makings through the visions of his spirit. In his younger days he was a trusted advisor to my husband, and apart from telling his fortunes he researched the secrets of the universe – people say he's actually found a way to make gold. He's of Greek origin, lives like a monk or a saint, but says that the good of any religion depends on the quality of those who practise it. To him Islam, Orthodoxy or the Catholic belief in Christ is, if not exactly the same thing, at least only distinguishable from another in the eye of the all-seeing Lord, who so intimately knows the human heart that nothing can deceive him. And like the vicarious eye of our Lord is this man's vision here on earth. In my deep despair I did not know where to turn but to him. Disguised as a peasant woman I left my palace behind because all of its flowers had withered, its fruit had turned bitter and its birds had grown silent. The gazelle was sad since the sun itself lacked the power to kindle its heart. Thus I set out, walking, straddling mules and donkeys for days and nights until I reached Menisa. There I went to see Zacharias who received me saying that he had expected me. He bid me to sit down in his house. It was filled with the strangest paraphernalia: jars containing exotic herbs, liquids, metals, concoctions and animals, vessels in copper heated by a fire from which fumes and gases were constantly emitted, and there were models of siege engines and instruments for observing the heavens. I asked him what it was all good for and he said he no longer had much use of them, except when he had to induce himself in a state of trance. He bid me sit down but I felt uneasy. Then he told me to fear nothing, gave me some wine to drink and bread to eat while he himself began to breathe heavily into one of his vessels while reciting magic spells. I wanted to tell him what my purpose was but he wouldn't let me speak and I soon understood why. Suddenly he sunk to the floor and I feared he had died right in front of me. As I rushed to his side, he raised his arms straight up and began to speak, with a voice that seemed to come altogether from another world, his very lips concealed under his long white beard. These were his words, engraved in my soul like an inscription in stone,

– You seek to overthrow the Lord of the World *sub lunae* but his might is great and his power waxing. For you to succeed you must travel to the place where serpents breed in great numbers and you shall almost perish by their venom. On the shore, gazing at the dome of holy wisdom, you shall die to this world, lonely, despised, abandoned like the saviour himself. Then from God there shall be a sign and you shall be carried away and then brought through iron, water and fire to your resurrection in the eternal city. There you shall meet with him who has hair like the sun and eyes like the sky, a mighty warrior with whom your destiny shall be forever linked, since the two of you are the edges of one and the same sword. Only united can you hope for victory. Upon your arrival you shall therefore thank God for having selected you to do his works and humbly confess and convert to the creed of the warrior. Remember, the two of you want the same. Two fallible human aspirations uniting in a perfect goal. Thus is the *mutatis mutandi* of the world completed and through darkness divine light shall shine forth again.

– Then his speech turned completely incomprehensible and foam began to spurt from his mouth. Again I thought he was about to die, but suddenly he sat up, opened wide his vacuous eyes and said: If, after all I have said, he still doubts you, tell him his sister's name is Elenor and that *she* is the reason for his being there.

Chapter 20

Giovanni was speechless. There was nobody else in the world except his sister who knew about the solemn oath he had sworn to seek satisfaction on behalf of her murdered husband. On the other hand, all she had was that name. A strange coincidence, no doubt, nothing more. But then the final blow was delivered.

– Rizzi was not only a good and honest captain, he was also a close friend of yours, wasn't he? I understand how you feel and the stronger eagle chick hacks his brother to death while the parents are gone. My son was that defenceless chick to whom no one could offer protection against the voracity of his brother. Do you now understand why we are, and must be, in all of this together?

Hadije was content to see her ruse succeed. Although it was quite true that she had met with the soothsayer Zacharias, and although he did deliver a prophecy, the very wordings of which had been faithfully rendered by Hadije to Longo, he had never uttered the words: "And if he doesn't believe you, tell him that his sister's name is Elenor". This name had been given to her by someone else. It was in fact a message from someone who was no more.

The battle had been raging for hours and it seemed inevitable that the Genoese and the Greeks would either have to surrender or let themselves be massacred to the last man. In this critical moment, she heard a thumping sound next to her. In the obscurity of the hold where she had been confined she discerned Daniello's young body covered in blood, still gushing forth from multiple wounds. His hands and face were singed by fire and she could tell he was barely breathing. Instinctively she tried to help him and reached for some fresh water. She lifted up his head, put it in her lap and tried to give him some water to drink. She ripped off her own clothes and tried to bandage the ugliest wounds, but realised there was little she could do for him except to pray for his soul. The boy, about to die as a hero, now opened his blue eyes, staring right into hers for about as long as it took him to stutter,

– Tell…Longo Venetians too… die… with… honour. His sister, Elenor… before I sailed with husband, captain Rizzi… I came back, but sister say… must come back… alive. She gave me… letter. Take…

At this point his voice broke and his eyes glazed over. Overcome by an irresistible grief, Hadije began crying, taking the boy's body into her arms as if cradling it in death. Tears streamed down her cheeks and suddenly she found herself kissing him, first on his head, then on his cheeks, his chin, on his lips, and finally in every place she could reach, covering herself in his blood, tasting the tar and the resin which had burned his body to death. She also searched for a letter somewhere on his body, but she never found it. However, it was from the fragmented message of the dying boy she got the key words which had induced Giustiniani to open his heart to her. In this way Hadije managed to successfully pretend she knew more than she really did. It was a gamble, but one worth risking. Luckily her intuition had led her in the right direction from the very beginning. She still had no precise idea in what relation the young boy stood to either Longo, his sister or her husband, but once the relations between the latter had been clarified, it didn't really matter what Daniello's role had been. Now he was dead, but he had brought the message Hadije needed in order to see the prophecy come true.

In the belief that Hadije really knew about the tragic story of his sister's husband, Giovanni rather candidly began to reveal his heart as well as his own family loyalties. In the course of these confessions, she was surprised to learn that as a young man Giovanni had contemplated becoming a priest, and that he only renounced the calling because he felt the weakness in his own flesh to be too overwhelming to allow him to successfully embark on the narrow path of virtue. All his life, however, he had been in awe of God's will and his creation, and he held Catholicism for the one and only true apostolic faith.

– You see, he said, the sufferings of Christ were real, and so were those of his mother.

Alone that phrase struck a powerful cord in Hadije's soul. Slowly and emphatically she said,

– Then I want to become a Catholic Christian myself.

Giovanni couldn't help laughing at the impetuousness of her desire. Amused he countered,

– We have a proverb back in Genoa that runs as follows: "Woman wants a priest but only after she has conquered the warrior".

– I'm not quite sure I understand the full meaning of that.

– What it means… It means that a woman wants to be married and virtuous but only after she's been able to get the most able man on the hook.

– That's right! Hadije exclaimed. – And if it takes for me to become a Christian to have him, then so be it. I want to convert to your faith and be baptised.

– But do you know anything about what it is to be a true Christian, about the original sin of our first parents, and…

– I know everything about sin alright, that's what the harem is all about, but I need no more of that. No, I want to be baptised in your creed.

– I'm sure that can be arranged one of these days.

– Why not tonight?

– Tonight? No, that's not possible, Giovanni laughed. – First you must be instructed in the doctrine and then.

– What if I die tonight?

– What?

– If I die tonight, I won't come to heaven, right?

– Why would you…

– Because I'm an infidel, and infidels don't go to heaven.

In this vein their conversation continued until Giovanni finally realised that she wouldn't give up her strange request. All he had to do on the other hand was to refer her to the Emperor, since he was the one ultimately in charge of her destiny, and as far as everybody else was concerned Hadije was a prisoner of war. Among the last thing prisoners of war usually came to think of, was to issue demands about their own baptisms. Giovanni could only chuckle at her near complete ignorance of what her real situation was as a hostage. But then something quite extraordinary happened.

Constantine, ever so curious to receive information about her, had returned to Blachernai. After having related the rather bizarre story of her prophetic quest, Giovanni arrived to the point in his report where she had asked to be baptised. To his surprise Constantine didn't even smile ironically at the proposal. On the contrary, he gave it great afterthought. Then he said,

– It makes sense. This could be exactly what we need to top off this day's astounding achievements. We will turn her into a princess of the Sagas, and you, dear commander, into the living embodiment of the dragon slayer, a modern day Saint George. This could have great moral value.

– Wouldn't it be of more moral value if she converted to the Orthodox faith?

– No, that's precisely the point. That would only make the impression of a premature political move and confirm the suspicions that she's a spy. No, this is much better. She was driven hither by the desire of so far unrequited love and now she has thrown herself at your mercy, converting to your faith, kissing your feet. That's beautiful. I can't really explain this to myself, but I can feel there is some important truth in all this. We must use her appearance here to our advantage as much as we can.

– And you're not worried this has just gone a little bit to your head?

– I'd be much more worried about her if I were in your clothes, Constantine smiled and gave Giovanni a paternal pat on his shoulder.

– You must play the game and try to find out as much as you can about her.

– But how do you know she's not an infiltrator on a mission?

– I don't, but we shall find out. Rather, you will. Just be very careful not to fall head over heels in love with her. She's a mighty fine specimen of her gender, commander.

It is possible that the Emperor to some degree believed his own words. But it is also possible – perhaps even more so because it was just a hunch, a feeling – that he consented to Hadije's odd request secretly hoping that Giovanni would become so attracted to her that in the end he could not imagine abandoning the city without bringing her along. The only thing Constantine needed to do, then, was to make sure she would not be given the chance to escape. So, besides making sure everything was being prepared for the baptism, he also issued an order for her house arrest, albeit one under unusually comfortable conditions, considering the circumstances. In fact, Constantine wanted her treated like a queen. In his view that would only enhance her beauty and make her even more irresistible to her chosen victim, who, as it were, simultaneously happened to be his right hand. And just as much as Constantine wanted to believe in Giovanni's unswerving loyalty to their common cause, just as much did he know that no living man on earth so far had ever been chiseled out of stone.

Chapter 21

The ceremony took place at midnight in the palace chapel. Fratello Lorenzo, an Umbrian friar of the Franciscan order hastily called to duty, conducted the ritual with Giovanni and Constantine as sole witnesses.

Candelabras in the apse illuminated the three deeply set vaults and their glass windows, depicting scenes from Genesis: Adam and Eve in Eden and the Tree of Knowledge flanking the centre piece, the Arrival of the Archangel Gabriel to the scene of the crime. The air was heavenly scented with Persian sandalwood, and from the baptismal font, in which hot water and essences had been poured, fragrant fumes rose toward the ceiling creating all kinds of fugitive and hap-hazardous shapes before dissipating in the cool air.

The walls presented mirrored images in stone, marble patterns arranged in the form of fanciful butterflies, seemingly flapping their decorate wings in the light of wall sconces; and in the otherwise near-empty room the murmuring voices of the friar – relentlessly chanting his liturgical melismas while swinging the censer – and the two others, from time to time whispering to one another, formed a responsory song of sorts.

The age old font itself, in black porphyry and said to have been transported from Kiev during the reign of Basil the Bulgar-Slayer, was remarkable not only because of its sheer size and volume – it was large enough to swim in – but also because of its extraordinary decoration. All along its rim ran a massive serpent, in the coils of which mystic runes had been inscribed as well as other symbols which to both Constantine and Giovanni seemed pagan in origin. The snake's head was a particularly rich rendering of a dragon, and its mouth, gaping wide to expose two enormous fangs, was in the process of swallowing the tail. Thus the serpent formed one continuous meandering, never ending movement.

From the interior of the sacristy Hadije, in a swathing arrangement of white linen, emerged and was led to kneel down before the Maltese cross under the key stone of the central vault of the apse. She recited, after the friar, first the Lord's prayer and then the *Ave Maria gratia plena*. She was also made to kneel before the grand mosaic of the *Christos Pantocrator*, and at this point she spontaneously raised her clasped hands towards him while silent hot tears, shimmering in the light like drops of dew on a bed of roses, began to stream down her blossoming cheeks.

Finally she was asked if she was ready to receive the baptism in the name of the Father, the Son and the Holy Spirit, to become a devout Christian thereby renouncing all the works of Satan. To this she nodded and was now led to a small ladder leading up to the font. She climbed the ladder and on the sign of Constantine the monk seized her head and immersed her under water. He kept her entire body and head under water for as long as it took him to recite the words "I baptise you in the name of the Father, the Son and the Holy Spirit, and your name in the face of God shall be – Felicia, which means Bringer of Happiness." When she was finally released from the font, she rose, gasping for air, and for a moment remained like a statue in the centre of it, her uplifted face overcome by rapture, water flowing down her slick hair, dripping off her white gown, thus subtly revealing the hitherto largely hidden splendours of her body.

Constantine couldn't help but associate this to a sensuous and remarkably suggestive antique statue of Nike, the goddess of victory, he had once seen on the island of Samothrace; Giustiniani on the other hand felt as though Mary Magdalene had made an apparition and announced herself pregnant – with *his* child. In everybody's mind, chaste or not, there was little doubt as to why Murad had taken a special liking to her. Apart from her undeniable physical charm, there was a mysterious charisma surrounding her, a regal, commanding something which made it very difficult for a person in her presence to resist her will and desire. And no one was more susceptible to her influence than Giovanni. The soothsayer had told her to convert to the creed of the warrior once contact between the two of them had been established. There was no doubt Felicia was immediately convinced of having found the one man she was supposed to look out for. As for Giustiniani, his sentiments had been strangely mixed from the very moment she set eyes on him. One impulse strongly and wisely advised him to prevent any woman, be it his own mother, from getting a chance to influence military matters in any way. In his view, women generally knew so little of warfare that their ideas invariably were either impracticable or downright disastrous. But even though what he came to hear in the wake of the baptismal ceremony alerted him to danger in every sense of the word, he did not seem to be able to successfully take her words off his mind.

– You will help me, won't you? she had said, bravely stepping in between the table and the door as he made for it.

She had been conducted back to the Emperor's bedroom and given some clothes worthy of a lady in her position, as well as some privacy in which to dress up. A satin dress in carmoisine red and some jewellery, from who knows what hidden Venetian chest, had been brought to her while her conversion to the Christian faith was communicated to selected officials and senior officers. Many Greeks – in particular Francis and his domestic enemy Lucas Notaras – together with not a few Italians raised eye-brows at the news, not quite understanding how to interpret that a Turkish woman, held honourably hostage by the benevolence of his Majesty the Emperor, had had the temerity to turn to the faith of westerners. Was it a provocation? Another ruse concocted by the Sultan? Questions would undoubtedly have continued to pile up had it not been for another call to arms over the entire length of the land walls as Turkish scouts had been spotted beneath them in several places, searching for weaknesses in the fortifications sufficient to allow for a breaching attempt. Longo had entered the room to announce that he would continue the interview at another time when he discovered his helmet left behind on the table. He went to pick it up. When he turned around she stood right in front of him, ostensibly blocking his way.

– You will help me, wont you? she said.
– Help you with what?
– To kill that animal before he kills us.
– There is no way either you or I can get to him.
– Perhaps no way I can, perhaps no way you can, but *together* we shall.

For a moment they just stood there, watching each other with the silent and inscrutable intent of two brute animals suddenly brought face to face. Then, before he had the time to react, she flung her arms around his neck and pulled his head towards her. It all happened in an instance. He felt the singeing touch of her red lips and tongue caress the pale cartilage of his scarred ear. Blood rushed through his body as she buried her fingers in his hair and beard in disarray and coiled her left leg around his waist. Instinctively he threw her onto the table in front of him. There he unleashed the full power of his loins. At the receiving end of this demonstration of brute force was an irresistibly pulsating cavern set in a mountain of exquisite flesh that had once been the exclusive refuge of the late Sultan. As if conjured up by the genie of the lamp it was now reopened, promising his tormented mind and body an enchanted garden of interminable delights. She too swallowed his desire so avidly that he didn't even find the time to ask himself whether its darkest recess indeed held a fiery dragon, or if the distant pearl, gleaming seductively inside its black oyster, dimly perceived through the oneiric waters of his wildest dreams, was just there for him to grasp.

Chapter 22

The next morning, some of the soldiers discovered evidence that the Sultan was trying to gain access to the city by digging tunnels under the defence walls. By way of a large goatskin drum, positioned in a deep well to detect any man made subterranean movements, the soldiers on watch had been able to perceive the thumping sound from many pick axes relentlessly working on the stony underground. At daybreak, however, the digging work apparently stopped. Lucas Notaras, who knew his Theodosian wall, informed the Venetian Mayor Minotto, responsible for the defence of the Blachernai area, that the Turks would soon give up their efforts to tunnel their way into the city at this juncture. The reason, he said, was that although the walls outside the so-called Prison of Anemas were more vulnerable than other sections of the wall, due to the comparatively poor workmanship of its original builders, they were nonetheless founded on solid rock. Although this was not obvious from either the inside or the outside, Notaras claimed to know this for a fact and categorically declared that it would be impossible for the Turks to successfully bring about the eventual crumbling of the walls by means of mining.

Whether he was right or wrong about this, the Turks apparently soon stopped their diggings around the Gate of Blachernai. But this did not mean that their mining efforts as such had been abandoned. On the contrary. They were just deployed on several other portions of the wall simultaneously. Luckily all defenders had been alerted to the potential danger of a surprise mole attack, and so wherever suspicious nightly activity could be detected, and the sounds of pick axes be heard though the ground, the defenders were on their guard and ready to strike back.

Now, this was a task for which Giovanni, having participated in several sieges of Italian cities. was not entirely unprepared. But although these too had required some unusual techniques and tactics, he had never experienced a sustained artillery bombardment of this magnitude either as an attacker or a defender. In his heart he knew that without re-enforcements from the outside world within the next two weeks or so, the Turks – springing forth clad in armour like the legendary soldiers of the dragon seed from the bowels of the earth – would eventually wear them out. In the end the only thing expected from Giustiniani personally would be to inspire others to follow his example and bravely prepare for their own heroic deaths. Although well acquainted with the grim realities of warfare, this was something he instinctively tried not to think about. Luckily, the Turks had so far been unable to gain a foothold inside the Horn. As long as this was the case a rescue fleet still stood a reasonable chance of successfully joining forces with the one anchored behind the boom. Together they would perhaps even be in a position to strike back.

Be that as it may, Giustiniani, thought. At present there was no time for day-dreaming, and yet that was precisely what he was doing. Whatever he undertook, no matter how hard the task and how assiduous the effort, he saw her image hover in front of him. She spurred him on, kept his desire for bravery and adventure glowing. For some strange reason she had given his quest a new spark as he was about to write off his own mission as impossible. Thus he begun to feel the power of the two-edged sword, but as yet he did not know where to direct it. And that same night, not even a full day after their first encounter, he met with her again.

Felicia was officially still a prisoner of war, but her confinement could hardly be compared to that of Turkish soldiers just barely holding on to their lives in dark, humid, filthy, rat, bat and lice ridden caverns. She had an entire apartment of a Roman style villa – one of the few still in existence – and a maid at her disposal, and Giustiniani, haunted by her presence, sought and obtained permission from Constantine to go and see her, officially to continue the interrogation which had been cut short by the alarm that the Sultan was now employing miners to get inside the walls.

The city after sunset was dark as usual and the single lamp from the two Greek soldiers who led the way only barely lit up the streets, dangerously pot-holed from the impact of projectiles and filled with all sorts of debris. Finally they arrived at the villa. One of the soldiers pointed toward two windows from which a faint light was emitted. There were two other soldiers on guard outside the entrance to the house and they now took over, conducting Longo up the stairs and opening the door to her quarters. She sat beside a table, working something with her hands. She was fully dressed in a red and yellow robe, her long black hair artfully arranged around her neck. As he entered the room, helmet in hand, she rose from her chair and moved to greet him.

– I knew you would be back, she said with a smile, squeezing his scarred and bruised right hand inside her palms.

– I'm here on the Emperor's orders, Longo said, trying to sound as official as he could while the soldiers were still in the room. He made a sign for them to withdraw. Once they were outside she answered,

– It doesn't matter what you believe your reason to be as long as you always come back to me. The important thing for now is that we are here together and that we start to work on our plan.

– What plan?

– Oh, please!

– I 'm sorry, he said – Whatever you have in mind, I don't have time for any other plans than those concerning our defence. Unless you happen to know of a miraculous way to successfully rebuild a crumbled piece of bulwark in two hours, then don't pronounce yourself on things of which you have no experience. Unperturbed Hadije replied,

– I heard Mehmet is now trying to bring the walls down with the help of miners.

– Yes, what about it?

– I was thinking, that if he can dig a tunnel to get to us, why couldn't we dig a tunnel to get to him, before he gets us?

– And what would be the purpose? We don't have anywhere near the manpower to mount an attack on any of his larger army units. It would be suicide!

– I wasn't thinking of attacking the entire army, only him.

– How?

– Well, from what I have heard, his tent is pitched at a mere stadium beyond the moat. Wouldn't it be possible to dig a tunnel from inside the Peribolos that goes under the wall, as well as the brick of the moat, and then head straight for his tent?

– Possible perhaps, if you had limitless manpower and a hundred years of tranquility. But let's say the Sultan would be in his tent a century from now, still trying to figure out how to best conquer the city. What will you do once your tunnel does reach him?

– The general idea would be to amass as much gunpowder as possible and then, at the right moment, ignite the compound and blow the tent, with Mehmet inside it, in the air!

– Yes, wouldn't that be just fantastic! And then, as Mehmet has been dispatched to the moon, there will be total confusion in the Turkish camp, the generals will have to meet to decide what to do, and unanimously vote for a swift withdrawal in spite of the fact that our walls look like a piece of torn and ripped lace. Yes, that's exactly what's going to happen!

Felicia did not immediately answer. She looked at him intently for a moment and then said,

– I guess you're right. It was just an idea. But no matter what, we've got to find a way of getting to him!

– No dear lady, that's not what *we* will do. What *we* have to do is to try to hold him at bay for as long as it will take for our reinforcements to arrive from overseas. Only then…

– You are naïve, Giovanni. If you only knew how little all the Franks, and their ilk, care about you and everybody under your command at this moment, you wouldn't be expectant of any help forthcoming.

– If you're right, we're all but dead.

– Maybe so, but we still have to get him. Now give me a kiss.

He now felt he should refuse this intimacy on principle. But her perfume acted as a powerful aura of persuasion. Once again he simply couldn't resist her. Her slender hands caressed his chest covered in gunpowder and coagulated blood while he drank the nectar of eternal youth from her mouth. In between her breasts a crucifix was gleaming. As he reached for her pomegranates, he felt her hand fixing into position the battering ram, which now began to pound at the golden gate with a steadfastness of purpose that would have put even the gunmen attending to the Big Bear Barrel of the Turkish artillery in awe. The roaring of the guns, the blood, the piles of dead, the putrid smell of decaying corpses, the constant effort, the constant vigilance, the constant responsibility, the constant allegiance to what now began to emerge in its true light as an utterly lost cause, had begun to wear him down. Although he was as yet in no position to surrender, he felt that there was no knowing if he, or anyone else for that matter, would even be alive tomorrow. Thus he found nothing in his heart or conscience – not even a faint fear of divine punishment and eternal damnation – to restrain him from committing what at least technically was a sin. His was the enjoyment of a professional courtesan, washed up for God knows what strange reason, on the shores of his deserted island in the midst of a volcanic eruption. Perhaps this in itself should have given him an even stronger reason to worry, since all the men who relied on him would rather see that he bothered more about the effects of the eruption, than about of a pair of dark eyes trying to harness his will for its own capricious purpose. Giustiniani, however, thought himself strong enough to both succumb to seduction and maintain his military integrity. Whatever the degree of truth in that assessment, the moment his semen was ecstatically discharged, the question as to whom he did in reality owe his loyalty and honour suffered a temporary eclipse.

Chapter 23

As soon as Longo was back at his post the Emperor was eager to hear first hand news. Longo told him about Felicia's idea of having a tunnel dug to the Sultan's tent. Apart from being impracticable the plan struck Constantine as quite inventive. Seeing the gleam in Longo's eyes, Constantine was able to convince himself that Longo did not take her plan seriously. But since Constantine also knew that if there was something Italians were known for – regardless of their loyalties, talents and flaws in other respects – it was precisely that they could resist anything but a beautiful woman. Ever since Constantine had decided that he had no other choice than to make a famous mercenary his right hand, he had also had an uncomfortable presentiment that if and when the ultimate hour of truth struck, he would nonetheless find himself grievously alone. And although he believed that by making the Turkish woman a Catholic and a privileged prisoner, he had also tied Giovanni even closer to him, his heart remained beset with an annoying yet persistent doubt.

As the two men stood together on the ramparts in the dead of night, the Turkish camp ominously silent and eerily illuminated by open fires fuelled by a night breeze pushing in from the sea under jagged skies, Constantine said,

– I know you are a very brave man, Longo, but I have this feeling inside me, persisting in spite of my efforts to rid it of all trustworthiness, that as we are moving closer towards our inescapable destiny, you will be obliged to seek a way out of all this. However, since I don't intend to let go of the verbal assurance you have given me to the contrary, I can only see this take the form of a betrayal, the consequences of which, were you to survive, will haunt you for the rest of your life. I therefore want you to know that I, by virtue of the honours and the responsibility bestowed upon me by my people, herewith seize the opportunity to absolve you from any future guilt in this regard, knowing that in the last instance you must do what you have to do, and that even though my loyalty is fatally bound to what my God, my people and my ancestors expect from me, I can't demand the same from foreigners, no matter how sympathetic they happen to be to our cause. When the time comes you must do as your conscience tells you. This I want you to know.

– Your Majesty, it saddens me to hear you speak of the future in this way, Longo solemnly replied. – First of all, we should not loose heart as to the possibility of reinforcements arriving soon. Secondly, I'm a man of my word. Rest assured that a betrayal such as the one you mention could never occur. Death alone can break the pact between us. Until then we shall continue to fight side by side, so help us God Almighty.

Constantine nodded thoughtfully but remained silent, not wanting to compromise this moment of supreme confidence. In this way the God Almighty invoked resounded through the night, impelling Giovanni to listen to the echo of his own words. It was a far reaching echo, magnified and illusive, like the nymph herself.

– I'm afraid I don't have much else to add at this moment, he finally said. – With your permission, I must return to the walls to make sure the repairs are sufficiently solid to withstand another day's sustained attack. Your Majesty need not worry further. We are in this together, and there is no other way out than through our doubled and joint effort to never give up.

Giovanni Giustiniani Longo's voice was composed and sincere. Seeing straight into his blue eyes the Emperor blushed inwardly at the mere thought of having suspected him of already making plans to abandon ship. His intended response was cut short by a messenger, arriving with the no doubt reassuring news that a group of Serbian miners had been intercepted inside their own freshly dug mine shaft. There they had been given a warm welcome with Greek fire which all but incinerated them completely. Panicking to get out they then kicked their own props with the consequence that the entire tunnel came down and buried the remaining force alive. This had all happen around the Gate of Charisius. Longo and the Emperor quickly set off to hear the heroic reports and make sure there were no further subterranean attacks in the making.

Chapter 24

In spite of the many precautionary measures taken among the defenders, there was no way to entirely avoid casualties, and some of the lethal projectiles constantly raining over the citizens were bound to hit their target. Each and every day brought its share of dead for which vigils had to be held. Day and night censers swung in chapels and churches, dissipating the persistent odour of putrefaction while priests intoned the halleluiahs and mourners spelled out the orthodox litany:

> *Thou only Creator Who with wisdom profound mercifully orderest all things, and givest unto all that which is useful, give rest, O Lord, to the soul of Thy servant who has fallen asleep, for he has placed his trust in Thee, our Maker and Fashioner and our God.*

The wailing of anonymous widows and fatherless daughters alternated with psalms and hymns soaring to the vaulted ceilings as flowers were strewn over simple stretchers of animal hide – no wood was allowed to be used for the making of caskets. In the small hours, the dead were brought to their final resting places, a single grave-pit hastily dug, soon filling up with corpses over which last blessings were showered while bearded priests in shiny satin caftans recited the Prayer of Absolution. To bells tolling throughout unforgiving nights bereft of stars and moon, countless icons and statues of Mary, carrying the son of God in her arms, were paraded, showers of last kisses bestowed on crosses and amulets. These were then thrown into the pits as the corpses disappeared under a layer of earth and stones, not only to signal the location of the grave but also, and no less importantly, to discourage the city's many starving dogs from scavenging.

One man who had made it his special duty to regularly attend the funeral masses was the learned monk Gennadi, a man renowned for the purity and zeal of his conviction. A sworn enemy to the union of the churches, he nonetheless rendered the Emperor, and thereby the city, a service of sorts by constantly setting the example of a God-loving man possessed by unwavering faith. To Gennadi miracles were not only possible but positively attainable, but only under the condition that all precepts of orthodoxy were strictly observed. He was practically indefatigable in carrying out prostrations. Somewhat more alarmingly, Gennadi had also let himself be convinced that the greatest of all possible miracles to visit mankind would be God's imminent decision to bring about its demise. In short, he did not hesitate to propound the message that the Sultan's siege was a tell-tale sign that the Apocalypse of John was about to become reality, and that the reason for this to happen was that God, precisely in the year 1453 AD, had grown tired of the wicked race he had once sired.

Constantine had been alerted to the potentially devastating effects of this fatalistic message – one dangerous implication of which was the idea that Mehmet had been chosen by providence to carry out God's last will – months before Mehmet had actually turned up outside the walls. In truth, Gennadi's declaration that the defection of the Orthodox Christians from the one and only true faith, as well as their willingness to allow Catholic ritual to desecrate the holiest of churches, Hagia Sophia, had unleashed riots in the streets threatening Italians in general, and their spiritual leaders, such as the Pope's special envoy Isidore of Kiev and his right hand, Bishop Leonard of Chios, in particular. Understandably, the Emperor, fearing far reaching complications, was hesitant to impose penalties on the ring leaders, although his Roman guests, who had in fact brought indispensable bowmen and supplies to the city, demanded that they be forcefully suppressed. Attendance in unionist church services was consequently symbolic at best.

As the siege wore on, however, Gennadi, considered by the faithful as the rightful successor to Patriarch Gregory – who had left Constantinople for Rome two years earlier exasperated at the suicidal stubbornness of its population – had broken his voluntary isolation. He could now be seen actively participating both in the city's defence and in the services held under oil lamps as numerous and glimmering as the stars of heaven. Whether he had changed his mind about the inevitability of the city's fall was not to be deduced from his public appearances, but it did give Leonard and Isidore an opportunity to try to converse with him. Consequently, and much to the astonishment of pious Greeks from all walks of life, Leonard and Isidore were on several occasions seen participating in the Orthodox masses for the fallen, humbly adhering to ceremonial minutiae.

It was well into the night when the two of them discreetly caught up with Gennadi making for his monastery in the presence of two monks. The Greek sage at first refused to have anything to do with them, making no secret of that he held them personally responsible for the corruption of his people. It seemed as though that would conclude the matter, since he refused to salute them, turned away and was about to disappear into a dark alley when Isidore, a Greek by birth, suddenly had a bright idea. He ran after him while exclaiming,

– Brother Gennadi! We're aware that you loathe our presence and thus shun our company, but let me tell you this: the church of Rome does not wish to see its brothers in faith fall prey to the caprices of Allah over a matter of preposition. Please, don't let the matter of Jesus' substances obscure the reality of the fact, that to the infidels Jesus is not even the Son of God, but a prophet subordinated to the authority of Mohammed, a common camel driver who eight centuries ago claimed to have received visions from the archangel Gabriel instructing him to disregard the Bible as the ultimate dispenser of truth. In view of the resistance which the *laetantur coeli* has met with among your flock, the Pope has declared himself willing to reconsider his stance on the question of independence and will issue an invitation suggesting a new council of the churches in view of obtaining, once and for all, a convivial solution to problems raised by local variations in theological interpretation.

It was diplomatic nonsense and the promise little more than a pious lie as the Pope's conviction in this regard was known to be more solid than the rock of Gibraltar; but it was also, considering the precariousness of the situation, a license taken with regard to the fact that if Constantinople ever fell to the Turks, the Pope's position on the matter of union between the churches would matter very little anyway. Surprisingly, Gennadi seemed willing to accept this pretext for a chat, but it wasn't until they had reached the monastery, and the three of them were installed in the refectory for a bowl of soup – the monk's only meal for the day – that he told them his real reasons for allowing this unprecedented meeting to take place.

Chapter 25

To the light of a single lamp the three men prayed together. Then they broke the bread and consumed their soup in silence. Isidore and Leonard refrained from posing any specific question to the eccentric recluse. But this didn't mean the two of them had no intentions of their own. Quite to the contrary. What they really desired to confirm, if possible, was an intelligence so sensitive that they hadn't even dared to inform the Emperor about their suspicions. Two days earlier, in the Church of the Holy Apostles, Isidore, hidden behind a drapery, had incidentally overheard a confidential confession between two monks revealing a rumour that Gennadi, through his secret contacts with the Mayor of Galata, had actually met recently with Mehmet in person on the premises of the Sultan's own tent. As a consequence Isidore began to make his own discreet inquiries among churchgoers. If and how such a thing would even be possible no one seemed to know. But it was indeed confirmed that some citizens of Galata, by virtue of its professed neutrality, moved freely in and out of their city through their northern land gates. These were all hidden from sight from any vantage point in Constantinople. Rumours again had it that spies in Galata volunteered information they gathered from close-hand observations and communications among the crews of allied ships in the Horn with the Turks, in exchange for food, wine, oil and other commodities. Most importantly, the information collected among the Genoese destined for the Sultan served the purpose of putting him in a benign and merciful mood. In this way the people of Galata hoped to be spared the atrocities that no doubt would befall the people of Constantinople if he succeeded in taking the city.

The resentment among the Orthodox against the cowardice, deceitfulness, wickedness and evil of their Genoese neighbours was based on centuries of mutual hostility. Sometimes the enmity had flared up in brutal naval battles, sometimes it had just kept smouldering. But in one way or the other it was always present. At this stage it only seemed to add confusion to hatred that seven hundred of the defenders were actually of Genoese extraction. People didn't know what to think, because they had by now had ample possibility to verify with their own eyes that these alien Genoese men fought every bit as valiantly and death-defyingly as the Greeks, and this although they believed in Christ for all the wrong reasons. But why, when their comrades on the other side of the narrow bay were about to sell them out, bit by bit, piece by piece? Or was it just hearsay, evil tongues? Nobody seemed to know for sure, except possibly this eccentric monk. And suddenly, in the dead of night, lit by a single lamp, with the waxlike faces of two Catholic officials framing the gilded icon of the Holy Mother on the opposite wall, he began to speak,

– To you, men of a church that allows its acolytes to split, divide and negotiate what God has intended to be a single, indivisible and non-negotiable truth, I have little else to say than this. You have brought the greatest danger upon all of us by allowing the Pope's maniacal resolution to force congregations of true believers, faithful to the very words of Jesus and the apostles, to seek protection within what is, and as far as I am concerned, always was, a heresy. There is thus little doubt that the Turk has been sent by God to castigate us for our apostasy. But it has, alas, become too late for us to atone for our sins, because even if we were all to repent, the divine command has already been given and cannot be reversed. The archangel Michael has flashed his shiny sword and the second Exodus from the second Eden is imminent. Yes, so overwhelming is the wrath of our Lord, that he has had his archangel announce, that as things have developed, he'd prefer the remainders of his herd to fall under the yoke of the Sultan, who will at least grant the children of the original faith the right to continue to ask the Lord for forgiveness, whereas Rome won't even pray for us in this hour of distress, much less send men to help us.

There was something almost prophetic in the monk's appearance, and his speech, cloaked in metaphors and learned allusions, did not fail to impress his Catholic interlocutors. But whether the gleam of madness in his eyes – possibly a consequence of his exalted zeal and self-imposed mortifications – was to be taken as a token of his honest beliefs, or concealed a more mundane ambition to survive regardless of the circumstances, was difficult for them to determine. However, there was one part of his harangue that intrigued Isidore, who by birth and habit knew the Greek tendency to get carried away with flowery orations. It was the statement that seemed to imply that the Sultan, as opposed to the Pope, would be willing to grant the Greek church complete freedom of worship. Isidore therefore said,

– Brother Gennadi, I'm not here to try to change your views on the proposed union, which apparently must remain in the negative, but I was just a little surprised to hear you utter with some confidence that the Turk, as opposed to the Pope, would allow you to worship freely, and that in this way there would be a real possibility for the true children of God to repent during a second Babylonian captivity and turn their faces away from the lure of Italian merchants dressing up their naked greed in saintly garments. (By now Isidore himself began to feel Greek eloquence descend upon him like a white dove from the dome of heaven). – But how, he said with a shrewd inward grin, – How can you be so sure that the Sultan, upon conquering the city, won't just herd you – men, women, children, yes even your dogs of the true faith (Isidore truly felt the inspiration!) – into the churches and utterly destroy every soul therein?

Isidore and Leonard, aghast at what they were about to hear, did not have to wait long for the answer. And it was now that the two men, without even looking at each other, unanimously arrived at the uncomfortable conclusion, that the leader of the Orthodox church, in the wake of Bessarion the Illustrious, had not only gone mad, but had also, in word and deed, betrayed his Emperor.

Chapter 26

– But how was it possible? Leonard said incredulously, – I mean, the entire city is completely sealed off from the outside world. How could you possibly manage to get in and out of it without anybody noticing you?

– Oh, you'd be surprised how many ways there actually are to leave the city even during a siege. But of course, you have to know these ways, he added with a thin-lipped smile that worked instant horror in his listeners. – Several tunnels, only barely covered with stones and earth at ground levels, lead into various parts of what is at present the Turkish encampment. As a matter of fact, one of them ends up right next to the largest of all their artillery pieces. But under the present circumstances tunnels are not the safest places, especially when you try to get out of them on the other side. Besides it wasn't really necessary. You see, I already had an invitation from Mehmet to come and see him.

– You had an invitation from the Sultan?

– Yes, he knows my religious conviction, and I guess he wouldn't want to leave one single option untried. Naturally he thought he could persuade me.

– Good Lord, how in all heavens did you manage to get to him, and where did you meet?

– As it already happened and I have nothing to hide – my intentions are solely in the interest of our sacred rituals – I might as well give you a hint.

The two churchmen did as best they could not to betray their sense of alarm. Leonard even managed to pretend he was suppressing a yawn. In reality the hair on their necks stood as straight up as the bristles on a porcupine.

– One of my reliable men in town is a pious fisherman who never misses an opportunity to show his loyalty to God. He and his family go to church every day and he sometimes comes to me to seek spiritual advice. This man owns a small rowing boat that he formerly used for fishing. Now, since the beginning of the siege his boat has been hidden away in the Contoscalion harbours on our Marmara coast line, and for those who know where to look for it, there is a tunnel, dug in greatest secrecy by iconophilic monks during the era many centuries ago when so many priceless works of art were destroyed by ferocious pseudo-Moslems calling themselves Christians. The tunnel was used for hiding and storing artworks in until they could be salvaged and smuggled out of the city, where the carrying around of icons, or any other divine representation, had become punishable by death. This tunnel leads straight into the harbour area, although access to it nowadays involves wading through three feet of water. But I regarded it a small price to pay in exchange for an audience with the Sultan, who through intermediaries, the names of which I mustn't disclose, had a message sent over Galata and brought to me by my good man. On a moonless night some days later he took me with him. In the cover of utter darkness he rowed me to the shores of Galata well beyond the point where the boom is attached. There I was expected, just as the Sultan's letter had said, and let inside the walls. The following day I was conducted outside the walls by the Genoese. A group of Janissaries rode up close to us, dismounted and said they had orders from the Sultan to escort me to his tent. I must come alone.

– Didn't that make you suspicious? Leonard asked inquisitively.

– On the contrary. I knew my life to be in the best of hands, because the Sultan already knew that I'm considered odd and difficult by the Emperor and his partisans. The Sultan thus knew I would make a useless hostage; in fact, displaying me as a captive would only make most of the pro-unionists, you bishop and cardinal included, very relieved. Because in this way I would be in no position to influence the population of the city, and that's exactly how the Latin-lovers would prefer things to be. No, I knew the Sultan had invited me for the sole purpose of trying to find out whether he could win me over. And I was of course not going to say that I wouldn't consider helping him as long as I was still in his camp – *that* would have been suicide. In this way, confident in my decision and with God as a witness, I was given a Turkish dress to disguise myself and thereafter conducted through much of the Turkish camp, where I got the chance to see their artillery and siege engines at close range. It was shortly before noon when I entered the large tent of his highness Sultan Mehmet II and prostrated myself in front of him as custom requires – anyone having the temerity to remain standing when introduced to the Sultan volunteers himself for instant death. No, it has nothing to do with his moods. From what I've heard the soldiers execute you instantly, on the spot, on principle, and before the Sultan has even had the chance to give the matter second thoughts. To remain standing – as the ill-mannered Frankish barbarians used to do when received by the Byzantine Emperor – in front of the ruler over all subjects from Belgrade to Manzikert – you might just as well spit directly in his face.

Anyway, as the preludes were dealt with and I had remained on my knees long enough, I was told to rise and was cordially conducted to a table set with food and beverages. I sat down and tasted some titbits so as to not offend my host. He dismissed his guards except for two statuesque Janissaries in conic helmets who took up positions as perfectly immobile pillars in the antechamber. Much of the loud noise from the outside was strangely subdued in this tent where voices, involuntarily reduced to whispers, found no resonance.

In looks and countenance Mehmet is not unlike his father Murad, whom I once had had the honour of meeting with as well. But Mehmet, this one senses right away, is a good deal more reserved and inscrutable than his father, who in spite of his ostensibly belligerent policies and rapacious lusts was at bottom a peace-loving, not to say jovial man. Seeing Mehmet face to face was enough for me to realise that the only thing that mattered to him was to achieve his goal no matter the cost. That's why I found myself in his tent, having to listen to a long explanation as to how and why the Ottomans had been chosen by God to take over Constantinople. Once taken, the city was destined to become the administrative centre of the *Jihad*, from where the perfect world order would be imposed on all subsequently vanquished peoples. I didn't even have to ask him what the mundane fate would be of the Greeks who had remained faithful to the creed of their fathers. The very first thing he assured me was, that if I were to help him, he would make sure that I and all the members of what he kept calling "my parish" – apparently not knowing, or not wanting to acknowledge, that I actually lead the life of a recluse – be spared slaughter and looting. It was for me to pick a church or monastery in which to await liberation. He would give personal orders to his men to save that church. I had his word on that.

Now, why should I believe in his word, knowing that he had broken it in the past whenever it suited him to do so? I mean, he did promise to keep up the peace treaty signed by his father. And what did he do with our ambassadors sent to ask him why he was suddenly seen preparing for war? He cut their heads off! I told him that a promise of clemency from a ruler dealing in this way with peace-treating diplomatic envoys of the Roman Emperor hardly seemed credible. Hearing these words Mehmet gave me an uneasy smile, no doubt intended to reassure me, while he waved the question off by saying that it had been accidental – the envoys had apparently caught him in a bad mood – and that his future plans for me, on the other hand, were of utmost importance to the future administration of his domains. He said he wanted me to become some sort of ecclesiastical minister or advisor to his government. Regardless of my protestations he also kept referring to me as Patriarch. His face was calm and his eyes, betraying nothing of the inner workings of his soul, stared intently into mine as he began, in a tone of voice that I strangely associated with crimson velvet, to tell me how much closer the relations were between the religion of Islam and our Christian creed, than between the latter and the Frankish heresy. How is that? I of course had to ask him, surprised at the astounding command he had of our beautiful Greek language and the range of his knowledge in matters spiritual, despite his young age.

Chapter 27

– Islam, like the Orthodox faith of Christians, he said, embraces the truth that all men are equal in the eyes of the Almighty. None among our spiritual leaders, the imams, is in reality superior to another, and as far as I understand the same holds true for the Byzantine Patriarchs, among whom the one of Constantinople is only – how do the Latinists put it – a *primus inter pares*? Inversely, the Pope of the Italians not only considers himself above his bishops and cardinals, but well-nigh above God himself. Meanwhile all his powers depend on the degree of cooperation he can obtain by alternately bestowing graces on or issuing threats to the Frankish lords, all of whom are worldly, greedy and selfish men with no or little concern for the common good. But this they are too cowardly to admit, just as the Pope is too cowardly to admit that without the continued support from kings, who in reality would all like to see him gone and replaced by someone of their own choice, he's powerless. So they hide behind each other's back, pretending to their subjects that they are righteous and God-loving while only pursuing their own individual interests, constantly ready to betray one another for the next sack of gold.

– In their organisation there is consequently neither unity nor truth. In Islam, as in the Orthodox Christian faith, on the other hand, it has always been acknowledged that there is no true existence except the ultimate truth, which is God himself. Therefore there can't be, as among Popes and Frankish lords, a question of a division of secular and divine justice – justice can only exist and be applied in the name of God, as well as in the name of him who simultaneously represents divine and temporal justice, which is the head of the divinely sanctioned state. To claim otherwise is to deny that God is everything, and that the codification of justice should consist in anything else but an attempt to interpret the laws for human conduct in a manner consistent with the way this same law was once revealed to prophets from Moses to Muhammad.

At this point I found it impossible not to object, so I said,

– Maybe so, but if you, in accordance with Islamic doctrine, deny that there can be free will and that wrongdoing is only a kind of obfuscation of the sacred law which Allah has pronounced and instilled in each and everyone of us, then we humans are little more than slaves to the divine master. If human righteousness is only about obedience or disobedience to a once and for all given law, then unselfish love, the *agape*, common to Christians of all denominations, loses all meaning, because it's based on human free will, forgiveness and love as demonstrated to us through the unique example of Christ.

– That's exactly the point! Mehmet exclaimed. – The immense advantage of the Islamic law is precisely that it treats everybody the same, without exception and without appeal. Everyone, including myself, regardless of my apparent wealth and power, is but another slave to Allah, and the only reason why I'm the head of state is that it has so far been Allah's will that I should be.

– But that amounts to nothing more than crude fatalism! I interjected, – In the name of which everything that happens can be justified by the sheer fact that it happened. How is there in reality a means of distinguishing between the will of Allah and the capricious whims of a tyrant whether he calls himself Caliph or Sultan? How does a believer come to know that the Sultan represents Allah when the will of that same Allah can only be made known through the actuality of events as they unfold in time and space? He who is eternally unknowable can never be the same as the God who sent his son to die for our sins and reveal to us the full extent of our free will.

– And did the son of God die because he himself wanted it, or simply because his father in heaven demanded it? I believe having read in the Bible that Jesus, when confronted with the prospect of death, decided that his human will would have to surrender to that of his eternal father. How free was he then? Wasn't that sacrifice as prearranged and predestined as the fate of Muhammad, and why discuss freedom in relation to God? There can never be an issue of human freedom in the face of God. Freedom or its opposite is in the human world and only in the relationships between human beings, and any ruler wise enough to kindle human talent will eventually reap the benefits of letting able men, whatever their creed or pedigree, freely make their way through man-made hierarchies to prove themselves worthy of offices and riches. And this is what we Ottomans do. It's assumed that the Sultan is Sultan because it so pleased Allah – that's our *a priori* as the great Thomas Aquinas would have said. Meanwhile, we don't assume that just because a man was born in humble circumstances he can't be in possession of a rare and valuable talent, or vice versa, that a man born to a dignitary must necessarily be the ablest man to succeed him as a minister. So instead of an inflexible hierarchy, based on the notion of birth and pedigree, weighing so heavily on Latin society and its mores; instead of the elaborate theocracy of the Orthodox which forces every other discussion in the market place to become one of hairsplitting theology; instead of the vain Jewish habit of always debating the will of God and squabbling about money, our society is at all times a fertile ground for the ambitions of brilliant men. We want the best to come forth, and that's why we allow them to compete freely with one another, because to succeed in this world mere strength is not enough; one also has to be able to outsmart the others. Strength *and* cunning, that's our recipe, and a recipe taken straight from nature, where the lion, though the strongest, is oftentimes fooled by the jackal. Our way of doing this is to prepare from a tender age all men for the realities of life. Future janissaries for instance are recruited among suitable boys of all nations that have been conquered in the name of Allah. They are then sent to serve for many years in the provinces to learn farming and forestry. At the same time they receive proper schooling, and those apt for higher studies and crafts are in various ways promoted. The most talented, ambitious and disciplined of these young men then become the elite of our army and government. In this way it's ensured that the ruling elite of our society is never allowed to become lazy and stagnant, since just as easily as a man from nowhere can raise through the rank and file of our administration, an influential man may fall from the heights of prosperity by a wink from the Sultan. This keeps us in form and makes every man vigilant.

As far as our courage in war is concerned, it suffices for the common man to know that Allah will provide for all his needs in Paradise, so that if he won't make it through a battle, his reward in heaven will be proportionate to his valour shown prior to death. In this way our soldiers can always hope for life even as they prepare to die. In prayer we are all united and the Sultan must prostrate himself before the Almighty as humbly as any of his subjects. That's the sacred law.

Mehmet here paused for an instance, and I took the chance to intervene. I no longer felt intimidated by his magnanimous pretensions, and as the voice of the Angel spoke through me, it once again assured me that the present misery of our people was a self-inflicted consequence of centuries of unrelenting sin. Seeing how sinful the Sultan himself was, I instantly knew that he had only been allowed to lay this siege because God had decided to chastise us, and that we must accept this ordeal with the same patience, faith and repentance as the Jews facing the destruction of Jerusalem. Eventually Mehmet himself will be destroyed as the reign and terror of the devil will come to an end on the day of doom now rapidly approaching. In truth, the last days are already here, let us pray for our souls and beg for mercy!

Gennadi suddenly grasped the hands of the two Catholic envoys and raised them towards the ceiling. For a moment, which seemed like an eternity to his guests, his body was torn by spasms and he hyperventilated, as though fighting some fiendish presence inside himself.

Then he just as suddenly calmed down, let all hands down on the table, dropped his chin to his chest and seemed to observe his own belly button. He then looked up and resumed his narrative at the very point where it had been interrupted.

– The Lord is now in our hearts, and he wants me to continue to tell you the whole unmitigated truth of what I saw and experienced in Mehmet's tent on that day. This is what I told him,

– You praise the alleged humanity and enlightenment of your rule, you maintain that birth-right and theological dispute are of no consequence to you. Meanwhile your methods of punishing those who do not in every aspect comply with all your ordinances at once are as merciless as they are abominable. In addition you allow men, and most of all yourself, to maintain promiscuous inclinations through the institution of your harems, which for no natural or divine reason turn women into prisoners and your own sinful lusts into their capricious wardens. There is debauchery in food and wine, and killing for the cruel pleasure of seeing people die. And then there is the practice of polygamy. Had God wanted Adam to have many wives he would have given them to him along with Eve, but in his wisdom he ordained that one woman should be enough for every man, which was just as much for the reason of propagation as for good measure in all things human.

To my surprise Mehmet seemed more bemused than taken aback by my critique. He calmly examined his finger nails, then looked at me and said,

– The old Hebrews, wise people of the Book, never had the idea to try to restrict a man from having as many women as he could cater to. It's attested in the Bible that Abraham himself, still able to procreate at the mature age of three hundred years, took himself another wife along with the many concubines he also had. And the Bible makes no mention of that as being sinful. The danger, on the contrary, to which Christianity in all its denominations has exposed itself, is to have exalted woman per se to such heights that she is now represented as presiding along with God and his prophet Jesus in the heavens. With all due respect to the mothers of prophets, but they must never be confounded with the will and essence of the one and only. And look what happened to you once you let women run politics and wars! It's through your infatuation and indulgence with women that you shall all be brought to your knees. A woman can't think clearly in matters of the state because her head is constantly clouded with love and hatred. We would like to believe that mothers love their children, no matter what. Well, bestow upon a woman royal dignity, and you will see her go to any length to preserve her power, just like your Empress Irene, who had her imprisoned son brought before her in chains and in spite of his pleas of innocence stung out his eyes only to let him slowly languish to death in a dungeon.

– But it's perverse of a woman to not cede the crown to an able son, and women should thus never be allowed to interfere with state matters of any kind. Their role is to entertain, to seduce, to become pregnant and provide new warriors. Countless are the destinies of powerful men who have been betrayed by their wives, or just lost their kingdoms because they actually loved their women so much as to take their advice seriously, such as was the case with the otherwise able Emperor Marcus Aurelius who, under the influence of his adulterous wife Faustina, was persuaded to abandon the very successful system of adoption to provide the best heirs possible to the title of Emperor, thereby unwittingly putting an end to the golden age of the Antonines. It was the woman, of course, who could not put the interests of state above her own desire to see her flesh and blood crowned Emperor, and though Marcus had the chance to change the disposition after her demise, he respected her will and made the mistake which spelled the beginning of the end for the city of Rome. To have women in a position of power is always a bad idea, and you shall see how, in the end, the entire Christian world shall dissolve from within thanks to relentless infiltration of female partiality and impudence in public affairs.

– No, the only way to keep women is to regard them as one would regard other kinds of property, such as houses, servants, horses, camels, jewellery, spices, gold, silver. They should be kept and respectfully entertained as mothers, wives, concubines, and they should be allowed to adorn the spaces of villas and palaces like colourful singing birds. But just as birds may fly away if you don't keep them attached, so women must be kept within the confines of the Eden created for their convenience. A man with many wives and concubines has been richly blessed by Allah and should thank the Almighty for his luck. However, he must never be tempted to let any of them have a say in politics. But this is the weakness of your Christian faith, that you have turned Mary, the mother of Jesus, into an idol, blasphemously worshipped in the name of God. For this you will eventually have to pay.

– However, it is not the Sultan's wish to impose on any of his conquered subjects the truth of Islam, since experience has shown that

God is so great that he will even tolerate those who do not worship him in the precise and final form prescribed by the Prophet, seeing in their worship an imperfect but nonetheless acceptable attempt to bring him due honour and gratitude. Our society is therefore one of religious and philosophical tolerance, and in case you accept the offer I'm willing to make, I shall personally guarantee that you'll be instigated as Patriarch of all remaining Orthodox believers in Rum. Now, are you willing to listen to my proposal?

Chapter 28

We had finally arrived at the end of the preliminaries, and it was a great relief to me no longer having to listen to the dreadful insults he inflicted on our chaste and holy virgin Mary, mother of God and the loving protector of all true believers. In truth, I had had enough of his boasting, but I had to stay to find out what he really wanted from me. It was the following.

– It has come to my knowledge, the Sultan said, that at the great church council in Florence fifteen years ago you were utterly dissatisfied with the behaviour of your country men, who at the end of long and largely fruitless negotiations proved dangerously weakened by fatigue. Finding themselves in a state of torpor they ominously signed the agreement of the union, an agreement which you subsequently tore up in public accusing the signatories of having made a pact with the devil. Rightly so, then you know as well as I do, that these godless Italians would pay lip service to any god as long as there's a reasonable chance that such allegiance would bring them a financial advantage. You furthermore, and correctly I must once again admit, realised that their brand of Christianity contains no piety and no respect for tradition; in fact, it only barely conceals considerations of the idlest and most pragmatic kinds. In other words, it's but a meagre pretext for more wealth and money. In contrast Islam and Christian Orthodoxy are in far greater proximity to one another, as they both acknowledge the infallibility of the heavenly arbiter and put their faiths entirely in the hands of the almighty. Consequently our prayers and rituals are as true as they are sincere. Since the *dar-al-islam* is neither fanatic nor negatively predisposed towards the religious doctrines and practices of vanquished peoples, it can even guarantee that there will be freedom of worship and ritual within its domains as long as general civic ordinances are complied with. We both know that the Italians and the rest of the Franks will only continue to consider supporting the people of Constantinople if the latter agree to a union brought about by insults, threats and ultimatums. It is and was a disgrace, but you also know your Emperor to be the helpless victim of his pro-unionist secretary Francis, of Italian and defected Greek members of the clergy, and last but not least, of Italian mercenaries and seamen offering services in the hope of being able to render the empire penniless so that they may populate the city with their own vile tradesmen, while conveniently deposing the last Greek Emperor in favour, once again, of some Frankish baron. You furthermore know the Emperor is weak and lacks the support of the people precisely because of his willingness to trade off, not only your sacred churches but faith itself. Seemingly the situation is hopeless because the faithful will lose regardless of the outcome. But I promise you, with Allah my witness, that you and your brothers in faith will still be able to worship as you always have under my jurisdiction, if only you would lend us a hand in bringing this siege to an end and set up a community of tolerance and mutual respect. Face it Brother Gennadi, the Byzantine empire the way your remote ancestors knew it is long since gone and will never return. It will fall under my pounding fist, and it is my hope that you will realise that I'm going to take it before any Italians arrive to bid on it. As I said, I can save you and your congregation from slavery and death, but only if you agree to help me.

– And what is it that you want me to do? I said, shivering inside at the mere prospect of what he was going to say.

– At the junction of the land wall and the palace of Blachernai there is a small gate in a postern called Kerkaporta. This postern and its small door can be accessed directly from the Blachernai palace. Now, if ever I must order a major assault of the city, I want you to use the confusion, and the by then empty palace, to steal unseen through the covered passage way that leads to this postern and unlock its door from within. If any of my men finds out that this door is open, we shall know that you have made the choice to save your faithful ones from death and destruction. As we enter the city you and the ones you wish to save must abandon your posts and barricade yourself inside the Church of Chora. In return I will issue orders to all unit commanders to inform their soldiers that anyone who breaks into that church must pay with his life for disobeying my orders.

– What about if there are still men who ignore or simply haven't heard of your ordinances, I mean, there will be thousands and again thousands of soldiers thirsting for rape, blood and revenge entering the city, surely they will not spare anyone and the churches with their marble, gold and silver will be their next target. Our holy Mother of Wisdom will be the first to suffer utter devastation and desecration.

– There shall be no looting inside the Hagia Sophia, on this too you have my word, Mehmet said.

– This you're in no position to guarantee, I objected, and I know that unless you don't have it razed to the ground, you'll turn it into a mosque.

– Perhaps, he answered, but then again, since you will lose it anyway, why not take steps to at least make sure that true Christians will have *some* places left to worship in, yes, that they'll even survive? I shall make you the Patriarch to the Orthodox church in the city, and you will have benefits and privileges to go with it.

– I don't wish to be a Patriarch, I only wish to be able to retire and contemplate the will of God intent on teaching us true humility and how to repent. Indeed, we have nowhere to go. Our predicament is akin to the one prevailing on Ulysses in the straits of Messina, where either side held lethal monsters.

– The simile is well chosen, Mehmet responded, but don't forget that by sticking to the middle of the current, Ulysses, although inevitably losing a few men in the process, managed to save the majority of his crew and come out safely on the other side. I offer you the same chance: spare the faithful the destiny reserved for apostates and live to reform your church in the true image of your God.

– I now realised that if I were to tell him that God had not only decided on the destruction of his defected Christians, but was bringing the entire world to its end by allowing the sins of Sodom and Gomorrah to make themselves at home in what had previously been his chosen city, he would just have laughed at me, believing me to be the prey of delusions. But I tell you, papal legates, that the signs are here, and that there will be yet other auguries for his kingdom come. Mehmet is but his sword, and that too will eventually melt away in the flames of Armageddon. In jest I therefore addressed the Sultan,

– Well, if you really want me to help you, I shall need a written guarantee signed by you personally and sealed with the Ottoman seal that you will spare the people I shall gather at the hour of our destiny.

To my utter surprise Mehmet immediately agreed to this. He called for a scribe and instructed him to draw up a document in both Greek and Turkish confirming in writing everything he had promised. Since I do have some knowledge of the written Turkish language, I could verify that the wording was identical in the two languages. Mehmet signed his name to the bottom, pricked his finger on the point of his dagger and added a blood stain next to the signature. Then he folded the document, poured melted wax over it and sealed it with the signet ring he was carrying on his left index finger. It occurred to me that the Sultan was in fact left-handed, because both his signature and the seal were issued by his left hand. In my experience left-handed people are not to be much trusted as they are possessed by sinister desires and have fickle characters. I only accepted his guarantee to finally be able to get out of there, offering to help him in order not to provoke the famously bad temper known to have caused the death of earlier emissaries. In this way I have likewise sealed my own fate, because once Mehmet is inside these walls, and unless I haven't already perished by then, he will have me brought before him and gruesomely punish me for what he no doubt will consider a betrayal. At this point I can only pray that God make our deaths quick and merciful. May the holy Mother be with us now, in the hour of our death, and in all eternity, Gennadi said, glancing sadly first at Bishop Leonard, than at Cardinal Isidore.

The two Catholics were one mind, but it was Isidore who dared pronounce the question,

– Where's the signed agreement right now then, he said as casually as he could while shifting the empty wooden soup bowl from one hand to the other.

– I of course consecrated it to the flames as soon as I had safely been conducted back inside the walls of Pera, Gennadi answered. The awkward silence that followed was again interrupted by the monk, discerning faint traces of disbelief on the two faces rendered mask-like by the pale light of dawn.

– You don't really think I ever intended to conspire against the Byzantine Emperor, his subjects and Christianity, do you? Oh, I can see it in your eyes though you try to hide it. But instead of condemning me, think of it this way. Why would I ever tell you, sworn enemies and renegades of our church, the truth if I really had the intention of giving the Sultan a helping hand? No, I wouldn't have told you, would I? Because you can now walk straight to the Emperor and tell him about my adventures. This is unfortunately also the reason why I can't tell you where the tunnel is located, it would undo the whole purpose of having a secret way out, wouldn't it? But I actually also know that you're not going to tell Constantine what I've just told you, because you know, deep at heart, that I've told you the truth, and that we shall all have to face the end, which our sins have brought upon us, as true martyrs of faith.

– Now, let us pray together… brethren… in the name of Christos Pantocrator: "O Lord, Jesus Christ, Son of God, have mercy on me, a sinner".

Chapter 29

Leonard and Isidore debated on what to do. Gennadi had clearly become so enmeshed in his apocalyptic confusion that he had lost most if not all of his wits. How else to explain the unheard of anomaly of a self-appointed clerical emissary, who in the midst of a life-and-death struggle decides to take a leisurely stroll over and into the fire-breathing dragon's den? It was a feat that only a madman could have pulled off. Unfortunately, however, this kind of lunacy could also instantly turn messianic and apocalyptic expectations presently smouldering among the general population into a flare.

The two seasoned envoys from the Roman See were only too familiar with the Greek penchant towards confounding delirious, incoherent theological ramblings with prophecy. It was a well known, albeit deplorable, side-effect of excessive asceticism. Carried to extremes, mortifications, flagellations, sleep-deprivation and fasting combined to induce in the individual a trance-like state accompanied by hallucinations that both the victims and their witnesses were only too keen to interpret as veritable spiritual revelations. It was assumed that monks on the brink of starvation were particularly prone to these epiphanies. Gennadi, after having taken the vow, both looked and acted the role of a true martyr in the making. Considering the nature of his afflictions it didn't seem unlikely that he had simply invented the whole story and put it in circulation – hence the rumours. But perhaps even more alarming than that he himself seemingly believed in his own story, was the effect it might have on fundamentalist believers inside the walls. If the défaitisme of Gennadi was allowed to spread it could rapidly undermine the already dangerously weakened public morale to the point where it would force Constantine to surrender. If this happened, any Italian rescue operation on its way would be in for a potential disaster. In other words, it was imperative for counter-rumours to be set in motion, declaring that Gennadi had fallen prey to delusions of grandeur since he now regarded himself as the Sultan's friend and most trusted advisor.

It was decided between the two men that the best way to implement this scheme was to reinforce the rumour, that Gennadi had met with the Sultan, with the sensational news that the Sultan had been so impressed with the arguments of the learned Greek that he had now decided to convert to Christianity. This would hopefully make Gennadi's claim seem completely ridiculous, and put a quick end to the unsound interest common people had recently begun to take in his eschatology. But as rumours designed to ridicule him began to circulate, Leonard and Isidore still had another daunting task ahead of them.

It couldn't be entirely ruled out that Gennadi had as a matter of fact met in person with the Sultan. In order to prevent such a claim from being confirmed by possible eye-witnesses, these must be tracked down and coerced into silence and cooperation. Potential witnesses in Galata were obviously of less importance as they would never be able to personally speak up in Constantinople until the siege was over. In the event there was only one other person prominently figuring in Gennadi's story, and that was the fisherman who allegedly held his boat hidden in the Contoscalion harbour. Their task was to find out whether such a small boat actually existed. If this could be corroborated the next step would be to find the man himself who so bravely had twice transported Gennadi across the mouth of the Horn under the cover of darkness.

They hoped to find nothing, but they needed to be sure. The very last thing they wanted to do – and on this point, mad or not, Gennadi had been absolutely right – was to inform the Emperor about their findings, as this would put pressure on him to incarcerate Gennadi, in this way sustaining the halo of imminent martyrdom above his head. Even worse(semi-colon)a standing subject of conversation between Isidore and Leonard was what they perceived as the notorious inability of Constantine to deal appropriately with signs of insubordination among soldiers, priests and civilians alike. In their eyes he was always far too lenient, and chances were he wouldn't even dare to question

Gennadi and his motives for fear of becoming even more unpopular with his people – both men knew that Gennadi only a couple of years earlier had publicly announced his support for Constantine's brother Thomas, as news of Emperor John's death arrived in Constantinople. Indeed, they must take care not to reveal their real intentions.

A third crucial issue was to find out whether the tunnel ominously referred to by Gennadi actually existed. Considering that the section of the wall where the tunnel was supposed to be was situated in the immediate vicinity of a monastery, and that Gennadi himself belonged to the same Hesychast monastic order as the monks inhabiting it, although he himself didn't actually live there, these men might even have planned the entire operation together. The same monks were also charged with the defence of the surrounding portion of sea wall where any military attack would have been seriously impeded by the proximity to the sea. Without their permission Leonard and Isidore were never going to be able to discover any tunnel, since such a secret passage way almost certainly would originate somewhere within the walls of the monastery itself. Gaining access to the monastery was not going to be easy. It would perhaps be even more difficult to persuade the inhabitants to talk, considering that Hesychast monks, apart from the habitual discretion of monastic life, had also taken a special vow of silence through which the normally invisible, unknowable and ultimately uncreated divine energies paradoxically were allowed to temporarily manifest themselves. The Hesychast doctrine and movement, though tenacious like sin itself and known to have infested the eastern Mediterranean for nearly a thousand years, nevertheless appeared enigmatic to Bishop Leonard.

– You know what? It certainly wouldn't hurt if the Lord right now made his uncreated energies just a little bit more created, he said as they decided to part and try to get some rest before they would be expected to reappear before Constantine and thereafter resume their respective positions.

– I just wish the weather would get a bit warmer, Isidore replied as they huddled together for shelter under an arch, pierced by a gusty northern wind stuffed with hail. Three weeks into the siege, at the end of April, the weather was still as unpredictable as it was winter-like, adding cold, physical discomfort and humidity to hunger and relentless bombardment. In such trying circumstances they had unexpectedly been treated to a steaming bowl of hearty soup. In addition to parsley, small carrots and spring onions it had contained rich morsels of lamb, and this at a time when all sheep inside the city had either been eaten or requisitioned by the Emperor and minutely rationed. Odd then to find such delicacies in the habitually most frugal of places.

It only slowly dawned on the papal legates that perhaps they too had just received a few crumbs from his highness the Sultan's sumptuous table. Meanwhile, they were surprised to find out that what they at first believed to be hailstones were in fact tiny grains of rock, not unlike the pumice spewed out by volcanoes. The strange thing here, though, was that there weren't any known volcanoes around the Bosporus. So where did the minuscule rocks come from?

Chapter 30

Iannis Papanikolaou made quite a living from the ferry services he provided to people wishing to be taken to and from Galata. So far all transportations had been across the Horn, where he could use the half-decked boat of his brother-in-law, Zachyntus, with whom he would share profits. Although no unauthorised persons were allowed on the harbour premises, there was a surprising amount of passengers, goods and services passing through it every day. There were informers from Galata, who in turn got their intelligence from Christian soldiers in the Turkish camp. There were loads of food, oil, wine, clothes and other commodities in response to the constant demand in the hungry city. There were diplomatic missions. Iannis wasn't authorised in any way, but he knew ways to work around the system. The main reason for this was that the crews of the ships were just as eager to lay their hands on extra supplies as anybody else. Their dilemma was that they couldn't simply leave their posts to obtain them.

Iannis was a fisherman, so he could always say he was going out to fetch oysters while hiding something or somebody under his nets. Initially the harbour commander – the tall, dark and fierce-eyed Venetian Alex Diedo – had tried to put an end to the illicit trade, but he too soon realised that in the end it was to everyone's benefit that the Galatians were allowed to discreetly help out where they could. So the trade rapidly turned into a very unofficial but nonetheless very real system of bribes and ransoms being paid according to unwritten rules. Iannis soon found out what went where, with the result that he became one of the few citizens able to always put food on his table. His naturally large family soon became even more extended as news spread about his ability to get extra supplies. At dinner time there were, apart from Iannis, his wife, her brother and his wife, as well as a total of seven children, typically half a dozen extra guests in the little house inside the wall of the Perion harbour.

In addition Iannis made money, money that he saved and kept hidden until the day when it would really be needed. He didn't trust that things would somehow work out in the end. He had seen enough of the Turks to know they were ruthless. Not even children were spared. So he had instructed his wife exactly what to do in case the city should fall. On the day of the decisive battle, if it ever came, she was to take the children with her and wait for him in the monastery of St Julian next to the Contoscalion harbours.

– The monks there, he said, know how to help you. – In case I never show up, you must ask them to show you the secret passage to the port, where you will find our boat which I have managed to hide at the end of the tunnel. You will launch it into the sea and intercept one of the many ships trying to escape. But wait until you hear and see people run for the ports. If they are reluctant to take you, your strongest argument with the Italians will always be this! he said, pointing to a leather sack full of coins. Once they hear the sound of money they will prove much more cooperative. But don't give it to them before they have taken you on board! And then only some of it!

Iannis' instructions were interrupted by a knock on the door. He peered through the key hole and recognised the people outside. In the faint light emitted from a lamp inside Irene too recognised them as Venetian mariners, but she was used to these unannounced visits and knew what was going on. She saw her husband return into the house, dig some bags out of a closet and go back up to the door. He gave them to the mariners who in turn handed over something smaller to him. The whole transaction was over in a less than a minute, and Irene could tell it had been a successful one because there was an even deeper ring to the money bag after they had left.

Later that same evening, however, after everyone had gone to bed, there was another knock on the door. Irene woke him up, saying there was someone in the street. Iannis cautiously opened the shutters ajar but could only make out that there were two men dressed like monks down there. He sneaked down the stairs and lay his ear to the crack in the door.

– Iannis, a voice whispered, – Iannis, this is brother Thomas, and brother Philip is next to me. We have a job for you.

A job? Iannis was bewildered. Whispering he said, – Why don't you come back tomorrow?

– Because it has to be done tonight.

Iannis drew the clasp aside, unlocked the chain, opened the door and let the two monks inside.

– What's this then?

– Iannis, we wouldn't be here at this inconvenient hour if it wasn't very important. We can't explain to you why, but we need someone to take our spiritual leader, brother Gennadi, over to Pera tonight.

– It's impossible, they have guards and watch towers all along the water front of the Horn, and what I can possibly get away with during the day I can't do at night. They'd kill me.

– Yes, we know, and that's why you must use your own boat, the one hidden in our tunnel.

– To Galata, but that's almost two miles of unprotected water!

– Slightly less. Anyway, we haven't got much time. Please come with us.

– And I suppose you expect me to do this just because you let me keep my boat over there?

– I suppose we would, if we had to. But you're very lucky this time, Iannis.

– How so?

Neither Thomas nor Philip answered, but from within his robe Thomas produced a purse and handed it over to Iannis. He opened it and couldn't refrain from whistling: coins, a multitude of coins in bronze, silver, even gold. He picked up one of the golden ones and held it against the light of the oil lamp. It weighed heavily in his hand.

– But this is a new Turkish coin, it has Mehmet's head on it, he said looking from Philip to Thomas. How on earth did you manage to get hold of it?

– Can't really tell you that, Iannis, but it is, so we have been instructed, part of your payment, the rest of which is also contained in that purse. Now please make yourself ready.

– How's the sea?

– Calm.
– No moon?
– No moon.
– What about the Turkish fleet?
– All anchored at the Double Columns.
– What about the guards at Galata?
– You will be expected. Head for the gate closest to the boom on the outside, and the two of you will be safe.

Iannis knew that the distance from the first gate beyond the chain on Galata's sea side to the nearest sentinels of the Turkish camp was way too great to allow anyone to see what was going on around the gate during a moonless night. But he would also need to keep sufficiently far away from the boom to escape attention from the defenders. Provided the Galatians were in on it, it could be done. For that kind of money anything could be done! He quickly went back upstairs and explained to his wife that he had had an urgent call to go over to the monastery and move their boat to a safer place while nobody was watching. She was too sleepy to protest, and didn't even quite realise what he had said. He kissed her on her forehead and told her he would be back first thing in the morning.

Chapter 31

When he eventually returned, another day and night had already come and gone. The house was in uproar and this for several reasons. Irene was consumed with worries, convinced her husband had been killed. But alarming as that seemed to her, still that was only one of her anxieties. As of yesterday the Turks had moved up some heavy artillery on top of a bluff dominating the Valley of Springs north-east of Galata and directly opposite the Petrion. During the entire day the walls right outside the house had been pounded. The children were terrified and cried helplessly, and the din from massive stone balls crashing into the defences was deafening even inside the trembling buildings. There was no way of escaping it. Reinforcements had been mobilised from other and presently less threatened sections of the walls, but all the defenders could do was to stand and watch as the projectiles continued to tear out chunks of stone from the ramparts.

At dusk the cannonade stopped as unannounced as it had started, and the defenders were relieved to see that although Zaganos Pascha and his artillery men had done everything in their might to put their guns to the best possible use, the destruction on the Petrion walls had been limited, as the aim of the guns had not always been very accurate. Although undoubtedly to the advantage of the defenders here, the same did not necessarily hold true for the ships anchored closer to the boom. From behind Pera, the Sultan had ordered his gunners to keep sending volleys of cannon balls over the inlet. The aim of these were even more random, but this fact only seemed to increase the risks of freak hits in places that wouldn't normally be targeted. And sure enough, suddenly one of the Genoese galleys, belonging to and anchored beneath the Galatan colony, took a direct hit and went down in a matter of minutes. Other stone balls too splashed dangerously close to Galatan ships, while only a few strayed as far as towards the Byzantine fleet. All this seemed to indicate that the Galatans had now also become drawn into the war. It might also help to explain why they seemed unaware of the extraordinary events taking place below their northern walls. Presumably the bombings, now directed at Galata's walls as well, prevented them from getting an overview. But regardless of whether their ignorance was real or just affected, Iannis was the first person to know exactly, and by first hand experience, what the Sultan was up to. Just as he had been the first to see the Turkish ships approach Constantinople from the sea, he was now also the first to actually witness them literally crawl over land, as though supported by the myriad of tiny insect legs he had initially attributed to them.

Once the children had stopped crying and Zacynthos had returned home safely with some crabs he had caught while running gauntlet on the beach; once his wife had begun to cook them in oil and garlic and Irene had had the time to finally compose herself, Iannis sat down at the table and began to tell them about the entire expedition. The expectation in the room was as intensely silent as the previous bombings had been loud. Iannis waited for the lights to dim and the stage to be completely set. Then, lit by the single oil lamp still miraculously dangling from the ceiling by a thin gut string, a fire smouldering in the oven, he began to display the entire range of his theatrical genius.

– So, the two monks come here in the middle of the night, and Irene wakes me up, you see? I said, Ave Maria, has the harbour captain finally sent out a warrant for my arrest? But no, it wasn't him. It wasn't any of his gaffers, nay. It was the ever silent brothers Philip and Thomas from St Julian's. Were they talkative for being mute monks! But I tell you what, the thing that persuaded me wasn't their talking, but the purse they brought with them. That was true eloquence, that was. Of course, I also owed Father Gennadi one, but there was somebody, I tell you, somebody who wanted this to happen real bad, so bad in fact he had them hand over a sizeable portion of the Sultan's treasure chest: there was gold, there was jewels, there was Aladdin's lamp – and the flying carpet, neatly folded together.

– Oh please, father, let us see the flying carpet!

– Not yet, children, because I was not to touch any of these wonderful treasures before I had accomplished my very dangerous mission. Only then would I reap my reward. And you shall have to wait until I have told you the story. Now, where was I? Oh, yes. It's as black as pitch outside, and they don't even light their lamp as long as they are beneath the wall for fear of being stopped by the guards. So we have to sneak very cautiously through the alleys and stop every now and then to make sure the coast is clear. After a while they do light up the lamp and we come out on the field where there are no soldiers. Then along the aqueducts and through the Forum down to Contoscalion.

– Now Father Gennadi is waiting for me there inside the monastery and says we have to leave right away. So I go up on the roof and look towards the sea. The sound of the reefs was not very loud so I gathered the sea was not too rough. And there were no stars either, but it was cold all the same. And then, under cover of the moonless night, we first go through the secret tunnel, and that is cold as hell for the water goes all the way up to the waist in places. Me and Father Gennadi had taken all our underwear off and placed them on our heads, because you go off at sea with them wet pants, and you'll freeze and get yourself a really bad cold. So we was dry as we dug out the boat and got inside. The monks was keeping watch for us both on the beach and on the walls, and unseen by any other parties, I got them oars inside me thole-pins and started rowing. We was lucky that boat had been floating in the water of that tunnel all that time, because this had prevented it from cracking up and I tell you, her deck was a dry as gunpowder, at least that was until the waves started hitting us. They'd said the weather ain't gonna give us no problem, but they was not sitting in that boat either. And though there wasn't much wind for sure, there was a nasty kind of choppy swell from the north and we was much wondering whence it came, when suddenly the cause became apparent: there was a big whale fish ahead of us and he stirred up all these waves with his tail. But Father Gennadi spoke to him and said it wasn't such a nice thing to do as we was on our way to save the city from a great danger. Then the whale turned around and wanted to help us, because he was the same enormous fish that had once swallowed Jonah and now he was regretful for what he had done to that righteous old man, so he let us tie a rope around his dorsal fin and then we fastened it to our prow. Oh, you should have seen the speed we made over the water, and he knew exactly where to go after we had pointed the direction out for him.

– As we came into the vicinity of the great chain we unleashed him. Only then did he dive back into the sea, and we could see his tail wave like a peacock feather made up of encrusted shells, and one of his eyes gleam like a black pearl, as he disappeared into the depths. Now we had to be very careful not to be seen from anywhere. On our side of the boom there was no activity to be detected, but lo and behold, over towards the Turkish port and the lands in that direction there was many fires and a lot of work being carried out in the dead, or rather the fiendish life, of night. We realised our folks could see none of what was going on from behind the chain, and we was very astonished at the magnitude of the operation. Apprehensively I stuck them oars back into their pegs and brought us safely to the shore without us being observed by nobody. When we had landed, Father Gennadi went straight up to the gate, brought out a lamp and lit it. Then he made signals by alternately covering the lamp under his robe and pulling it out again. Soon there was a signal from the top of the tower and he returned to the boat with five men who helped us carry it inside the gate, which was opened and then immediately closed behind us. We was now inside Galata.

Chapter 32

There we was and a lot of that Genoese being spoken too. Father Gennadi speaks that language himself, and it's a story as true as that I'm sitting here right now, that once, while living as a hermit in the Cappadocian stone desert, he was kidnapped by the devil who wouldn't release him until he could talk to him in Turkish. So he had to learn that dreadful language to be allowed to return to his cave. I believe the devil later had him study Persian and Arabic as well. Anyways, there we was, and he just telling me to wait for his return. And everybody was much occupied with him and what was going to happen to him, and all that, so nobody even noticed what I was doing. Out through the back door I went and saw a staircase leading right up to a tower. There was nobody to be seen or heard around or inside that tower, but I was curious as you can understand, because I had seen all that activity in the Turkish camp. So I climb all the dark stairs to the top of that tower, and what do I see? There was big fires scattered over the entire valley. And then there was an enormous wooden ramp, stretching from the waterfront half way up the hillside. I saw dozens of men heating up animal grease in barrels over fire and then smear it out evenly on the ramp. Beside there was a large number of oxen ready to be harnessed. As yet I couldn't quite figure out for what purpose. The ramp itself was more like an entire wooden road, twenty feet wide and a hundred and fifty feet long, and it was coming all the way up the hill, it was. It was a bit far away for me to see everything in detail, but with all the fires lighting up the place, there was no mistake about it: you could see that the Sultan was around because of all them important people in fancy military attire, and they was all watching and shouting while their soldiers was building a road for them boats to be shipped over land into the Horn!

– I couldn't believe what me eyes was seeing. And I would have liked to stay to follow more of them strange procedures, but by then I could hear the Genoese had started to look for me and I thought it best not to make them angry, so I went down from the tower and went back unseen into the house where they had taken me and Father Gennadi while they were shouting in the streets. But when they finally saw me, that's when they arrested me and locked me up in a room on the fourth floor so I couldn't get out and around anymore. By that time Father Gennadi was nowhere to be seen and those damn Genoese wouldn't tell where he was – for all I knew he could be locked up in another room, and wouldn't that have been a pretty situation: the two of us arrested for trespassing? Guess who would have been popular when that news reached home!

– Well, deep inside I knew it was probably just a precaution, and the reason they kept me like this was that I was simply a bit too inquisitive for their taste. You see, I asked them what they make out of the enormous military operation going on right below their damn walls, and they just shrugged them shoulders and looked at me as if I was some kind of buffoon They even pretended they knew absolutely nothing about it and I could see they didn't want to make no explanation. But how daft can you be, I mean, they wanted to remain neutral, right, but that was not being neutral, not sending as much as carrier pigeon over to tell your own countrymen what in glowing hell was going on. No, they had decided to say and know nothing, which I can't interpret otherwise than that they must have traded with the Sultan and struck a deal that he would look kindly to their interests once this siege was over and we others was all dead, but only if they kept their mouths shout about what was going on. Otherwise I can't understand why they was in such total denial. They didn't even have anybody up in their towers! They must have been told to stay real low if they wanted to get out of this with all their wives and children and possessions intact. He probably told them straight up that if they didn't stay indoors and he could see anybody on them walls, he would pummel them too.

– That must have been the reason, because I had the time to see that not only was he preparing to drag them ships over land, but he had an entire battery of guns placed right beneath their walls, and as dawn came along I could hear them stone balls whistle through the air above our heads, and that's when I knew he was shooting at the harbour from behind the walls of his ally. If only you knew how sad and worried and angry I was when I was thinking of how you was now in the middle of the firing line. I prayed to God, Jesus and our most Holy Virgin all the time that she'd protect you all. And when I wasn't crying and praying, I looked at those mural paintings on the opposite wall of my prison. You know how incredibly narrow them streets are, and how the buildings rise six, seven, sometimes ten stories high even when the alleys is no more than six feet wide. And that's why it seemed to me like having my own illumination in a wide open book. I stared over and over again at them sea monsters and them sirens, half human, half fish, like the centaurs, half horse half man, and the griffins half lion half eagle. Finally I began to feel half, half myself, and I thought what about if I had a pair of wings, then I could fly out of the window, take a closer look during daylight at the Sultan's camp, and then come back to the room before anybody noticed. But no wings would grow on my back.

The children, on their way to falling asleep, exhausted by the day's tumultuous events, suddenly quickened and begin to whisper, and then there was his daughter Anna, ten years of age, who said,
 – But Father, why didn't you remember to bring the flying carpet?
 – Exactly my dear. I now did remember that I had actually carried it with me all the time, and I just came to think of it. It was in my back pack. So I brought it out, unfolded it, put it down on the floor and whispered the secret pass word so that only the threads of the carpet would hear it. And then, before I even had the time to count to three, the carpet took off through the open window. For a while it flew me through lanes so narrow I could touch the walls of the buildings with my bare hands, but then it changed direction and we went straight up to the tower, first in and around the first ring of arcades, then up to the second level, and finally we made rings around the spire, before it headed straight for the Sultan's war machines. We flew in and out of siege engines towering as high as Hagia Sophia, I saw elephants fitted with turrets, horses, camels carrying two bowmen each, and guns with barrels so large that three men could fit inside them. And the Sultan I saw, with an enormous turban in the form of a white flower, and I saw all his wondrous women, behind the bars of his portable harems, the Janissaries with their sloping headdresses, and the soldiers from all corners of the world, Tartars with long pointed beards, Bulgarians with moustaches so long they that had to be tied around the neck so they wouldn't trip over them, Serbs with conic helmets, Anatolians with no special characteristics, Christian Syrians with a battering ram in the form of a crucifix, and Nubians blacker than the night itself.
 – And then I saw them ships being hauled one after the other onto the track by three dozens of oxen and countless soldiers steadying them. And inside the ships there was a ghostly crew of skeletons, pretending to row the boat upwards while cymbals, flutes, horns and drums accompanied the procession, yes, believe me words, even the sails was up, so as to make the illusion complete. It was an eerie sight I tell you, but then they discovered me in the air and began to try to bring me down with their cannons and their cross-bows, but the carpet saved me and we took a wide turn over the Marmara sea. From this altitude I could clearly see the Black sea and the Dardanelles at the same time, and there was schools of hundreds of dolphins and islands of turtles. I saw dust and rubble fall everywhere from ramparts and the cannon balls whizzed criss-cross all around us. In the midst of this I saw Hagia Sophia as I

have never seen her before: a golden sphere floating in a sea of haze and gun smoke. In the air, suspended above it, was the face of Mary, and when we came closer she spoke to me and said: – Iannis, don't despair, I shall protect your family from all evil. Even though they may destroy my temple, they will never be able to destroy my heart which is harder than diamond, deeper than the cave of St Cyril and full of blood and tears from all mothers who ever lost a son in war. O Iannis, trust me, and I shall protect you and all those who are dear to you.

– This is when I knew Mary had heard my prayers, and I asked the carpet to return to Galata, which it promptly did. Before I knew what we was back inside that room and I was staring at that wall again with them frescoes that so intrigued my mind. It became dark. I ate a bit – see, they had been nice enough to leave me with some bread, cheese and even wine, so it wasn't exactly like sitting in the dungeons together with the bats of Blachernai. Suddenly, out of nowhere, Father Gennadi stood in the doorway and says we had to go back to the monastery. I asked him were he'd been, but he put his index finger over his mouth and looked down on his own stomach button, a strange habit he and all these other monks have when uttering their prayers. So I posed no more questions and by midnight we were off the same way we had come. This time there was no whale to help us, but it didn't matter since we had the wind from the back and I could hoist the small sail. In no time we were at the secret opening of the tunnel, whence Father Gennadi gave his signal. The monks appeared on the walls, we dragged the boat inside and waded back to the entrance. There we were most warmly welcome and given dry clothes and some warm soup. I was very tired and fell asleep. I woke up at dawn and realised that I had to get home, and here I am, my friends, after an adventure which Homer, Virgil, and even Harun the Great would have envied me.

– But what happened to the magic carpet. Do you still have it with you?

– The magic carpet, my dear boy Manuel, is inside that boat. It can only fulfil three wishes. I already used two, one to take me out of the room, another to come back. But there is a third wish to be fulfilled. But only when you come to the boat shall you know the secret word and you will ask the carpet, and listen now very carefully, to take you as far away from here as it can.

– But why, Father, why? Are we going to leave Constantinople for ever?

Iannis, who had told his story with incomparable bravura and spellbound everyone, even the adults, always bemused by his hyperbole, suddenly grew serious while silent tears moistened his eyes.

– Children, it's late. You must get some sleep. Tomorrow you will be able to see the ships yourselves and then you will know that everything in the story happened exactly the way I told you. Now, say your prayers and go to bed.

Once the children had made their round, wishing good night and receiving blessings in return from from all family members, they climbed the ladder leading up to the loft housing their beds. When out of sight, Iannis turned towards Irene and Zacynthos. Leaning over the table, speaking in a muffled voice, he added gravely,

– And there's absolutely nothing that can be done to prevent it from happening. Tomorrow we'll have the Turk in our backyard. Once there, only a miracle can save us.

Chapter 33

– Anna... Anna, are you awake?

It was Manuel, her brother, whispering in the dark. Scared by all the bombing, then animated by his father's incredible story, he now refused to sleep.

– Yes, she said. – What do you want?

– Can I come and sleep in your bed?

Anna, two years older, pretended it would be something of a sacrifice on her part and sighed, just to demonstrate her benevolent indifference. But in reality she felt scared and lonely too and was glad he'd asked.

– Are you afraid? she asked mockingly while he stole under her blanket.

– No. Are you?

– Absolutely not.

– How come you're not scared?

– How come *you're* not?

– I asked you first, so you must answer first.

– I can, but I don't have to.

– Alright, you don't have to, but will you tell me why you aren't scared?

– Because God protects us and, because God is angry with him, the Sultan can't win.

– How do you know God protects us, have you spoken with him?

– You don't talk with God, silly! You can only pray to him. Him and Mary.

– What about Jesus?

– Yes, you can pray to him too.

– But you can't talk with him either?

– No, they can only listen to you, but if you're heart is open and your prayer sincere, they can make your wish come true.

– Hmm. That's good. But I still wonder why nobody has ever talked to any of them.

– I think some of the holy people actually have.

– You mean the priests?

– And some of the monks too.

– Like Gennadi?

– Yes, people like him.

– I wonder what God told him!

– Oh you're so silly. They aren't just talking like we're talking right now. It's more like they're talking and listening to themselves, and then suddenly they can hear God's voice inside themselves. See?

Manuel nodded and was silent for a moment. His sister didn't miss the opportunity.

– So why is it that you're not afraid? she said. When we were hiding in the cellar today you were whining and sobbing, I heard it.

– Yes, and you were wetting your underwear.

– I wasn't.

– You were, because there was a puddle on the floor.

– That wasn't me!

– So where did it come from then?

– If you don't stop you'll have to go back to your own bed.

– Alright, I'll tell you why I'm not afraid. Because our father has hidden the flying carpet in a safe place, and all we need to do if the Sultan comes is to find it and fly away from here and live in a magic cave for ever.

– Why would you like to live in a cave?

– 'Cause it's a magic cave, it becomes whatever you want it to be. It's a palace and a tree house at the same time. And it has elephants and monkeys. It's a fantastic place.
– You really believe in that story about the flying carpet, don't you?
– Of course. Don't you?
– Naa, that's just a story. In reality there are no such things as flying carpets.
– That's 'cause you don't believe in them. And why would our father be lying to us about such a great thing?
– He isn't lying, he's just exaggerating.
– What do you mean?
– Oh, like he said about the boat, that they put a whale up front to pull it forward, like a donkey in front of cart, that was to make the story better too.
– So you don't believe in whales either?
– Of course I believe in whales, only that they don't pull boats along in the middle of the night.
– And what about that man and his boat swallowed by a whale and then spit up on an island somewhere – was he not real to you?
– That's a story from the Bible.
– And the Bible tells the truth, doesn't it?
– Yes, why?
– So if you must believe in that whale and that he could swallow a man and his boat, what's so strange about our father using another one for his boat?
– Oh, stop it now, I get a ringing in my ears from your talking. Now, go to sleep because I am.

Anna turned demonstratively round and faced the wall, and she really was very tired, so she soon fell asleep. Manuel though was bewildered by this new and unexpected information. If the flying carpet didn't exist, or at least couldn't fly, or perhaps could only fly a little, how had it been possible for Father to take a long tour in the air around all of Constantinople? And what if there was no whale?

Meanwhile, the Sultan seemed only all too real, and the cannon balls most certainly were. Maybe then there wasn't any possibility of escape, which meant Manuel couldn't even trust his father's words. The idea was upsetting. But then he saw something strange. In one dark corner of the room, where normally the cat used to sleep – there was an old crack in the wall which allowed the mice to enter – he saw a small but distinct light. At first he believed it to be the cat's eyes, because they too would sometimes gleam in the dark. But they were always in the shape of two circles, and this was just one light, swinging gently back and forth. Manuel tried to focus on it but as soon as he raised his head he could no longer see it. Only when he remained stretched out sideways on the bed could he see the light. So he tilted his head ever so slightly so as not to lose sight of it, then followed its movements. And now, as the light moved closer to the bed, he beheld a miniature man who would hardly have reached above Manuel's own knees had he himself been standing. In his hand he carried an oil lamp, its wick strangely illuminating his face and curious costume. He was dressed neither as a Greek nor a Turk. Although he did wear some kind of turban on his head, it was different from any of the Turkish ones Manuel had seen. He also had golden slippers on his feet; and the pointed tips were so long and winding that they curled up like ram's horns at the end of his toes. He wore white balloon trousers, a red ribbon around his waist and a red, short, embroidered velvet jacket. His face was very distinct, with bushy eyebrows, small piercing eyes and a sharp, almost birdlike nose. At last he stopped near Manuel sniffing around as though he was trying to pick up some scent, swinging his little lamp back and forth.

– Who are you? Manuel said, almost sending the little figure reeling back to the wall, so surprised was he.

– Oh there you are! the miniature man exclaimed while collecting himself. – Wasn't expecting to hit upon you so soon. Sometimes I have to look for people for days, even weeks, but *you* were very easy to find.

– Who are you, and where do you come from? Manuel repeated.

– Who I am? You should know that since you sent for me.

– How could I send for you when I don't even know who you are?

– Hmm, that *is* strange, the man said scratching his curly beard. Well, let me see here.

While he was fetching a papyrus scroll from his pocket and unfolding it he asked Manuel to hold the lamp for him so that he could read the text. The lamp itself was of shiny brass and had a circular handle in the form of a snake. The light emitted was even stranger though. While the miniature man was searching for some entry on the scroll, Manuel saw a flame spew out of the spout. Again it was the figure of the little man himself, but constantly changing in appearance as the draft through the room blew the flame in this or that direction. And again the light disappeared altogether whenever Manuel tried to sit up the better to discern the human looking figure in the flame. Manuel lay down and looked into the flame.

– Is that also you? Manuel asked pointing at the wick in the lamp.

– Mmmm?

– The figure, the figure in the flame, he looks like you!

– Ah, here we are! Your name's Manuel Papanikolaou?

– Yes, but there's a man inside the lamp, a man of fire. I just saw him!

– Says very clearly here your father has asked Sim Saladin to grant you a trip on the flying carpet, but only if and when the Sultan has entered the city. Well, young man, this means you have something very special to look forward to...

– But the man of fire!

– Oh don't bother about him. Looks a bit odd, but quite harmless really. I tell him to stay inside the lamp, but he doesn't listen to me. He wants to get out. Problem is he then promises things to the children that I'm unable to deliver. It's really most annoying.

– But he looks exactly like you!

– My brother. We both act on behalf of Saladin, but he's the more volatile character really. Now, if your trip is not scheduled for now, I wonder why we were sent here in the first place? Has there been any doubts expressed around you as to the extent of Saladin's realm and power?

– It's my sister, she doesn't believe there are flying carpets. She says it's just a story.

– Ah, there we have the crux! No doubt she also considers herself more grown up and wiser than you for not believing in the power of magic.

– She makes fun of me!

– Common, indeed common. It happens to a lot of children as they grow up that they suddenly cease to perceive us, the 'small folks' as even we sometimes are wont to call ourselves.

– And what do you otherwise call yourselves?

– Oh, we are the Saladinos of course. And you do believe in flying carpets, don't you?

– I want to, but she said I was silly to believe my father had actually been on one.

– Your father, let me see... Iannis Papanikolaou, right?... Oh yes, he was on one of our special carpets as late as yesterday night. Full tour of

Constantinople and the Bosporus. But you, it says here, you want to fly all the way to Saladin's cave.

– Yes, how did you know?

– Somehow you must have expressed that wish, otherwise I wouldn't know.

Having said this his brother suddenly shot out again through the spout of the lamp, performing a salamander dance as a gesture of farewell.

– We have to go, said the Saladino giving his intricately flaming brother a weary glance. By the way, my name is Hattun, and that of my brother is Ignotus. We'll soon see you again. "See you again", mimicked the figure in the flame, making big round cat eyes while waving a furry fire-tail.

Hattun set off towards the crack in the wall. Before Manuel had had the time to respond he slid through the opening. Manuel could still see the flickering flame from the lamp, but when he sat up it disappeared, just like before. When Manuel lay down this time he felt an irresistible urge to sleep. But he forced himself to stay awake another moment. Again there were some lights at the level of the crack, but this time it was clearly the glowing circular hollows of the cat, because Manuel knew exactly what they looked like and he was not afraid of them. He wanted so much to wake up Anna and tell her the wonderful news about the flying carpets, but then he realised she wouldn't believe him unless she too actually met with Hattun, who could then explain it all to her. Manuel was quite content though to have encountered the strange brothers, and although he still feared another day of bombing, he felt that there was hope and a way out if or when the dreaded moment came when they all had to leave. In that case Hattun and Ignotus would surely be back and spread the red carpet right before their eyes. Strengthened in his belief Manuel then fell into a deep sleep.

Chapter 34

Come morning, Iannis' predictions were proved alarmingly correct. To the horror-stricken amazement of the people gathering on the ramparts, innumerable cradles carrying entire ships and their crews were slowly but surely lowered into the Galata bay. Iron wheels, metal tracks, logs, planks, ropes, tackles, winches, live-stock, soldiers, all worked as perfectly together as the body and limbs of a giant crocodile pushing its lethally serrated jaws onto the surface of the lagoon while its scaled body meandered the hill sides and its tail still dipped into the open sea. The hauling, which had mastered a maximum elevation of 200 feet, lasted the entire day, with the Sultan and his retinue intently supervising the operations from the shore-line. The bombardment too had resumed as the juggernaut continued.

The consternation among the defenders well-nigh transformed into panic as shortly before sunset a total of over seventy ships, among these several large galleys, had been witnessed entering the basin beneath the Valley of Springs. For all their mounting discomfort and fear the Emperor, Giustiniani, Gabriel Treviso, Lucas Notaras, Alex Diedo and other commanding officers, couldn't help but reluctantly acknowledge, even admire, this astounding feat of military engineering. But witnessing the impossible take place right before their very eyes didn't exactly boost their sense of security. The sheer force, speed and technical mastery whereby this had been accomplished sent cold shivers along their spines. How, everyone felt, was it going to be possible to resist an enemy that showed such undaunted resolution in face of obstacles hitherto held to be insurmountable?

It became clear that the already dangerously stretched out defence line now had to be spun so thin as to make it likely to snap whenever and wherever a sudden and unexpected increase in pressure occurred. Men urgently needed to man the ever weakening land walls would henceforth have to be deployed along the sea sections, which were much less solid precisely because they were considered highly unlikely targets of attack as long as the Byzantines were able to defend their sheltered harbour. Previous sieges of the city had ultimately failed because the enemy had not been able to take control over the Horn, whence vessel-borne attacks were far more likely to be fatal than those launched from sea. In addition the Turks were supported by heavy artillery on this side too. The noose tightening, the city gasped for air.

The Emperor called for an immediate meeting and instructed the terrified Francis – to whom the ships in the bay seemed, in his own words, "more numerous than drops in a rainstorm, leaves in a forest and stars in the sky" – to gather its participants in utmost secrecy. And as though that was not enough to worry about, he also had to face the fact the he was running short of money. Though gallantly abstaining from any claims to remuneration on his own part, Giustiniani felt constrained to inform Constantine that in order to keep his forces united and motivated under the extraordinary pressure they had to endure, nominal payments must be forthcoming. Without them Giustiniani could find his leadership questioned; perhaps he would even be in for an insurrection, which, as a direct result of recent developments, would be tantamount to a desperate run for the ships.

Constantine, realising the precariousness of the situation, ordered silver plates, chalices and other valuable metal objects in the churches to be melted down and minted. Bishop Leonard maliciously confided to Isidore that this was about the first good decision the Emperor had made since the beginning of the siege, and even the stoutest supporter of the Orthodox church, who, as it happened, were also the harshest critics of his policies, were all too scared to speak up against it. As for the Emperor himself, he calmly justified his action by saying that if God were to save the city, he would make sure God was paid back many times over.

The only two non-Venetians participating in the emergency meeting were Constantine and Giustiniani, held in high esteem even among his Italian rivals. Present were thus the Venetian mayor Minotto along with the harbour commander Alex Diedo, and some of the more prominent sea captains, such as Gabriel Trevisano, Zacaria Grioni and Giacomo Coco. Altogether there were no more than twelve men around the table. The atmosphere was heavily charged. Everyone agreed that an immediate counter-measure had to be taken, and taken fast, but there was loud and agitated discord as to how to go about it. To Francis it was a smarting sting that Constantine had not asked him to also be present and take notes, but he was too worried that the answer would be in the negative if he were to recommend himself, so he never dared to ask for the reason as to why he had been left out.

After Constantine had thanked them all for coming on such short notice, realising the urgency of the situation, he left the word to whomever felt inclined to seize it. It was Zacaria Grioni, a tall eagle-like Roman, who opened the score,

– I believe we, reinforced with all the Genoese ships, should make a concerted attack against their harbour fleet during broad daylight. As we have seen, the high hauls of our carracks effectively prevent them from boarding and if only we can quickly surround them, they will incinerate as we unleash Greek fire on them and then drown like cats. Those who are still alive after that we'll finish off with spears and pikes.

– That might sound good in theory, Gabriel Trevisano, a bearded, barrel-like figure from Verona, objected. – What we mustn't forget here, though, is that the enemy has a battery of guns stationed well above and around his fleet. If we attack by daylight, they'll withdraw as close towards land as they can, and we'll be pulverised by their artillery before we even get a chance to engage them in close combat.

– Yes, well, we might have to sacrifice one or two ships to get close to them, but once there we can practically burn them to hell.

– One or two ships! Trevisano exclaimed. – You don't even know what you're talking about. We need every single raft still afloat here. We can't even afford the loss of one single ship. This must be done with just as much stealth and surprise as the Sultan's manoeuvre. Besides, bringing in the Genoese on this operation is going to be tricky considering they're sending every issue over to Galata to get the point of view of their mayor there. And you've got to forgive me, Giustiniani, for what I'll have to say here, but I don't trust for one second the professed neutrality of your countrymen in Galata. How come not even a stray rumour about what was going on beyond its walls ever reached us? Rome wasn't built in one day, you know. Neither was a track the length of three hippodromes and capable of transporting 72 ships over a hill of 200 feet. But just because we obviously don't get intelligence from them, it doesn't necessarily mean that the Turks are not getting any either. I'm positive there must be Turkish agents and collaborators over there, all the more so since we have no means of forcing them to clarify their position vis-à-vis us. So whatever we do, and let it be known that I say this for the first and last time: we can't trust any of the Genoese who are not here among us and have declared themselves willing to honourably and valiantly defend this city of God. There can be no question of involving Genoese ships from Pera in this operation. In fact, the risk of alerting informers even excludes the possibility of a surprise attack involving *any* Genoese ships!

Without either overtly consenting or disagreeing with the speaker, Giustiniani suggested,

– Suppose there was a way we could make a surprise sortie over land and destroy, or at least render inoperable, their cannons. Then there would be a realistic chance for the fleet to quickly move in for a decisive hit.

– Yes, hero-curled Alex Diedo, said – But any such detachment of soldiers will jeopardise the defence of the walls. Just as little as we can gamble with our ships can we afford to calculate another major loss of men, even if some part of the force would be able to reach the gun batteries and turn them over. I don't believe it can be done to our advantage.

The discussion went on in a similar vein for two hours. In the end, though, it was the plan proposed by Giacomo Coco, normally sailing on Trebizond, that won the day. Coco hadn't said much during the earlier stages of the discussion, which no one thought strange considering that he was a man known to prefer action to words. Perhaps that was also the reason that when he finally did speak, his few words of advice, uttered through the impenetrable tangle of his beard, seemed to weigh heavier than the all the others taken together. Unanimity could not be achieved, but since there only seemed to be bad and less bad options available, consensus settled in favour of his idea. And although all Venetians heartily agreed that the Genoese must be kept outside the entire operation, it could in the end not be kept a secret. Speed, timing and smooth coordination was of the essence, and it was decided that the operation should take place the following night, but the preparations, kept as discreet as possible, were still such that they caught the curious eye of the Genoese captains, who quickly sniffed out that there was something in the making that they too wanted a share of.

As soon as the leading Venetian captains had returned to their harbour stations they were besieged with questions from the Genoese. For the time being the captains tried to avoid confrontation by locking themselves up in their cabins, only to discreetly walk the deck at night. But even then they were spotted and the protestations finally grew so loud that they compromised the security of the entire port, precarious at best under normal circumstances. The century old animosity between the representatives of the two Italian republics was about to flare up again. And since every single movement on Venetian ships was eagerly followed by hundreds of Genoese eyes, glowing with curiosity and indignation in the darkness, the necessary preparations of the ships, no matter how discreet, were ruthlessly revealed and duly reported to Genoese commanders. The night was not even over as the Venetians – with the exception of Trevisano who at the risk of his own life had categorically opposed Genovese involvement from the very beginning and now stood by his word – caved in to the Genoese demands. By dawn order was restored among the arguing and fighting seamen. But the price for this internal truce was high. The Venetians declared they would be ready to strike the following night. The Genoese protested, declaring they had been deliberately deceived and needed another day to get their ships battle-ready. In the end it turned out they needed two. As a consequence the entire operation was delayed for four whole days, leaving the Turks plenty of time to set up their own defence lines.

Trevisano, who had had his ship ready to leave on schedule without arousing suspicion, muttered over what he felt to be a devastating rivalry between two small fish fighting over territory, not realising that the closer they argue the easier it becomes for an even uglier fish to snatch both of them at the same time. Trevisano had his misgivings, but when the critical moment did come, he couldn't deny the others his assistance.

Chapter 35

The night was black as pitch and the sea calm. In the Galata bay an armada of ships were gently swaying on their anchors. After five days of intense vigilance the Turkish mariners had begun to feel a bit safer as signs of preparations for a counter-attack continued to shine with their absence. Admiral Hamsa Bey himself had lessened the rigorous watch duty of fully armed crews and there were now only two lookouts in shifts throughout the night on the bigger ships, as well as on the smaller ones anchored farthest from shore. For once it wasn't as cold after dark as it had been on previous nights, and the calm wind conditions added to the comfort, allowing the seamen and soldiers to actually doze off an hour here and there before dawn would inevitably force them to rise again.

But the seemingly motionless night held ominous secrets. A number of high-decked fustae, veritable maritime spearheads, one-masted battering rams with a lateen sail that could be deployed by one simple pull of a rope, easily manoeuverable with one row of oars, cannons and gunners on front deck and the helmsman behind the canopy in the aft, silently and ever so gently heaved their anchors and gathered in the waters outside the harbour of Galata. Soon both smaller and larger vessels added to their number, among the larger, two sturdy merchants, padded like horses for bullfighting – one Genoese the other Venetian – as well as two Venetian galleys under their commanders Grioni and

Trevisano. As the latter slowly moved up to join the ghost fleet, he discovered that the night was indeed dark except for one small but intensely luminous point on top of one of the Galata towers. Seen from their anchoring position in the harbour the light was almost invisible, but it's faint gleam hadn't so far alarmed anyone since look-outs on the Galatan side, who had little reason to fear direct gunfire from the Turks, would often make fires on the ramparts to warm themselves. But what Trevisano, ever suspicious of the Galatans, now came to witness convinced him that their operation must be immediately abandoned. The light wasn't steady. Considering the unperturbed sea around them it could not be accounted for by capricious gusts of wind causing it to flicker. For sure, it was a sign. But not to their Christian brothers. It was a sign to the enemy.

And here he was, the last to pull out, having one of slowest ships to move by oars. During daytime orders and warnings could be shouted from one ship to another, carried on in a long chain of command, at the top of which Trevisano would find himself. But any loud noise at this point would instantly blow their cover and make them exceedingly vulnerable since they had not yet had the time to group in tactical formation. So the only thing he could really do now to stall the mission was trying to delay his own arrival to the scene so that dawn would forestall them and force all ships to return to harbour before they had been discovered. Trevisano, hating to be right again, clenched his fists and teeth while powerlessly staring at a light signaling treason to everyone not completely blinded by prejudice, wish-thinking and a sudden lust for glory.

Trevisano's deliberate attempt to slow down the convoy made everyone nervous. Some captains correctly inferred that there must be a reason for Trevisano's prolonged absence, and impatiently waited for his arrival. When he finally caught up with them, his worst fears were confirmed. Coco, the man of action who resented Trevisano's caution and reserve, had lost his patience and taken things into his own hands. Instead of waiting for the fleet to gather and strike in formation with two "gun-proof" transports up front, as their plan prescribed, he had set his rowers to go ahead of all other ships, forcing these to catch up with him as best they could. The bulk of the fleet was now less than half a mile from the outer perimeter of the enemy line; by now Coco had to be right up there ready to strike. In the worst case scenario he could be instantly surrounded by Turks who would sink him and then set out to attack all the other ships still not properly lined up. It could spell disaster, but at this point there was nothing else to do than trying to close the gap between the first and the last vessels of the armada. Easier said than done, though. The faster ships were already up front while the slower ones lagged behind. Having to coordinate their efforts at all costs, the decision was at last taken to give Coco the support he would soon be in desperate need of.

Suddenly the intense darkness around the fleet was interspersed by a series of quick lightnings originating in the Valley of Springs. Seconds later the roaring of gun batteries tore the stillness to shreds around them. The first volley hit very randomly, but the light from the cannons had been sufficient to allow the gunners to aim their second battery on stand-by to greater effect. Once located, Coco's fusta at less than a hundred yards from the shore turned into a sitting duck. The next round of firing brought down a huge stone-ball amidships, instantly smashing six rowers to pulp, and breaking the vessel up in equal halves that sank to bottom of the bay faster than it took its terrified helmsman to recite the Lord's prayer.

The gunners on the foredeck, armed with cuirasses, helmets, swords, daggers, and pulled down by ropes, gun racks and cannons, didn't stand a chance, and were dragged down as quickly as though they themselves had been cast in bronze. Survivors for the moment jumped over board only to discover that they didn't know how to swim and drowned. The rest, trying to swim in the cold water, or holding on to the jetsam and flotsam of their only seconds ago so menacing vessel, faced the dilemma of easily being able to reach the shore teeming with Turkish soldiers, or perish by hypothermia before they could make it back to Constantinople.

To most, except Trevisano and his crew, the barrage out of nowhere came as an overwhelming shock, and before the remaining fleet had the chance to even form a much needed defence-line, allowing for their retreat, Turkish ships set out at appalling speed to intercept them while the gunfire continued unabated. Alessandro and Stefano, two of Trevisano's most reliable men, had been injured by stray arrows from the approaching Turks and carried under deck to fend for themselves. As they lay there, moaning from their wounds, the didn't know that their situation was about to change from very bad to the worst possible. Minutes later, two well aimed cannon balls crashed through the hull just above the water line, failing only by inches to transform their torn flesh to ground meat. The ship, now having to stand up against waves from oars, projectiles and ships around them, began to take in water. Allessandro and Stefano found themselves swimming, realising that if they couldn't stop the water, they would all go down to the bottom of the sea, since on deck there wasn't one single man to be spared. In fact the fight up there was ferocious. The war cries of the Turks chilled their blood to the point that their brains actually began to work. Quickly they amassed anything they could to stop that water from continue pouring inside the ship: wood, cloth, ropes, sails, jars. The water inside was all red from their blood but at least it only rose so slowly as to give them a chance to make it back to port. That was if they could get away from the Turks ruthlessly engaging them on all sides. For the time being this was not the case, and the water kept rising.

Trevisano and his men on deck were eventually able to disentangle the ship from the many smaller predators trying to bite through its carcass, and under heavy bombardment, slowly but definitely not so surely, limp back to port. When they arrived there Allesandro unfortunately was dead, but Stefano was found holding on to a barrel he had propped up against the hull, his bluish face covered in blood. Around the barrel there were only trickles of water sifting into the ship, and although the survivors had to swim inside to liberate him from his heroic task, the ship had somehow managed to stay afloat. Hours later, when the broken arrow had been artfully extricated from his arm and he was sufficiently warm again to be able to speak, Stefano explained that Alessandro had ended his life by propping himself up against the hull to prevent the water from coming through the other hole. Without him they would never had made it.

Meanwhile the padded, near immobile, carracks had been spotted, separated as they had become from the rest of the fleet. The fight here was if possible even wilder, but both the Venetians and Giustiniani's force in the Genoese ship, fought bravely, knowing that it would be the end for them all if they were killed or forced to surrender. Since the larger ships stayed further out in the bay, the guns had no luck in reaching them and had to stop their cannonade as the Turkish vessels pulled up along their sides. Luckily an early northern wind allowed the Italians to set a few sails. The ships, once in motion, drifted back towards Constantinople and after one and a half hours the Turks, though thirsty for blood like never before, had to return to their anchor position not to fall prey to Greek fire and artillery.

Early morning, cold and bleak, revealed a sad story. Coco's ship, as well as a few smaller vessels, had been sunk. Nearly ninety able crossbow-men, archers, gunners, rowers, mariners and commanders, including Coco himself, were dead or missing. One Turkish fusta also rested on the bottom of the bay, but that indention in their force was negligible, as a hundred missing Turks was not in any way comparable to the same loss of Christians. To the Sultan human lives were dispensable, to the defenders not. All now wished they had listened more attentively to Trevisano, but the one other captain who had the strongest reason to publicly regret and excuse his disobedience could no longer be held responsible for his actions. He was dead. With him the hope was also buried to drive the enemy out of the Horn.

Chapter 36

Why on earth did it take the Latins so long to arrive with a rescue flotilla? With their help, the now seriously weakened Turkish fleet remaining at the Double Columns would make an excellent target. But where were they? It was the question on everybody's lips. Not because it had suddenly become more likely that a rescue fleet would actually appear, but because it was the only thing, short of divine intervention, which at this time still offered a glimmer of hope.

Constantine received the news of the failed assault with outward composure and inward despair. But as he hopelessly brooded over the irreplaceable losses, messengers arrived with news that was to turn the day of April 29 into one of the most sinister events to have scourged the city in the course of its millenarian history – and it had indeed seen a few fateful ones before. Once all the ships engaged in the battle had returned to their anchoring positions, it turned out that in the general confusion of the night some 40 Italians had neither drowned nor been able to make it back to the city. Instead they had ended up on the enemy shores, where they were captured.

The grey of the sky was dull and unforgiving. The face of Allah was as impassive as the *Jihad* was active. On the walls of Galata there was no sign of human life. Yet, no doubt someone had been up there during the night, warning the Turks of the imminent attack. The gunners had had everything prepared in the dark and once the signal was given they had their fire-breathing dragons spring into action. Their success had been undeniable, and the informers inside Galata had reason to believe that they had won themselves a star in the Sultan's book of merits. But to Mehmet this was still not enough. When he returned to his tent after the battle, he felt a tidal wave of voluptuous desire mount inside him at the mere thought of how he was now going to capitalise on his victory. The moment had come to set an unforgettable example as to what would happen to anyone trying to destroy, or even impede, *his* forces. With any bit of luck it might even terrify the remaining defenders to surrender. For this reason it was paramount that the stage for the second act was set so that it could be beheld from the walls of Constantinople.

Around noon the unlucky survivors were paraded on the shore, partly to show the population of Constantinople that they were there, but more importantly to deliver them to their gruesome fate in full view of the besieged. The Greeks began to divine the horror as they received the echo of Turkish axes simultaneously working on forty wooden poles in order to turn them sharp at one end, and prepared to be driven into a pre-dug hole in the ground at the other. One by one, under desperate cries for mercy, trying in vain to run away, the prisoners were first prostrated before the Sultan, then thrown onto a rack, violently stripped of any remaining clothes. The executioner, armed with a sledge hammer, then approached the victim. Two horses strapped to the victims with ropes pulled his legs apart. One of the sharpened poles were then enforced betweens his buttocks. The preparations in place, Mehmet made a sign with his finger. With full force, unleashing in the victim a scream so full of agony and pain that it was easily carried over water into the Greek harbour, the executioner hit the sharpened pole as hard as he could. Being trained for the purpose and having the necessary experience, he mostly managed to drive the pole through the rectum a full eight to ten inches into the intestines of the victims. Sometimes though he would have to hit twice or thrice to achieve optimal effect, which was to make the pole stop just short of the heart so that death would regrettably not be immediate, but the torment as excruciating as possible. Then the pole skewing the hapless man was raised and fitted into the hole so that the intended prolonged suffering of the victim could be enjoyed to the full among the bystanders.

Constantine, having witnessed how some of the men he had seen fighting valiantly next to him on the ramparts were subjected to this atrocious humiliation and terrifying death, felt a black cloud descending on him. There wasn't much he could do, but there was one thing he had to do, one thing that all the outraged people around him asked, demanded and craved for. At the beginning there had only been tears and loud lamentations among the spectators on the Greek side, but as the ghastly show went on, Constantine resolutely issued his awaited order. From dungeons and caverns they were all scrambled together, tied up in a long row and marched off to the walls of Petrion. There a platform with a scaffolding was erected and Constantine sent for a number of his most trusted men of Varangian descent. Armed with the famous long-swords of the ancient Norsemen they set to work.

During the course of that single afternoon, no less than two hundred and sixty Turkish prisoners of war were beheaded by Varangian swords and long axes, their blood streaming down the outer walls to colour the bay purple. Seeing what had happened to their Italian counter parts on the other side of the Horn, the prisoners knew there was no mercy to be excepted. Realising that the Sultan dispensed with their lives as though it had been that of cattle, some of the men might have seen things in their true light. Others, and those were perhaps in the majority, still hoped that the promise of rich rewards in the after-life for brave warriors would be honoured. Whatever their sentiments, the vast majority of them faced the inevitable with dignity. Constantine regretted it, but from the masses gathered beneath the platform, on the walls and below, a cry of triumph soared at every chopped head rolling down the stairs. The heads were then collected, carried to the land walls and dumped outside together with the bodies. When the Turks later in the evening tried to retrieve the headless corpses and the many severed heads, they were fired at by the infuriated soldiers, sprayed on with Greek fire and showered in liquid tar. At nightfall the grisly spectacle had come to an end. There would be no more taking of prisoners.

Chapter 37

The Turks, invigorated by their success, continued to fortify the pontoon bridge they had constructed across the Horn just north of the junction of walls around the Blachernai. This enabled large army units to quickly move from one position to another, constantly forcing the defenders to keep a watchful eye on all their movements to prevent a sudden attack from occurring on any thinly protected section of the walls. The Sultan also repaid his informers in Galata by intensifying the artillery fire passing straight over their heads and aiming for any target around the boom and the waters between Constantinople and Pera. In many other places as well the bombings were carried out from dawn to dusk, forcing the citizens to constantly keep up their repair work.

A delegation of citizens in Galata, concerned by his apparent lack of consideration for their well-being in spite of the vital piece of intelligence he had received from them, set out to seek audience with the Sultan. However, they were only allowed to meet with the Grand Vizir, Halil Pascha, who summarily explained that once the siege was over, his Majesty the Sultan would repay the Galatans for their losses, including but not limited to the twelve thousand ducats worth of silk, wax and other products that had constituted the cargo of their now irretrievably sunken merchant. That was all. The Sultan was obviously in no mood for excuses, and the Galatans now had good reason to fear that their neutrality had become a trap ready to be sprung at any moment.

Mehmet was in his tent. After walking to and fro while absent-mindedly running his hand through a chest loaded to the brim with gold coins and precious stones, he impatiently turned to his General Zaganos Pascha.

– Well then, he said, – Do you think we should increase the pressure on them by demanding that they let go of the attachment to the boom inside their town? After all, they would only have to endure the shame for as long as it would take us to destroy the fleet, now caught between the pincers of our own. Once we control the harbour there will be no stopping us. Afterwards we will obviously deal with them in any way we find appropriate, but if for now we promise that trade will resume like before and that they will enjoy special privileges as allies of the Sultanate, we can perhaps coerce them.

Zaganos Pascha, a Greek convert to the Moslem faith, wasn't quite sure what his master really wanted to hear, so he decided to take a gamble and speak his mind,

– It's my opinion, your Majesty, that we should be careful about demanding their full submission at this time. So long as the citizens of Constantinople can only speculate on the extent of Genoese cooperation with us, they can still pretend to be neutral, albeit with a few unpredictable elements in their midst. If they were to cut the umbilical cord to the mother city, however, it would be an act resounding of treason throughout the entire Christian world. More specifically, it would cast a shadow of eternal disgrace on the Republic of Genoa and its dominions. Confronted with such ultimatum, they literally would have to opt for martyr death, since the Pope of Rome would feel compelled to issue an almost interminable array of excommunications and interdicts. Although the Christians will soon have to accept that Constantinople has been graced by the presence of Allah, and bow to his might, the stain on the Genoese coat of arms can never be washed clean. In short, the churches, Catholic and Orthodox, will never forgive them.

– Hmm, assuming you're right about the Pope – I don't know his thoughts and policies well enough to question your judgment – I'm not so sure the same applies to the Orthodox camp. You see, I had a meeting with their spiritual leader, a certain George the Scholar, an erudite theologian who has taken the vow of chastity – as if he ever needed to promise God, or himself for that matter, to never look twice at a woman – and assumed the name of Gennadi. The other day I had a little chat with him, and even though he seemed predictably outraged by my suggestion that he should help us, I had this hunch that he just as well might. The truth of the matter is that to a majority of Orthodox believers, Islam, with is superior unity of faith and the simple purity of its rituals, appeals more to the average Orthodox believers than the corruption of 'the one true doctrine' and the ineradicable pagan tendencies of the Latins. I made him understand that we will not prohibit their displaying of icons and other pictorial representations of the divine a long as they keep it to themselves, and that Orthodox communities will consequently thrive like never before under our magnanimous rule.

– With all due respect, your Majesty, but the Galatans are not Greeks, they are Latins, and they are bound to uphold loyalty to the head of their church. It's far better for us to let the Genoese, skilled in all types of maritime activities, continue to trade the Black Sea against set tributes to us, than to eradicate them here and now and possibly force Christianity to summon another crusade against Allah. If Venice and Genoa come out of this with what seems to be only moderate harm done to their interests, they will be keen to forget that Constantinople was ever Christian in the first place and go on fighting each other like they have for centuries. As long as they are divided in between themselves we have nothing to fear. We may even begin to plan how to eventually overrun and add the entire Italian peninsula to the glory of Allah. From what I've heard, the city is in uproar and everybody is accusing his neighbour. In a few days time they will be so exhausted by internal strife that they'll have to give up. Food supplies are running low, the Emperor is melting church bronze and silver to pay the mercenaries. Best of all, their high commander, the Emperor's right hand, Giovanni Giustiniani Longo, apparently has got himself a Turkish mistress.

– What?

– A mistress from among your subjects, your Majesty.

– Who is she?

– Rumours say, although I believe this to be a piece of deliberate deception, that it's not just any of the Turkish women attending to the traitor Orhan, but a woman of the highest standing who somehow managed to get inside the city during the siege.

– But that's impossible!

– That's what I thought too, but our informer insists that not only is she a noble woman, but that she held an important position at the court of your father – may his soul be eternally blessed.

– And why does she now want to be inside the walls of a city we're about to storm?

– It seems she has fallen in love with the Genoese condottiere.

– Obviously, yes, after she came to the city. But what on earth brought her there in the first place and who is she?

– We don't know that, Majesty, but we can do our best to find out.

– Your best isn't good enough. Just make sure you get her name and history right. I want to know.

The Sultan made a sign that the discussion was over and Zaganos Pascha respectfully retreated. Although he had somehow managed to get out of the fire into the frying pan, he was content that Mehmet, at least for the time being, didn't seem to want an open conflict with Galata. The Sultan, he had to admit, could be both head-strong and impetuous, but he was far from stupid. As long as one agreed with him that it was necessary to prolong the siege for as long as it took to see the city fall, he was willing to listen to advice. Strange, though, that the mere existence of a Turkish woman in the city should make him so upset. Zaganos Pasha had to admit that he was quite curious too. And now he had another order to pass on to the Sultan's secret agents.

Chapter 38

– I told you, I won't do it! Giovanni was determined but Felicia was not prepared to give in.

– If you can only convince Constantine that the best thing for him to do is to accept your offer and go aboard that galley of yours and disappear for ever – just tell him that the ship will take him to Peloponnesus so that he can gather new forces there and return with them – then the city, bereft of its leader, will surrender. All you have to do is to hold out for another two weeks, at the very most, and then accept the final outcome of events. Without the Emperor present all fighting morale crumbles and there will be riots in the street after the rumour spreads that he hasn't gone off to seek reinforcements, but has abandoned his people in cold blood. Nobody is going to want to fight any longer, no matter what they had previously promised, and you can accept the final ultimatum from Mehmet – oh, they always send that ultimatum to the besieged before they are about to massacre them. It will not be disgraceful for you to do so, because the fighting spirit of the population has been broken, and, even more importantly, no help from the Latins has been forthcoming, so there is no one there to guarantee the soldiers their pay. Thus you accept the terms, which give us, you and me, and all the others in the city a chance to get on a ship and sail out of here. The Turks take the city peacefully. Asked about what happened you truthfully answer that you and the officials of Constantinople persuaded the Emperor to go and gather reinforcements, quite especially to look out for Papal, Venetian and Genoese ships. But as you have told me, in all likelihood the Signoria of Venice has instructed all her captains and fleets to lay low and rather negotiate with the Sultan than risk a confrontation. As far as your fellow Genoese are concerned it should be pretty clear by now where they stand. Add the infuriated Greeks to the picture and you have no less than three compelling reasons why the situation became untenable. All you have to say is…

– Insidious, absolutely insidious! Giovanni interjected.

– Yes, but think about the alternatives. When I first came here I was convinced that God was going to show us a way to bring Mehmet down. But now, since I saw what you actually do and have done for all your men in order to motivate them to keep on fighting, I realise that God didn't send me here so that I could get revenge for the murder of my child, but for me to offer my life-long loyalty to you. I was set straight already when I first laid my eyes on you, but now my heart can no longer bear to keep its secret. I must declare my love. All that matters is that we both get out of here before it's too late. You have a duty to return to your sister. She knows you could never achieve what you really set out to do, she knows it was an impossible mission. All she wants is to have you back, safe and sound. The population of Chios, to which your family is attached, soul and heart, will welcome you with open arms. Genoa itself will hail its prodigal son. You were unable to save Constantinople from falling, but you did save the lives of almost a thousand Genoese soldiers and citizens trapped inside a moribund city. Don't ever think that the magistrates will hold it against you that you choose to do the only reasonable thing once the Emperor had been removed to safety.

– But what about the people? What about all the Greeks, they have nowhere to go. Should I just leave them to their fate?

– People are resilient. And the Sultan has no interest in forcing new subjects to convert to Islam if he knows he can count on them as reliable taxpayers. The Orthodox church, believe me, will even thrive under Ottoman rule. The most bitter thing to swallow will be the transformation of the Ayasofya into a mosque. But once that's a fact, life will go on. And this is what counts, that life goes on. Please, don't have us all killed because of some stupid principle! The battle can't be won, I was wrong. I admit that in the beginning I myself thought I had come here just to use you for my own selfish purpose. But I was wrong. Can you find it in your heart to forgive me although I don't deserve it?

– Felicia, you can never deserve to be forgiven. You can only be – forgiven. May God forgive me too for listening to what you have to say. And, yes, if I had ever suspected anything else, I would forgive you, but you see, there's another thing, and that is that you can't ask for forgiveness where there is no offence. It never crossed my mind that you weren't trying to use me in one way or another. But that's alright. And you know what, maybe I'm just using you too, Felicia!

He loathed the way she argued. It had all the accoutrements of sincerity and reason, yet he had the uncomfortable feeling its implication was perfidious, false and rotten to the core. It occurred to him that he sounded almost desperate. All the same she was not inclined to show him mercy,

– No Giovanni, you don't understand. I have discovered that I love you. From now on I'll do anything for you, give my life for you, yes, give up my life for you. This is the sword of unity that Zacharias, greyer than mist itself, spoke of. Our love is like a two-edged blade around which a wondrous energy spirals. That's the force of our love, destined to conquer centuries still to come. It's invincible, I know it. And its force must not be wasted on a lost cause. Oh, love of my life, kiss me, kiss me as though it were for the very last time…

Rebelliously they fell in each others' arms, engaging in a kiss as unceasing and passionate as the thunderous fiery sparks lighting up the night sky above them like so many shooting stars. Impatiently tearing the clothes off one another, not knowing how to enter Eden fast enough, they engaged in a fierce ritual of special propagation, step by step working their way up the ladder to the zenith of their desires. Felicia, clinging to him like a squid to a moist rock, was overcome by the intense sensation that a series of lightnings were being released from her uterus, traveling in rhythmic pulsations throughout her body. It was an ecstatic embrace unlike anyone she had experienced. Enveloped in a sea of fluids, flowing in and out of her like ebb-tides swirling around a fixed pole, she became the very mortar in which the seeds of life itself are pounded and crushed. Mixed with liquid and supplanted with leaven, it mysteriously expands to become the dough of life. But as the mortar was pounded and its content reduced to finer and finer particles, it transformed to a golden chalice emitting an intense light. And the mystery was not that she actually saw the light within, because she didn't. She just felt it.

Giovanni too was overwhelmed. After having satisfied his lust, he was overcome with a sense of morbid weakness. This mollifying of his brain was a threat to all he believed he stood for. Suddenly he no longer felt a noble hero, but a simple thief calculating the risk of being caught *in flagranti* while stealing. It wasn't rational, but it was his feeling. His own lion heart seemed no more than a hare locked in an eagle's talons and vowed for death. A wave of disgust at the mere thought of his cowardice came over him and he rejected her kiss as though it had been of hemlock.

– What is it, Giovanni? What's the matter? Felicia exclaimed, unable to recognise in his sudden contempt her ardent lover.

With a mind as dark as the circles under his eyes he stood up and brushed her aside so violently that she fell over the table, hit her head against one of its corners and ended up lifeless on the floor. The blood, meandering like a red river over the cool white marble, gushed forth from an ugly wound. Giovanni stared at it, unable to move. For a moment his mind was paralysed. He just stood there, looking at her with broken eyes and open mouth. But then the bile clouding his brain ceded and left him painfully aware of the gravity of the situation. He took her in his arms and laid her on the table. He ripped pieces of her garment to shreds and dressed the wound with them. He had to change the bandage three times, but by then the blood flow stopped. Still, she was unconscious. He carried her over to the bed, sat down by her side and held her slender cool hand in his, remorseful and sad to the death.

Then, at last, her eyelids came to life. She moaned and moved. Giovanni's sigh of relief filled the room like a hot gust of wind. When he looked back at her, he saw her teary, dark eyes fixating his. And these could but stare back into hers.

He wanted to speak and if at all possible explain himself, but as he opened his mouth to tell her what horrible yet irresistible urge had come over him, there was a hard knock on the door. Giovanni turned round, appalled at the mere possibility of literally being caught with his pants down,

– One moment! He yelled towards the door while desperately searching for his belongings, haphazardly strewn around the room.

– Sorry, Sir, didn't know you were there, Sir. Been looking for you everywhere, Sir. Very urgent news, Sir.

The voice behind the door was as loud as it was respectful. Giovanni was relieved to hear it obviously belonged to a Genoese.

– Just hold on, I'll be with you in a moment! Giovanni replied hectically in dialect. Damn, how could it be so difficult to tighten a pair of trousers! He hobbled over the floor, still holding his trousers up with one hand, to open the door. At last he felt sufficiently prepared to face the intruder, knowing that he would have to make up a credible story very, very quickly. Finally he stood ready, sword in sheath at his side, pants up and shirt down. Blond hair still in disarray though.

– Oh, is that you Luca. What's the matter?

– Sorry to interrupt Sir, but beginning of breach has been made at the Romanus. Enemy attack might be expected as soon as the Sultan realises what has happened.

– Alright, let's go.

– Horses waiting, Sir.

At this moment Giovanni realised that Luca had discovered the pool of blood on the floor as well as the pale, half unconscious Turkish prisoner in bed.

– Yeah, Giovanni said thinning his lips while making a furtive gesture in her direction, – Had to use a little persuasion to make her talk. Strong reason to believe she was hiding something. Got what I wanted though. Believe she's innocent for the rest. So just have the maid take care of her. No, she'll be fine. A mere scratch resulting from a small blow. Female skin, you know. Delicate.

Giovanni didn't care to look Luca in the face to find out whether or not he bought that whimsical explanation. But Luca was too upset about the recent breach in the wall to have the time and leisure to ponder the subject further. Giovanni himself knew he had finally made up his mind about where his loyalty and life belonged: with his men. Knowing that he had almost killed her, he also knew she would never forgive him. His manhood was restored. He could feel his strength return with every breath of air. At every step down the stairs military discipline and the call of duty made themselves incrementally incumbent upon him. The mortal danger of succumbing emotionally to a woman in the midst of a siege had come and passed. Now the two of them must for ever be enemies and act accordingly. It was a great relief. "Thank God I crushed the serpent under my heel!" he exclaimed inwardly. But under that stentorian affirmation, more unshakable than a statue in a square, there was another man, shaken, breathless, horrified, ashamed and utterly convinced he would never, ever deserve to be forgiven for his despicable deed. It was the end of his love, and he knew it. Now there was only one thing left to do. To fight as a man and die with honour.

Chapter 39

Spurred on by the turning tide of the battle, the Sultan had ordered bombardments to be resumed, and with even greater force, on the walls surrounding the particularly vulnerable Gate of Saint Romanus. After an entire day of pummeling a chunk almost thirty feet high finally gave away from the top of the wall. Tons of loose stone and rubble tumbled down, creating natural stairways on the outside from which the enemy could now more easily attempt to throw their ladders. Luckily the wall collapsed just as a the ramparts were swept in a rainy fog arriving from the sea, preventing the Turks from actually seeing how successful they had been. Nonetheless it was a threat to the city that needed to be addressed immediately. However, both Constantine and Giovanni were absent from the scene when the disaster struck. The able veteran Luca was in charge, and he quickly organised a repair squad and began directing its operations. Word was sent to Constantine and Giustiniani. The former soon appeared and relieved Luca of his command only to send him off to find Giovanni, whom nobody had so far been able to locate. It was Constantine himself who tipped Luca that the commander might be found somewhere in the vicinity of the Turkish woman. It was in the same house, at the opposite end of town, where she was held in honourable house arrest that he found him.

By early morning Giustiniani was so tired from the Sisyphus task of rolling stones back up the hill that he simply fell asleep standing, and was awakened only by the fact that he had hit the ground. The sun, cold and bleak, implacably rising over the hills of Anatolia, was accompanied by a renewed cannonade from Urban's monster. Giustiniani fell asleep in between the thumpings. Around midday the enormous gun surprisingly grew silent. The gunners operating it had discovered that smoke leaked out from around the barrel and that shots had begun to drop dead at only half the distance to the target. The Sultan was furious, seeing himself tantalizingly close to opening a decisive breach, and called for the monster's father to answer for himself and his creature. The trembling Urban inspected the barrel inside and out. Regrettably he must confirm that a large crack had disabled the gun so that it had now become a lethal weapon against the attackers themselves. If fired it could simply blow up and kill everyone around. There was, however, nothing he and his helpers could do to repair it in its present position. To be mended the gun must be brought back to the foundry. Once there Urban could try to fill the slender air pockets with a mixture of molten iron and bronze. But the work could not be done in an instant. First he needed to make sure that the liquid metal penetrated every nook and cranny of the crack and not just its surface, in which case the gun would once again have the innate capacity to cause potential mayhem.

Mehmet, impatient to bring the siege to a close, now took a rash decision. Around three o'clock in the afternoon, when Giustiniani's men had finally managed to fall asleep for a split second, the trampling of thousands of feet, like a stampede, accompanied by blood-chilling fiendish outcries carried by the ghostly flutter of castanets and the shrill shiver of tambourines, put a sudden end to their comfort. The Turks had been signalled to attack and sent wave after wave of orderly formed aggressors. Giovanni had no choice but to quickly rub his eyes, resume command and organise his forces. Luckily the eerie sound of the enemy gathering for the attack had also alerted other and more rested soldiers on other sections. Bells chimed all around the city and from everywhere weapons and soldiers were rushed to Giustiniani's aid, preparing to face what was to become the closest hand-to-hand combat so far along the Theodosian wall.

Indeed, a hellish welcome awaited the death-defying Turks, who perished by the hundreds alone in their initial assault. But instead of retreating they only kept coming, using the heaps of dead bodies as bridges and trampolines in their ever increasing efforts to overcome the ultimate obstacle. This obstacle was the inner wall, originally designed and erected under supervision of the ingenious Roman architect and engineer Anthemius, who had wisely taken steps to anticipate the urgent future needs of the still adolescent Emperor Theodosius II at a time when the terrifying Huns, under their chief Attila, ravaged Roman provinces from one end to the other. This had all happened a full thousand years earlier, and though the city had occasionally been taken and sacked by invaders, the occasions on which the walls had thankfully prevented them from doing so were far more numerous. But the circumspect and cautious Anthemius had only had the capacity of the largest imaginable stone-throwing catapults in mind when he decided on the final dimensions and dispositions of his wall. How could he possibly have foreseen the effect of gunpowder on future warfare? But here, exasperatingly real before their very eyes, the devastating effects of explosives had been demonstrated. In its wake the Turks were determined to sacrifice any amount of men to obtain their goal.

The Turks mobilised siege towers, horses, carts and chariots; they climbed over dead and wounded bodies to reach the inner wall and latch their hooked ladders onto the inside. And they came close to succeeding, on several occasions very close. However, with Giustiniani in the lead like never before, they didn't stand a chance and died like flies under a swatter. It was a carnage of mythical dimensions. Afterwards the not easily impressed leader of the Varangian guards was moved to say that Giustiniani had appeared to be what their ancestors called a berserk: a man who without regard for his own life and safety cuts lose on the enemy in an unstoppable frenzy. In this way he inspired his men, on the verge of collapse, to fight back like true saga heroes. Some regrettably fell, joining the dead and wounded Turks littering the peribolos, but in the end the enemy horses stumbled, the siege towers crumbled, collapsing in a heap of wood and animal hides on which more corpses gathered like autumn leaves carried thither by a strong wind.

Others perished like chaffs under a reaping scythe. Swords and axes cut heads in halves, leaving skulls and brains like an embroidery on the grim tapestry in the making. Yet, the enemy cries, their castanets and tambourines, refused to abate. Like a scene out of the Apocalypse, dancing, swirling dervishes in the background spurred on the soldiers like devils armed with glowing tridents. Only at nightfall did the ghastly music stop. The waves receded into its human ocean, leaving thousands of dead to be eaten by scavengers, gathering from all directions of nowhere. Greek and Italian losses had, in spite of the ferocity of the attack, been moderate. But once again, if the defenders' losses, however small in comparison with those of the enemy, were to continue at this rate, there would soon be nobody left to man the walls. In this situation Constantine urgently summoned all commanders to yet another meeting.

Chapter 40

It wasn't actually Giustiniani who said it, but once the proposition had been made it surprisingly quickly enthused many of the participants. And at this time it did give Giustiniani the opportunity to offer, without in any way compromising his position, the Emperor his own superb galley. He was well aware that it had originally been Felicia's idea. He was also painfully aware that he had almost killed her for expressing it. His blood boiling after the great battle, his body bleeding from various wounds, he had nonetheless not dared to visit her in person. Good old trusted Luca had been sent over, though, and reported back that she was in good condition. It reassured Giovanni. Nevertheless, he was still too ashamed to go over there himself and expose himself to her wrath.

The idea was in fact put forward by Alex Diedo. The Emperor, thus ran the suggestion, was to embark on a reconnaissance trip in an attempt to locate the now long expected Venetian, Genoese and Papal ships. The reason why it was necessary for the Emperor to do this in person was – according to the diplomatically seasoned Diedo – that if any ship crews out there were confronted with a commander or captain of their own nationality, they could easily deflect their mission to better suit their common interests. But no commander of any ship would be able to refuse following in the keel waters of the Emperor in person once the precariousness of the city had been clearly explained to him. As a worst case scenario – by which the absence of any Italian flotillas on the Lake of Marmara, or even in the Aegean sea, would have to be assumed – the Emperor could head for Mistra on the Peloponnesus and there gather every fighting man and every vessel available, and then return.

It was in many ways a carefully argued plan in a situation where really good plans were virtually excluded. Constantine, seeing himself surrounding by heroic warriors prepared to carry on the resistance while he would be temporarily gone, felt intensely touched by their display of solidarity. But he also realised it couldn't be done, and that the crew of the largest galley of them all, the crew of the battle ship Constantinople, would rise in open mutiny once its captain was gone. Leaving Lucas Notaras or any other member of the aristocracy in charge would only work for a hitherto unknown but nonetheless limited number of days and hours. And as far as Mistra was concerned, Constantinople could easily be sacked and massacred three times over before he even got there, let alone returned with reinforcements. No, there was no way he could save the city in this manner, Constantine, while still preparing his answer in a bitterly prolonged silence, broke out in tears,

– I praise and thank you all for your counsel, which I well understand to be in my best interest. But tell me, gentlemen, how can I possibly do this, leave the priests and monks, the churches of God, all its people and the Empire itself? What would the world and posterity think of me? I pray you, tell me how it can be done? No my lords, no. It can't be done. I'm so sorry, but I must stay here and die with you.

When Constantine had said this he took a few steps forward, and bowed so deeply to everyone that he almost fell over. Many priests and other Greeks wept with him in silence. The Italians too were visibly moved, and it was strange to see so many men, who only hours ago had bravely slaughtered a hecatomb of enemies, cry like children having lost their parents and having nowhere else to turn in the world.

Finally Constantine got a hold of himself and came up with another suggestion which all then agreed upon. He proposed that the Venetians should immediately send out a ship westward to look for signs of Italian marine activity. The Venetians consented, and before anyone had had time to ponder the issue further, twelve volunteers stepped forward from the rank and file of both Greeks and Italians. The meeting was dissolved, a brigantine rapidly put in order. That same night twelve men, dressed like the Turks, flying the colours of the Turk, were discreetly towed towards the boom. Only a subtle rattle of chains against wood indicated that the boom was lowered on one side. A northern night-breeze helped to make the launch as uneventful as everybody had hoped. The ship unfurled its sail and zig-zagged unmolested through the infested waters. At the height of the Princes islands it was safely on its way, relying on the reports from the Venetian captains arriving a month earlier, that Turkish ships were nowhere to be seen from there to Gallipoli. Once past that stronghold they were in the Aegean, where the rescuers, if not actually already triumphantly beating up the Marmara, had to be.

Chapter 41

Constantine too was tired. Not only, and like the rest of his men, from the fighting, but tired of the sad state of his imperial legacy. Even before the siege begun he had been contemplating – like so many of his predecessors fortunate enough to ever approach the age of 50 – the prospects of abdication and monastic retirement. Over time this possibility had become like the mirage of an unattainable Eden. The Mistra of his childhood and youth – with its green hills in spring, its pagan ruins overrun with vine, its venerable churches and its famous philosophical academy under the illustrious Plethon – now seemed more distant than ever. Nothing appeared more desirable to him now than a small cell in one of its monasteries tucked away in a secret valley under a blue sky whitened by hammering noon, surrounded by the accompaniment of sun-drunk cicadas. But no matter how modest a dream this would have been in times of peace, it was now a luxury he could not allow himself to even contemplate in moments of weakness and solitude.

"I'm tired!" he sighed, looking emptily over the wasteland separating the walls from the nearest villages of the interior. At some distance from one another were covered campfires around which soldiers and citizens huddled for warmth in the night: "I'm tired", he sighed again, "tired of this stench of death, urine and excrement (in fact all the towers and ramparts were so full of foul smelling waste that there was no way to avoid stepping into piles of it, especially at night),"but there is simply nowhere I can take this fatigue. I can't even, like my men, visit the brothels to get a moments' relief in the arms of a woman. The mere thought of it is forbidding, and yet, heroism apart, what is there left? Giovanni has the beautiful Turkish princess running after him. Should keep him warm. And other unmarried Greek women now give themselves up to whomever in exchange for a morsel of food or a blanket. Our recent success in repelling the enemy was a temporary respite at best, while I still pretend to meet destiny with resolution. But that's only because I feel I must. Were it up to me alone, I'd let go of it all. Oh God! I should have accepted their proposal to back out of this just as much as it was their own weakness in disguise. It was a plan for abandonment intended to save lives at the expense of our moral dignity and the future of my people. It would have involved their sacrifice insofar as their future would then be in Turkish hands. But maybe that would have been best for everyone Now it's too late. Forlorn – the very word chimes like a bell. And tired! Tired! Tired of empty empire and hollow family name. Tired of trying to mend the schism of the churches. If the issue hasn't been solved for a millennium, why would it be solved now? Just look at me. Since the beginning of this calamity my beard has turned all grey. I'm not fit to assume the Herculean task of putting ancient Rome back together. There are lives to be saved here and now – in time God will count his own. But this dying for a cause, however righteous and noble, is repulsive to me. My very sentiment of resignation to this end is repulsive. If people only knew how I felt, they'd turn themselves over to the Turks right away. I feel I'm defending something I no longer believe in. In whatever outward direction I look from up here, I see only provinces taken over by the enemy. We don't even have a single piece of land left before our door step. So what in reality are we defending? A memory, a petrified memory of something that once was and is no more. Yet I officially maintain that this ghost of a glorious past, and a long past at that, is worth dying for. Ah, what a mess. What a terrible and inextricable mess. And out there, hidden in the dark, is Death himself abiding his time, ready to wreak havoc in the name of Allah, the One and Only.

Constantine was about to descend the stairs of the inner wall where the had taken refuge in solitude to regain his fighting spirit, when his eyes fell upon state secretary Francis mounting the same staircase.

– Your Majesty, please forgive me for intruding on your well deserved privacy.

– Oh dear Francis, don't excuse yourself. Actually, I needed to speak to you.

– I thought you well might.

Francis, reading the slightest shift of mood in his childhood friend as though it had been from pages in an open book, held back what he was about to say and changed course.

– No, your Majesty, he said, no, you mustn't give in to that.

– How did you find me? Constantine replied in a vain attempt to divert Francis' attention.

– Never mind about that, but we must not lose heart.

– Of course not, what makes you think I would ever...

– I see it in your eyes, I see that you are on the verge of giving up.

– I've never heard of such preposterous...

– Call it what you want, and please, again, forgive me for knowing you so well, perhaps even too well for my own good.

– You can say that again! Constantine interjected, his face darkening. But Francis, having the presence of mind to for once let go of his courtly *delicatezza*, stood his ground replying,

– But if that really is the case, why didn't you seize the opportunity when you had the chance? Giustiniani, all the Venetians, the Genoese, Diedo, I myself, even Lucas Notaras, your enemy in disguise, were willing to grant you the benefit of the doubt and let you off the hook. But there you were, commiserating and forcing everybody else to sob with you in tears.

– You know just as well as I do what would happen if I left the city.

– Yes, your Majesty, I do.

– So, what is it that you advocate, that we open our gates?

– Not while you're here. It would be unbearable to your sense of dignity, I know.

– And you think my dignity would be less hurt if I stood on a ship deck somewhere, knowing that I had abandoned my people at precisely the moment when they needed me the most?

– With all due respect your Majesty, but what difference does it make if you are here or there at the moment when a hundred thousand bloodthirsty Turkish hounds are about to climb the walls and kill everyone inside the city. All that matters then is that you can appear in shining armour before our Lord that same day and testify to your valiance and fidelity. But apart from this, and that this is what you believe future chroniclers of history are expecting from you, nothing will have been achieved, and we shall all perish together with you.

– So, what is it you're implying? Should I give the order to surrender before it's too late, and then live with shame as I see fit and let posterity judge?

– No, your Majesty, that's precisely what has now become impossible. There was a moment when you could have slipped out of world history through the backdoor, while our people passed from one governance to another. But like Jesus in the desert you refused the temptation of the devil. You told him to return whence he came. The dice have been cast. You have traversed your Rubicon. Now you must prepare to face God and his angels on the day of Last Judgment. Only an act of supreme faith, akin to that of our Lord Jesus, can bring you into that grace where everything, at last, will be determined by the highest will there is in the earth and heavens. And this is what I came to tell you, only to find you the prey of doubt no longer befitting the situation. Because there is still hope. Listen to this. I just had this report from the people around Blachernai after our last heroic battle. At the very moment when they were almost entirely overrun by the enemy they felt the salvaging presence of divine intervention. Out of the blue Virgin Mary appeared to them. Moreover, witnesses are unanimous in their description. She was seen hovering over the inner wall. She then disappeared in a cloud, making a mysterious sign with her hand. In the next instant several assailants, about to crawl over the outer wall, suffered a devastating explosion, the cause of which nobody could later explain since we had had no guns stationed there. Unless it be assumed that the Turks had by mistake fired a heavy gunshot into their own, it remains inexplicable. The immediate effect on our soldiery, however, was such that the initiative swung back in our favour. Step by step the enemy was forced off the ramparts and trapped in the peribolos, where they were cruelly annihilated by our archers, stone-throwers, gunners and crossbow-men. And the strangest thing of all was that so long as the epiphany lasted all enemy projectiles came to a halt in mid air, as though all the people seeing her had been protected by some invisible shield.

– I just returned from the city, Francis continued – and the apparition of our most Holy Lady and Mother of God has had an incredibly invigorating effect on people. Even though they have had to reassume their heavy duty of burying the dead, they do so with joy and confidence in their hearts, knowing that their losses and sacrifices have not been in vain. Again, incense and wax candles are lit as the miraculous vision is fervently invoked in hymns and prayers. Just as difficult as things have been, people now regain faith in God's almighty hand. This is something in which we too should find strength and confidence. Thus, so far so good. But I would be lying to you if I didn't also report that there are other omens of more sinister portent.

– And what is that, dear Francis?

– Rumours, your Majesty, rampant rumours.

– About me?

– No, your reputation, on the whole is untarnished, although there are some, mostly Italians and consequently members of the Catholic affiliation, who think you're acting weakly in the face of open insubordination among our own. Unfortunately there are some people who take advantage of what they perceive as a lax state of affairs, knowing that you would not at this point lift a finger to punish them, and so they allow themselves to fall prey to delusions.

– What are you insinuating, Francis?

– Christ's second coming, your Majesty. The rumour of his imminent return runs like a wild fire inside our walls. And I'm afraid to say I believe our envoys from the Holy See are the major driving forces behind it.

– You mean Bishop Leonard and Cardinal Isidore? What interest would they have in seeing Christ back on earth?

– None of course. As far as they're concerned it's but a pretext. They want to get out of here before it's too late, but they can't advocate open betrayal, so they mobilise the masses against you.

– But how can they? You know how little liked these western church men are by our people. Anything they say would sound like anathema

to them. They would rather do the opposite even if they knew the Catholics were right.
– Exactly, so they use a different tactic.
– Which is?
– Gennadi. They have concluded a pact with Gennadi, promising him the complete independence of the Orthodox church in return for his agitation that the third age of the Holy Spirit, of which the Catholic heretic Joachim of Flores prophesied already centuries ago, is now finally dawning.
– But that's a message of universal brotherhood and love regardless of ecclesiastical hierarchy and the sacraments. It's completely contrary to Catholic faith; in fact, it entails the undermining of their entire creed!
– Correct, but that's how perfidiously they operate to make sure they will survive this with no harm done to their own interests. They want to launch us on our path to destruction, so that we, not they, can be accused of having brought about our own ruin. Most dangerously, the central message in Gennadi's propaganda is that even if Mehmet will in the end succeed in entering the city, Christ will appear in front of Hagia Sophia and deny him entrance to its holy interior. In this way Mehmet will be forced to leave and we shall oust all Catholics and reaffirm our true doctrine.
– But that's nonsense!
– Of course, but very dangerous nonsense, your Majesty.
– What do you suggest I do.
– You must arrest Leonard, Isidore and Gennadi at once.
– But the two former are commanders on the walls, I have myself appointed them such. We need them desperately. And what do you think the rest of the Italians will say and do if I arrest their religious leaders? There will be rebellion, mutiny, call it what you will, and that, if nothing else, spells the end of all this. I can't do that.
– What about Gennadi?
– Also impossible, he's too popular with the crowds.
– Well then, I'd say the least you can do is to have a good heart-to-heart with these dignitaries. Because if the effects of this propagation is not stopped right now, there is virtually nothing to guarantee that one gate or another is not just swung open to welcome the enemy into the city in the insane belief that by so doing Christ and his glorious celestial army will appear in their midst.

– Alright, Francis. Let's go and find them.
– Look, your Majesty, on the eastern horizon now dies the phantom of morning. In an hour the real dawn will break, announcing yet another one of our many sacred days, which is the day of the traditional parading of the most holy Hodegetria. If I'm not entirely mistaken, it's in connection with that event, ideal for the dissemination of insidious propaganda among naïve souls, that we will find the ones we should really be looking for.

Chapter 42

When young Manuel Papanikolaou woke up next morning, he vividly remembered his encounter with the little Saladino who had promised to keep a flying carpet ready for them "if need be". But since the Saladino had said that people need to believe in miracles for them to come true, Manuel felt that for the time being it was best not to provoke his skeptical sister into further disbelief. It could jeopardize the whole deal. Most likely Mother would react the same way. The only person Manuel felt confident to tell the secret to was his father. But he was gone early that morning, and Manuel had been told to stay put inside the house because of the bombardment. But since he resented his sister saying he'd been a coward, he really wanted to show them that he wasn't afraid. Manuel knew he wasn't. Even though he couldn't pass unnoticed by his mother and his sister in the kitchen downstairs, he could still make it up to the roof terrace, which was even more dangerous and exciting than being in the street. Without making any noise he climbed the ladder to the roof. Once up there he spotted the high tower of Galata above the Petrion seawall. He could actually see most of upper Galata, and he made it a new game to try to spot the cannonballs being fired from behind its walls and predict where they would hit.

The morning sun had just risen above the upper reaches of the tower, enveloping it in a bright halo. Manuel tried to look at its roof, but the light was so intense that he had to avert his eyes not to be blinded. Then, as he again directed his gaze towards the conic top of the building he beheld a luminous being suspended in the air right above it. It looked like an angel, an angel with eyes of fire, fuming nostrils, a wide open mouth, a glowing sword in his hand and golden wings. The angel didn't remain still, but swirled round frantically in circles until the sword – it too describing wide luminous circles in the air – was pointed downwards, striking the spire of the tower while setting off an intense lightning. Manuel couldn't hear the sound of it, but the lightning alone was so powerful and travelled so fast towards him that he stumbled over a pile of bricks, fell head first and lost consciousness.

When he woke up he was back in his bed. Irene and Anna had heard the thumping sound on the roof, and when they didn't find Manuel upstairs they immediately knew where to look for him. It was obvious he'd had another one of his seizures. It had been a while since the last one hit, so long in fact that they had almost begun to hope he had somehow been cured from his affliction altogether. It was now clear he hadn't. It was the same spasms of the limbs and the same frothing around the corners of his mouth as always. They had to force a piece of wood wrapped in cloth into his mouth to prevent him from biting his own tongue. Anna then helped her mother to carry him over to the ladder, where she took him over his shoulder and descended back in to the dark. Together they managed to get him in bed. The seizure was now over but Manuel was still unconscious. And no sooner had they carried him back to safety than the weather, which had been very fair all morning, took a thunderous turn for worse. Shortly the rain poured down so heavily that it seemed the gates of heaven had been suddenly swung open.

As the heavy rain hit Iannis in his small boat, he was forced to speedily return home, that day's risky trade mission between Galata and Constantinople unaccomplished. But he was happy to have done so when he saw his son. At this time Manuel was again in his usual cheery mood, if only a bit pale to his cheek. Even though the whole family of course knew about Manuel's epilepsy, it was only Iannis who knew about his son's supernatural visions. At least he was the only one to take them seriously. So when Manuel told him in confidence about the angel he had seen just before losing consciousness, Iannis was all ears.

– He had a sword in his hand, you said.

– Yes, father, and there was fumes coming out of his nostrils, and fire through his eyes, I swear!

– How was he dressed?

– Oh I don't really know. I believe he was dressed in angel dress. Yes, that's it, in angel armour, golden plates all over, but his face was scary, like he was screaming, but there was no sound except for the guns.

– Manuel, you must promise me never again to go up on the terrace alone and without permission. It's very, very dangerous to even be outside right now and you must be here.

– To protect my mother and sister?

– Yes, my boy, Iannis answered with a compassionate smile. – To protect our women.

– Father…

– Yes.

– Anna says you was just exaggerating about the flying carpet. She says there's no such thing, that they only exist in adventure story books. Tell me, honestly, is she right 'bout that?

– Yes, Manuel, she's right about that.

– So you was just lyin' to me about all that travelin' in the air!

– I wasn't lying.

– Well, extravagating then?

– No my son, not even that. You see, it is true that flying carpets are only to be found in adventure story books. But thing is we're right here and now inside the greatest story book ever written in the whole world, because it's the adventure book of God himself. And in that book there is certainly flying carpets, but only for the ones who believe in them. The ones who don't believe simply can't see them.

– But if this is a book, where is the letters that tell the story, because I know too that story books is written in letters.

– They're there alright, but they are so big they reach all the way from here up to the heavens. In fact, the angel you saw was probably one of them letters.

– But what about the Saladinos, they're so small though.

– The Saladinos?

– Yes, the Saladinos. You know about the Saladinos, don't you?

– Hmm, but of course.

– So what do they look like?

– The Saladinos?

– The Saladinos.

– Ehrr, well, the Saladinos, with whom I have been in much contact over the years, are small men from Happy Arabia, about this high with red hair, spiral slippers and strange conic hats, and if I'm not entirely mistaken they are also in charge of flying carpets. As a matter of fact, I talked to one of them just today.

– Did you?

– Yes, and they confirmed to me that if we call for them in a time of emergency, we'll be on the next carpet out of here.

– I'm so happy you met with the Saladinos; I think they might even be letters too. Especially Ignotus, cause he was changing all the time, like he was really writing himself.

– Manuel. I want you to stay here now and get some rest. I must run an errand but I will be back before dark.

Iannis gave his son a long melancholy glance, wondering whence he had received that strange gift of seeing things hidden to others. The angel seemed no small matter. Iannis had never heard anyone, not even archangel Gabriel, being described in this manner. But he knew his son to have perceptions and insights of the super-sensible world. Irene, as the reliable and sensibly down-to-earth woman she was, naturally thought Manuel's imagination just got overheated from all those violent seizures. But Iannis, in spite of being just a fisherman with little education, was a spiritual man and knew better. As late as yesterday afternoon soldiers at Blachernai had seen the Virgin in a vision. Iannis got to know all about it. Now his own son had been face to face with an angel. It had to be a sign, but of what? Iannis decided he must consult Gennadi on the matter. And it only confirmed his sense of urgency that just as he was on his way out of the door, he met with the two monks the hermit had already sent to his house to ask him over. Indeed, the atmosphere was growing thick with omen. Truly there was not a moment to lose.

He was asked by the brothers to accompany them back to the Monastery of Panaghia Hodegetria, so called because it was here that the most venerated icon in all of Constantinople, the Hodegetria (meaning "She who shows the way"), was kept and regularly put on display. The Hodegetria – a gilded picture of the Holy Mother, pointing towards the Christ child sitting in her lap, crowned by praying angels – was pregnant with holiness. It had been in the travel chest of the 5th century Empress Eudochia, who had visited Jerusalem and brought back with her relics of priceless value, such as a splinter from the cross on which Jesus had been crucified, a piece of the mantel of the soldier who pierced Him in the side with a spear, as well as the said Hodegetria, painted by the apostle and evangelist Luke himself. The patina of time had perhaps even given the gold a darker luster, but in the eyes and minds of her worshippers, she was like a battery, charging every time deep and sincere prayers were directed towards her and kisses dispensed.

Iannis was admitted into the dark and humid monastery and asked to wait in an antechamber for Gennadi to finish his daily prostrations. When he told him about his son's story of the angel on the ramparts, Gennadi grew silent and gave him meaningful glances. Iannis asked him if he believed that it could have been a real angel, but instead of answering him directly, Gennadi led him into the chapel where the Hodegetria, set in a heavy wooden case, was kept. He made Iannis swear to God that he would not reveal to any other human being what he was now about to see. Iannis fell on his knees, kissed his crucifix, made the sign of the cross and swore. Then Gennadi removed the cloth covering her and asked Iannis to tell him what he saw. Iannis still had to get used to the twilight in the sparsely lit chapel, but then, as he looked closer, he too came to witness the miracle. From the corners of her eyes Mary shed red tears, and they didn't just stay in her eyes, but trickled down her cheeks and garments to the exact point where they met with Christ's hand poised on her heart.

– Tears … of blood? He said slowly looking at Gennadi and then at the picture again. No doubt about it, they still kept flowing and disappearing under the Jesus child's index finger. – What does that mean, Father? Iannis whispered and fell to the floor crossing himself in desperate devotion. Gennadi looked around twice before he answered. In a low, confidential tone of voice he continued,

– The Hodegedria has only been known to shed tears of blood twice before. The first time was during the first Arab siege of our city in the year of our Lord 674, the second was shortly before the Franks brutally invaded us in 1204 and put the barbarian Baldwin on the throne. This is the third and final time. What it means? It's a sign that the end of times is drawing near. Christianity as we know it will cease to exist when God punishes the apostates for their wickedness. The Hodegetria sheds tears for the impiety and countless sins of man, and when these tears are red it's a sure sign that the last days are upon us. Antichrist shall now act in the name of God, and the angel your son saw departing from the walls was neither Michael, Raphael or Gabriel, but his rejected son Satanael, now brought in to announce God's will to destroy the world.

– You see, the first time her bloody tears appeared, it signalled the centuries of suffering which the pagan religion of Islam will one day impose upon us. The second time was when we accepted the Franks and their abject rituals into Hagia Sophia. The third time is now, and it heralds the victory of Antichrist. For a thousand years to come a Demon is going to rule over the earth and all her people. In the guise of Mehmet Bey, son of Murad, Satanael is taking over where Christ, his Mother and all the good angels have failed. The only thing that can ever change this outcome of events, is if God, in his inscrutable wisdom, decides to send his son a second time. In that case he will be here to meet Satanael right in front of Hagia Sophia and deny him entrance to it.

– But how do we know when and if this will happen? Will there be a sign for that as well?

– Yes, there are signs said to presage that, but they are indeed strange and unheard of. First, it is said, the moon, though full in her second quarter, will suddenly disappear and leave the bright night sky filled with stars alone. Then there will be a rosy hue descending over Hagia Sophia, signifying that the Holy Spirit intends to take her in his possession. Then, as a token that the Son's return is well under way, the rosy veil enveloping the basilica will lift again and that is the sign that the Holy Spirit has delivered Christ to us. Nobody will know, however, that he's about to enter the city, because according to secret scriptures his arrival is destined to take place through the smallest of all gates of our city, which is a postern called Kerkaporta close to the Blachernai palace. For this reason, but only if the other signs have been witnessed, it is crucial that someone makes sure that the Kerkaporta, although closed, must not be left barred on the day of the final battle, so as to allow our Lord and Savior to enter the city through that small gate when the moment is ripe.

Confused and upset by the cosmic drama unfolding before his very eyes, Iannis set off home. He didn't want his family to share his forebodings, and then there was the solemn vow he had taken not to tell anybody about what he had seen. He understood that anyone allowed to witness the bloody tears of the Hodegetria must be a privileged human being, even if such a vision was also, necessarily, a harbinger of evil. He decided to make everything ready for his family's escape. A Madonna that cries blood, that was definitely not a good omen in Iannis' book of revelations. Not to speak of the rest.

Meanwhile, back home, the rain had stopped for a while, allowing a fan of sunshine – like an angel's wing suddenly descending from the transcendental reaches of heaven to grace the earth – to pierce the heavy cumulus of clouds and dart through the open shutter next to the glowing hearth above which a cauldron, black with soot from years of faithful service, was bubbling with fish and clams. The sudden light hammered so intensely on the incrusted, dented copper that one could almost hear it resound as though it had been a church bell set in motion by an invisible hand. Irene, standing in the kitchen, turned round to her daughter saying,

– I can see there is a moment of sun. Would you please help me to hang these clothes back on the lines in the garden. They're still wet and I don't know how we're ever gonna get them dry in this unpredictable weather.

In the same instant, they heard the hissing sound of one of the Sultan's larger projectiles. A moment later it must have hit something inside the city, because they could hear distant agonizing cries and the shouting and trampling of soldiers and equipment being moved on the ramparts. It had not been too far from them, and a stray stone could certainly hit them too at any moment. But there was nothing to do about that. The house couldn't be moved, and they couldn't just go down and live in the cellar. Luckily their house was also situated so close to the wall that most direct hits had so far been absorbed by it. Obviously a chance volley could change all that in an instant. Even so, life had to go on and to remain hidden in the cellar for days on end was not an option. They simply had to get the clothes dry before they would start to mould.

Anna dropped the quill onto the loom and got up from the bench. She was helping her mother with a rich piece of tapestry, commissioned by a Venetian nobleman's wife in town, depicting a peacock and a princess in a Persian garden. It was slow, minutely detailed and painstaking work, and they had started it even before the siege begun. Under the circumstances it was doubtful whether they would ever be paid for it, doubtful even whether the fine woman would even care to remember her commission, not to mention to honour it. When life itself was at stake, art and luxury had to wait. Which didn't prevent mother and daughter Papanikolaou from dutifully working on the motif whenever they had a spare moment.

– You never know, Irene told Anna, when a piece of work like this comes in handy. – I learned the art from your grandmother, who had been a prisoner of war for many years among the finest silk weavers of Arabia. Her work was famous from Baghdad to Palermo and the ladies of this city, when she finally came back here, all wanted their fine lingerie crafted by her hand. And if Lady Vicenza doesn't want it, someone else will, sometime. Who knows, maybe one day it'll end up in your own dowry chest!

They laughed together and went outside. While busy hanging clothes, Anna looked obliquely at her mother. She hesitated for a moment, then said softly,

– Do you think Manuel is really ill?

Irene, at first dumbfounded by the question, took some time to respond.

– He's had these terrible seizures for many years now, and there is no one who's been able to find a remedy. But he seems to get along, don't you think?

– I don't just mean the fits and all that.

– What do you mean then?

– I mean, if he's sick in his mind?

– What on earth makes you think that?

– Well, for one he asked me if he could sleep in my bed last night.

– And that makes him sick?

– No mama, of course not. But you see, I didn't want to argue with him about something so I pretended I'd gone to sleep. But I was awake, and you know what?

– How could I?

– He then started to talk with the cat as if he'd been a human.

– You mean calling his name.

– No mother! He was talking about a lot of strange things with that cat and he answered it back as though he got answers from those two silent circles in the dark. It was scary, Mama!

– So what did he say?

– I can't even remember, it was like abracadabra the whole thing, but I swear to you, he was listening to our cat talking 'cause he was answering it back and waiting for it to respond.

– Hmm, I'm sure it was just a very intense dream, and that he was talking in his sleep. You know he sometimes has a very lively imagination.

– Lively? It scares me hearing him talk about things I can't see. He even believes Father really went on a flying carpet the other day. I told him there was no such thing as flying carpets, and then he got upset with me. It's so childish to believe in that.

– Well, he's a child, and you're the older one, so you will have to show some understanding. And as long as believing in flying carpets can't hurt him, I see no reason why you can't let him. Alright?

– Alright... But I still wonder what's the matter with him.

– That's it! All the clothes back up on the line. Let's hope it stays sunny until nightfall.

While the two women returned inside the light in the garden turned all deep blue and green from the sun shining through a cluster of heavy clouds. For an instant it became so still out there that one could hear a single grass straw grow. It was as though time itself had stretched out and become infinitely long within a single moment. Soldiers, guns, walls, humans, animals, even land, water and heaven grew distant and utterly silent, while that which was near and nearest appeared magnified in the extreme. Within that same curiously unlimited moment, Manuel woke up from his dreamless sleep and, inhaling the aroma from the kitchen below, began to look forward to supper.

Meanwhile Irene, although making a virtue of her faith in almighty God, was a good deal more worried about her son's health and the family's future prospects than she wanted to show. She and Iannis had previously lost two children, one boy to the plague of 1447. Two years later a girl was born but she had been blue in the skin and died within weeks. She was afraid Manuel too, though otherwise of robust constitution, would eventually succumb to the holy frenzy, as his affliction was called among monks. And she was also concerned about her husband's tendency to fuel their son's imagination instead of tempering it with sober reality. As she and Anna now kneeled down in front of the icon, she put her whole motherly heart into the prayer, asking the Virgin to forgive her all intemperance and give her strength to endure what must be endured. She also prayed for Iannis' safe return home.

Even though Anna could be annoyed with her brother Manuel at times, she loved him dearly and would conclude all of her prayers with a special request to God that her one and only brother be always protected from the hazards of life. For her own part, she had at 12 years reached an age when girls and their families begin to plan for marriage, and she hoped her future husband would be as good and kind to her as Iannis had been to their mother. And it wouldn't hurt if he's handsome too, she cautiously added unfolding her hands while making the sign of the cross.

Chapter 43

– Cards for divination of the future, are they? The Doge – receiving an impromptu visit in his sumptuous newly built palace by the Canale Grande from his consigliere Piombini and the philosopher and humanist Patricio Battista – turned the cards in his hand not quite knowing what to believe. He looked at Battista, then at Piombini, then again at Battista.

– Si Serenissimo, Battista said, that's exactly what they are. And I should know because I was in Peter Bembo's studio when he was working on them. Indeed, my presence there, which could only be explained by the confidence and close friendship we have always entertained, was surrounded by great secrecy. No one except Visconti himself was allowed to see the cards while they were still being designed – I was the exception. Bembo told me he had some very specific instructions as to what figures should be depicted on different cards, and so there are, for instance, heretical images, such as this showing a female Pope. The majority of the cards, however, correspond to regular playing cards in four suits, where the only difference is that in addition to Knight, Queen and King, there are also Pages in all four suits, so that there are actually, in all, 56 of them. Philosophers and alchemists refer to these more regular cards as the lesser arcana, or the smaller secret. Then you also have the *Trionfi*, 22 cards of supreme significance and meaning, which philosophers call the major arcana, or the greater secret. These cards represent forces beyond human control, whereas cards of the minor arcana represent forces that can be influenced by human will and circumstances. The total number of cards is 78.

– So how does it work? the Doge asked.

– Some of the symbols on these cards go all the way back to the Pharaohs of Egypt, others originated in our own pagan antiquity. But it was a Bishop Cuthberto of the monastery on the holy island of Lindisfarne – which in the ancient Gaelic language signifies "Land's Corner", and is to be found off the distant coast of Northumbria in the unforgiving Northern Seas – who first made these powerful images known to Christians. He had some of them incorporated as illustrations in the silver cased Lindisfarne Gospels, which only very few people in this world have seen, not only because they are still in the remote land of the Anglo-Saxons, but because they were first hidden and then carried to the mainland, together with the body of the dead Bishop. You see, many, many centuries ago, the barbarians whom the Greeks call Varangians, and we call the Goths, Vikings or, most recently, Normans, came over the sea and brought terrible destruction. In the annals of the monastery it says: "... and in the year 793 fierce, foreboding omens came over the land of Northumbria. There were excessive whirlwinds, lightning storms, and fiery dragons were seen flying in the sky. These signs were followed by great famine, and on January 8th the ravaging of heathen men destroyed God's church at Lindesfarne. The heathens then poured out the blood of saints around the alter, and trampled on the bodies of saints in the temple of God, like dung in the streets."

That was of course a terrible thing to happen, but in order to save the Gospels from falling into the hands of ruthless pagans, Cuthberto ordered it to be hidden under the crypt of the monastery, whence it was eventually saved by survivors. By then Bishop Cuthberto, as I said, was already dead, but when they opened the book of the Gospels they found inside it his instructions concerning the usage of single parchment copies of the images in the book, which they had also manage to save, to make predictions for the future. In this way monks, faithful to God, should be better prepared for forthcoming unexpected events, and never have to endure the same fate again. And now I will show you the order in which the cards singled out for divination must be distributed and arranged according to the venerable Cuthberto. The formation that you will see is appropriately called the Celtic, or the Irish, cross. This particular cross is not oblong like ours, but symmetrical and in most representations surrounded by a circle depicting the snake-dragon, which to the northerners of these distant times was a powerful symbol of the world itself. For the sake of simplicity, and in order to avoid confounding the circle cards with the cards making up the cross, it's customary to align these four cards vertically on the right hand side of the cross. Now, the only thing we need is a question.

– A question? Piombini said.
– Yes, a question, a query into the future.

– Any query? the Doge said.

– Basically yes, but I think it would be more worthwhile asking if Venice will ever see Milan as one of its dominions than asking if we shall get fish or poultry for dinner.

– Of course, the Doge said, his impassive pale face suddenly lit up by a grin, a streak of malice in his eyes. – Well then, let's ask, let's ask about – what will happen to Constantinople? Can these cards tell us anything about that?

– We might as well give it a try, Piombini said.

– Alright, this is what we do. You Serenissimo, concentrate on the question and try with all your might to visualise Constantinople at this very moment. Meanwhile, you Signore Piombini, shuffle the cards. When I tell you to stop you give me the cards and arrange them in three stacks. I will then cut the deck by merging the three stacks into one again.

– Are you're sure this is not to dabble with the tools of the devil?

– Of course it is! That's the whole point!

– But wasn't this Cuthberto a true man of God?

– Indeed, but the times were different then, and to these pioneer Christians of the ultimate north, the pagan gods, although officially rejected, were not considered as non-existent or completely powerless for that matter. In extreme circumstances some of them were even called upon, although they were obviously never mentioned by name, so as to not offend the Christian God, mightiest of them all. In this case I happen to know that there was a figure of the Underworld which both the Goths and the ancient druids called Mimer, who was in possession of the secrets of the future. It was Mimer and the Snake, i.e. the circle, which gnaws at the roots of the tree of life, i.e. the cross, who were invoked in the Lindisfarne tarot. Now Gentlemen, are you ready to bring Mimer and the Dragon back to life?

Although both Piombini and Foscari felt apprehensive, their curiosity had already got the better of them, and so the cards were shuffled, cut in three stacks, and united again. They were then distributed to form the pattern of the Celtic cross. The procedure began with the placing of the first card in the centre of the table. Battista explained that this card signified the question itself. And the card was the The Wheel of Fortune, the meaning of which was not difficult to discern, since it was the blindfolded figure of Justice surrounded by four jesters dressed like kings, caught in the perpetually concentric movement of the wheel. Above the one at the top of the wheel the words "I reign" were written. Under the figure below the wheel the words "I have no reign" were written ", while the two figures to the right and left hand side of the wheel were indicated as either ascending to or descending from power. – The wheel, Battista explained, is one of the *Trionfi*, thus a card of extra-mundane power. However, I don't think it needs much explanation. The question has been posed: Who will reign next in Constantinople?

The second card to be pulled from the deck and placed on top of the first, signified the immediate influence on the specific situation indicated by the question-card. It was the Two of Swords from the suit of swords. It was obvious to all that the two swords were obviously symbols of Islam and Christianity in open conflict and pitched for battle. Then Five of Pentacles – a card signifying a more distant past conducive to the present situation – appeared and was placed directly to the right of the first two cards. This one depicted some poor, destitute and mutilated human beings struggling through a blizzard outside the stained glass windows of a church. – The meaning of this, Battista said, is that the already impoverished and maimed city has seen a lot of hardships lately and that the winter, as you can see, has been catastrophic.

The fourth card, placed directly beneath the two central ones, was The Devil in person. This card signified the immediate past, in other words, the most recent events pertaining to the situation outlined in the question card.

– That's Mehmet! Piombini exclaimed triumphantly.

– Yes, that's no doubt the most immediate association. But take a closer look at the two human beings below his throne, chained together by his might. In the Tarot, you see, The Devil doesn't primarily symbolise wickedness and evil as such, but specifically the human sexes and their tenacious interdependence in the flesh. Seen in this light, I do suspect that even though the Devil, as a figure, might still be interpreted as Mehmet, the implication here is that under his sceptre we have two lovers irresistibly drawn to one another. Let's see if we can find them. Ah, what did I say? Here is the card showing the consequences of the immediate past on the future, and this, is as you can see, The Knight of Wands. It's a mature, but still younger man who has not as yet achieved the status of king, so his relation to the woman of his desire is still that of wish-thinking and courtship. The wands, being the symbol of fire, suggest he's a warrior, and my guess is that he's of either

Venetian or Genoese descent, probably Genose. It's a charismatic, creative personality, and a much needed remedy for the lamentable figures in the Five of Pentacles.

Who can the woman be then? Foscari really began to take an interest in the way things developed.

– The woman, Battista said, while posing the last card of the cross on top, is … The Queen of Swords. A woman of belligerent intent, a Salome of sorts, demanding someone's head to be presented to her on a tray. This is the lady whom our knight pursues and desires. But though sensuous, even lascivious, she has something secretive about her, and her own lust is strongly influenced by a higher idea, an idea which she will harness her knight to turn into reality for her. The Queen is also positioned in such a way that she comes to represent the goal towards which everything pertaining to the question strives. Knight and Queen are both seeking union in the sign of The Devil, which means that even though they may think that they have a choice and a free will, in reality the master of the underworld has them under his thumb.

– Now we come to the actual serpent-circle, which for the sake of convenience we arrange in a vertical row on the right hand side of the cross. The first of these cards will show us the question once again, but now in its objective form, that is, it will demonstrate what Constantinople really is and represents at this hour of its destiny, and this regardless of the subjective interest of the querent. And the card is called – The Hanged Man.

– Why is the hanged man showed as hanging upside down? Piombini wanted to know.

– The hanged man is actually the allegorical emblem of supreme sacrifice, and the closest the tarot deck comes to representing the crucifixion of our Lord. In this context it can only be interpreted as the city's present calamities and the sacrifice that it demands from all its citizens.

– Next card signifies the factor that could bring about the final outcome of the question.

– And what is that outcome? Foscari asked?

– That is exactly what remains to be seen. The very last card will give us the result, which concludes the answer to our question "What is now happening to Constantinople?" Depending on whether this answer is in the positive or the negative, the present card will be seen as either benevolent or malefic. It's the – Hierophant. The Hierophant carries the insignia of the Orthodox Patriarch, and so represents the eastern church in general. Seen here the Hierophant symbolises the belief of Orthodox Christians and their spiritual leader. As far as I know the last Patriarch to Constantinople abdicated when the union wasn't upheld, and so for the time being I don't know who's their leader. Do you? No? So, in the event, we must postulate that there is someone there, and that this person will be absolutely crucial to the outcome.

Now we come to the penultimate card, and this is a delicate one, because it tells us about the deepest fears of the inquirer. In other words, this card will show us the nature of our fear in relation to the question. And it is – The Emperor.

– The Emperor, Foscari said, why should *I* have anything to fear from the Emperor?

The Doge's tone of voice was too peremptory not to alert Battista to a sensitive spot – suddenly what had been "*the* question" had turned into Foscari's own question. Diplomatically Battista continued,

– The matter of the fact is that there are no representations of either Sultans or caliphs in the Tarot, so The Emperor could just as well symbolise Mehmet, the greatest threat to the outcome of the question.

– But you just said that the fear in regard to this card was not in regard to the object of the question, but to the person asking the question?

– That's correct, but as the querent and the question are fundamentally one and the same thing it could mean an Emperor and an Empire in one form or the other. It could represent Mehmet, but strangely, and perhaps, even more likely, The Byzantine Empire itself. If we thus assume that the greatest fear here is our presentiment of what might happen to the besieged city, quite especially in view of the tardiness in our preparations to come to its rescue, then the last card will now tell us whether or not Constantinople will for any length of time remain a Christian stronghold on the threshold between the Mediterranean and the Black Sea. And the last card is – The Tower.

It became dead silent around the table as the three men stared at the card supposedly giving the answer to their question. There wasn't really much to be explained about it. A fortress tower on fire was stormed by soldiers, and the people on the tower itself were shattered by a lightning from heaven, throwing them out of the tower and down to their deaths on ground. It was an unequivocal image of destruction, and it very probably didn't concern Castel dell'Angelo in Rome.

Battista finally took a deep breath in order to recollect and take a last look at all the threads weaving through the root of time.

– To conclude, there is a strong sensuous love between a man and a woman, which is somehow related to the spiritual leader of the people, or that people itself, possibly somehow implied in their story too. Meanwhile The Emperor and the Empire are isolated and the victim of fear. Whether it's The Devil or The Hierophant or The Emperor, or all together, who ultimately bring about The Tower, I don't know. But with The Devil in play one can always be sure that there's illusion and betrayal at work on some level of all this.

– Please note, though, that more than half of the cards drawn in this divination were *Trionfi*. When this is the case Destiny, being super charged with divine energies, allows for a bonus.

– And what's that?

– A last card, coming down like a heel across the serpent's head.

– Oh please let me do that the Doge said, and eagerly grasped for the remaining deck. Before Battista even had the time to consent, Foscari pulled the very last card granted by faith and placed it above the very image of destruction: It was another trump card: The Lovers. It showed a man and a woman united by the vows, gestures and bonds of love, though without being visibly chained to one another as in the card of The Devil.

Chapter 44

At dawn on February 2, 1453 the volcanic activity of the remote and uninhabited island of Kuwae, some 1200 miles off the coast of an Australia still unknown to Europeans, reached its peak. The pressure inside the crater had been building up for months, raising the rocky ground at a speed of several inches per hour. In the early morning a terrific explosion sent the entire island up in flames and smoke. Molten rock and lava flew like pre-historic birds through the air and crashed into the ocean shooting columns of smoke into the sky. An enormous pyroclastic cloud, raging high into the stratosphere, was carried by winds to nearby atolls and islands that were instantly incinerated – once the cloud had passed there were only stumps of blackened palm trees left; the rest of the flora and fauna was literally gone with the wind. The more finely grained particles of lava, gases and pumice then spread in all directions of the Pacific, initially creating a cloud of fire and smoke so thick that it blocked out the sun for weeks. Day and night the continuously dark ocean reflected the flames of this thick cloud. Eventually it began to thin out and allow the sun to shine through.

However, the Polynesian survivors of the tsunami which devastated hundreds of Pacific islands within hours and days of the volcanic eruption and the seismic thrusts from the seabed beneath it, soon noticed that there was something strange about the weather as well. On islands normally basking in pleasant warmth, calm seas and sunlight this time of the year, ferocious hail storms, lightning, even blizzards struck and covered palm-lined beaches in a layer of blackish snow. It didn't make the sight less eerie to notice that the same beaches were littered with thousands of cadavers, humans and animals alike. On the islands of New Zealand, at the height of summer, and as far away as on the Japanese islands, as well as in the southern Yangtze river valley in China, it snowed uninterruptedly for 40 days. The Maoris had simply never seen anything like it; temperatures plummeted and crops were instantly stunted in iron nights so cold that the water of lakes home to tropical birds froze over. And if it wasn't snowing or raining cats and dogs, there was a constant excretion from the sky of a fine dust, descending on the landscape and covering it in a greyish hue, making it seem all but dead.

In Constantinople the sound of the Pacific explosion, though many billion times more powerful than anything the Sultan could possibly throw at them, was not heard through the roar of the more nearby cannon. But just as the devastating radiation of an exploding star in our cosmic neighbourhood would have to travel aeons through empty space before impacting us, so the effects of the Pacific eruption took its time to reach the shores of the Black Sea and the Bosporus. By mid-May, however, the air above Constantinople was full of electrically charged particles and of microscopic dust from the late Kuwae. Of course nobody knew this, but there was not one Turkish soldier or Byzantine defender who didn't notice that the spring had been quite unseasonable. The sun, if at all present, seemed noticeably fainter, as if covered by a thin veil even on otherwise bright and fair days. Then there were the hail and rain storms, suddenly piercing ash-grey clouds, unleashing such torrents that it seemed God had decided to send a second deluge to earth to punish its wicked inhabitants. The spring crops – usually abundant in a walled city which had its ever shrinking population to thank for its now plentiful planted gardens and fields – were not forthcoming as expected. The early blooming almond trees kept their flowers well into late April; cherry, apricot, peach and apple, normally setting fruit in early May, had hardly sprung in bloom by the middle of the month. Spring onions were stunted and frail, carrots, salads and cabbages small, and the grass, providing food for the livestock, was levelled to the ground by grazing, lean animals competing for any haphazardly remaining patch of green.

In the city the shortage of food supplies made itself felt more and more. The rations to soldiers and citizens who already worked around the clock to plug the holes in the walls were getting smaller while their sense of danger was increasing. It was not a favourable equation and there was, as far as the Byzantines themselves were concerned, only one way to make the citizens forget temporarily about their own hardships, and that was to concentrate on that of Christ and the Holy Mother. Easter, celebrated at the end of April after the last full moon, had given such temporary relief, but then again there had at that time still been pieces of bread and lamb for all to eat and wine to drink on Holy Sunday.

In all the churches, except for the ominously empty, cold and dark Hagia Sophia, incense burned while candles threw their flickering light on glittering mosaics evoking happier, more prosperous days. Everything from stumbling whispers to outcries of despair over the recent loss of a loved one soared to the ceilings and were conducted back by echoes dripping off pillars and arches like bitter vinegar. Most of the city's long, chequered story could be deciphered frame by frame in elaborate sequences: solemn coronations, brutal executions, nose-slittings, castrations, horse races, baptisms, burials, nuptials, public holidays, sieges, harvests, courtiers, officials, priests, monks, metropolitans. And the people, in all its infinitely rich and varied plurality, century after century, recorded in painstaking detail by patient miniaturists specialising in the art of making reality come to life through the arrangements of myriads of coloured facets. There were also all the wondrous scenes from pagan antiquity: Ulysses and Jason, seamen turned into dolphins, Neptune and his horses, Dionysus, Aphrodite, satyrs and nymphs. But all silent now, as though standing on the cusp of Hades, slowly fading from the memory of this world.

Last but not least there were the Biblical scenes. From Abraham, Isaac, Jacob and Joseph to Herod, Salome, through the Holy Family and its entourage to the Apostles and Barnabas. And the Pantocrator, an elongated face and nose, long dark hair, surrounded by an aureole, the fingers raised in the sign of teaching: "Look, I'm speaking, I'm bringing you the happy message", filling every other apse with his dignified, yet melancholy presence. The whispers of slippers brushing over marble, of praying widows, sighing elders, fatherless children, officiating priests and last confessions. The crosses and the talismans, the icons and the amulets. All kissed and then kissed again, and again, until the paint itself had given way and made the annual rings of naked wood saturated with holiness. The foul stench of death blending with the over-sweet fumes of incense, interspersed with wild war cries, trumpets, tambourines and castanets, accompanied by the steady drumming of the guns. The ecstasies and comas; the mutilations, gangrenes and infections; the lack of food and elementary sanitation; the dead enemy piling up outside the walls and while almost still warm buried under earth, sand and rubble to form new mounds; the disease-ridden brothels, the religious fervour, the intrigues of commanders and clergy, the Emperor feeling his strength abandoning him, in short: the atmosphere of Constantinople had become the breeding ground for visions and revelations stranger and more ominous than even Pharaoh's dream.

In the monastery chapel, inspired by that glorious example of ultimate self-mortification set by Simeon the Stylite, Gennadi, a knotted leather whip in hand, forced himself to endure hours of prostrations before the Hodegetria, while occasionally administering a few well deserved lashes to his aching back and shoulders. No one was allowed to enter the chapel while Gennadi carried out his daily routine of spiritual purifications. And after four hours of intense torture in the name of the Holy Spirit and the Virgin, and consequently soaked in blood, Gennadi finally saw the divine light appear behind the four riders of the Apocalypse galloping towards the city gates through the night.

Amongst the echoes of rhythmical lashes he was heard moaning as the fourth and final pale rider arrived beneath the city walls. In one giant leap he steered his steed clear of the embankments and then flung himself into the city followed by a swarm of locusts with human heads devouring everything in their path. The moon itself was red and dripping with blood and around Hagia Sophia griffins circled, diving into the masses of fleeing humans to tear their flesh to shreds. Through the Golden Gate entered the Babylonian harlot, dressed only in pearls and jewels, straddling a lion with ten horns, followed by a thousand naked slaves, all chained together in one long procession. The scythe of the pale rider swung incessantly, the locusts satiated themselves with blood and raw flesh. And those who were not dispensed of in this way were crushed by gigantic hailstones or masonary falling down from all the buildings as earth quakes split the ground open, sending everyone, invaders and victims alike, down to the eternal flames of the burning Gehenna.

Then there was silence. Gennadi himself was much surprised to wake up on the ramparts and seeing beneath him, washed in star light, a group of people dressed in white garments, stretching their arms towards an intensely luminous celeste vision of a lamb surrounded by a cross and a chalice. As the lamb approached earth it took the form of our Lord and Saviour, likewise dressed in a white robe and preceded by the luminous archangel Gabriel pointing his double-edged sword to the sanctuary of the Church of the Holy Mother. Led by the sword, the survivors marched off into the church and closed the doors behind them. There, in the apse, through the very image of the Pantocrator, Jesus Christos himself descended to earth to embrace the few who had remained faithful to him and bring them to their new home in the heavenly Jerusalem, the gilded towers of which could be seen through the hole made in the heavenly dome by the lamb, the cross and the chalice containing its sacrificial blood. The angels, awaiting the faithful, formed one concentric circle after the other in the seemingly endless vault of a cloudy heaven. At the centre of luminosity there was a throne, still empty, waiting to be occupied by the Lord. Bestowed with wings the human beings now followed the ascending Christ in pious procession and slowly drifted through the air up against the sky. Never in his life had he seen anything so beautiful and mysterious.

Gennadi's return to the refectory was long overdue, and given the excruciating nature of the ordeals he had imposed on himself, it wasn't strange that the monks had begun to worry. When he didn't answer to repeated knocks on the door separating the penitentiary chapel from the aisle, they decided to open it in spite of the instructions they had received. They found him, stark naked, on the floor surrounded by a pool of blood still being added to by the open wounds on his back. Seemingly he was still alive. But even though he was unconscious, his right hand still clasped the seven-knotted whip while the left held on to the crucifix so hard that they had to force his hand to release it. And still he wouldn't wake up from his coma. They carried him out of the chapel, cleansed his wounds, applied some balm to help to heal them and wrapped him in linen. Then they put him on a bunk, chest down, to allow him some rest. Nonetheless, as he remained unconscious they began to believe he was about to die and had the mass read while anointing him. In the middle of the night, however, Gennadi came to life and the first thing he saw was a monk praying to an icon on the opposite wall. Then his nostrils registered the smell of incense and he realised, that in spite of everything he had experienced, redemption was still only on its way for the few and just. But the angel had spoken clearly and unequivocally to him. It was time to prepare everyone that had reason to believe they had kept the words and love of God in their hearts and not strayed from virtue in their actions for the imminent apocalypse. He found it hard to speak. At first he heard himself trying to form coherent words while nothing but blabber came from his lips. Given water he managed to lean onto his elbow, and then utter, in a voice so shrouded in transcendent mystery, that the monks were all struck by awe: – Go and find my faithful servant Iannis and tell him I have a task of the greatest honour for him to perform on the day of redemption. Go now. There is no time to lose. I need to speak and explain to him the will of the heavens.

Chapter 45

The Sea of Marmara had been ominously quiet and empty. Here and there a fisherman's boat, a tiny triangular sail on the horizon, even some larger traders, but nothing more promising than that. The ship and its crew, after vainly having scanned the shores of the Dardanelles, found themselves in a larger and even emptier sea. The brisk northern breeze of summer, the Meltemmia, already seemed to have the Aegean in a firm grip, darting the ship like an arrow towards its first port of call: the island of Lemnos, so far as anybody knew still in Byzantine possession. If anywhere, news of an approaching Italian flotilla was to be found here. With some luck they might even meet them on the open sea. But although they spent an entire day under clear blue skies, on a frothing sea stirred by a northern wind providing excellent visibility in all directions, there were no major vessels to be seen.

They passed the north-eastern tip of the island but could detect no signs of a fleet hidden inside its northern bay. It would, on the other hand, have been strange to find it anchored there considering the prevailing wind, and so the crew raced against sunset to reach the Cape of Skandali on the south-eastern tip of the island before dark. This they managed, but then they cast anchor as soon as they could in one of the outer parts of the wide bay, not knowing what to expect from the townspeople after dark. At dawn they began to slowly tack up the bay only to discover the main harbour gaping discouragingly empty save for a few cogs. Once they had declared who they were and what their mission was, they were warmly greeted by the inhabitants of the island all of whom were still loyal to the Emperor. It turned out that the islanders were informed about Constantinople's great distress, since news had been brought to them by local sea and fisher men gathering rumours in mainland ports. Thus they feared greatly that they would be next in line if and when the holy city fell. Unfortunately they hardly had the resources to even defend themselves, so there really was nothing they could do to help. There were also many Italians among them but all they knew was that both Papal and Venetian ships, according to reports, should be on their way. That meant little or no reassurance to the crew, and the brigantine, manned with twelve brave souls of both Greek and Venetian origin under its captain Luca Gritti, left again for the sea, desperate to find a trace of the illusive fleet.

In the days to come they combed through most of the northern Aegean from the northern Naxos as far south as the island of Chios, where there were both mercenary soldiers and plenty of ships in port, although none of them explicitly sent to come to the aid of the besieged city. Furthermore, the mayor of Chios, anxious not to compromise the professed neutrality of the Genoese in Galata, and in spite of Giustiniani's presence in Constantinople – not only was the latter born and had grown up on the island, but he belonged to one of its most prominent families – refused to mobilise any of his forces without orders from Genoa itself. This infuriated the Venetians on the reconnaissance vessel to the point that it almost resulted in them being thrown in the dungeons. Thanks to the soothing eloquence of captain Gritti this new and very unnecessary threat was just barely averted and the crew was allowed safe conduct back to its ship under the escort of suspicious minds and spiteful comments. While they hurriedly took to the seas again Captain Gritti realised that the time had come to make a crucial decision.

Seeing the malicious intent of the Genoese, realising that with such lack of consideration, even for their own kind, there was little chance any rescue operation would feel motivated to consider coming to the city's defence, one of the Venetians prevailed upon the captain to take them to safety on an island controlled by their kinsmen, for example Crete.

– If we go back to Constantinople now, Bartolo Zorzi, a bearded, dark-haired, and over time even dark-skinned, mariner from Venice, said, – we will ll only return to see Turkish banners flutter above the towers. There is no way the city could have held out unaided to this point, and even if against all odds they are still putting up resistance, knowing there are no signs whatsoever of help on the way will only demoralise them in the same way as it has demoralised us. I say, let's cut our losses and come to terms with the fact that in all probability the city can't be saved.

In secret some of the Greeks actually felt sympathetic towards Zorzi's suggestion since they imagined they could always blame the Venetians for the betrayal. But Captain Gritti, though Venetian himself, looked around among his men and said: – Is there anyone else who is of the same opinion as Bartolo? There probably was, but before anyone had the time to voice such support, Georgios, a tall, handsome Greek with curly fair hair like that of the great Alexander himself, spoke,

– You ought to be ashamed of yourselves even considering this. How can you imagine living on with such stain on your conscience, such sin in the eyes of God? Not only have you solemnly promised to bring our Emperor news of what he might or might not expect, but your own countrymen have put their faith in you. If we defect now, what would our expedition amount to other than that we used their need and peril to ignobly abandon them in the hour of destiny? No my friends, we can't do that. We shall have to return to Constantinople regardless of whether it's in Christian or Turkish possession, regardless of whether we return to life or death. Let us set sails!

Gritti couldn't take it upon himself to contest Georgios' flaming appeal, so although many felt that it was a rather sad thing to return to the lethal dangers in and around Constantinople after they had been able for two weeks to both eat and drink well, yes, even to see some willing women in the ports, they dared not object to the idea. A change in the wind direction from northern to southern may have helped to make the island of Crete seem uncomfortably distant in a geographical sense too, and so – off they went. And again, what irony of fate! By doing this they missed the possibility to actually meet up with any of the Venetian ships. Face to face with the reality of the situation, their captains could not have denied the Constantinopolitans the assistance they so desperately needed.

At daybreak on May 23 a small brigantine, visibly belonging to the Turks, was making good headway over the Marmara when it was sighted. This time the Turks were prepared, though, and hardly in the mood to sit back and watch another enemy charade. As soon as they understood that the ship didn't belong to them, they assumed it was the vanguard of an Italian armada. Instantly they mobilised en masse from below the Two Columns, the fastest fustae rowing against the wind for all they had to intercept and crush the daring intruder. But the crew held their advantage, since this time the wind didn't fade under the Gate of Santa Barbara. On the contrary it increased and the ship slipped unscathed under the protective barrier.

As soon as the ship arrived the citizens all flocked to the harbour to hear what they hoped to be good tidings. The news was then reluctantly passed on from person to person that the ship had made its voyage to and back from Lemnos in near splendid isolation. The potential for deception corresponded with the degree that expectations had been exalted. From the moment the ship had been sighted everyone believed, or wanted to believe, that help was on the way. It was heartbreaking to the brave mariners to see the last glimmer of hope vanish from the cavernous eyes of haggard and exhausted men and women, and worst of all was to witness the teary-eyed Emperor embracing them one by one, thanking them profusely for having had the courage and determination to return with the awful news, and then break into tears, helpless like a child.

What nobody knew – and would it have been of any avail to the city's defenders had they known it? – was that Venetian ships were carrying out an intricate dance of tactical and strategic manoeuvres along the coast of Crete and off Negroponte on mainland Greece. But the only result of this was a deliberate arrest of any concerted assistance to the citizens of Constantinople before sufficient intelligence had been gathered concerning the Sultan's plans and the city's actual state. All in all the Venetians behaved as though a diplomatic solution to the conflict could still be envisaged, and they were in no hurry to find out otherwise. To the men who only hours before had captured and tortured Serbian miners of the Sultan's army in order to obtain information about a tunnel armed with explosives, this passivity would have seemed an act of utter indifference – to say the least. Perhaps the sight of twenty incinerated and mutilated enemy bodies dragged out of one these freshly discovered tunnels, and finished off with axes and swords if they still showed signs of life, would have convinced Venetian commanders to finally take decisive action. But so strong was the conviction among those not directly and experientially aware of the reality of the present situation, that they couldn't, or wouldn't, imagine that a city which had managed to withstand violent attacks for a thousand years could possibly be at risk from one day to the next. Instead they just pretended to be ready to spring into action. It was all arranged in a carefully designed chain of command where one movement had to be completed, one condition fulfilled, before the next was initiated. The end effect, however, was invariably the same: delay.

And if the Venetians seemed recalcitrant, what about Pope Nicholas who had as yet not even received the galleys he had commissioned from Venice? "Oh, they always want money and goods for nothing," he had been heard muttering when Gregory Mammas, the former Metropolitan to Constantinople, prudently asked why no further military help seemed to be forthcoming from the papacy. – The Byzantines want money for nothing? Gregory asked, somewhat surprised. – No, no, no, of course not, Nicholas answered impatiently, – The Venetians, the Venetians!

Chapter 46

It was an age-old belief among the citizens that whatever fate befell Constantinople, she could never be overtaken by an alien force on a waxing moon. Part of that legend was perhaps due to the fact that the Islamic arch-enemy, ever since his first appearance beneath the city walls, had carried the new born moon as the chief emblem in his banner. Perhaps it was intuitively felt that the young moon belonged as much to an uncertain future as the full moon was part of tradition, maturity and wisdom. By all means, the moon had wandered silently through seasons and centuries, casting its changing lights onto the copper of domes and palaces, the Bosporus, the Horn, the Marmara and its islands. It was as much a symbol of the city as the many holy relics inside its monasteries and churches, and it spoke to the people in a myriad of secret ways. To many the mystery of holy motherhood was more convincingly conveyed in the whispering silence of the moonlit night than in the glaring light of day. Although the one could not exist without the other, there was something in the Byzantine faith itself that prompted a disinclination to respond to any light not broken down in countless refractions and reflections. The mosaics themselves were such vehicles of refracted light, the furtive reality of facets, of intricate meanders and convoluted interpretations. The churches too were full of nooks and crannies where the only light ever seen was that of wax candles, the shadows of which outlined ghosts and demons on the walls. It was in the magical ambiance of a lavishly decorated grotto, full of wizardry and divine grace, that the Byzantine faith unfolded itself and found its true expression. And the icon was not only holy because of its professed relation to the holy family, but for reasons wholly unseen. The most vivid part of it was not the one shown, but the part hidden in that which was shown. An interplay between the visible and the invisible worlds, like waves of time breaking over reefs and shorelines, cradling anchored ships, licking the very foundation of Constantine's city. And yes, a thousand years later it was still a Constantine's city. How different though its spiritual atmosphere; how much older, more melancholy and, precisely therefore, deeper its hope.

The age of Constantine the Great lived in people's memories as an unimaginably distant past. Many institutions and practices from these almost pagan days still survived into the present time but few people knew their original function and meaning. If asked about them, they would shake their heads and say: "Oh, it's tradition, that's the way it has always been and the way it's supposed to be." One such holy tradition, dating back to a time of zealotry so intense that the very existence of the Christian religion then pivoted around the question whether or not it was permissible to even try to create an image of the invisible, was the official parading of the Hodegetria. It was a symbol so old and venerable that it had become identical with the city itself. When the Hodegetria was brought out in procession for public display, she *was* the city.

On May 23, the valiant and untiring efforts of the Scottish master engineer John Grant and his able miners had finally managed to successfully flood and smoke the enemy out of every single mine shaft running criss-cross like so many mole tunnels to and from the city walls and the Turkish encampments. The props had been removed and the shafts collapsed, conveniently killing and burying entire enemy detachments all at once. It would have been a most heartening victory had it not been brutally shattered by the arrival of yet another group of heroes, forced to impart the news that not only the Marmara, but the Aegean sea as well lie waste and empty like a desert.

As though he wanted to voice his fury over having been stalled in his subterranean activities, Mehmet intensified his artillery fire during the whole following day. By dusk the cannonade stopped and a silence, as intense as it was unexpected, intervened. When the clouds of smoke dissipated, the sky revealed itself a sparkling blue. It was a night of spring so clear as anyone had ever seen, the fragrance of garden roses and the song of the nightingale suddenly filling the air with harmonious resonances. The scene was set for her Majesty the Moon. But one hour after sunset she didn't appear as expected. Instead only a thin sliver of the moon could be seen rising over the hills of Anatolia, while the rest of her was covered in rusty red. It was a blood-chilling experience because it was like seeing the scimitar of Islam rise triumphantly in the east. The Turkish camp was a boiling cauldron of expectation. All the soothsayers and astrologers were unanimous in their interpretation that the extraordinary celestial phenomenon heralded a victory soon to come, quite especially because the moon was in conjunction with a bright star, easily identifiable to astrologers as the planet Jupiter, ancient ruler of the gods.

Inversely, Byzantine spirits turned sombre and inert like lead at the ominous sight which lasted four hours. Discouraged they followed the moon sickle as it rose in the heavens preceded by a dark red halo, and although she then slowly re-assumed her normal shape, each and everyone knew that the waxing moon, supposed to culminate in a glorious full moon, token of the might and invincibility of the city, had failed to materialise in the very moment she was crucially needed. The following night would be in the sign of a waning moon, a time of the lunar cycle considered potentially sinister, particularly in matters military. With nature too set against them it was little wonder that the citizens turned to prayers in the hope that somehow, in spite of it all, God would ultimately show mercy and deliver them from death and destruction through some miracle. Constantine himself, deeply troubled by the lunar eclipse, took the decision to have the Hodegetria brought forth from the church of the Saviour in Chora, where she had been moved from her monastery, and paraded through the streets in a solemn procession.

Chapter 47

Gennadi was most definitely against it but could not refuse an order issued by the Emperor. He tried to prevent its execution for as long as possible though. Finally he admitted the reason for his reluctance to some monks whose discretion he trusted. But when they entered in the presence of the icon, neither the monks nor Gennadi himself could detect any traces of blood on it, and it was believed that it might be safe to bring her outside. The icon was quite heavy and placed on a wooden pallet carried on the shoulders of four trusted men, who would move and change directions in unison although no specific itinerary had been prescribed. The reason why such guidance was considered unnecessary, was that the icon itself possessed a mysterious power to direct the steps of her worshippers.

A large crowd had met up in the early morning around the church. After customary prayers and sprinkling of holy water the doors to the church swung open and the Hodegetria herself appeared in all her divine majesty. The procession set off and "She who shows the way" led them in the direction of Blachernai. As more and more people flocked around the holy portable shrine – chanting, praying, begging – the unthinkable suddenly happened. One of the icon bearers stumbled over a stone and dragged the others with him so that they could no longer hold on to her. Shell fell to the street and became so deeply embedded there that she was almost completely covered in mud. If this was the reason why she now also became heavy as lead it is not easy to say, but the fact of the matter was that many men, struggling to raise her from the ground, had to battle arduously just to get her back up onto the shoulders of the bearers. And even after she had been cleansed with water and wiped dry with pieces of cloth, the bearers unanimously, and ominously, confessed they now felt like *Christoferos* himself.

Christopher was a legendary ferryman helping people to cross a difficult river. In the summer time, however, the river ran so low that he couldn't launch his boat and so, strong and shoulder-broad as he was, he used to take people on his back across it. One day a young child approached him and asked to be carried to the other side. That would be no problem Christopher said, seeing how little the child weighed in comparison to most of his passengers. But there was something very strange about this particular child, because when they entered the deepest and most torrential part of the river, Christopher felt the child on his back get heavier. Christopher didn't want to admit to himself that he could only continue with utmost difficulty, but as the water began to stream more vehemently around him he felt the weight on his back increase unbearably. In his distress, Christopher cried out: – Who are you little child and why are you constantly growing so heavy that I, grown and strong, can now hardly endure your immense weight? Whereupon the child replied: "Christopher, I am your Lord and Saviour, and the burden you carry is not that of me, but of all human sins that I have taken upon myself. Go in peace, Christopher, and preach my word to everyone you meet, because I have chosen you to share with me the burden of all mankind. In that same instant the child was gone from Christopher's back, but the relief he felt was not only of a physical nature. Tears filled Christopher's eyes and as soon as he reached the other side of the river, he fell down and praised the Lord for having let him meet with Jesus Christ and for a moment share his burden. Only now did Feros, as he had been called up till then, become Christoferos, because that name means the Christ-carrier, and he spent the remainder of his days on earth preaching the Christian message of remittance of sin through love and compassion with all beings' suffering.

In truth the comparison with Saint Christopher was more than just a passing metaphor in the minds of these men, struggling with an icon of Mary holding the Holy Child who now seemed as if cast in solid bronze. And if that were not simile enough, a thunderous roar was heard, this time not from enemy artillery, but from the sky itself. A horrifying darkness descended on them, interspersed with a continuous series of lightning flashes. Then the sky split open, as if torn to shreds by the wrath of God himself, sending bullets of hail, some as big as fists, over them. Last but not least came the rain, pouring down, not in drops but in cascades so violent that small children walking in the procession were carried away in the gutter and were saved only by adults rushing through the streams to prevent them from being washed off the face of the earth. Several cats and dogs did indeed disappear for good, and the Hodegetria had to be hastily brought inside the nearest still roofed building before something still worse happened to her.

In this dense atmosphere of rain, confusion and despair, it was only all too evident that someone had to be blamed for the disastrous outcome of the procession. In the midst of the torrential downpour a voice – nobody ever learned to whom it belonged – suddenly cried out: "It's the Turkish woman. She's a sorceress and she's been sent by Mehmet to destroy us all!." No sooner had these words been uttered than the whole crowd went ablaze. Although there were one or two individuals who knew this allegation to be apparently quite absurd, their arguments in favour of restraint were powerless against the overwhelming sense of panic and the hysterical need for a scapegoat it engendered.

– Yes, yes, that's right, she's got both our Emperor and Giustiniani under hell spell! yelled the uncouth tongue of one of the city's ambulating and self-appointed quacks. Then there was a third and a fourth, beggars and other members of the rabble, who joined in screaming: – As long as she's here we won't stand a chance. What can we do? – We can burn her! came the answer, and with that their entire argumentation came to an end.

Iannis was among the few who instinctively and actively opposed the idea of the mob taking justice into its own hands. In vain he had invoked the harsh punishments reserved for any willful attempts to pervert the course of justice. He voiced his objection accordingly: there was no proof that the female Turkish prisoner was in any way implicated in Mehmet's efforts to conquer the city. On the contrary, it seemed she had provided the military command with much useful information. But Iannis' brave attempt at reason was cut short by the idiot who had proposed her guilt in the first place. Though it was quite obvious it had to be a lie, this man, a bald and shaggy character known as Barnabas by the local rabble, following the procession in order to jealously fight over the doles traditionally dispensed on the occasion, again raised his coarse voice, yelling,

– And who do you think she spends her nights with? The Italian, of the same corrupted blood as the dogs in Galata! He's in on it too! Are you blind or what? It's just obvious. Together they've been double-crossing our Emperor all along and made him believe they're all for him and for us. But they only really care about one thing, and that's to save their own fine arses. So they concluded a pact with Satan himself. Against safe conduct from the city after its fall. It was *his* idea, but *she* did it for him.

– What, what, what idea?

– To signal over to Galata the other night to tell them traitors' guards that we were on our way over to the Turks to kick their backsides.

– What? Did you see that?

– You bet I did. I was close by, up on the street leading there from the Forum, when from the the roof of the villa Agusta in which they house her, a light signal became visible. I saw it clearly with me own eyes, a beacon, a torch lighting up in the midst of curfew, intended of course to look as if paraded there by chance. But I knew better, of course. I've seen that Giustiniani come out of that villa more than once with his pants half-way down his legs. He's doin' her good alright! And when they finally had enough for the moment of each other in sin, he decided she must go on the roof to give the signal which was then relayed to the Turks. Treason is what it is, and if we don't get her now, we'll never get the chance again. She's none of us, but a Turkish harlot and a bride of Satan fornicating with the Genoese in the hope of carving out for herself a pretty little kingdom in the lands of the Franks. The Emperor himself will be grateful to us when he gets to know the truth. Now, let's go and get Mehmet's special whore!

What originally had only been a single person, taking his chance to randomly pinpoint a target for the pent up frustration of the crowd, thus became the starting point for a peregrination considerably less holy in its intent than the one that preceded it. It suddenly seemed very easy to accept that witchcraft must be at the root of the attack on the Hodegetria, as well as at the dismal defeat of the sailors the other night, which everyone knew for sure to have been caused by ruthless traitors in Galata. But from whom did they ever get the information, But of course! From the Turkish woman! In addition, the catastrophe of the fallen Hodegetria was such that citizens, who under normal circumstances would have been appalled at the mere idea, now joined in as though possessed by one and the same demon. Yes, so compelling was this call, that people who had already found shelter from the rain felt prompted to brave the inundation of the streets and join the motley crew. It only seemed to further their collective irresponsibility that the mud stuck not only to their clothes, but that their limbs and heads were completely camouflaged as well.

Spurred on by one another and unrestrained by the soldiers, all deployed along the walls, the mob stumbled down the Mese to the Forum of Constantine, where their number was increased by the market traders who had also had a bad day, much of their merchandise having been ruined by the rain. From there they found their way to the antique hippodrome. The assembly, comprising well over two hundred people armed with rakes, pitch-forks and pointed sticks, eventually arrived at the villa Augusta in which Felicia was kept under surveillance. The two soldiers guarding the entrance put up a token resistance but found themselves grossly overwhelmed. They quickly gave in to avoid getting themselves killed. And now, unleashed like a pack of rabid dogs, the crowd stormed through the old, artfully decorated loggia. From there it continued into the rooms of the princess and tore her out in the street like a rag doll. Since a formal *auto-da-fe* seemed impractical under the circumstances, a gable wall offered a jutting beam from which a noose could be suspended. Felicia, who with mounting apprehension had heard the mobsters approach, tried in vain to declare her innocence. She was dragged further out in the muddy street and soaked there until someone had the brilliant idea to slit her nose before execution and approached her with a scythe in hand. She wrestled for her life, but the only result of that was that she tore her own clothes, and in her half-naked state further confirmed the opinion of the mob that she must be a witch, because only witches could be that sinfully beautiful. It was all becoming clear: She, the infidel who had had the temerity to receive the Catholic baptism in the city eternally vowed to the one and only true faith, had led Protostrator Giustiniani and Emperor Constantine astray to the point that they were now voluntarily handing over the city to the devil. This must never happen. A choir of diabolical voices, united by the anonymity of its individual members, resounded around the helpless woman. And the text to their ghastly song was neither hard to discern, nor difficult to repeat, since it ran as follows: Hang her! Hang her! Hang her!

The mob moving in, she felt leathery, lizard-like, skinny hands and ugly nails pinch and hurt her everywhere, while the foul smell of a hundred bellowing jaws descended upon her like the corrupted breath of Satan in person.

Meanwhile, Iannis, appalled by the atrocious turn the religious procession had taken, made up his mind on the spot that he must do what he could to prevent the Turkish princess from being lynched by mobsters. But since he held no sway over the crowd, the only remaining possibility was to run as quickly as possible to the walls and alert commander Giustiniani to the lethal threat to his fiance. Iannis didn't know why he felt sympathy for both her and the Italian, but like the rest of the city's inhabitants he was well aware of the intimate attraction between them. Soon after the event itself had taken place it became public knowledge that Felicia had undergone Catholic baptism in the presence of the Italian commander. Some of the palace people close to the scene must have been responsible for circulating the rumours in the first place. Once pronounced, however, this piece of precious gossip was on everybody's tongue. And not always with approbation. On the contrary. Some pious Orthodox people were outraged at what they felt to be a disgraceful provocation thrown in their faces, and they accused even their Emperor of being a dupe and a victim of foul play – little did they know that Constantine had been, if not the instigator, by all means the chief counselor to this surprising arrangement – and so they partly blamed Giustiniani, whose attention to the city's defence was obviously not as undivided as it ought to be, but most of all her, because she was both a foreign intruder and a strikingly beautiful woman. Thus it didn't take long before the insidious emotion had taken root among envious souls that she really was a witch and a spy, capable of turning men's head in any direction it pleased her. So when Barnabas finally seized the opportunity to vociferously blame the fatal downfall of the most holy Hodegetria on Felicia, it was like blowing Greek fire into a dry haystack. The reason of the populace went out in a whiff. All that remained was blind and unchecked fear, frustration and hatred attempting to seek satisfaction.

Although Iannis was himself a pious man he lacked that particular strain of moral fanaticism so characteristic of many other devout believers. Even more importantly, he respected Giustininiani and admired his heroism almost as much as did his own son, Manuel, presently recuperating at home from his epileptic seizure. He also instinctively knew that if anything were to happen to Felicia, Giustiniani would indeed give everything up and escape the city as soon as he could. To Iannis the thing was clear. Felicia must be kept alive, because she was *his* inspiration just as much as the Hodegetria was *theirs*. And the downfall of the one was not attributable to the malice of the other. This much, Iannis felt, was beyond a shadow of a doubt. And so he ran for all he was worth along the Mese back up towards the majestic land wall. He was lucky to catch Giovanni as he was about to climb the stairs.

– Commander, You must listen! he panted out of breath while approaching the long staircase.

– What is it that you want? Giustiniani said, turning round, visibly annoyed by Iannis' peremptory tone of voice.

– It's your wife.

– Wife? I don't have any wife, Giustiniani retorted curtly and with a wry smile destined to impress his military entourage.

– Well Sir, the Turkish Princess, if you will Sir.

– She's by no means my wife, but what about her?

– Oh please listen, there is not a second to lose, they're about to kill her?

– Kill her? Who?

– A terrible mob, Sir, it's on its way to her quarters as we're speaking. If nothing is done I'm afraid she'll be ….

He was about to say "murdered" but Giustiniani, during the split second it took Iannis to impart the fateful news, had taken a single tiger leap down the stairs and flung himself onto the back of his horse in full career as he finished his sentence, after which Iannis collapsed to the ground, exhausted from the sprint he had made to bring the horror in the making to the commander's attention.

A hail of emotions ran like flames of lightning through his brain while he spurred his steed down the Mese towards Felicia's house. All he could think of was that it mustn't be too late, hoping they hadn't dragged her too far away from her prison. The streets were in terrible condition after the torrential rains. Horse and rider sometimes struggled so deep in mud that they were both almost buried in it. But somehow Giovanni managed to again and again put the horse on stable footing and almost miraculously pull them out of every pitfall.

Had it been only seconds later, Felicia would have been dead, ignominiously strangled. But the outer rims of the mob seemed to become aware of the sound of the furious warrior from afar and hesitatingly to cast glances in the direction of the Forum. In the centre of the action, Felicia had had her hands tied up with a rope, a noose cast over her shoulders. The only thing now separating her from death was the clumsy attempts of her executioners to throw the other end of the rope over the beam jutting out from the facade of the villa. It wasn't until someone managed to get hold of a ladder and raise it against the wall that the ringleader Barnabas was finally able to secure the rope around the beam and blood-thirstily cry out that they could now start to haul "the bitch" up into the air. This is also what the men on ground would undoubtedly have done, judging from the fiendish acclamation by which Barnabas' latest success was greeted, had not the commanders' horse in the same very moment began to make his way through the crowd. The people next to the victim were still unaffected by his approach, and the rope in their midst was steadily tightened to the point where it only needed another vigorous pull to leave Felicia irrevocably dangling between heaven and earth. Moments later, the outer circles of the mob, terrified by the stentorian voice thundering from horseback, as well as from the incessant and deadly blows from its sword of vengeance, started to recede in panic, eventually leaving Giovanni with a frantic free run up to the ladder and the still unsuspecting Barnabas at the very top of it. The blow he struck through to his astonished forehead was so violent that it cut the man literally in half all the way down to his belly, squirting a tapestry of bones, brain substance, blood and entrails over the entire right flank of horse and rider, after which the hideously mutilated body slowly fell from the highest rung of the ladder down into the mud, where it remained, utterly unrecognisable and instantly abandoned by the crowd, now quickly taking refuge wherever they could as they realised with whom they now had to deal.

Felicia hung lifeless in the noose, but she wasn't dead. The rope had never been pulled to the full, because the final clearance had never come from Barnabas. As soon as he was dead, the henchmen on the ground disappeared faster than weasels, leaving the whole scene empty save for the valiant knight bowing down over the pale face of his beloved lady. It wasn't until she was well inside the house that her deep, dark eyes reappeared under flickering eyelids. With her face lit up by the faintest of smiles, she added meekly,

– Ah, here at last. I was just beginning to think I would never see you again.

Chapter 48

– I can't thank you enough for in the end saving my life instead of trying to take it, she said with a beautiful ironic smile and gave the commander another kiss that made him feel all warm inside. Distancing her still moist lips slightly from his, she continued in a half whisper, – But to be perfectly honest, these disgusting people are actually right about one thing. I am guilty of the crime they accused me of. Although I have nothing to do with Mehmet and his consort, I do want you out of here alive. If that means bailing out while there's still time to do so, well so be it. Because if it weren't for all that talk about honour and duty, you would actually have come to your senses by now, realising that your loyalty should be with your family and not with a lost cause. The future needs you more than heaven does; you'll be of no use to anyone up there. So you better make sure you survive after you helped me to do the same!

– Felicia, my love, I understand you're both worried and upset about what happens now in this place, Giovanni responded in a voice which attempted to be both calm and reassuring, – but please try to understand also, that even though dying at this moment is the very last thing I would consider a viable option, the men on whom I rely for our survival, and who in turn trust me with their lives, actually are my family. Not in the sense that my next of kin don't matter any longer, but insofar that right now the Giustinianis can help me just as little as I can help them. My very real sentiment is that every time we lose one of our men, I lose a brother I never even knew I had. But in death he reveals himself as such. And it's ultimately my brother who will stand or fall by my side in victory or defeat. What one man can never accomplish alone, we can accomplish together precisely because we stick together. If the men under my command can no longer feel that I'm risking my life for them, as they are risking their lives for me, the sense of mutual trust breaks down and the entire chain of command collapses. You seem to think that for me it's some matter of chivalry, but that's very far from the truth. It's a matter of complete interdependence: we have no choice but to trust each other until death do us part.

– Well, maybe you should marry all those men instead of me then! Because I too am willing to stand by your side until 'death do us part', but I simply can't see the point in witnessing your being taken away from me like a bull destined for slaughter when I want to live by your side, give birth to your sons and daughters and, with God's mercy, see them grow up in happiness and prosperity. If you die in this battle I shall never see this happen, and there is not one thought more unbearable to me than that of not being allowed to carry and deliver your children to this world. But just as much as I love and adore you, I want you to know that if that line you were talking about ever breaks, I'm going to make sure that I'm out of here and … Oh, Giovanni, for God's sake please understand. If the Turks storm the city they aren't just going to rape me a hundred times and then do what the mob already did. I'd be very lucky if that's the case. When Mehmet gets to know that they found me, he will subject me to the slowest most gruesome torture his vicious mind could ever imagine. If I can't escape the city I shall consequently have no alternative but to kill myself. That's all.

She gave Giovanni a long silent look full of tenderness and added,

– Who knows if I will ever get the chance to say goodbye to you for real. I might just seize the opportunity and do it now.

It was as though she was reading his mind. Ever since they met for the very first time he had been haunted by the image of her falling victim to the people and the ruler she had betrayed. He didn't want to think about it, but every time he had been fighting on the walls, and the enemy appeared dangerously close, that image presented itself in uncannily clear outline. He literally saw them beat her to a pulp and drag her before the Sultan, who would immediately realise she had tried to mount a rebellion against his authority, and punish her accordingly… "It mustn't happen", he thought. "I simply can't die…"

They fell in each others arms, both knowing that the deep and tender kiss they now exchanged acted as a living token of their love. Just as much as they felt the burning desire to unite and become one, they also feared that once nature had been allowed to take its course both of them would have to walk out of that room to face separate destinies. To Felicia the idea of losing Giovanni seemed absolutely exasperating, and Giovanni himself, though harnessed against bullets and swords and hardened beyond his years by the grim reality of warfare, had next to nothing to protect himself from the more subtle but no less deadly arrows of Cupid, capable of bringing the greatest of heroes down to his knees. And this was exactly what happened. Giovanni fell down on his knees:

– Please forgive me if this seems vaguely inappropriate at this critical hour, but I really wanted to ask you, before it might be too late I mean... in itself, a simple question. May I? She looked away, secretly, or not so secretly, crying for joy and in trembling anticipation. While remaining in that position she nodded, and Giovanni finally found it in his heart to pronounce the very words she would sacrifice her life to hear from him, – Felicia, will you marry me?

In this moment Felicia felt a wave of heat surge through her body, irresistibly drawing it even closer to his. Her lips then trembled in his ear: – For the longest time I believed that true love would never happen to me. I had got used to seeing myself as a cold, impermeable shell, the secret of which would never be revealed to anyone but God himself. And I had decided to just use you to achieve my objective. Now I understand that so many of the things we think we do by our own will are in reality preordained, and that the breaking of my crust was a miracle that God had reserved for me because I admitted his light to my being. He sent you, Giovanni, to break my resistance, even to beat me, in order to show me that vengeance and hatred, strong and mighty as these forces are, will only bring the thorns of love, but not its sweet fragrance and taste. But I want it all, and I have decided not to die with any love unexpressed in my heart. Therefore, Giovanni Giustiniani Longo, my unconditional answer is: Yes, I will.

Chapter 49

Bishop Leonard and Cardinal Isidore had been more than busy making sure the sections of the walls they had been entrusted with were not going to prove the weakest links in the chain. Meanwhile their suspicions of a conspiracy against the Emperor, led by the brilliant but mentally unstable leader of the anti-unionists, George The Scholar, also known under his monastic name Gennadi, hadn't exactly been disproved by more recent developments. On the contrary. Not being able to check for themselves who went in and out of the monastery in which Gennadi had revealed the details and circumstances of his alleged meeting with the Sultan to them, Leonard and Isidore had paid a Greek boy to constantly survey the cloister and report to them the nature of all movements. The boy, receiving payment for every piece of information he could provide, told them that the only conspicuous anomaly in the monastery routines was the frequent coming and going of a certain fisherman from Petrion.

– Do you know his name? Leonard asked.

– Yes, I believe so, but my memory is getting weak from lack of stimulation, the boy boldly added, correctly estimating that the two ecclesiastics would be prepared to chip in an extra coin for this piece of information.

– His name is Iannis Papanikolaou, and he lives together with his wife and two children in the house of his brother in law close to the Gate of Petrion.

The two churchmen exchanged meaningful glances and decided to pay an unannounced visit to Iannis. Fate forestalled them though, because it so happened that on the ominous day when the Hodegetria fell from her pedestal, Iannis was in the procession. The boy was also there and pointed him out to Leonard and Isidore, who caught up with him under a vault where he had taken refuge from the heavy rain just menacing to turn into hail again.

– We know you have a boat and we know you keep it in the Contoscalion harbour! Leonard shouted in a attempt to outdo the sound and fury of the elements while catching his breath. – What we would like to know is if you have ever transported him to and from Galata?

Iannis, seeing that he had been trapped between the Catholic church inside the vault and divine vengeance outside it, decided to cooperate and responded,

– I suppose him is meant to be Father Gennadi? And yes, since you're so keen on getting to know everything I know, I'll tell you all because that won't take me long. I rowed him there once during one night and rowed him back on the next.

– Did you know where he was going?

– Oh, no, he wouldn't tell me about that. They even kept me locked up.

– Who kept you locked up?

– The wretched Genoese, who else?

– Did you know he met with the Sultan?

– No idea, but it wouldn't surprise me.

– Why is that?

– Because he knows that Antichrist is about to take over here and he might have wanted to have a chat with him before he's installed on

his throne (Iannis was very careful to avoid letting them know that the prophecy also said that in the end Christ would not allow it and that on the day of his second coming an angel would prevent Mehmet and his men from entering Hagia Sophia).
– And so he might have gone to see him?
– Absolutely. He ain't afraid of anything. And I might as well tell you, venerable Montsignori of the Frankonian church, that you better start planning for how to get out of here too, since you can see for yourselves that all hell has already broken loose.

In the same instant a terrifying bolt of lightning struck nearby; they could even hear the air crackling before the bang hit them and almost threw them to the ground. Involuntarily they all crouched.
– So where is your Gennadi at present? Isidore shouted through the roar of the elements.
– I have no idea. He most surely would have participated in the procession since he and his monks are the keepers of the Hodegetria. But I ain't seen him nowhere. And you take it from me, her falling into the mud like that was no chance event; it was a sign, it was, and a bad one too! Now Montsignori, you must excuse me, but I really got to go.

There was another cracking sound announcing thunder. Isidore and Leonard both covered their ears and involuntarily closed their eyes while waiting for the bang. Once again it well nigh knocked them over, but as they opened their eyes Iannis had merged with the crowd, now crazed to madness by all the evil portents, and again stirred to action, this time by the trouble-maker Barnabas who incited the gathered mass to go and seek satisfaction for all its humiliation by killing the Turkish princess. Because of their distance from the scene, and because of the constant thunder and roar around them, neither Isidore or Leonard could witness Iannis's attempts to dissuade the mobsters from following up on their destructive instinct. And when they finally dared to leave their hiding place behind, the people were already well under way down the Mese while Iannis was running in the opposite direction for all he was worth. The two officers and clergy men therefore decided they ought to return to their posts, and could only regret their failure to obtain the information they had so eagerly sought for.

Chapter 50

The hail storms, the torrents of rain and the ominous portents didn't only contribute to bring the morale down among the defenders. Even the roof of the Sultan's tent sported a couple of holes pierced by icy projectiles, and there had been severe injuries, even casualties, throughout the Turkish encampment among soldiers who were not fast enough to take cover, or had been foolhardy enough to believe that their helmets and unplated chests could successfully withstand the impact of hail the size of small cannon balls. All army quarters were cold and damp and the soldiers themselves wet to the marrow. As soon as the wretched weather had passed – and it could not be ruled out that, in spite of the good omen which the moon sickle covered in blood had brought, the subsequent deluge had been administered by an Allah in a far less benevolent mood – Mehmet ordered all camp fires to be lit again. However, the rain had dug deep furrows and canals in the terrain, undermining everything and soaking unprotected wood supplies, some of which had simply drifted off into the Lycus valley. Barrels of gun powder, though more securely stored, were not wholly impervious to air saturated with moisture, and at least for the time being most of the guns were inoperative. Clouds of smoke announced the resistance of the logs to catch fire, and as hours went by spent in vain attempts to get the army dried up and on its feet again, discontent was stirring.

Realising the potential danger of a situation in which the blame for the fruitless siege could easily be shifted from the impersonal force of nature to the ineptitude of the army's high commander, Mehmet decided to summon his generals and ministers to a meeting. He had good reason to believe that the Janissaries still remained committed and loyal to him. This was very fortunate, since tradition and experience strongly suggested that if a Sultan ever got the Janissaries against him in conflict, the most likely outcome would rather be a new Sultan on the throne than two thousand new Janissaries. On his last round of inspection though, groups of unidentified soldiers had been heard shouting disparagingly at their ruler in the thick mist. There were signs of disobedience and rebellion in the making, especially after the rumour circulated that the Greek brigantine able to slip past the Turks and into the Horn had been the forerunner of a huge armada presently crossing the Sea of Marmara. Reliable sources also reported that the Hungarian king John Hunyadi was on the march with a vast army that could be expected to arrive any day. To this was to be added the rapidly increasing toll of deaths, and the piles the corpses that had to be thrown in while their still living comrades dug out mass graves on the muddy plain.

At the beginning of the siege, those of the dead whose religion, or lack of it, permitted cremation had been placed on funeral pyres and properly consumed. Not only was wood scarcer now, but it was so wet it wouldn't burn by itself, let alone burn when weighed down by hundreds of bodies soaked in blood and mud. And with the dead waiting to be buried came the risk of infectious disease. Another sudden change of weather could bring the heat of summer upon them, and corpses rotting in the sun had never been known to foster health and optimism in any army camp. For nearly two months Turkish guns had been pummeling at the walls, but these had always been repaired, and every infantry attack on them had resulted in dreadful casualties. In truth, the besiegers too were profoundly demoralised and exhausted. In order to forestall riots among the rank and file of his army units, Mehmet let it be known he had sent a proposal to the Byzantine Emperor to the effect that the latter would be free to leave with his people on condition that he surrendered the city and everything in it against possessions elsewhere and an annual appanage. The only alternative was that the city committed itself to pay a yearly tribute of 100, 000 bezants, an amount Mehmet knew would clearly exceed the depleted reserves of the imperial treasury.

But Mehmet was not the only one to see the inconvenience of the solution he himself had devised. A peaceful surrender would more than likely oblige Mehmet to forbid his soldiers to loot and plunder, whereas under the laws of *Jihad* this would be an expected reward for his marauding army. The soldiers themselves, eager to revenge the deaths of all their comrades, would probably prefer to hear that a final attack was imminent, than receiving the news that the city had simply given in to the Sultan's demands. Both sides had witnessed public executions of their own at the hands of the enemy. To be forced to show pardon now would be an insult. But this also meant that a failed general attack could back-fire so seriously that Mehmet would have to retreat ahead of his troops to avoid being deposed and killed by them. It was at this critical juncture, in the spirit of irreversible war, that Mehmet received the commanders of the army and his advisors.

Upon entering his tent they were much surprised to find it empty save for a large quadratic rug on which a red apple had been placed. Suddenly Mehmet appeared out of the dark and everybody fell to their knees to pay him customary respect and honour. As the sign was given for them to rise, Mehmet wasted no further time on ceremonies. Instead he asked them,

– Is there any of you generals and ministers who can suggest of a way of picking up this apple without stepping on the rug?

The pashas and the advisers looked at one another in bewilderment, each one of them wondering if he was the only one not initiated into this practical joke.

– I know you all believe I'm trying to trick you, but I will show you that it can really be done if you're prepared to go against all conventional wisdom and think, so to speak, outside of the rug. Any idea, anybody?

One would have heard a pin drop. The military assembly stood gaping in disbelief as Mehmet, mischievous like a child and shrewd like an old Jew, slowly began to roll up the rug until he reached the middle. When close enough he just stretched out his arm and picked up the apple, where after he rolled the rug back into place, took a bite from the apple and sat down, bidding his advisers to do the same.

– Now we all know what that apple signifies. And some weeks ago I might have asked you the question: is it possible to enter the Golden Horn with numerous ships without ever breaking the chain protecting it from intrusion? It was proved that it could be done, and I would like to believe that if we only put our minds to it we can also design a solution enabling us to reach the apple without having to step on the rug. However, I have not called you all here to prove my genius, but to ask from each and every one of you your honest opinion as to whether this siege should be discontinued or prolonged. I will take all your advice into consideration, and you need not fear to disagree with my secret wishes.

The last remark was obviously intended to make Halil Pasha, the first vizier to the late Murad, feel comfortable enough to step forward and deliver his expected speech in defence of a swift withdrawal on favourable terms.

Halil was an old-timer fostered in an atmosphere of pious devotion to Allah. But he had also been one of the architects of the late Murad's policies, advocating friendly tolerance of Christian subjects within Ottoman territory as well as the entertainment of cordial relations with Constantinople. He had opposed the siege from the very beginning and was not expected to suddenly have changed his mind.

– Gentlemen, in my days I have witnessed and participated in enough battles to know that the outcome of war is uncertain, and that instead of leading to increased prosperity it often has the reverse effect, antagonising subjugated peoples and creating a desire for revenge. When dealing with city populations diplomacy is always an option to consider. Constantinople may seem at her breaking-point but her allies are rapidly approaching. If the Venetians arrive our reduced fleet in Diplokion may come under fatal attack. Even if we go out to meet them they might be joined by the ships behind the boom, and I'm sure I don't have to call to mind the painful experience we had in connection with our first naval engagement with the enemy, and that against only four of their ships! What do you suggest we do if they bear down on us with ten, fifteen, even twenty large heavily-armed vessels? And what about if Hunyadi simultaneously were to appear on the horizon? And what about if the naval command decides to bring in the reinforcements and surround our ships in the Horn – they would have nowhere to go, and we might just lose them down to the last plug and plank. No, what I propose is for us to ask for a large but not enormous annual tribute. This would initially allow for a fair distribution among our soldiery while simultaneously guarantee a steady influx in your Majesty's treasure chest in years to come. And as soon as the first installment has been made and the treaty signed we should all retreat in good order.

Halil's speech most certainly did not express the Sultan's secret wishes, but true to his word he didn't betray any impatience or dislike. The next speech, however, was definitely more to his liking. Zaganos Pasha, tall, courageous and ambitious as only a renegade Greek could be, had started his career within the Ottoman administration as a Janissary, but it wasn't only his good looks and intelligence that eventually earned him the title Vizier and Tutor-Counsellor in Mehmet's cabinet. Zagano's grandfather had been a Grand Vizier; other and even more distant ancestors had held important positions among the early Seljuk rulers of the Middle East. In other words, Zaganos came from a much respected family composed primarily of politicians and military men, often, as one might expect, both at the same time. More importantly, he had been in favour of the siege ever since Mehmet first whispered about it, and he now spoke forcefully about delivering the final blow,

– The city is ripe for conquest. The discord between the different factions inside it is literally tearing it apart from within. The Italians are all divided and very, very anxious not to let any single contender gain a major advantage, so they will first and foremost keep each other under surveillance. More specifically, the Venetians are afraid that Sforza, recently the new leader of the Milanese, will try to attack them back home. They consequently have few mercenaries to spare. Genoa obviously, and wisely, has decided to stay put and await the outcome. This means we have little to fear from them for the time being. Without the help from Scanderbeg in Albania and George Brankovich in Serbia, Hunyadi is not a threat, and he knows it. So far we have had no reports saying that either Serbia or Albania is taking to arms against us. The House of Aragon and Naples would only lift a finger to help if Alfonso sees a realistic chance to become the next Emperor, so that would rule them out. The Pope's appalled at the fact that the union of the two churches is not upheld as convened. In addition he hates spending money and fears that Rome, as a consequence of too many over-seas enterprises, will lose its dominance over the Italian peninsula. He might in fact be the one encouraging the others to go and find out what's going on here, but both Venetians and Genoese want to see the Pope himself sending ships and soldiers across the Mediterranean before they risk a major deployment of forces towards the east. In other words, they're still mainly watching one another. Thus the moment has indeed come, but we can't wait for long, because we have discord among our own and we need to appease the men by not only promising a final attack, but also that it will take place very soon. To remain here for weeks and even months to come will not be an option, as this will eventually force all Italians to take action. If that small vessel had been a vanguard of the Italian fleet, the main force would have been here already. No, I believe it was sent out by the citizens to look out for a rescue flotilla. They didn't find it so they returned, but the word is out now and the Italians will have to act soon. If we strike now it will luckily still be too late for them to do anything about the new order of things. Instead we can call them to negotiations and offer continued trade between the two seas completely on our own terms.

It all sounded like music in Mehmet's ears and to his satisfaction he now heard General Turhan Bey and the religious leaders join the choir.

The few individuals supporting Halil had little to come up with against Zagano's magisterial exposition of the present state of the balances of power, and so remained silent, leaving Halil with the uncomfortable feeling that if, against his advice and belief, they were nevertheless to overrun the city in the next couple of days, he would soon not only be short of a career, but of a head as well.

It was decided that Zaganos should take a ride through the different encampments and positions and ask what the men themselves thought about going back to the walls for a final assault – a relevant question no doubt since those were the ones who once again would have to risk their lives. Zaganos duly returned with the reassuring answer that every single army unit endorsed the idea of attack, in fact they were all incredibly enthusiastic about it.

Addressing the entire assembly a few hours later Mehmet declared:
– Zaganos, you set the date for the battle. Make sure Galata is properly surrounded and prevented from coming to the city's assistance. And one last thing: do it quickly!

Chapter 51

The day of thundering lightning, hailstorm and torrential rain, was followed by another in which the entire city and its surroundings were shrouded in a fog so thick that the Turks lost sight of the city altogether and the defenders couldn't even discern the towering relief of the inner wall while they stood guard on the ramparts of the outer. This thickness also enabled the crowd guilty of attempted lynching to disperse and vanish utterly – while Giustiniani, the man who had single-handedly rescued their chosen victim from a certain death, didn't have the time or energy to press charges against a crowd unknown to him. Barnabas's heavily mutilated body had remained abandoned in the gutter and was eaten on to its bare bones by dogs, rats and vultures during the night. There was now only parts of a human skeleton to be seen, and then only at close range. Beside it appeared the ghoulish remains of a dirty, torn rope with a hanging noose.

The Turkish artillery too remained silent because the target had become utterly invisible and the rain had undermined the gun positions, rendering their aim arbitrary. Yes, so saturated with moisture was the air that any gunpowder still considered dry had to be ignited immediately to set off an explosion. Put to the test five minutes later it was useless. To the soldiers the mist seemed so dense that one would be tempted to use a sword to blaze a trail through it, as though the slowly drifting clouds that it mainly consisted of had been the tightly intertwined leaves of an oily mangrove marsh. The ominous silence was perhaps even more unnerving as it gave no hint of enemy positions and movements. The greatest danger for the besieged lay in the possibility of a sudden massive strike at a weakly defended section of the walls. But then again the Turks didn't see more of the city than the defenders did, and they couldn't, as would have been the case during an attack at night, light up torches to guide themselves. It was a stalemate.

Fields, orchards, churches, monasteries, houses, villas, palaces, squares, streets and alleys – all enveloped in the same thick moisture, slowly depositing itself on every roof, dripping down, drop by drop, as though descending the insides of a gigantic watery time glass: tick, tock, tick, tock, like a clock still moving but showing no time. In once bustling loggias and open court yards made slippery by fungus and lichen, vast mosaic frescoes majestically sunk into a sea of no return. Neptunes, tritons, sirens and dolphins, dispossessed of their pagan innocence and exuberant gaiety, gaping empty-eyed at the forlorn silence over and around as they disappear into the depths of oblivion. Neptune's horses, the very emblem of the Meltemmia at the height of summer, dragged out of sight by a giant octopus; the sirens dissolving into foam. Strewn all over the floors, flowers massacred in the prime of youth, left to wither and litter the cool marble turned sickly green and sulphurously yellow in a misplaced autumn. Red roses nipped in their bud and thrown to the ground by showers of hail, rain, pumice and sand. All exquisite art, all venerable tradition, covered in debris, disintegrating, rotting, sinking, and, most disheartening of them all, a magnificent statue of Nike, split in two by a falling beam infested with snails.

Into this vortex of time luminescent saints and glorious Emperors vanished alike while the eyes of the black granite Judas Iscariot dripped belated tears like so many silver coins. The squeaking in the ribs of an abandoned ship minutes before being torn apart by waves and reef, the melancholy music of churches, lamenting with Jeremiah as they succumb to the elements. A mist so thick and all pervasive it obscured the interiors of palaces and churches – the starving raven herself becoming too old and decrepit to attempt to leave her nest. Not the slightest hint of daylight, not the slightest hint even of a sky; only the thick, impenetrable silence and the dullness of relentless decay. Vesper approaching, vapours and darkness merged indistinctly.

Then, as the grey broth was absorbed into the pitiless night, spotted by all the men on the walls, by worshippers fumbling their way to their soaked churches and chapels, by friend and foe alike, an eerie fluorescent light suddenly rose from the base of Hagia Sophia, embracing her in a fire of cold flames. The light was not stable, it streamed up and down the entire height of her walls, enveloping the dome, licking the sky itself. Inside the flames people saw signs and portents: letters, figures, animals, humans, even the indescribable and terrifying face of God.

George Francis brought the phenomenon to Constantine's attention and the two friends stood gazing at it, amazed by the reddish liquid flow which intermittently spilled out around the base of the church only to regain vertical energy and send glowing sheaves way into the dark sky where the light was eventually dispersed by the fog and suffused, first into crimson, then violet, before it disappeared altogether.

Even more alarmed was Mehmet who summoned all of his astrologers for an impromptu conference, believing that he and his army must have unwittingly offended Allah, now using the Aya Sofya as a beacon of warning – had Halil been right after all, and was the tide of luck indeed about to turn? Was this the announcement of troops and fleets rushing to the city's rescue, and would Mehmet and his men soon have to turn their backs on the city only to perhaps spare themselves a humiliating defeat? And what if this was actually the Christian God, who although he wasn't really allowed to exist in Islamic imagination, had nonetheless sent a sign to his flock to hold out and believe in the power of the eternal fire? And what was the connection between this light and that of the moon, recently appearing as a crescent when it should have been full? None of his astrologers had ever seen anything like it, although one of them had heard about remote peoples of the ultimate north claiming to have witnessed strange moving lights, green and pink, suspended over an entire horizon as a gigantic curtain wafting in an intangible breeze. Whether this light was similar to the one described by the northern barbarians, he couldn't tell, and so far south as the Mediterranean no such augury had ever been reported. Mehmet didn't exactly know what to do with this information, and though it certainly aroused his curiosity, it didn't calm his forebodings.

Meanwhile, in the city, Iannis finally, uneventfully – so he hopes – is on his way back home when he freezes in his tracks, struck by a vision more powerful and overwhelming than any of the ones he had previously experienced, the blood-crying Hodegetria included. It didn't take him long to recall that this was the legendary and never before witnessed omen Father Gennadi had related as the prophecy for Christ's second coming. As a matter of fact, it was the second and unequivocal sign, the consuming of the bastion of faith for the rebirth of all sinners in fire and Holy Spirit. Iannis felt every fibre in his body grow stronger, his soul bend like a composite bow and his spirit change into an arrow ready to spring into action.

After hovering around the basilica for some time, the light slowly crept upward, leaving more and more of the church in darkness. In a while all that remained was a flicker on the dome, struggling, it seemed, to sustain the flame against the onslaught of darkness. Then the light turned into a slender column, ascended and disappeared into heaven for good. Not even bothering to return to their churches, men, women and children fell on their knees, beating their fists against their chests, tearing their own hair and clothes while imploring God for mercy. Desperation, wailing and tears filled the streets as the unstoppable message spread, that the Holy Spirit had created a final emanation for himself only to depart from Hagia Sophia and deliver the people of the Holy Mother to Antichrist. The Turkish scimitar had appeared in the guise of an anomalous crescent moon. It was the final answer and reversal of the Christian aeon announced in a vision to the very first Emperor of Constantinople more than a thousand years ago.

The Hodegetria had fallen from the shoulders of the most trusted bearers in the city, the light of the Holy Spirit had been snuffed out like a candle. At this instant everyone seemed to recall another ancient prophecy. It held that just as the first Constantine had had a mother called Helena – the feminine form for Greekness itself – so the last was also going to be a Constantine with a mother Helena. And the name of Emperor Constantine's XI Serbian mother had been precisely that – Helena…

All the signs were noticeably coinciding, but Mehmet was not all that easily convinced, overcome by a fear that maybe, at times, he had come dangerously close to believing himself superior even to Allah, and that Allah had detected his secret ambitions and decided to give him a lesson he would not so soon forget. Mehmet's mullahs and astrologers all tried to convince him that the departing light, eerie and unreal though it had seemed, was the tell-tale proof that the false light of the Christian faith was to be replaced by the True Light of the True Faith, and that the Sultan had nothing to fear. The Sultan himself, however, knew his own heart better and didn't get much sleep that night. But before he finally dozed off, the crescent moon enveloped in red, that he had seen next to Jupiter some days earlier, appeared before his inner eye. According to his astrologers, this was an unequivocal sign of his imminent victory. Seeing it again, on the threshold of sleep, Mehmet solemnly promised Allah to make the crescent moon and the star immersed in a pool of blood the emblem of a new Constantinople.

Running muddy streets, sliding over slippery marble, brushing through dying vegetation, in between antique statues lacking heads and limbs, the fisherman could be seen making for Father Gennadi's monastery to receive his final instructions.

The soldiers posted along the central sections of the land wall kept seeing countless lights flaring at such distance beyond the Turkish camp that they couldn't be attributed to the Turks. Many believed the lights to come from a multitude of camp fires belonging to John Hunyadi, finally arrived with his army. Others, less inclined to subjugate their senses to their wishes, pointed to the fact that while these lights, though at a great distance, obviously could be seen, why was it that the Turkish camp so much closer still remained invisible?

CHAPTER 52

– What do you make of that, dear friend?

Francis looked at him and had to resist the impulse to start crying when he saw his pale face, marked by the lack of sleep and the mask of unflinching bravery he had to carry at all times in spite of never ending adversity. Because there, in the intimacy of confidence, Francis saw how vulnerable the man behind the mask really was, and it dawned on him that it was precisely this weakness that forced Constantine to refuse to meet his destiny here and now. If Constantine wouldn't himself have felt that one weakness, Francis might at some point have been able to persuade him to leave the city. But he knew that Constantine was more afraid of being remembered as a coward than having to die while doing his duty.

Maybe it would be false to assume that Francis did at this stage have a ready opinion, but he most definitely had an ominous presentiment. To him the imperial institution as such meant more than the lands, cities and peoples it was supposed to bring under its fold. To him Byzantium was something which existed in heaven, something which neither wars and conquest, nor politics and policies could essentially change, much less bring to an end. There were perhaps temporary setbacks, but even if Constantinople would eventually have to succumb to an aggressor, as it had indeed done in the past, Francis' belief in its inherent strength was such, that he thought it could and would be reconquered once the world had realised that it could not be without it, and, even more importantly, because God would not allow his own city to fall into the hands of the infidels for any length of time. It was an ordeal, just as Babylon had been an ordeal to the Jews. But it wasn't final. Loud he therefore said,

– I believe you should call every concerned party to a meeting tomorrow and prepare them for the inevitable. In all likelihood the Sultan will interpret this light as a sign in his favour and try to convince his army that it means Constantinople must fall. The next days will see the Turkish camp preparing for a final assault. If we can withstand that last attack, I believe the Sultan, at great expense to his prestige no doubt, will be forced to abandon the siege, since his losses will have been such that he can't risk another setback. So, everything now depends on our resolution and remaining strength.

– But what about the sign, what about the light suddenly enveloping our Holiest of Holy and then cruelly departing again. What do you think it means?

– I really don't know. But there is something very strange about all the weather phenomena we have experienced recently. Look at this! He dug his thumb into the balustrade and showed the result to Constantine. – It's not just water, it's water mixed with black mud. Maybe, I say maybe, the light has something to do with that?

– You mean it wasn't a divine sign at all, that it can somehow be explained as an effect from a natural cause?

– I wouldn't dare to swear on it, but I remember when I visited Santorini many years ago, that the island had recently had a volcanic outbreak. Weeks after that the air was still full of black dust that mixed with rainwater and became dirty like this. And then there was a light similar to this, not in the air, but in several bays of the island which could be seen glowing in iridescent colours at night. I don't know if this could have been a similar thing.

– But we have no volcanoes around! Constantine said.

– That's true, and I'm of course only speculating. The only thing I'm trying to say is, that maybe God hasn't abandoned us, maybe his just testing our capacity to the utmost to make us worthy of his ultimate grace.

– You don't really believe that, do you?

Francis' silence was more eloquent than a thousand words.

– So what do you believe?

– I believe you should leave the city and gather forces to deliver it. Meanwhile we pay as much as we can of the tribute Mehmet asked for and tell him that he will have to wait a little for the rest. Then you come back at the head of the entire Frankish world and drive him out of here.

– Sometimes you reason like a child, Constantine said, a faint smile playing on his lips. But the meeting, as you said, will be held tomorrow.

And so it was. As a matter of fact Constantine didn't even have to call a meeting; it appeared spontaneously. The constant bickering between Venetians and Genoese had reached such intensity that it threatened to tear to pieces the precarious Treaty of Turin which 70 years earlier had brought a prolonged armistice, if not exactly peace, between the two republican arch-enemies. For every Mediterranean island and piece of coast over which Byzantium had lost control over the past centuries, Genoese and Venetians had fought like hyenas every time the dominant Turkish lion had been called to defend his turf elsewhere. Now the old enmity was about to flare up, and as far as the Greeks were concerned, the timing couldn't have been worse. Not only were their city's defences strained to the breaking point, they also found themselves right in the firing line between two factions of Italians who needed someone to blame for not being able to cut each other's throats. The scapegoat naturally became the Greek community who had lured them into this mess in the first place. On the previous evening Giustiniani had requested that a number of the cannon deployed along the walls of the Horn be relocated to the wall facing the Lycus valley, and this for an apparent reason. The enemy, as could be easily inferred by the myriads of fires lighting up in the dark, was about to concentrate his strike at the very point he had now tried to weaken for almost two months. Yet, Lucas Notaras argued that without the cannon there would not be enough fire power to hold the enemy fleet in the Horn at bay. At this point Giustiniani could no longer hold his horses,

– You have five hundred skilled archers and cross-bowmen under your command and now you also want to keep the guns simply because you feel so good about them? Because you figure that if the city falls tomorrow, your personal honour will be saved because at least you were not to be blamed for it? Oh no, you and your men stood up to the test while the Emperor, putting his faith in fickle Italians, allowed himself to be overrun by the enemy. But do you really think that when they finally get to you, after having walked over *our* dead bodies, they will all fall down on their knees in reverence saying: "Oh look at this brave commander who knows so well how to organise his forces, we must spare him from being killed, and decorate and make him a general of our own army. Is that what you think – ehh? Well then, let me tell you. They'll stick that sabre right into your intestines, then they'll pull them out and while you're watching yourself dying they just might chop your head off, if you're very, very lucky! So get real, commander, and let's discuss this again when the battle is over. Tomorrow morning I'm going to have those cannon moved to where they are needed the most. Just tell me if I shall also need to bring a signed order from the Emperor. Because you know what, knowing that I shall be fighting three steps away from him, he just might consider it desirable to have me on *his* side.

Needless to add that Notaras felt insulted and swore to revenge himself once the danger was over. However, it couldn't be excluded that the Emperor himself did indeed stand behind the requisition, and so he grudgingly consented.

Then, on that morning of May 28, as heated arguments in the wake of the crucial meeting between Greeks and Genoese escalated into outright skirmishing, something unheard of happened. People of all walks of life, whether Greeks or Italians, suddenly, as though prompted by an invisible yet imperative command, took to the streets and brought every sacred relic of every church, chapel, monastery and private house out in the open. The Turks, busy filling the moats, dragging their cannon into new and even more threatening positions, moving their troops in preparation for the major assault, involuntarily looked up as the belligerent music from their own camp suddenly stopped. Along the ramparts of the inner land wall a long procession could be seen slowly moving ahead. Icons and crosses were lifted high into the now miraculously blue sky – highest and most triumphantly the previously so ill-fated Hodegetria herself – incense spread in all directions of the winds, and the age old hymns, intoned by thousands of penitent voices, were carried on ethereal cushions of air far and wide. The Emperor himself joined the procession and scenes of rare piety took place. Seeing the Emperor being the first to forget and forgive, others followed suit and once the train of people had passed by all the holy places, all the bitter trouble and strife of the past two months was instantaneously dissolved. Instead of discord and mutual suspicion a sense of brotherhood for good, for bad, even for worse, descended on people like a dove from on high. Meanwhile Mehmet, seeing the religious piety of his adversary and fearing repercussions from Allah, decided that the necessary preparations were now in place and ordered his entire army to cease work, and to consecrate the remainder of the day and evening to prayers and ablutions. Thus silence fell on both camps.

In the presence of all his military commanders and their subalterns Constantine rose to speak. The silence preceding his words was intense as his gaze wandered up and down, scrutinizing each and every face, however briefly.

– Venerable generals, estimated officers and honourable comrade fighters. You know that the hour has come when the enemy of all Christendom, with all the might and cunning in his possession, at sea and on land, like a venomous snake shall try to sting us and devour us like a lion. Because of this I address myself to you, encouraging you to bravely stand up, as you have stood up so many times before, against the enemy of our faith. In your hands do I command this glorious and famous city, father and empress alike of all others. Comrade fighters, you know that there are four things for which we must rather die for than continue to live without: our faith and our religion, our country, the Emperor as the Lord's anointed will, and finally, our families and friends. When alone one of these reasons is sufficient for us to boldly accept a fight to the death, how much more compelling must all four of them be together! To give our lives for the holy faith which Christ himself gave us through his own blood, that is the highest! If someone were to gain the entire world but take harm to his soul, what really would he have gained? Then there is our fatherland, and then our

Empire, once so powerful but today sadly reduced – do you want to see it utterly humiliated under the rule of an infidel tyrant? Then there are our wives and children who would all be taken away from us and sold as simple slaves. Now how do you feel about that?

– For fifty-seven days the wretched Sultan has been besieging us day and night, trying every trick he could possibly come up with. Thanks to the mercy of our all seeing Lord Jesus Christ he has so far been rejected and forced to wallow in his own shame. And now again, brethren, don't give way. Even if some of the walls have been demolished, you can see that they have been repaired as well as they could be. We put all our trust in the invincible majesty of God; they on the other hand believe in wagons and horses, and in the sheer power of superior numbers. We too believe in the force of our arms and hands, but the reason we believe in them is because God has given them to us to use against the enemy. I know that these hordes of many tens of thousands will come at us once again, and with their wild cries and self-conceited confidence try to scare us into submission. You yourselves know all too well what jester's tricks I'm talking about. And they will let stones and cannon balls rain over us again. But I hope they shall not be able to harm us, because when I see you like this all around me, my confidence grows strong again. Although we are a small force, we are all in a good mood and well experienced in warfare, vigorous, strong and of one heart. So brethren, just cover your heads with your shields and stretch your right arm holding your sword as far out against the enemy as you can. Your helmets, your harnesses and your plated breasts are well-placed and safely secured, and they will serve you well during the battle. The enemy has none of this. You're well protected behind the walls, whereas they, unprotected, with great effort must try to scale up ladders to get to you.

– Now, do as Hannibal's elephants. They were only a few but the mere sight of them and the sound of their trumpeting sent the entire Roman cavalry into flight. And when that could be accomplished by simple animals, how much more must we men, who have been set to rule over them, be able to impose ourselves on an enemy who is just as much an unreasonable animal, if not of even lower standing? The Sultan broke the treaty, the Sultan has set fire to our fields and farms, the Sultan has killed or enslaved every single one of our brothers in faith whom he could lay his hands on, the Sultan – enough! has in his mind to turn our holy churches into temples for his blasphemous doctrine, into a sanctuary for his devious and lying prophet, into a stable for mules and camels! Think about all this, brethren – comrades, so that the memory of you, your glory and your freedom, will live on forever.

– Last but not least I would like to take the precaution to ask you all for forgiveness, in the name of our Lord Jesus Christ and His holy Mother, if in any way I have wronged you. A situation as difficult as ours sometimes calls for draconian measures. Though I have always tried to listen to what everyone had to say, I have sometimes been forced to make decisions that were bound to hurt the pride, and perhaps even honour, of some. Though this has been inevitable I want you all to know that it was never my intention to overlook anybody's legitimate interest and opinion. But there is one thing that I will not regret and not atone for, and that is that I have called the Galatans traitors. This they have been and this is what they still are, because instead of fighting the Sultan like men, they have made friends with him.

Constantine looked around for a moment and it seemed as though his face grew dark with subdued rage, but then he bowed down in front of the cross, inviting everybody to follow his example. When he rose he made no sign for the assembly to disperse but went round to each and everyone in the hall, embracing them one by one. Returning to his place at the end of the long table he drew his sword and held it out. – Brethren, he said, – Go in peace and prepare for battle. May God be with you all.

Chapter 53

Moved by his speech, all the soldiers thronged around the Emperor to pledge their loyalty. Constantine received their resolution to die rather than to give up their faith with tears in his eyes. But it hadn't escaped his keen eye that the two fighting clergymen Isidore and Leonard were conspicuously absent from the meeting. If Francis' judgment were to be trusted this could only be interpreted as a refusal on their part to loyally commit themselves to the fateful task ahead. He felt he had little choice but to actually bring them in for questioning, whatever such a display of overt distrust would entail. And the Emperor shuddered from head to toe at the mere thought of having to conclude that they were actively conspiring against him.

On the other hand the show of loyalty on the part of the men who were present hadn't just been formal gesture. In everybody's mind an event which had taken place two days earlier was still reverberating. In vain had Constantine in person appealed to the Venetian captain to stay put. But his pleas, pronounced in such a way as to fatally undermine what was still left of his imperial prestige, seemed only to strengthen the man's resolve. He didn't contradict Constantine in words, preparing his treason in silence. And when he finally spoke, it was in order to inform his men that he had an indisputable duty to deliver his ship's goods to Venice at all costs. The crew saw the chance to save their lives without having to answer for the defection themselves and anxiously embraced the opportunity. Thus, as soon as it had become overwhelmingly clear that the Sultan was preparing a massive assault they set to work. Under cover of darkness the large Venetian merchant – needless to add that it too was crucial to the maritime defence of the Horn – somehow managed to have the boom lowered and slip unnoticed into the Marmara. Come the morning, the remaining Venetian mariners were seized by panic and may well have mounted a mutiny had they not suddenly become witness to the afore mentioned pious procession appearing on the ramparts. Its candid display of faith and trust provoked a change of sentiments as sudden as it was unexpected.

Notwithstanding this surprising turn for the better, Constantine had no idea how close he had actually come to losing the battle before it had even begun. Even though there was not at the subsequent meeting one man who did not swear on his honour to do battle, there was yet another man – and not just any man – who had not been present at the meeting. He of course had a very understandable reason for not being there since he had been wounded the night before. Incidentally that night had also seen the eerie glow envelope Hagia Sophia only to later allow the Venetian galley to disappear. As soon as the fatal news of Giustiniani's wound reached Constantine, he ordered the Venetian surgeon Niccolo Barbaro to make sure he was taken care of in every conceivable way. Without the trusted Genoese general at his side, Constantine knew he would lack the power to convince the Italians to carry on the fight. It was an unbelievable stroke of bad luck: Giustininai seriously weakened on the very eve of what was no doubt destined to become the final battle.

What had happened? After his heated discussion with Lucas Notaras, Giovanni Giustiniani Longo had returned to his post at the

Gate of Saint Romanus to survey the endless repairs. There he waited for Constantine so that he could have his order to move the cannon from the Petrion next morning endorsed by the supreme commander without encountering further resistance from the megadux. Routinely his eyes ran up and down the walls and his men climbing up and down on ladders, when suddenly, he discovered a Greek woman of the people, tirelessly carrying buckets of pebbles and gravel to the walls and handing them over to the soldiers. At first Giustianini was more bewildered than worried. But then came the moment when she dangerously exposed herself by actually climbing over the wall, a bucket in each hand, and stretching out her arms to empty the gravel on the outside. It was a dangerous action. By leaning too far over the edge of the wall she was spotted by what appeared to be a faint shadow – barely visible on the rim of the haze. Giustiniani caught a sudden glimpse of the slowly moving shadow and immediately realised what was about to happen when he heard the faint but unmistakable sound of an arrow being loaded to a crossbow. A moment later, in the corner of his bloodshot eye, he saw the familiar triangular outline of a crawling cross-bow gunner aiming right at her from a distance of, at the most, fifty feet. Reacting instinctively he threw himself down the wall to push her out of the line of fire. While practically still floating in the air he heard the ominous snap and the arrow whizzing invisibly through the air.

He fell on top of her with the full weight of his entire body, covering her under his broad shoulders. A fraction of a second later the arrow-head struck a metallic chord as it made a substantial indentation in his shoulder plate. It didn't pierce though and the arrow itself shattered from being brought to a sudden standstill against the protective metal, the resultant debris delivering smarting stings as it literally shattered into flying needles burying themselves in his neck and cheek. One of the deadly nails pierced just above his right eye and released a stream of blood covering his face. Rolling to the side he pulled the wooden splinter out of his head and used his fingers to establish that the wound, though hurting, was not very deep. He could only hope that the poor woman had neither been hit nor sustained substantial injury from their collision. Thank God, she was still moving. He moved closer towards her while soldiers began to flock around them and their own crossbowmen and archers unleashed a wild barrage in the general direction of where they assumed the shot to have been fired from. In her fall the hood she had been wearing had been pushed down her neck and her features were revealed. And it wasn't a Greek woman. It was Felicia.

– What are you doing up here? Don't you realise you could get yourself killed a second time by parading on the ramparts that way? And for God's sake, cover your head again so that the others don't recognise you!

– I'm sorry, I got carried away, she panted. – I just realised how desperately we all need this particular wall to look sufficiently impressive and repellant by dawn again. I wanted to help, but I didn't want people to maybe suspect me of trying to sabotage you, so I dressed up a bit. Anyway, thanks for once again saving my life. You didn't even know it was me, did you?

– No, and now we've got to get you out of this. Unfortunately I don't have the time to accompany you back to where you stay and…

– I'm going nowhere, Commander. My place is here by your side. You tell me what I can do to help you rebuild that wall, and that's what I'll do… Please.

Giovanni was about to say something he would perhaps later have regretted, and so he caught himself. Wiping the blood off his face he added,

– Actually, in that case, why don't you just continue to carry those buckets up and down the stairs. This time, however you empty them on this side of the wall, and we'll take care of it from there, alright?

– Yes, Sir!

Her energy and determination was apparently not there to produce melodrama. During the entire night, until dawn made them visible and prevented further work from being carried out, Felicia kept delivering bucket after bucket with stone and gravel. She carried logs, branches, sacks full of debris and sand, yes, anything that was considered good enough to serve as a provisional bulwark. And she did it silently, without asking for help, without complaining, although her body was aching and bleeding all over from the bruises she had contracted when Giovanni brought her down on the unforgiving boulders. Giovanni, energised by her relentless determination, couldn't help glancing at her. She glanced back at him every now and then, her flashing eyes betraying a paradoxical mixture of pride and tenderness. And it was now, as their flaming eyes met in the bull's eye of imminent death, that the full weight and intensity of his love for her came over him. This realisation was followed immediately by another, no less alarming. When he looked down inside his harness he saw that it was not only completely soaked in blood, but that blood was still pouring out of an open wound somewhere under his metal jacket. He went inside the tower and was helped to undress. On his left shoulder the culprit was found. A sharp metal piece about an inch long had lodged itself right under the collarbone, just above his heart. There were no two ways about it. It had to be removed. Under the circumstances it meant immediately undergoing the knife with a few mouthfuls of tsipouro as the only anesthesia. Lead by torches held close to the commander's chest by soldiers, Barbaro executed the operation with the greatest possible care. The irregularly shaped scrap of metal had to be removed so as to not cause further damage and to prevent festering. As soon as he had swallowed the alcohol he was offered a piece of rope to bite into when the knife entered the wound. He stoically refused it but the intense pain, accompanying a procedure lasting several minutes, turned his face pale and convulsive.

He was laid to recover in a simple room partly hewn out of the living rock, partly masoned with stones dating back to the earliest days of the city's existence; in fact, most of them had once been used as building material for the original Constantine's city wall, now long since gone. The vaulted room had been furnished with a stretcher and a single chair. An oil lamp placed in a niche illuminated the wall; through one of the wood latticed windows the suffused moonlight, breaking through a rift in the haze, weaved mysterious patterns on the blanket enveloping the patient.

Chapter 54

By a combination of threats – some involving the more complex prospect of eternal damnation, some promising a more immediate, palpable castigation – Leonard and Isidore were able to force the brothers of the Contoscalion monastery, to which Gennadi also belonged, to tell what the end of times was expected to hold in store for them. At divine sword point, so to speak, a truly grandiose story was revealed. Its centre piece was Gennadi's apocalyptic prophecy of Jesus' second coming at the very moment of Turkish triumph, and the miraculous salvation of every human soul who at this point had taken refuge in the church of the Saviour in Chora. Christ himself, however, was not destined to materialise in the church carrying his name – it would just be protected by his grace. Leading an army of angels he would instead appear in front of the Hagia Sophia, denying Anti-Christ and his hordes entrance to the inviolable sanctuary. Asked about whether this scenario also involved the brethren deserting from the military posts assigned to them along the sea wall, Leonard and Isidore were told that in case the city was in the end overrun, the monks had the means to reach the harbour and the ships beneath their monastery faster than the Turks could knock down the front door. Knowing that no Turkish soldier would want to miss the opportunity to loot the city while there was still something left to take, a barrage of the small harbour by Turkish ships would be an unlikely occurrence. In other words, taking to the sea potentially remained a last resort.

Neither Leonard nor Isidore were unfamiliar with the *Parousia*, as the Greeks called the belief that Christ must one day return to establish his kingdom on earth. But whereas in the Catholic realm 'kingdom come' was mostly regarded as a gradual process in which the church took a very active part as forerunner – and in the event was expected to assume its eternal form within the confines of a now heavenly Rome – various Orthodox congregations throughout the ages had expected His arrival to be both sudden and literal. It wasn't just a question of the Holy Spirit permeating the minds of true believers to the point that they all began to shine from sheer other-worldliness. It was a matter of Jesus returning in the flesh, just as it had been written in *Acts*: "This same Jesus, which is taken up from you into heaven, shall so come in like manner as ye have seen him go into heaven", by which many Orthodox believers understood a simple reversal of the original event when Christ went from body to spirit. Now his spirit would become flesh again. With general despair at boiling point, any belief that still seemed to offer some hope was feverishly embraced by the common folks.

Needless to say, both Isidore and Leonard considered such blatant disregard of dogma plain heresy. However, in the circumstances both cardinal and bishop were willing to show leniency vis-à-vis popular sentiment if they could only get the monks to help them escape the city if and when it had become clear that its continued defence would amount to nothing but a senseless waste of human life. But before they got round to that, they did have the presence of mind to give the thumbscrew a final twist. Why, Leonard asked, were the followers of Gennadi convinced that they would be safe if, on the day of the final assault, they took refuge in the chapel of Blachernai? When he didn't get the answer he wanted he simply grabbed the monk by his throat and pressed him hard against the wall, telling him that if he didn't speak the truth here and now, he, Leonard, would hold him personally and solely responsible for conspiring against the empire and drag him in front of the Emperor to answer for himself. The monk, who had never experienced a Catholic priest behaving like a ruthless mercenary, capitulated.

– Father Gennadi says he has obtained a promise from the Sultan to spare his congregation if they gathered in that church and didn't put up any resistance.

– How's that? Why would he spare them just because of that?

– Because … because… Father Gennadi swore that he'd rather continue worshipping God under Turkish rule than accepting the supremacy of the Catholic church in Constantinople. And to prove his willingness to let the Sultan have it his way, on condition that he spared the lives of those faithful to God, he told him that he would make sure that… that…

– What?

– … That Commander Longo was going to be forced to retreat at some point during the battle, leaving all his men utterly confused, and that this was the great moment when the Sultan could finally seize the initiative and force his men through the breach at St Romanus.

– That's a lie, and you know it! How would he ever be able to predict such a precise and crucial event? Clearly you're trying to hide something from us.

– I swear to you, that's all I know, that's all he ever told us.

– And where is he now?

– I don't know.

– You rascal! Leonard shouted. Do you really think we're so gullible as to believe that you don't even know where you're hiding your master! And what did he really promise the Sultan? Answer!

As Leonard was about to once again jump to the monk's throat, Isidore, by virtue of his higher rank, interceded and put a sudden end to the interrogation.

– Enough! he exclaimed, – Let the man go. The only person who can obviously clarify this mess is Gennadi himself. Taking Leonard aside, he continued, whispering in his ear. – Don't you see, we need to get the Emperor to issue an order for Gennadi's arrest before he manages to have us all delivered to Hell.

– And where is he?

– Who, Constantine or Gennadi?

– Let's start with Constantine, as you say.

– Probably on his way to Hagia Sophia. All those people gathering in the streets this afternoon are on their way there to pray for their lives and ask for God's forgiveness. Constantine will be there and we have to get there before him. Once seated next to the altar it will be difficult to get near him as there will be hundreds and hundreds of Greeks wanting to touch him and cry with him.

– But we've got to be able to get out of this too. Let me at least ask them where their tunnel to the sea starts inside the monastery!

– No, Leonard! We simply haven't got the time. We must stop this man and we must do it now. Right now. I have a terrible presentiment of what's on his mind.

– What's that?

– I'll tell you on the way. Let's go.

Chapter 55

Constantine's guard, frantically searching the city, finally found the unsuspecting Bishop Leonard and Cardinal Isidore outside Hagia Sophia. Declaring themselves unaware of the imperial meeting taking place as they were speaking, the leader of the guard concluded that the foe they were purportedly pursuing must be imaginary. In his view their testimony affirmed the suspicion that they were currently trying to escape the city. Unable or unwilling to communicate to the common soldiery the real reason for their defiance, they were unsentimentally put in chains and marched off to the imperial head quarters – which was exactly what they wanted. Under the circumstances it was the only way for them to obtain an audience with the Emperor, apparently not present in Hagia Sophia at this time.

Constantine received the prisoners in the palace where the meeting of all higher officers had just been concluded. With Francis' deprecatory words in regard to the Catholic dignitaries still ringing in his ears he was at first disinclined to believe their fantastic claim. However as two monks named Philip and Thomas of the Contoscalion monastery were referenced as witnesses, he decided to have them brought in for questioning as well. Meanwhile Isidore, surprisingly composed and eloquent in spite of the heavy chain hanging around his neck, explained the matter as follows,

– Most noble and venerable Majesty, we have the strongest reason to believe that the unofficial leader of the popular religious movement aiming at the full restoration of the untainted Orthodox faith to Constantinople, George the Scholar, also known as the monk Gennadi, has in fact been conspiring with the Sultan against your Majesty and all remaining honest, trustworthy men and women of the city. A rumour – willfully sustained by this traitor disguised as a man of God – runs wild in the streets that Christ's second coming is to be expected in connection with Mehmet's anticipated assault, and that those singled out for redemption must meet and lock themselves up in the Blachernai chapel during the impending battle. In reality, though, Gennadi, during an impromptu and secret visit to the Sultan in his war tent weeks ago, struck a deal with him to the effect that the selected people seeking refuge in this particular church shall be spared against their active help to bring the city down. This much we know for sure. What we don't know, alas, is when and in what form this help will be forthcoming.

– So what do you want me to do? Constantine answered in genuine consternation.

– You must have this man arrested at once and make sure that none of his followers will be able to take refuge in the chapel. The crowd must be dispersed and neutralised. Once the Turks have been effectively repelled we will be able to provide you with ample evidence of his guilt. For now the only thing that matters is that this man's evil intention is brought to a halt.

– But how is this even possible? Constantine said, I mean I have been in several intimate discussions with Gennadi over the past months and…

– It doesn't matter your Majesty. The man's a traitor. We don't have the time to prove it to you right now, but we shall, God willing, be able to do so. If it turns out we were wrong, you may punish us as you see fit. But please understand that by now we've been on his trail for a long time. He's willing to do anything to drive Catholics out of here. And he knows you won't have the power to do so. Thus…

– But! interjected Constantine, still unable to grasp the entire picture, – how come you haven't informed me earlier about all this?

– Majesty, we had to make sure our suspicions were well founded before we could make a move. There's still time to get to the root of this if only Gennadi is immediately apprehended.

– Aha, and where do you think he is to be found right now?

– He's almost certainly inside the monastery adjacent to the Contoscalion harbour. The monks there refused to reveal his hiding place, but that's doubtlessly where he is, celebrating his own black mass and scheming our downfall. Please hurry before he will be able to turn his plan into reality!

Constantine looked at Isidore, then at Leonard, then at Isidore again. Unable to understand why these two men would simply invent such an insidious scenario in this moment of utter crisis, he realised he had to make a quick decision. Turning to his guard he said,

– Send an attachment to the monastery of Saint Jerome and look for Gennadi. You have the right to apply any means of interrogation to find out where he is. When you find him, arrest him and lock him up. Bring those two monks with you as well.

Half an hour later the monks in question were brought before Constantine. But although they had searched the place inside and out, the guards had been unable to find Gennadi on the premises. In spite of the fierce flashes emanating from under Bishop Leonard's eyebrows, the monks seemed at first unwilling to concede any information whatsoever. But a white-glowing iron rod that had been prepared already before the arrival of the clergy was now brought in dangerous vicinity of their eye balls, quickly untying their tongues. Trembling with fear of the age-old Byzantine punishment of blinding they confirmed that Gennadi had in fact, under the cover of darkness, been taken to Galata from the Contoscalion harbour in a small rowing boat owned and operated by a fisherman named Iannis. This had all happened some days ago, but the monks swore on their lives they had no idea he'd subsequently gone from Galata to meet with the Sultan in person. All they knew was that he hadn't return to the monastery until the following night. Thus the only one who could possibly corroborate the allegation of treason against him was said Iannis, known to be Gennadi's trusted agent.

Hearing this Constantine immediately issued an order for the arrest of Iannis as well, since in all likelihood he had been duped by

Gennadi and charged with a mission to deliver the city to the enemy. There was indeed no time to lose. Constantine, releasing Leonard and Isidore from their shackles, received their pledge of loyalty. He convinced himself they'd spoken the truth. Instead of being conspirators they had done what they could to apprehend the culprit. Constantine took them both in his arms after having raised them from the floor onto which they had both flung themselves in a reverential gesture.

– What a pity, he said, that I shall perhaps never know the full truth of all this. I can only hope that you're both wrong about the real nature of Gennadi's intentions. By all means, we must all stand fast as though we were rocks in the sea. All the gates are manned with reliable and steadfast men such as yourselves. I thank you for bringing this strange possibility to my attention, and I believe your honest intention. However, I must now ask you to take up your positions again while I pay a visit to general Longo, who this afternoon sustained a wound while saving a woman of my people from being shot dead by a sniper.

– If I may speak for both of us, Leonard solemnly replied, we too hope to be wrong. But you have heard the testimony of the man's own monks. Admittedly their story sounds confused, but we have had the doubtful privilege of also listening to Gennadi himself bragging about his alleged visit to the Sultan. He might of course be inventing something out of the blue. But for what purpose? Why would he go round and promise people these things? What does he hope to gain from it? Maybe he's just crazy. Let's in God's name hope so. But it can't be ruled out that he's put this fisherman to work to carry out some act of treason and destruction.

While Constantine pondered an answer the guard returned and told him that the chapel of Blachernai was chained shut. Not a single soul had been be found inside its walls. Constantine again turned to the papal representatives.

– At least that was a false alarm, he concluded shrugging his shoulders. – We'll continue to look for both Gennadi and his alleged messenger Iannis, but deep inside I refuse to believe that something so insidious as this could be in the making. It simply must be some kind of misunderstanding. Monks, you're allowed to return to your posts.

Leonard and Isidore were incapable of feeling equally optimistic, but they resigned themselves to the fact that little could be done unless Gennadi and Iannis were actually caught and put behind bars. Since the imperial guard had been instructed to continue their search all through the night if necessary, Leonard and Isidore realised that Constantine had indeed understood the gravity of the situation. The problem was not so much unwillingness on his part as the terrible scarcity of time. Respectfully Isidore therefore changed the subject saying,

– We pray for Giustiniani's health so that he may appear tomorrow like a Gabriel in front of Satan. God bless your Majesty. We shall all faithfully battle at your side.

With these words the two churchmen retreated and obediently made for their respective ports of call. When outside Leonard was the first to break the silence. But he had hardly opened his mouth before Isidore anticipated him,

– You never said it, I never said it, but I do hope we'll be able to see each other again under somewhat more pleasurable circumstances. And please don't doubt my innate heroism, but I've always found that carrying some money in my pockets during battle can make negotiations easier if and when a retreat is unavoidable.

A faint, somewhat surprised smile lit up Leonard's face. The two men then kissed each other on both cheeks and parted in the dark, each to see his own destiny.

As soon as Leonard and Isidore had left, Constantine sent for his horse. Entering the house in which Giustiniani was kept, he made a sign for the surgeon Barbaro to leave them alone. The latter, having done everything possible to ease the suffering of the patient, withdrew. Constantine sat down on the chair next to Giovanni. The latter was still a bit hazed from alcohol and the burning pain from the cauterisation of his wound by glowing iron.

– How are you, my friend?

– I'm sorry about this, Giovanni replied. – It was such a stupid thing. Here I am, practically running the gauntlet between enemy projectiles every day. And then, when I had the least reason to expect it, bad luck strikes.

– I understand how you feel, Constantine said, – But the fact is you unselfishly risked your own life to save that of a woman of my people. Considering your responsibility in general it was a foolish thing to do, since we could in all earnest do without her but not without you. Anyway, you did what you did and earned yourself a respect that will travel before you in life like a beacon. The important thing right now, however, is that you don't lose your nerve and sinew. The decisive moment, as you know, is here: it's now or never that we shall repel the enemy for good. When that moment comes – and it will be sooner rather than later – all these brave men will look to you for courage and support. Just by seeing you they will fight on with superhuman strength. In this very moment you're the Emperor of the Italians as I'm the Emperor of the Greeks. As long as you and I stand up, there's a good chance they will do the same. I pray to the Almighty that by this dawn all your strength has been restored to you, because for our edifice to remain standing you have to be to your men what the key stone is to the vault. On the secure and inflexible positioning of that one piece the whole vault and, by extension, the whole wall depends. So get in shape, my friend. Sharpen your angles and fit yourself precisely into that centre of the vault, because only then can we let go of the scaffolding. *In hoc signo vinces…* he added thoughtfully.

– I'll be up there when the trumpets sound, Giovanni said, but his smile, intended to be reassuring, turned into a grimace as he simultaneously tried to move. – Oh, don't worry, it's nothing, in fact I never felt better...

– My friend, Constantine continued, visibly moved, – You have no idea how profoundly grateful I am having had you to rely on since the very beginning of this calamity. It's my conviction that without you, personally, we would have been run over ten times by now. Just in case I shall not be given another opportunity, I would like to express this feeling here and now. We've both done everything we could, and even a little more, to defend our faith at a moment when it has been threatened like never before. As long as we continue to do so, we shall always be free of blame. The rest is all in God's hands.

With these words their conversation came to a close. Constantine had scrupulously avoided briefing Giustiniani on the alarming news of possible internal enemies. In truth he couldn't afford to tell him since it might bring down his morale. With this key issue off limits, little else remained to be added. Constantine consequently rose, leaving Giovanni to recuperate.

An hour later the moving patterns on the blanket had turned even fainter, while Felicia, recognised only by the loyal and ever discreet Barbaro in the adjacent chamber, was allowed to steal unseen into the room. For a moment she remained immobilised on the threshold looking in what she assumed to be his direction. Then she moved forward. He woke up as a consequence of feeling her lips alighting on his forehead.

– It's already the second time you saved my life, she said wetting his hand with her tears.

– Oh, it's really just another flesh wound, but they insist on keeping me here to make sure I'll be fit for tomorrow.

– So it really is now that all is going to be determined, is it?

– Certainly looks that way.

There was a silence during which Felicia's finger traced the blanket's runic meanders, now about to disappear altogether. Giovanni felt her hand moving over his body. Then, as her dark eyes turned even darker, she said,

– So this might be the last time I ever see you.

– Why is that?

– Because if you climb that wall again tomorrow there will only be one choice for you, and a choice without an alternative is no choice, but an ultimatum, an *imperative*.

– Oh, we could still win.

– You make it all sound so easy, as though it was only a matter of another day up there. But that's not how it is. This time there will be as much bloodshed as it takes until… until…

– Until what?

– Oh, Giovanni, please don't pretend not to understand.

– Felicia, how many times do I have to explain this to you? I have a duty to be there. I have just given the Emperor my word – once again. Without me he could just as well accept the Sultan's offer and leave the city together with his people, or convert to Islam.

– And why doesn't he? Why does he want to die and drag everybody else with him into the grave?

– It's a matter of faith – and of honour. And apart from that, what would all my men think of me if I deserted them in this hour of direst need?

– What good is duty, faith and honour to you when you're all dead?

– Maybe I shall be able to appear in the face of my Creator and tell him that I stood up for him.

– But what about if he never stood up for you, what then do you owe him?

– I owe him my life, he gave me my life.

– Yes, but only to take it away when it so pleased him.

– Felicia, do you realise that you're blaspheming the very God you have accepted as the one and only truth and light of your life?

– *You*, Giovanni, are the truth and the light of my life. I did it for you, not for him. I did it so that I could be with you without jeopardising your reputation as a soldier of Christ. But whatever I did, it's too late now. You just go out there and have yourself killed over some principle. Besides I'm late too… I'd better be going.
 – Late for what?
 – Three weeks late, my love.
 – Three weeks?
 – Yes Giovanni, I'm pregnant.
 – Pregnant? With my, I mean – is it *our* child?
 – Who else's do you think it would be? No, Master and Commander, I'm carrying *your* son under my heart. If I stay in the city both of us will soon be dead.
 – So what is it you suggest?
 – There is a ship, tonight. Another Venetian captain has had enough and has decided to leave before it's too late. I spoke to him. He would take all of us, but there really isn't much time. He'll be sailing before midnight. In a matter of hours we must steal over to the harbour.
 – You know I can't do it, just as much as it's the only thing I'm dreaming of right now. But I want you to go. Go to Chios. I shall write a letter and instruct my family members; they will take care of you and you'll be safe until I arrive there.
 – I won't leave without you.
 – But you must. This is our only chance. You go ahead without me. You have nothing to worry about, because I promise you that if during the decisive battle I see that everything has been lost and all that awaits us is to be massacred to the last man, I shall turn round and make for the ships. Believe me, I will get out of here, and I'll come to Chios to get you.
 – You can't force me to leave Constantinople without you.
 – I'm not forcing you Felicia, I beg you, I implore you to leave. Don't you see how this changes everything? How could I possibly allow myself to die now, now that the two of us have become one?
 – Ask your God how you could?
 – I don't need to ask him. He'll give me all the strength. But that's how it will have to be, an escape at the very last moment, when there can no longer be a doubt that all that remains to lose are more Christian lives. This I promise you in the name of the Lord, of me and my family and, last but not least, in the name of our still nameless child.

– And what if, in spite of your brave will, you won't make it, what then shall become of me?

– I'll take care of that. Do you think you can find me a piece of paper, a quill, wax and some ink?

– I'll try.

An hour later, after having mustered all her natural resourcefulness, she returned with the required items. Propping himself up against the wall Giovanni set about drawing up the letter while Felicia guided his eyes with the aid of the lamp. When it was all done he carefully folded the parchment. The wax heated by the flame dripped down onto the folds, uniting all four corners under a hot red dot upon which Giovanni, liberating the signet ring from his finger, sealed the coat of arms of his family – a crowned eagle above three defence towers.

– Everything you need for your protection on Genoese territory is contained in this letter, Giovanni said looking intently into her eyes. Now, make sure you keep it out of contact with water, and don't hesitate for another moment. Go, save yourselves. Remember, I love you – both.

The oil lamp flickered when Felicia returned it to its niche. She came back and leaned over him. Her face, no more than a silhouette to him now, then blocked out all of the remaining light. Her seal was not of parchment, nor of wax and ink, but of red blood circulating in torrential thrusts by a heart in uproar, expressing itself in lips that trembled as they finally met his, in a kiss deeper and more passionate than words can tell.

Chapter 56

With mixed feelings Doge Francesco Foscari received the news that his one and only remaining child had been summoned from Crete, where at the moment he endured banishment, to once again face the Council of Ten, this time accused of having conspired against the Republic of Venice through treasonable correspondence with the Duke of Milan and – hardly less worrying – with the Turkish Sultan. In the midst of the polemic surrounding the proposed rescue operation to Constantinople, the investigation of Jacob Foscari, on-going ever since he had been suspected of complicity in the murder of a much respected member of the Council, had reached a point where a new hearing of the defendant was considered indispensable. The Doge learned that the order, without his knowledge, had been brought to Crete by one of the captains in the fleet destined for the Bosporus, but before Foscari's own subsequent letter (admonishing the son to placidly comply with all requests) reached its recipient, it was preceded by one from Jacob himself. In it Jacob once again swore on his complete innocence. He did admit, however, that before the Turkish siege began, he had overheard some Genoese seamen from Galata, seeking refuge on the Cretan coast during a storm, discuss the existence of a rare map allegedly in the Sultan's possession. This map, it was said, had come all the way from China to end up in Mehmet's hands. And so valuable apparently was its contents that it sufficed for him to briefly show it to the Genoese delegation seeking audience at his court, to make them bend over backwards to accommodate his wishes, in exchange, that is, for the map itself.

The reason the map was so valuable was that it didn't just show Europe, Asia and even the vast African continent in clear outline. It also indicated the precise location, way towards the east of China, of a hitherto not only unknown, but also enormous land mass, which a Chinese fleet under Admiral Zheng He had discovered more than thirty years ago. Realising that Mehmet considered the map a curiosity without consequence, the Genoese of Galata were quick to reassure him that in the event of a Turkish siege of Constantinople, the Galatans themselves would remain officially neutral in the conflict, implying that in practice they would even help him to succeed in exchange for the map. The Sultan listened attentively to their proposal and promised, in his turn, that if this were to be the case – and he did stipulate his criteria for what such tacit cooperation would entail – the map would indeed be theirs as soon as the city had fallen. As a result the Galatans now declared themselves willing to help him as far as they could without overtly compromising themselves.

Listening in on their discussion from behind a door in a tavern owned by one of his local friends, Jacob had also been able to deduce that the map was the main reason why commander Giovanni Giustiniani Longo had been given such extraordinary, albeit secretive, support from the Great Council of Genoa, as well as from his friends and family in Chios, to go to Constantinople. Officially he was supposed to help the Emperor, but it had been made clear to him back home that in case the holy city did fall, the very generous remuneration, and the honours which the city of Genoa held in store for him, was to be obtained only in exchange for the Chinese map. The Galatans, subordinate to Genoa in all major political decisions, were to get it from the Sultan and then turn it over to Longo, responsible for bringing it home. The problem for Longo, the mariners chuckled, was that in the name of the one and indivisible Republic he had been forced to serve two mutually exclusive goals. In case of military victory, no map. In case he got hold of the map, it would be at the price of thousands of deaths, including those of his own men. "Poor devil" one of them said. Emptying his cup to the dregs he added,

– I don't even understand why a map of something so far out there could be of any value to anyone. I don't think I'd even like to go to China in the first place. I'd rather go to India and stay there. They say the women are so beautiful and smell like flowers. And you can get rich trading in all those spices and textiles. Pepper, did you ever hear of pepper for spicing wine, meats and all that? What's worth its weight in gold over here is used for land filling over there! India, that's something! You know, there is this Portuguese prince, Henry the Navigator they call him. From his residence on the Atlantic coast he's been sending ships down the coast of Africa for years; rumour even has it his crews have found Christian peoples in India. I'd go with one of his boats one day, given half a chance.

The face of the helmsman, lost in reveries at the very mention of beautiful, fragrant women, suddenly expressed sober realisation,

– You're right. And even if there actually was another Atlantis out there, it would be much too far away to make trading profitable. I mean, if the Chinese themselves don't give a tinker's cuss about it and sell the map to whomever is willing to suggest a price, then it can't be of much value, can it? So what's the big fuss really?

– Don't really know. The only thing I could come to think of is if the earth, as some people say, is actually round and not flat.

– What do you mean?

– Well, if the earth was round, like an orb or something, it might just be that one could reach this island easier and faster from say Portugal than from China. You'd just have to sail to the west instead of to the east to get to it.

– Oh yeah, sure. If the earth is round, everything would just fall right off it, wouldn't it? It'd be like pouring water over a melon, there'll be no sea left, so how are ye gonna sail then?

– Hmmm, guess not. But you know what? Explain then to me why when I'm on deck I only see the masts of a ship on the horizon, but when I climb into the look-out I can clearly see the hull as well?

– It's because you have a better view from up there because you're higher up thick-head! Now, let's stop this nonsense and get out of here. Storm's over and the Captain's waiting.

– So why is it that they're all after that map?

– I already told you, I don't know. Come on, we mustn't be late.

In the letter to his father Jacob didn't reveal all these details of conversation, and he didn't have to. Francesco Foscari, although initially sceptical about the notion that the earth was round, had been familiarised with that idea through discussions with Italian philosophers and men of learning claiming that an ancient Greek named Eratosthenes had made a calculation of the actual circumference of the earth based on the following observation. At the height of summer the sun would be exactly in zenith over the Egyptian town of Syene, while at the same time of the year in Alexandria, situated farther to the north, the apogee of the sun at summer solstice fell seven degrees short of exact zenith. Knowledge obtained from camel drivers of the approximate distance between Syene and Alexandria in stadia then enabled him to make a trigonometric extrapolation of the earth's entire circumference. All of course based on what was no longer debatable to him, namely that the earth had to be spherical.

In Venice, always a patron of the muses, the teachings of Pythagoras, recently translated to Latin by Greek men of learning fleeing the political turmoil in the east, was also held in high esteem. The notion of a universe consisting of concentric spheres was so central in Pythagoras's teachings that it could scarcely be separated from his more empirically based musical theories and mathematical demonstrations. In Italy the *harmonices mundi*, as the Pythagorean clockwork of the heavens was called by Latinists, had become a catchword in vogue for practically any learned contemporary debate on the origins and purpose of music.

Against this background it was not surprising that the Doge, although officially maintaining ecclesiastic decorum in matters of heresy, was immediately alerted to the possibility of a *terra incognita* to the west holding fantastic riches. The sensational news that the Genoese arch-enemy overtly conspired with the Turk to gain a commercial advantage over and against Venice in the event of Constantinople's fall was, nevertheless, eclipsed by the realistion that, regardless of this treacherous act of collusion, all terms and conditions of maritime traffic between the Black and the White Seas would henceforth be dictated by the Turk. An overture to the west beyond Gibraltar and the remote Azores islands had to be considered a new possibility. Foscari doubted that Venice, even after his own demise, would ever seriously consider financing such a risky and highly uncertain expedition as to try to sail west of the Azores. But since there was no doubt that the ocean did also extend in that direction, it couldn't be excluded that somebody would attempt to go farther, perhaps even get very rich by so doing. For this reason he was determined to do what he could to prevent the map from ever reaching Genoa. Otherwise – an uncomfortable hunch told him – that city just might give it a try.

After realising how immense all the kingdoms and empires were that the jewel in the crown, Venice, was up against, he decided to appeal both to the Pope and his own people. First of all, the notion that the earth could be round must be officially dismissed as an ancient saga, on par with that of Atlantis, a pagan dream, that's all. Secondly he must personally get hold of the map, even, and he knew this to be a potentially fatal declaration of war, if the Treaty of Turin had to be torn up. There would be an overwhelming Venetian fleet to meet any surviving Genoese; even more importantly, the Venetians could engage them from two directions simultaneously. If only he could get the order out there that the priority now was to obtain the map from commander Longo if and when he tried to escape Constantinople. Though they were well into the month of May, a speedy boat, blessed with good wind and good rowers, could make it to the Peloponnesos in less than a week. If it left now there might still be time to gather the Venetian fleet and send it to ambush the Genoese off Chios, undoubtedly Longo's first port of call once the city had fallen. The Doge felt he had heard enough to conclude, that if the Galatans had been willing to trade Constantinople to the Sultan before he even arrived beneath the city walls, they must be up to something unusually wicked.

He penned a letter to Pope Nicholas in Rome and told him about his suspicion that the Genose were conspiring with the Sultan against Christianity. He also affirmed, that even though Ptolemy might not have been absolutely right about absolutely everything, his cosmology, honoured throughout the ages, was the only astronomic view considered consistent with Catholic dogma. If that foundation was allowed to be questioned, the church might suffer damages it could never repair. It had come to his knowledge, the Doge gravely underlined, that the Genoese, in addition to their treason, were preparing to propagate the heresy of a round earth and to incite European kings to financially back maritime expeditions intent on demonstrating that India and China could more rapidly be reached from Europe by a western than an eastern trade route. If the church did nothing to meet this new threat, its spiritual authority over the same kingdoms and their peoples could soon be but memory.

Foscari took pains not to mention the alleged map showing a land mass acting as a divider in the ocean, separating the far east from the far west. He contented himself to point out to his Eminence, that if the proclamation of a spherical earth ever was to be made, it had to come from within the church itself; any expedition purporting to find evidence for this hypothesis must consequently be sanctified by the papacy. Expressing his will to remain a good and loyal servant to the papal state, emphasising the similarities rather than the differences between it and Venice, Foscari certified that as long as the church wouldn't change its stance in this regard, he would personally make sure that anyone officially holding such views and propagating them among his people was to be treated as a potential heretic and handed over to the Inquisition for questioning.

In reality Foscari had no such thing in mind. Philologists, historians and philosophers were tremendous assets for a city striving to liberate itself from the rigidity of its own inherited theological debate. The show was put on to make sure the Pope would look the other way when news arrived that Venetian ships had routed Genoese vessels in the Aegean and taken commander Longo prisoner on trumped up charges of heresy. Cleverly Foscari also counted on the Pope's willingness to refrain from scrutinising Venice's motives, because if he did abstain from this, he might just find an excellent pretext to refuse to pay for the ships and crews he so recently had commissioned from Genoa, and instead pay his outstanding debt to Venice. Meanwhile the smoke screen would dissipate and everything be declared a mistake. Except that the map now would be in Venetian rather than Genoese possession.

Delighting in these prospects Foscari suddenly saw two tarot cards flash before his inner eye: The Wheel of Fortune and The Tower. It served to remind him that there's nothing stable under the sun and that one person's loss is often another person's gain. He had held on for three decades to the title of Doge, but he was getting tired of it, hoping his son would finally be admitted back and eventually become Doge. After all, it was the highest distinction a Venetian citizen could receive, and Foscari had nothing against institutionalising Dogeship as a hereditary title. The very worst thing he could think of, on the other hand, was for his son to reappear in Venice only to once again be found guilty and condemned by the Ten. "If I could only arrange for my son to be the one bringing the map to Venice…" he thought, "then everything would be different, and we would both come out on top of the wheel." He ultimately reminded himself that his own new palace had been built on the recently demolished remains of an older building known since times immemorial as The Two Towers. Even more important, and indeed symbolic, was the fact that The Two Towers had belonged to the same Francesco Sforza who, by marrying into the Visconti family, had now become Venice's and, thereby, Foscaris' personal enemy. Thus to Foscari, the ominously looking Tarot card depicting the crumbling tower didn't necessarily reflect treason and the impending fate of Constantinople; it could just as well be the sign of his own imminent success. All he needed was one last, favourable *trionfo*. Was there not also a card named The World? Indeed, to lay the foundations of an empire had always been the implicit goal of Venice's expansion on the Italian mainland during the quarter century it had been headed by its charismatic and belligerent leader Francesco Foscari.

Chapter 57

For months the Basilica of Holy Wisdom had remained an enormous dark and inhospitable cavern attended solely by a meagre body of faithful priests. From the moisture gathering under its domed ceiling stalactites had begun to form, conducting water to the floor from an invisible man-made heaven. The church no longer seemed an expression of God's concern for humanity but rather of his magnificent indifference, petrifying time itself into the slimy pillars of a sunken cathedral. But on the evening of May 28, 1453, a miraculous restoration took place uniting the melancholy compassion of the Madonna, the otherworldly joy of the Pantocrator and the inscrutable wisdom of the Holy Emanations, with the indelible and eternal sign of true brotherhood and love.

Wherever one turned in the immense man-made grotto, the twin-imaged marble slabs, the mosaics and the frescoes were lit up by innumerable wax candles gathered from every nook and cranny of the besieged city. From the incense burners columns of fragrant smoke rose towards saints and angels. The basilica, hitherto the cold, damp and unforgiving refuge of a handful of souls, had been magically transformed into one single, all-forgiving instrument of divine embrace. Warm, alive and vibrant like never before, the church spontaneously hosted and witnessed what centuries of elaborate church councils, extensive diplomacy and intense warfare had been unable to achieve: the unity of the western and eastern churches. Threatened by death and extinction, Catholics and Orthodox kneeled down together before the same icons and crucifixes, sharing the same *hostia* of the same sacrificial lamb, participating in each others' rituals and simultaneously speaking the word of God in Greek *and* Latin. Suddenly the cry of centuries for unity and peace, the *Laetantur coeli*, had come to rest in the folds of Mary's blue robe; the message of God's one and only Son finally delivered, turning each and every human being into a child of God. In a moment of despair the true strength of Christianity manifested itself in the universal sentiment of love and forgiveness. And the fact that this general feeling was also saturated with the wailing and sorrow of so many people taking farewell of one another, didn't change it in essence. If anything, it made the unity in Christ even more sincere and real.

In front of the central altar priests of both creeds administered mass together in a single ecumenical service. The Emperor, seated to the left of the altar – the right side being reserved for Christ himself – dispensed forgiveness to each and everyone while atoning for his own sins by asking members of his people to forgive him in their turn for any wrongdoing.

Then the *Kyrie eleison* was intoned. As soon as the priests had set the tone the ancient melody with its invocation of Christ was transmitted from one voice to another. Soon the entire congregation had joined in, and the melismatic meanderings, modulated by a thousand voices, rose like a cloud of sound to the inner rim of the dome, came dripping back down its stalactites, echoing off the walls, only to again reach the ears of each and everyone below. In this way the angelic music was magnified, well nigh appearing as the voice of God himself, indistinctly blending with the tumultuous murmurs, whispers, confessions and prayers of a distressed mankind. Swayed to ecstasy by the music, eager to settle their accounts and escape eternal damnation, people from all walks of life fell passionately in each other's arms, singing, crying, embracing and kissing. Small children were held up to holy icons in desperate attempts to gain divine protection for them. From the many prostrated widows rose the litany of the dead; flowers and garments lay strewn all over the marble floor.

Constantine had the mysterious sensation of being physically present at a last supper. Yes, so uncanny was the similarity to the biblical scene that, involuntarily, he looked out for his own personal Judas. He was of course nowhere to be found. The union of the churches was for ever anathema to him whose sole concern now was to deliver the supreme symbol of Christ to the mongers of the temple. Wearily Constantine's eyes scanned the *paroikia* in the vain hope of finding, against all odds, a conciliatory Gennadi dispensing blessings in its midst. It made his heart heavy having to suspect a fellow pious Greek of actively conspiring not only against his Emperor, but against all of Christianity, because at this particular juncture in time there was indeed a miracle of faith taking place. It was as though a millennium of discord was suspended as people lent their hearts to divine wisdom and their nostrils to the fragrance of the Holy Spirit. "Perhaps it's only when we must die that our eyes are capable of seeing for the first time the true grandeur and beauty of God's creation", Constantine thought while melancholy tears of joy obscured his vision. "And perhaps there is only one God for all of mankind, although we constantly strive to break him up into many so as to better serve our temporal interests. Maybe what we ordinarily call faith is but a perversion of the divine message meant to embrace friend and foe alike. Maybe there is nothing more inimical to life than the need to impose one's own particular creed on one's fellow men, because in the end they are all praying to one and the same, though under a thousand different names."

Constantine saw the thought for a moment hover in the air above him. It then majestically spread its wings and ascended into space. Meanwhile, on the outside of the basilica, a flock of seagulls, silently drifting in from the Marmara, began to encircle the dome, solemnly, and invisibly to any human eye, forming a perpetually moving white crown of thorns, slowly lowering into place to fit the head of Christ.

Chapter 58

The old monk spoke in a low but incisive voice as Iannis bowed down next to him to make sure he received the sacraments together with his final instructions. Earlier he had sent his wife and children ahead to the Hagia Sophia to celebrate mass with the rest of the city's civilian population. He then scurried over to the monastery. He gave the secret sign – three fast poundings on the door followed by three slow ones – and the heavy oak gate was opened to let him inside the old cloister, sparsely lit up by a series of torches casting long and strangely life-like shadows on the marbled floors.

– You know what to do? the monk said.

– I know what to do, Iannis ominously repeated. "Tomorrow I will take my family to the church of the Chora and then complete my mission. Tomorrow is the day when the Saviour shall be received and I shall be the first Christian soul to behold his presence. I acknowledge the responsibility which has been entrusted to me, and I know that, if necessary, I shall defend this task with my life. Even so, all just and faithful human beings will be resurrected by God's grace, death itself being but an ordeal, a needle's eye to pass through before entering the kingdom."

– In the name of the Father, the Son and the Holy Spirit, I bless you and our undertaking to the salvation of all true believers, he said pouring water over Iannis' head. – And remember, whatever happens to me you must press on with your task regardless of circumstances, because your accomplishment is *the* sign that the faithful are prepared to receive him.

– I shall not let you and our brethren down, Iannis responded gravely.

Just as the monk was about to ask him to raise to his feet and be on his way, they heard excited voices and a consistent hammering on the monastery gate. "In the name of Emperor Constantine, open the door or we shall have to bring it down by force". The coarse voice, though obviously still outside the convent, could be heard loud and clear. There was no doubt it meant serious business.

– Go, go now through the secret tunnel. Go and do what you have to do.

– But what about you, what about if you are the one they're after?

– Don't worry, it has been written that during the days preceding the return of our Lord, all righteous men shall suffer persecution from Satan.

– But it's not Satan, I heard them say they come in the name of the Emperor?

– That's exactly how evil he is. He'll try anything to prevent Christ from throwing him right back into flaming Hell. But don't worry about me, I know how to handle him. I'll be alright, but you must go. Now!

Iannis, still in bewilderment, nonetheless precipitated himself through the narrow passage that sprung open through a mechanism hidden behind one of the altars. Before he even had the time to say goodbye to his benefactor, the altar was rolled back in place and he found himself in the complete darkness of the tunnel. Luckily it wasn't the first time he'd used this secret entrance and escape route from the monastery, so he knew what to do, letting his hands and fingers direct him down towards the bifurcation where the tunnel split in two, one way leading down to the harbour, the other to an ingeniously hidden entrance on the inside of the sea wall. Apart from the holy brothers Iannis was the only person to know about the two tunnels and how to get in and out of them. Soon he smelled fresher, less moist air and knew he was approaching the exit. He cautiously rolled the stone, then the bush aside. When he peeked out he could see from a distance that the gate to the monastery had been opened from within. The soldiers being out of sight, Iannis seized the opportunity to steal into the night.

Meanwhile the monk was found kneeling on the floor chastising himself with a thorny whip as he ecstatically regarded the image of the crucified before him.

– In the name of the Emperor of Rome and the Byzantine empire, you, George the Scholar, also known as Gennadi the Monk, are under arrest. You must immediately come with us.

– What is it that I'm accused of? Gennadi calmly replied while a trickle of blood made its way over his back onto the floor.

– That's not for us to discuss. Now get up, we've got a fitting accommodation waiting for you.
– And how do I know you've really been sent by the Emperor and not by Satan.
– Well, for one Satan would probably not have the keys to the dungeons.
– Is that where you're taking me?
– Enough questions. On your feet, monk!

Chapter 59

After having returned from his visit to Giovanni, Constantine sent for Francis. As soon as he had arrived Constantine asked him to accompany him to the Blachernai palace. There they met with a house in mourning. Every member of the household was in tears and Constantine, once again moved by the affection of his subjects, seized the opportunity to embrace all and ask for the remittance of sin and guilt. Then, leaving the sorrowful crowd to their own devices, he passed over the threshold to his old bed chamber and closed the door behind him. He hadn't been sleeping in his own bedroom for the last two months, even though the room, transformed to a military quarter, still held his bed in the alcove. The oil lamp illuminating the two inlaid dolphins was lit, spreading a faint glow onto the walls of the niche. Watching the silent pantomime of the dolphins, who seemed to move in and out of a changing sea, he was suddenly reminded of the last dream he had had in that bed. He remembered having searched for his late wife, ever elusive in that dream, and by awakening he had run his hands through empty bed linen. But there had been something else before that … oh, now it all came back to him, an eerie figure, half man, half beast, with ivy twined around the horns crowning his head like a helmet. Mounted on a chariot behind two fire breathing horses, the driver had stopped in front of him and said: "I am the god of these ancient lands and I have come to claim it for my people. The time is drawing nearer and the sign shall be a purple cloud rising to heaven." Then the earth had split open and the apparition disappeared.

"The purple cloud we saw all right", Constantine thought, "but what about the strange centaur? Even if demonic, Mehmet's still a man worshipping a single deity, not some pagan monster. So who could this figure possibly have been?"

Ransacking his memory he came to recall a legend of old Thrace, according to which all the land from the Rhodopes mountains to the hills of Anatolia had once been the sacred realm of the pagan god Dionysos. Associated with wine and sensual ecstasy he had sometimes been depicted as half man, half goat. As far as Constantine remembered, the dream figure's head had been crowned with ram-like horns and his feet had resembled hooves. But wasn't that also the figure of the devil? And didn't Dionysos meet his death at the hands of giants tearing him to pieces, only to subsequently resurrect in a manner similar to the Lord himself? Perhaps, perhaps not. Unable to clarify the matter to himself, the exhausted Emperor leaned his head against one of the pillows and instantly fell asleep, dreaming of nothing. Two hours later, as convened, Francis knocked at the door, awakening his master. For a moment Constantine didn't recognise his own bedroom and looked at its painted walls in utter bewilderment. He then realised where he was and prepared to face the night.

The two of them mounted their horses and rode along the wall, stopping every here and there to exchange words with the men posted all along its meandering back. Constantine encouraged each and everyone to bravely endure the coming onslaught. He in turn received signs of loyalty from the soldiers, many of whom were positioned in the tightly secured towers from which no one could now enter or exit. At the hour of the first rooster cry the two men found themselves at the so called Shoemaker Tower where they dismounted. Through the darkness they heard a consorted murmur, the sound, as it were, of a thousand voices, like the continuous breaking of the sea against a reef. The guards here told them that it had been like this since nightfall, and that the constant din came from all the war machines the enemy was dragging into position. Along the coast too the enemy ships were in motion, and over the hills next to Galata guns were moved to achieve maximum striking ability against Greek ships and the walls defending the Horn.

Standing on the wall, out of hearing from the soldiers on the towers, Constantine turned to Francis,

– At last I have only one person to ask forgiveness from, and that is you my dearest, oldest friend and most loyal servant to our millennial empire. But it's not as your Emperor that I want you to speak your mind. It's me, your childhood friend and playmate, your true brother, who asks you: in case we shall not meet again in this life, is there anything we still need to sort out? Dear Francis, I beg you an answer.

Over the years George Francis had grown so accustomed to regarding himself as the mere extended arm of the imperial system, that he at first couldn't recall any of his more personal feelings in relation to his master. Once upon a time, in the gardens and streets of Mistra, as innocent children, they had played hide and seek together, discovered rivers and sources, climbed mountains, wrestled, fenced and swam in the sea. Although different in temperament, and at times separated in space from one another, they had always remained close friends. Still, Francis felt that when Constantine became Emperor, he had to move on to a plane, the heights of which were forbidden to Francis himself. No matter how close they had once been, Constantine was now *also* the embodiment of God's will and was to be revered as such. Nonetheless, there was one thing that had bothered him, and he thought it might be just as well to get that one last thing off his chest – just in case… So he said,

– Dear Constantine, and please forgive me for addressing you as such and not with all your customary titles. There really is one thing, and only that one thing which I would like you to explain to me, and that's why, when you had me summoning all the captains and higher ranked officers to debate how to best counter the Sultan's move over land, you would not invite me to sit in on the subsequent discussion. That's something I've really been thinking about, because I think … when I think about it … that it really did hurt my feelings.

Constantine looked Francis in the eyes. Moist-eyed he then broke the silence,

– But why didn't you just say you wanted to participate in the discussion? I didn't think it was of any importance to you.

– Of any importance? The Sultan moves his fleet over land into the Horn, posing a deadly threat to our own ships and harbour, and you think it's not going to be of "any importance" to me?

– But I never intended to keep you out of that. Of course you would have been welcome to participate.

– I understand, but you didn't actually ask me, and my feeling is, and was, that I wanted *you* to want *me* to be there! You know that I'd do anything for you, because I always loved you. Unintentionally or not, you shoved me to the side, and this is what I can't understand. I would have been ashamed for the rest of my life if I had met with your disapproval. That's why I didn't dare to ask.

Truly, Constantine had not had in mind to exclude Francis from participating in that urgent discussion. But it was also true that he didn't consider him much of a military strategist. Constantine now realised his friend already knew this to be the reason why he never asked him to be present. He also realised that he might never get the chance to repair the damage by acting differently in the future. Instantly he dropped the pretense and went straight to the heart of the matter,

– Dearest Francis, will you forgive me my negligence? I never meant to humiliate you in any way, you must know that, don't you?

Sensing a profound relief in the making Francis slowly and pensively answered,

– If that's what you say, I believe you. But please also remember that I have always loved and admired you. I know you will never, ever fall short of yourself. And that's why… that's why…

He didn't manage to finish the phrase. Instead Constantine stretched out his arms to help Francis get off the ground to which he had fallen in reverence. Once standing, both irresistibly fell in each other's arms, shedding heavy tears while silently closing the last page of a book they had been writing in together for so long. Francis experienced a moment of unmitigated bliss as he recalled that while staying in Trapezunt exactly two years earlier, in the early morning of May 29, 1451, he had had a dream in which the Emperor raised him up and kissed his eyes, profoundly grateful for his advice in matters matrimonial.

Regaining his composure Francis felt it would only be fair to ask Constantine to speak up in case he also had sentiments unexpressed. It seemed unlikely to Francis that Constantine, who had always the authority to speak his mind on issues as they occurred, would have anything to add to the protocol. But after having reflected for a moment, he said,

– I thank God that I have always taken all your political advice into serious consideration. On so many occasions you have been absolutely right, and I would have strayed had I not heeded your carefully argued recommendations. Still I think there was one decisive moment when I should have let my own spontaneous inclination overrule your well reasoned objections, and that was on the question of marriage. Of course, with hindsight it becomes so much easier to see and evaluate mistakes. Notwithstanding the advantage which time itself bestows on us, I still believe we made a serious mistake by recalling the marriage offer made to the House of Foscari in Venice, quite especially by letting it be generally known that the daughter of the head of a near legendary Republic was not sufficiently noble to be accepted as a bride to the Byzantine Emperor. This rumour alone was enough to permanently mobilise the Doge against us, and I'm sorry to say this might be the decisive reason why help from the Venetians to this date has not been forthcoming. Foscari simply wants his revenge. It's unfortunate, but I'm sure it's the case. It was perhaps the one moment when I shouldn't have listened to you. Now I must ask you to forgive me for doing so anyway.

Francis, taken off guard, was dumbfounded. Though he realised that boasting of the Emperor's incomparable superiority in rank – while his actual dominions had been reduced to little more than a shrunken head on a pole – was inappropriate, Francis had ever since tried to rid himself of his gnawing sense of having committed an irreparable diplomatic *faux pas*. Now, in the hour of destiny, that same blunder was used to ruthlessly poke him in the same eyes which seconds ago had received a kiss. Involuntarily, he mumbled something to the effect of "yes, of course, and I'm so sorry", but his mind was all confused and his heart on fire. Quickly wrapping ceremony around this freshly opened wound, he prepared to respectfully withdraw and leave his friend and master alone. Divining his intention, while simultaneously sensing the devastating impact his last statement had made on the speechless secretary of state, Constantine took two steps towards him exclaiming,

– Please, my brother, stay with me here for a while, stay and wake until the rooster announces the fateful hour! Can you feel the fragrance of the flowers in the air; do you remember the olive groves of our childhood?

Enthused he turned away, dreamily facing the breeze from the sea, gazing out over the dark expanses. Then he closed his eyes, envisaging the lovely hills, meadows, towns, churches and monasteries of their native Peloponessos. Eventually he saw appearing before the inner eye his first love. Feeling the need to ask Francis if he, per chance, remembered her as well, he finally turned round. But when he opened his eyes Francis was gone, as if swallowed by the earth itself, and the only answer he got to his question was from a strangely vibrant voice deep inside himself: "To the encounter ahead you can only invite – yourself".

Only now did Constantine understand that he had forgotten to bring the question of Gennadi's treason and arrest to his secretary's attention.

Chapter 60

The soldiers, immobilised in attentive postures, appeared mere silhouette figures on a painted wall. The night, for all its frenetic movement, seemed curiously two-dimensional, like a tapestry, an embroidered commemoration of some impersonal yet vaguely familiar scene. So far Constantine was only dimly aware of the majestic historical prefiguration of his predicament, but as Francis' abrupt departure began to sink in, an overwhelming sense of alienation seized him. At first it was no more than a sensation of increased weight and gravity. He felt his limbs grow stiffer and heavier, then his head began to droop. Over his shoulder it was as though a yoke had been placed and he gradually slid down the side of the wall until he reached a sitting position, his legs stretched out. Towering above him the richly attired mare seemed immobilised too. Looking back into the city he recognised beneath him the shadows of the imperial olive grove. Beyond the olive mound were the imperial vineyards. But olives and wine no longer held power over his mind, clouded as it was by an ever deepening sense of solitude: "Eventually, and contrary to every promise and reassurance, they will all abandon me, just as you, my dearest and most trusted brother, have left me when I needed you the most."

The thought, dark and bitter like vinegar, had a voice of its own, emanating from the immense cavity once the seat of his heart. Now it was an echo chamber, a tomb erected inside his chest, in which all voices of the past slowly died out, depositing on the bottom of his soul a sterile layer of futility: "Oh my God, how did it ever come to pass? Why wasn't there a timely way out of all this? What did we not do, what did we not try, and how did we fail to show You, Lord of all Things Created, Light of the World, repentance, devotion and obedience? Where and when have our deeds, sacrifices and sacraments been displeasing in your eyes? The union of the churches – You know there was nothing I could do to prevent that from happening? Without it we would have stood even more isolated in the world. Yet it has been Your will to chastise and punish us. For what? How can you punish us without even letting us know what we're punished for? Oh Lord, where and when have we failed you, and why is it, that in your infinite love and wisdom, You are sending us the Turks as a swarm of so many grasshoppers to devastate our venerable city and allow the greatest, most glorious church in all of Christendom to be desecrated? Please forgive me my pride and for not understanding why you want this to happen. Is there, perhaps, a truth to the rumour spreading through the city like fire, that you're actually intent on sending your Son back to this world and put an end to men's disunion and wickedness? Is that what it is? And have I had your inspired prophet and harbinger of the *parousia* arrested just as Pilate had Jesus apprehended? Am I thus unwittingly simultaneously the Judas and the wicked judge of this drama? What horrible irony that I shall perhaps never know whether Gennadi really betrayed us, or if for all eternity I shall be held accountable for opposing your inscrutable will!

"Alas no, regardless of the circumstances it's but a mirage. Gennadi may be guilty, or he may be innocent. In either case Jesus' second coming is not for now. It's just hope in its most illusive and impotent form. Insofar as it turns the citizens into fatalists, it weakens their fighting spirit. So whatever the truth, if Gennadi has been nourishing the belief that the end of days are near, in one way or another he shall have to face the consequences for not keeping such heresy to himself. That's all I have to say in regard to him for the time being. But then again there is of course the very real risk that he's been counteracting us all along, and has taken steps to actively help the Sultan to enter the city. We've had every single gate checked and double checked tonight, but to what avail if traitors are among us?

"I'd prefer not to think about that now, as I must ask You, my Lord and Master, to give me the strength to endure what I can no longer change. Yet, oh Lord, I have never felt so lonely in all my life. If you ask me: "Are you scared"? I would be a liar not to admit that although I'm prepared to die, death itself seems uncomfortably close at hand. Oh Lord, is there really no way out of this? Shall I have to empty the cup filled with hemlock to the dregs? Will you not help us to repel the enemy and save your city? Are you in earnest about letting it all go and leaving us at the mercy of the blood-thirsty tyrant, or are you only dangling the executioner's sword in front of us like you had Abraham swinging the knife before Isaac?

"And what about me? Did you ever think twice about the hardships you have visited upon me ever since I was crowned in your name? You gave me two wives and you took them away. You left me no heirs, and now you want to end the life of a childless father and leader of a destitute but nonetheless deeply devoted people. God Almighty, I have never betrayed you. I have never uttered your name in vain. I have observed the rituals, honoured the saints and to each and to everyone tried to give his due. But You don't answer. You don't have to. Because You're God and I'm just a man. But what about if I too were your Son, once begotten, never created? Oh blasphemy, oh my God – as the starless night moves towards its inevitable close, I see things clearly. Not as I would like them to be, nor even as You would like them to be, but as they really are… Oh night surrounded by darkness! There really is nothing out there. Nothing whatsoever, and we are but victims of our designs. Oh God … Oh God, why hast Thou forsaken me?

Constantine, feeling a terrible weight crushing him to the ground, managed to turn round and embrace a stone. Clasping his hands round it, he remained dumbstruck and silent. At last, at the hour of the second rooster cry, he was brought back to himself.

– I can fight the Turk, and today I shall kill as many of them as I can, he muttered, – but I can't fight You. Do with me as You please. No, not the way I want it, but in the way You see fit. Finally… finally … Nothing remains to be said but this: In thy hands, implacable Master, do I place my soul. Amen.

Moments later Constantine felt the strength return to his limbs and his mind clear. The only weight he was carrying was that of his cuirass. He adjusted it, mounted the horse and road along the walls to reach his commanding position next to Giustiniani. As soon as he was on his way, the frozen silhouettes of the towers began to move again.

Chapter 61

The onslaught, accompanied by drums, torches and gunfire ripping the curtain of darkness to shreds, was vehement beyond imagination. Spurred on by their commanding officers and mercilessly mowed down from behind by their own at any sign of retreat, no matter how involuntary, the frantically yelling bashibazouks of the Ottoman army hit the walls in one wave after the other. Virtually unprotected and armed only with bows, scimitars and slings they scurried across the now thoroughly filled in moat and raised their ladders to overcome the stockades that the defenders had erected wherever the original wall had been demolished. But once they were within reach of crossbows, archers, spear throwers, swordsmen, guns, muskets, culverins, liquid pitch and Greek fire, the defenders showed them no mercy. Ladders were swung back into space, balancing for a brief moment in the air before crashing onto the ground, breaking the bones of those holding on to them. Though perishing like flies under a swatter, the enemy was so numerous that some of them succeeded all the same to reach the battlements. Once there they were literally cut in halves by Varangian axe men and sword fighters furiously forcing their heavy blades through their heads. The blood from severed necks spurted in fountains, soaking the defenders from top to toe. Other attackers were welcomed with Greek fire which stuck to them like glue. Impossible to remove, it slowly burned them to death, and the agonising cries of the helplessly incinerated added a gruesome melody to the relentless racket from enemy pipes, castanets, horns and drums. The bass line was upheld by the big bear and her cubs. From the city itself the uninterrupted pealing of church bells alerted every remaining man and woman to their duty, while those too old and too young to help out sought refuge in the churches. Meanwhile, without any consideration for their own men, the Turks fired their guns right into the melee, oftentimes reducing an entire group of climbing bashibazouks to a pulp. The screams of dying men, the smell of blood mixed with that of gunpowder, pulverised stone and tar, the flames from torches and gun barrels, completed the inferno.

 Seeing the enemy come on to them like this, there were more than just one or two defenders wetting themselves. Though well accustomed to the fighting conditions, trained and hardened to withstand any military threat, the sight of so many wild warriors filling the moat like a stampede of panicking buffalo nonetheless weakened their knees, shrank their bladders and made them gasp for air. When they finally regained their breath, sporadically indulging in the vain hope that the withdrawal of these savages after two hours of uninterrupted slaughter spelled the end of the offensive, the scene was set for an even more terrifying spectacle.

Fighting shoulder to shoulder on the stockade between the gate of Charisius and that of St Romanus, Constantine, together with his most trusted nobles, his cousin Theophilus Palaiologos, the brave but elderly Don Francisco of Toledo, likewise claiming kinship with the Emperor, his old brother in arms John Dalmata and, last but not least, Giovanni Giustiniani Longo, again directing the defence in an upright position after having been carried to the battle front on a stretcher, now witnessed regiments of Anatolians rush in to fill the void left behind by the disorderly retreating irregulars. Unlike these hordes, the Anatolians were not only superbly disciplined but also adequately equipped with breast plates and helmets to protect themselves against the hail of missiles awaiting them. But although their task was hardly easier than that of their unfortunate forerunners, it now became clear to the Greeks and Italians that the attack of the bashibazouks had been a mere preamble destined to wear them out.

For all their discipline and bravery, the concerted attack of Ishak Pasha's regiments in the end proved no more successful than that of the irregulars. Like the former they were either cut down before they even had a chance to reach the upper parts of walls and stockades, or they did actually manage to crawl over the ramparts in small groups only to be quickly surrounded by defenders instantly hacking them to pieces. Pushed back into the growing piles of corpses below the stockades they presented a formidable obstacle to their own as every dead or wounded man was now in the way of the one coming up from below. Then, when the Anatolians too were on the verge of withdrawing, a terrific roar from the raging mama bear announced the arrival of another giant demolition ball. Seconds later a considerable portion of the stockade beneath Giovanni and Constantine gave away, sending barrels, human limbs and sacks of sand into the air. A thick dust cloud, momentarily enveloping the carnage, added to the confusion. The Turks quickly seized the opportunity and before the defenders even had the time to regroup, hundreds of Anatolians managed to climb the pyramids of their own dead and enter the area between inner and outer walls.

As soon as Giustiniani realised that the fire breathing dragon had managed to wedge his head between the walls, he shouted to Constantine to summon his men and rush over to the breach to support the suddenly outnumbered defenders desperately trying to close the gap. There was not a single moment to lose as the Anatolians now also attacked the Greeks from the rear. Throwing himself onto a horse

Giustiniani, followed by his Genoese, rode straight into the many Turks about to fall upon the defenders from behind. He was quickly surrounded and the enemy tried to seize hold of the horse's reins and straps and pull it down. Giustiniani, fighting for his life, swung his sword among their numbers and brought down one after the other. Still, had not his Genoese men finally succeeded to make way through their ranks, the Anatolians eventually would have got the better of him. It really was a matter of seconds only, then sneaking up unseen from behind, one of the Turks carefully aimed his crossbow at Giustiniani's neck at a distance of only six yards. He would surely have killed him instantly had he not, when about to pull the trigger, been pierced by the first Italian javelin seemingly appearing from nowhere. Turning around at the sound of an arrow whizzing by his helmet, Giustiniani first beheld torrents of blood spurting forth from the bowman's mouth, and then a spear on the end of which a human heart was still throbbing. Moments later the Genoese managed to close in on their leader. While protecting him they gradually forced the Turks down the stairways into the peribolos. At this moment, Don Francesco of Toledo, seeing what was about to happen, quickly detached a force from his part of the wall presently in no immediate danger. With his men he rushed down another steep staircase like a whirlwind, while from the opposite direction John Dalmata and his heroic Peleponnesians did exactly the same. The result was that once the Turks had been driven down into the peribolos they were trapped. Although the breach above them was still under heavy attack, Constantine's presence there gave every man superhuman strength. Indefatigable, he delivered mortal blows to every new head and body emerging from below, inspiring his men to follow his example. Luckily the blow to the stockade had tipped good sized stones inside the walls, with which the defenders now wreaked havoc among their foes. Eventually the outnumbered force on the breach managed to bring the surging enemy flood to a halt, even forcing it to withdraw, while the remaining Turks in the peribolos were quickly reduced.

Realising that death was only moments away the doomed Turks fought like wounded lions. Although they perished to the last man, they didn't leave the Greeks and Italians unscathed. A good number of defenders also lost their lives and John Dalmata himself, always at the cutting edge, was seriously wounded. Barely alive he was found under a pile of Turkish corpses resembling a monstrous hedgehog, so many were the upright standing spears and arrows adorning him. In the end, and garnished with the odd Greek and Italian, about three hundred Turks lay dead while the defenders made short history of those who in contortions and spasms still betrayed signs of life. The second major attack, miraculously it seemed, had been averted as well, but the prize paid by the defenders an hour before dawn was exorbitant. They were thoroughly exhausted. More than anything else they needed some time, however brief, to recuperate and prepare themselves for what was to follow. That respite was not to be given them.

Chapter 62

Giovanni and his men had fought with a bravery equal to that of the Spartans at Thermopyle. Though in every moment inches and seconds away from death they had held their lines and twice forced the enemy to withdraw. Giovanni himself had felt the wing of death graze his head and knew there was no certainty he would survive the day. Yet a deep-seated feeling told him that for the sake of his wife and child death was not an option. No matter what he'd simply have to make it. Knowing that Felicia had by now been safely conducted out of the city and was on her way to Chios, he felt the strength of a conviction overpowering even mortal fatigue. He was lucky not to know the truth, since that knowledge could only have made him the victim of invisible qualms instead of tangible arrows.

Because at the very moment of the Turks' second withdrawal Felicia was not at all on her way to Chios. She wasn't even outside the city. In spite of Giovanni's admonitions that she'd leave with that last Venetian ship, she had made a firm, albeit secret decision, to stay and help the citizens. Guided by the furious roar of the cannons and the pale light of dawn, she had taken it upon herself to run across the city from the walls of Petrion towards the gates in the Lycus valley where she knew her husband and his men was fighting for their lives. If he were to die today she was going to share his fate. It was a resolution as vainly heroic as it was foolhardy, because even if she would have reached the inner wall, she would have found its gates and passageways locked, as this had been ordered by Constantine to prevent desertion and any conspiracy from within. Discovered by the defenders the news would quickly be carried to Giovanni, who could then do nothing but once again worry about how to also get her out of there. That concern, more than anything else, would have seriously hollowed his motivation to remain a living target.

Felicia had just reached the western side of the Forum of Theodosius when she was intercepted by a woman fleeing with two young children. In the darkness of the square they practically ran into one another.

Watch your step! the mother shouted as they nearly collided. Felicia instinctively stepped back trying to bypass her. But then the unknown woman took a second look at her, exclaiming: "But you're that Turkish princess, ain't you?". Felicia quickly nodded and continued her way, but the woman, dressed as a fisherman's wife, wouldn't let her go. She grabbed her hand and said,

– And where do you think you're goin'?

– What business of yours is it!

– I'm makin' it mine!

– Let me go! Felicia made an effort to cut loose from her grip but the other woman was stronger and kept her where she was.

– You're not foolish enough to run to the walls, are ye? she said staring intently into Felicia's eyes. – You ain't thinking you'd be of some help over there, is you? she continued as Felicia refused to answer.

– I can see it in your eyes that you're about to do something very stupid. But I'll tell you what. That will only be the end of you and the man you love.

– Let go of me!

– No, ma'm, you're much to pretty to die for nothin', and that Turkish animal ain't gonna spare you. He'll put you on a skewer together with that Orhan and roast you alive over slow fire, he will. Now, you come with me.

– Why should I come with you?

– Because I'm the only one who knows a way out a here. Because I alone can save your life.

– We can still win!

– No we can't.

– How do *you* know?

– Listen, there ain't no more time for arguing. This is the end, come with me.

– I most definitely will not! Felicia pulled herself away, dodging the other woman. In the same instant she received a violent slap in her face and reeled back. When opening her smarting eyes, the fierce unknown woman stood yelling over her,

– I'm not letting you go, ye know!
– You will regret this!
– No ma'm, I won't! You leave me with no choice. Because you will either be dead today or you'll be grateful to me for the rest of your life. So get goin! I've got kids to take care of too.

The slap did have the advantageous result of making Felicia realise she really was in a hysterical state. Although still in shock, something told her that regardless of the strange woman's horrible manners, she had to trust her.

– Where are we going? she said, wiping an involuntary tear off her cheek – the slap had been sharp alright.

– You'll see.

Felicia, who had been running westward in an attempt to reach Giovanni fighting on the walls above the Fifth Military Gate, was now dragged along with the children towards the Contoscalion harbour on the Marmara shore. It was only a five hundred yard walk but the streets were littered with beams, stones and gravel. They advanced with difficulty, having to help the smaller children to overcome obstacles and prevent them from being hit by falling debris. Meanwhile cannon balls whizzed through the air randomly crashing into buildings around them. Here and there houses became giant torches as flaming arrows dipped in burning tar fastened themselves to thatched roofs. The suddenly erupting bonfires, terrifying though they were, had the advantage of illuminating the streets sufficiently to guide them along. At daybreak they arrived before the gate of the monastery only to find it solidly shut. Even though they pounded the gate with lumps of stone and cried out for help, the monks didn't answer their calls. This was not because they refused to do so, but because they were all deployed on the sea walls and unable to hear what was going on at their gate through the roar of the guns. To Felicia this spelled the end of all hope and she fell down in despair. But once again the other woman forced her to get up. She then led her and the children towards some shrubbery next to the wall some fifty yards to the left of the monastery gate. There she bent a few branches to the side and pointed to a particularly large stone in the wall.

– Help me, she said, and began pushing the stone inward with her left shoulder. The bewildered Felicia put her hands next to the woman's head, reinforcing the pressure, and suddenly, as by magic, the slab began to move inward revealing a tunnel.

– Take this, the woman said, and pulled out a torch out of a long goatskin bag and handed it to Felicia. She then bent forward and with great skill struck fire to a bundle of tinder with a flint stone. Applied to glowing tinder, kindled with thin dry branches, the torch rapidly caught on fire, providing them with enough light to illuminate their way. With her feet the woman pushed the slab back in place, thus sealing the entrance from inside the cave. The tunnel roof was high enough for the children to move along in upright position, but the two women frequently had to bow their heads to advance. Nowhere was there enough room for two people to stand shoulder to shoulder. As the tunnel led downwards it became more moist and hefty drops of water occasionally threatened to extinguish the torch. They arrived at a bifurcation in the subterranean system. The woman told Felicia that if they continued to the left they would reach the harbour, while the tunnel to the right would take them inside the monastery. – Eventually we might have to get down this way, she explained, – but for now we must try to reach the monastery.

They arrived at the far end of the tunnel and faced a slab similar to the one blocking the entrance. A large iron ring was fastened to it. When she turned it half way round and then pulled, the stone gave away and they emerged under a grand altar from which a second slab was opened with the same kind of device. They crawled out and found themselves inside the same chapel which Iannis had used as a transit when escaping the soldiers sent out to arrest Gennadi and himself the previous evening. The woman told Felicia to stay put while she peeked out through the door separating the chapel from the aisles and the inner courtyard. When she couldn't detect a single living soul, she returned saying: – For now we're safe, but we must be ready to use that tunnel again at the shortest notice. Felicia, still amazed at the transformation around her, just stared at the unknown woman and her children. Finally she opened her mouth and said, each word resounding like a clapper slowly tapping the bell: – Who…are…you?

Chapter 63

Poor Iannis! He was a good man, always planning ahead. His Achilles heel, however, was the inverse side of the very same talent which made him such great company among friends and a hero in the eyes of the children: the ability to tell an incredible story as though he had lived through every moment of it himself. And this was not just an aptitude, because Iannis, through the ardor of his imagination, could identify with a person to the point where his own destiny and that of the protagonist became one. Now, at the end of the eleventh hour, he identified with Christ. In the church of Chora – like a smaller and more intimate version of the grand Sophia, a haven for childlike credulity and pious faith – votaries had gathered in the inner sanctuary intently staring at the mosaic representation of Adam and Eve forcibly led out of Paradise, not by the archangel Michael, but by the Saviour himself. It was believed that just as Christ, being the eternally preexisting Son, once forced the children of God out of Paradise, he was destined to come back and open it for them again. Iannis was among the believers, but when all gazes, as though carried aloft by the monks' incantations, soared towards the ceiling, the moment came when he must discreetly slip through the sacristy and make his way towards the nearby Gate of Charisius.

The walls around this gate were not only the highest, they were also built on the highest hill of the city. From this vantage point he would have a view along the entire stretch from the Marmara to the Horn. It was in fact the only point on the walls allowing such an overview. But it was still dark outside, the streets abandoned, and the only reason for Iannis to climb the many stairs leading up to the battlements was to get an idea of when and from what direction Christ would suddenly appear and demand entrance to his promised city. When he got closer the amount of missiles darting through the air steadily increased, and he clearly sensed how easily he might get hit by one. Directly beneath the wall this incandescent rain was less intense since the very height of the bulwark alone forced the enemy artillery to either aim at the walls or much farther into the city. Indeed, there was a constant subdued thumping sound from cannon balls hitting stone. Iannis, his heart jumping higher and higher as he climbed the stairs, heard the sound of guns and chilling war cries intensify. At last he looked down into the dark city from its highest elevation. One false step and he would instantly be hurtling to the ground. Leaning on to the wall of the battlement was hardly a better idea, since it was under constant fire. Still, Iannis went down on all four and slowly approached one of the gun openings. Peeking out he realised there was only a handful of soldiers manning the inner towers, manoeuvering cannons which from this elevation had some lethal impact on the nonetheless relentlessly advancing enemy. Beneath them, on the battlements of the inner walls, there were hundreds of soldiers engaged in battle. But at this particular point of the inner wall, midway between two towers, there was nobody present except him. Gazing unseen into the valley he had the privilege of witnessing a truly apocalyptic scene.

Along the walls, lights from the many torches paved the way for attackers who like frantic rats sought a way to overcome the obstacle in their way. The walls were under assault almost everywhere, but the deeper the terrain descended into the Lycus valley, the denser became the fiercely burning clouds of enemy warriors. Partly supported, partly massacred by intense gunfire emanating from the Maltepe hill – practically on the same level as the Gate of St Romanus but ideally placed to inflict substantial damage on the lower lying walls around the Fifth Military Gate – one Turkish battalion after the other crashed onto the bricks and fell back wounded, dying. Intermittently the sky and the land was lit up by the gun explosions, showing the moat, no, the entire Lycus valley littered with corpses. Over mountains of bleeding flesh, new packs of rats renewed the efforts to reach over the walls while being mowed down from behind at any sign of hesitation. And as soon as they reached the walls, they received a warm welcome from Greek and Italian soldiers who knew they now only had their own lives left to lose.

The fighting around the Military Gate itself was unbelievably intense. Iannis strained his eyes to determine whether or not the fortifications were still intact and the enemy kept at bay, but he couldn't really tell, the distance was too great. What he did see, though, was the impeccable formation of thousands of Janissaries still waiting on the surrounding hills to be called into action. Somewhere among the gun racks on the Maltepe Hill he suddenly thought he saw the Sultan's purple turban being lit up by an explosion; a pale determined face, with two dark eyes, like those of a predator not for a moment letting his prey out of his sight. Iannis, feeling the oppressive presence of Antichrist, looked over the city to the east to find the first hues of dawn, but the eastern horizon was still plunged in darkness. Then, again turning to the west, he suddenly beheld the intensely luminous cross against the dark sky and the lapidary words, not uttered in a thousand years, reached him through the aeons: "In this sign thou shalt be victorious!".

The light was so intense that it forced Iannis to shade his eyes with his palm, but the message was clear and unequivocal. Christ was arriving. There was not another moment to lose.

Dangerously close to falling into the abyss, Iannis set off down the stairs again. Reaching ground he directed his feet towards the Blachernai palace. It wouldn't take him long to get there. But the problem remained how to find the small gate Gennadi had spoken of. Iannis had been in its vicinity some days earlier to acquaint himself with the surroundings, but he had only seen it from above the inner wall opposite the postern in the outer wall in which it was located. Its name was Kerkaporta. Though small it had a special significance in the city's history as it had often been used by children in religious processions celebrating Christ the infant. Since all the gates of the inner walls had been locked on the Emperor's orders, there was no way he could reach it through any of the regular gates. But Gennadi had told him there was a way through the palace itself leading directly inside the postern. Once there Iannis had but one task, to remove the bars blocking the door and leave it ajar for Christ to enter.

Seeing the characteristic silhouette of the Palace of the Porphyrogenitus, placed at an angle high above the ground, Iannis knew he was closing in on his target. The Blachernai palace then emerged, dark and unforgiving. There were no guards to prevent him from approaching it. At first astonished, then convinced he was guided by divine providence, Iannis found the main entrance open and stole into the court yard. Above him he heard the yelling from the Greek soldiers under the command of Lucas Notaras, making sure no one would get over the walls at this sensitive juncture. This provided Iannis with the opportunity he needed. At the far western end of the courtyard, just as Gennadi had told him, there was a door in the wall. It first led into a chapel but a second door, located behind and beneath the altar, led to another secret courtyard. From there steps led down under the peribolos and there was a passageway there, some fifty feet long. At the end of this, steps again led up into the postern. Iannis found himself standing inside a vault directly in front of the Kerkaporta, barred with three solid beams of oak running through iron angles. He dismantled them and then pushed the door ajar, waiting with pounding heart for Jesus to appear so that he could throw himself to his feet and be the first to welcome him back on earth. Iannis found it almost impossible to believe that divine providence had chosen him and nobody else to be instrumental in the world's salvation. This was the greatest moment of his life.

On the outside, some Turkish soldiers, led by the faint lights of dawn were alerted to what they at first thought must be either an illusion or a trap. However, it could be seen how one of the smaller gates in the wall was suddenly opened, then closed again, and then… well, they weren't sure, but it certainly looked as though the small gate had not been quite properly closed again. Another wave of attackers sustained heavy casualties as, once again, they tried to approach and climb the walls around the Blachernai palace. But there were some of them who nevertheless reached the gate. Amazed they confirmed that it was actually open. Iannis, overhearing the commotion from behind the door, knew that the clamour he heard and the excitement of many voices heralded His arrival. He stretched out his arms to welcome the Lord. Then the door swung open, and though Iannis saw neither the saviour nor the cross itself, he did have time to glimpse eternity as one of the angels pierced his mind with a dazzling array of light entering his forehead only to escape through the other end of his brain. Lifeless Iannis fell to the ground while a detachment of Turkish soldiers worked themselves through and began to spread in the space between the walls. In the first rays of sun the crescent moon was suddenly seen fluttering above one of the major defence tower. Like a fire the rumour then spread along and inside the walls: "The city has fallen! The city has fallen!"

In spite of this Lucas Notaras and his men soon managed to isolate this detachment of Turkish soldiers and were about to kill it to the last man while simultaneously closing the haphazardly open gate, when a handful of Turks had managed to find the same subterranean passage as the one used by Iannis. Moments later they found themselves on top of the Blachernai palace where they proudly hoisted their flag. Still only moments after that, they too had been surrounded and liquidated and their loathed flag was rapidly brought down. But, alas, the rumour had been carried off on wings. Too far away to be called back it quickly ascended the heights of Charisius.

In the very moment it arrived there, Giustiniani, soaked in sweat and blood, looked up towards the tower of Charisius expecting to see the Lion of St Mark triumphantly appear above the ramparts in the early morning light. He was confused by its absence. It only meant a few seconds of inattention on his part, but those were enough to allow a Turkish soldier still surviving in the moat to aim a culverin at him and pull the trigger. The shot rendered his left arm more or less useless. And it was from this moment onwards, fearing the worst from the absent Venetian standard on the most crucial lookout post of the Theodosia wall, that Giustiniani began to lose heart. Suddenly he felt blood streaming down his body. A chilling sensation seized hold of him from head to toe. Sounds and movements became strangely remote. As if in a dream he heard an Italian voice shout: "It's over, it's each and every man for himself!"

Had Giustiniani been quite himself he would have re-assumed leadership, regardless of the wound, and made sure the line remained intact. Apparently even the last Janissary attack, headed by a Goliath-sized warrior answering to the name of Hasan, had not been able to break their resistance, and there really was no reason for them to consider flight and surrender. But something had happened to him, something that had broken even his iron will. "Where am I? he thought. "Am I already dead?".

It was only now that Constantine became aware that his general had been wounded. Knowing that without Giustiniani visibly in the lead, the utterly strained defence line would actually break, he rushed to his side and urged him to get on his feet and show himself to his men. In spite of Constantine's desperate attempts to reanimate his fighting spirit, Giustiniani, in a voice that no longer carried conviction, asked to be put on a stretcher and carried away. For Constantine, unable to persuade the man to stand up and continue the fight, the truth that had dawned on him on the olive mount finally sank in. The end was no longer near. It was here.

– You bastard! You coward! I knew you would betray me, I knew it! He shouted after the man carried down the stairs to the battlements on a stretcher.

– I did everything I could! Giustiniani shouted back. – But look, the Venetian standard on the Charisius is gone. It can only mean one thing. The defence has given in there!

– I can't see the enemy up there! Constantine replied.

– Stay long enough, and you will! Now, for God's sake, give the order to have the gate opened for me!

– You know I have to refuse!

– I swear to you, I'll be back as soon as I can.

– If you leave there will be nothing to return to, and you know it!

– Let me through!

– I utterly refuse!

The shouting between the two men continued for a while, but through the din neither could hear the other as the distance separating them grew larger. Constantine's reappearance on the walls may have bestowed new courage among the Greeks, but just as he had predicted, the disappearance of Giustiniani caused the remaining Genoese to waver. In spite of hastily renewed imperial promises of glory, gold and land, they began to back away from the breach. When that happened, the thinly spun silver thread lining the walls broke. Although the Greeks still fought on valiantly, they could no longer withstand the pressure. The Turks, unstoppably, poured into the moat, over the breach and into the peribolos where they quickly brought up the rams destined to break through the Fifth Military Gate. Because of the steady increase of enemy soldiers inside the peribolos, the defenders couldn't prevent them from starting to ram the gate. When Constantine saw all the Italian mercenaries flee inside the peribolos in both directions, he knew nothing could be done to reverse the situation. In the most crucial moment of the entire battle, a moment they could still have fought and gloriously won, he had been abandoned by the very man who less than twelve hours earlier had pledged him loyalty to death. The discovery was indeed sobering. The time, on the other hand, to enjoy this new insight was sadly limited. For Constantine only one thing remained. To die.

History, legend, heritage, responsibility, valour, dignity – those were the elements invisibly but nonetheless compellingly shrouding his presence. If he kept his apparent imperial insignia, he would perhaps be spared for the moment, then, however, be brought in chains before the Sultan and forced to kneel down in front of him, humiliated and defeated in the eyes of all of those he had promised victory and survival. What would happen next was of little importance. The Roman empire was no more and would never rise again. Incarceration, execution, impalement – mercy? … No, this was it. Constantine had long since decided for himself, and the immortal memory of his people, to perish with them.

Impetuously, wild-eyed, he threw off his purple regalia. With a roar he drew his sword one last time, rushing into the melee at its thickest, slaying one man, two men, even a third before a scimitar found its way into his intestines and left him bleeding to death on the ground. The last thing his dimming gaze perceived was the gate opening above him, and an endless stream of wild warriors chasing the scattered remainders of his military force as it dispersed and fled in panic back into the city.

Chapter 64

Meanwhile, Giustiniani, on his own request, was hurriedly carried uphill inside the peribolos the four hundred yards separating the barred Fifth Military Gate from its neighbour to the south, the Gate of St Romanus. Once there and brought up on the outer wall, he could see that the enemy was about to overcome the breach in the valley and kill everybody left in the peribolos there. He ordered his stretcher to be put down and was helped back on his feet. At St Romanus too the defence was in disarray ever since the soldiers had been able to convince themselves that the Emperor and his men in the valley had irrevocably lost position. A trail of Genoese and Venetians running up the hills in both directions of the potential mass grave separating the walls quickly persuaded the soldiers manning the inner tower to open the gate to let the Genoese commander through. The remaining force on the outer wall, seeing what was happening, unanimously decided to follow suite and abandon ship. Through the heroic leadership of the venerable Don Francesco of Toledo, who had decided to fight to the last drop of blood for his cousin and Emperor, the retreat was nevertheless organised in such manner as to give the better part of the force the possibility to escape, while a handful soldiers stayed back to give the impression of continued resistance. The Turks, seeing more and more men disappear from the outer walls, rushed ahead to raise their ladders. They would surely have prevented many more defenders from reaching inside the main wall had it not been for Don Francesco himself. Taking on one after the other of the Turks, he swung his Toledo blade with great skill, killing a good dozen of them before sustaining a lethal thrust. The bravery of Don Francesco, straddling the stairs together with a handful of die-hard Castilians, allowed many hundreds of defenders to reach temporary safety behind the main wall before the gate had to be closed at the imminent onslaught of the enemy. Five surviving Castilians, finally ceding their blocking position, were the last to reach the gate before it had to be locked to prevent the enemy from winning immediate entry. Consequently nothing could be done for the unhappy lot still struggling uphill towards the gate. They all met their fates at the hands of an enemy growing a hundredfold in strength by the minute. Locked out, a contingent of Giustiniani's mercenaries desperately pounded their fists on the gate but nobody dared to respond to their call. They gate remained shut. Soon they were surrounded and mercilessly slaughtered.

Once inside the great wall, Giustiniani's men surprisingly found some horses tied up against it. Every horse had to carry two men, and Giustiniani was helped to take place behind his closest and most trusted officer Zeno. The rest of the force had been told to run for their lives towards the Golden Horn. The order was quite unnecessary. Everyone understood the game was over and ran like the devil in the hope, of course, to get on board one of the vessels that would try to take to the sea as soon as the word reached them that the city was lost. It was a good bet that Giustiniani, having the advantage of a horse, would be the first to tell them in person. That's what happened. Though rumours preceded him and the port was in uproar when he galloped in there, he did become the living harbinger of the catastrophic news. – Comrades! he shouted from his horse, – the city has been taken. We must do whatever we can to… (here the unlucky commander paused for a brief moment) only to collect himself, and at the top of his lungs, continue – Get the hell out of here!

The effect was immediate. With the rumour confirmed captains in unison began preparing for a break-out. It was at first believed that merchant cogs, biremes and triremes would have to fight their way to open sea, a prospect less enticing than ever. But here the pent up lust for booty and rape on the part of the Ottomans came to their rescue. When the Turkish navy in the Marmara saw one Turkish banner after the other fly into the sky, they became so eager to bring their ships to shore that some captains just ran them onto the nearest beach, whereafter the crew swam or waded to land to be part of the imminent carnage and looting.

Nor did the Turkish fleet in the Horn waste time to attempt to overcome its opponent in a seaborne attack. They simply drove their ships alongside their own pontoon bridge, allowing their crews to make it over to the *terra firma* around Blachernai, and then returned to their anchor positions, each vessel manned by a few men only. Behind them, the entire body of the army stationed around Galata under Zaganos Pascha, moved in for the kill as well. By now gates were opened all around the city and the fleeing came in droves – that is, those individuals who for some reason had been weak in faith and not put their trust in the prophecy that Christ himself would deny the Sultan entry to the Hagia Sophia. For those poor souls, on the other hand, the awakening to reality was to be rude.

A multitude of old, incapacitated men, women and children had gathered in the side entrance, beneath the majestic mosaic depicting Constantine I offering a scaled-down model of the the city, and Justinian I one of the Hagia Sophia to Christos Pantocrator. Their hymns and prayers were brutally cut short by the first Osmanli soldiers breaking through the wooden doors. After that the soldiers went on a leisurely killing spree, cutting down as many helpless victims as they could. When the initial furore abated, children, not killed in the first assault, were herded together and dragged out in the open, destined for the slave market; old men and women were mercilessly put to the sword, while the ones lucky enough to be younger and more attractive were dragged away and violated. Other soldiers, still able to resist the desires of the flesh, avidly went straight for the immense treasures they imagined would be kept inside the basilica. When they didn't find what they expected they accused the priests of hiding them – indeed, most gold, silver and gems had been stored in secret places long before the final assault took place – and killed as many of them as they could lay their hands on. Meanwhile, men and women who had tried to escape by running up to the galleries were tracked down, cornered and finished off. A steady stream of warm blood washed back and forth like a turbulent sea over floor mosaics and gave exuberant life to the cool marble slabs before dripping down below, like a drizzle in hell, sprinkling the dead on the ground floor. To many it later seemed an odd coincidence that the corpse of an old man, known to have been of Norse origin, was found embracing the balustrade, a spear in his back, at the point where Halvdan Viking had famously chiseled his signature in runes centuries ago.

Elsewhere in the city the scenario was similar. Some fleeing defenders with a late start, not quite knowing where to turn to escape disaster, were intercepted by Ottomans and cut down. Civilians were dragged out of their houses, killed or raped, or both. The houses were then looted and things without much commercial value destroyed. Finally, to enhance the visual effect of the victory, buildings became spectacular fireworks, setting the scene for the stately entry of Mehmet the Conqueror.

Thus, not only did Constantinople fall on the early morning of May 29, 1453, she literally went up in flames. By the time the Sultan entered the city by the gate of St Romanus – around which the corpses had been hastily removed so as to not offend his eyes and keen sense of smell – she was no longer more than a glowing memory turning to ashes.

Chapter 65

– Who I am? The woman repeated, her voice echoing in the spacious room. – Does it really matter? I mean, I'm so inferior to you in rank and birth that you, once this is all over, will prefer to forget everything about me, so that you don't have to be grateful to me for anything.

When Felicia didn't say anything and no longer seemed in the mood for protests, the other woman took the liberty to eye her from head to heel, touching her clothes, stroking her hair.

– You're beautiful, princess, and I'm sure you will make your prince happy – if you want to. Maybe he deserves it, maybe not. I don't know, but I do know that if it wasn't for him, you wouldn't be here. Anyways, who I am? I'm just a fisherman's wife, can't you smell it? My name is Irene, and that of my husband is Iannis. And these are our two children, Anna and Manuel, who is just like his father: he believes in anything he's making up! He'd lie to you even if he didn't have to! No, don't be put off, you're a good boy, just imagining things, like Papa.

– And your husband, where's he at the moment? On the walls?

– Naaa, he's on some kind of secret mission. He wouldn't tell me what, but you ask me, and I says its that Father Gennadi who put things into his head and makes him do crazy things. I don't trust that Gennadi no more. At first, when we heard him talk about the doctrine and all that, and that our church is a thousand years old, and Rome was always our enemy, I wanted to believe him. But then I understood that in the name of that holiness, he was actually going behind the back of the Emperor, betraying him, and us, to the Sultan. To the Emperor he pretended he was loyal all the same, but I tell you, he's made sure he'll have his cake and eat it at the same time. And I believe he made my husband even more crazy than he already was. You see, my husband told us to wait here for him, because he knows that if the city will be no more tomorrow, we at least have a chance to get out of here. But he says it won't happen that way because there will be a miracle and he will come and get us to show it to us. Now, a miracle would be fine, eh? But you know what, he said it couldn't be produced without him. Without him I says to myself? What do he mean? That God can't make a miracle unless my husband helps him? This is where I think that Gennadi has filled him with a lot of bull. And I'm worried, I am, that he will do something to hurt himself before he even get a chance to help the city. Anyways, he told us to wait here until he either come and get us or the city has been taken. So whenever we hear the monks come running, we know what's gonna happen, and that's when we go back into that tunnel and down to the sea level, where he says the little boat is hidden. Now, he says that if the Turks come, we must look out for Italian ships trying to make it to the Marmara, and that's when we have to be out there, trying to be picked up by one of them.

– And what if the Turks won't let them escape? Felicia asked.

– Then we have another problem. But you see, we can always wait here, we'll be better off the longer it takes for them to discover us, because at the beginning they just wanna murder and plunder… But, what am I saying? If they discover you, you're lost. So at least we've got to get you out of here one way or the other. Your prince, by the way, why didn't he come up with a plan for you to get out of here?

– He did.

– How come you're still here then?

Felicia didn't quite know what to answer, then opted for the truth.

– Because I don't want to be separated from him.

– So he don't know you're still here, eh?

– No, he thinks I went on that last Venetian ship to sail out from the Horn, and that I'm now already with his family in Chios. I suppose I just couldn't stand worrying about whether or not he would survive, so I decided to stay. It was foolish, of course, to think that I could do anything to help. But I really feel so sorry for all these people, many of whom have been so good to me in spite of my Turkish blood and of the awful circumstances we're in. But now you've made me realise that if he dies today, I can't join him, not even in my mind, because a part of him is still alive inside me, and I have a responsibility to protect that life to the limits of my capacity, and even beyond.

– So you're pregnant! Irene said laughing.

Felicia nodded.

– Do you think it will be a boy or a girl? Anna, intently listening in on the conversation, asked.

– It's a boy.

– How do you know? Manuel interjected.

– I just know it.

There was a moment of bemused silence, then Felicia continued,

– I guess I should consider myself very lucky to have met you, because there is, as you say, obviously nothing I can do to prevent that which must happen from happening. But since experience has taught me that most things in life happen for a reason, I have not been able to give up the idea that I will one day be able to share my life with him and be the mother of his children. And if there is only going to be one, well, then that one child will be my mission in life. Right now it's my only motivation to carry on. I've already lost a child, you see, and it wasn't God who took his life.

– If that's how you feel, I believe your prince has figured out a way to come back to you.

– No, no, he's too proud, talking about duty and to die rather than going back on your word. I won't see him again.

– Sure you will. What was that word again?

– To fight to the death… That's what he told me he had promised the Emperor.

– Why would he do that? He has only been hired to do what he's already done, ain't he?

– No, he came here because he wanted to, that's how he is.

– Alright princess, listen. There are always more motives than the eye can see. So things might not only happen for one reason but for many, sometimes different reasons, and even reasons as seem to be contradictin' each other. I don't know that much about politics, but I know this: Your prince ain't just come over here with seven hundred of his own hand-picked men only to realise they were all gonna die without some kind of compensation. After all, the Galatan Genoese are staying put, ain't they? How do you think that ties in with the policy of their republic and all that, and their mayor givin' fancy speeches? No, I think they wanted your prince there on the walls for another reason than for him to win. If he wins, well fine, but he ain't being abandoned if he loses, because they have a plan for that as well.

They've been smart, you see. Like that fox Gennadi they are pretending to be on nobody's side, while in reality they'll both expect to end up on the winnin' side. You can be darn sure those Galatan dogs will back up your prince and make sure he gets out of here in a flash before the Sultan finds out the two of 'em have been in it together all along. Whatever he told the Emperor, he won't have to answer for it before he's dead himself, and that's not part of his plan right now. He wants you, and he wants that boy. And then he wants something else too. Mark my words. Them Genoese are out for something bigger than just another contract with the Sultan. I don't know what it is, but I know your prince is in it up to here! Irene concluded and grabbed around her own throat with two hands to illustrate how deeply involved she considered him to be.

Chapter 66

Her words echoed and finally died out in the gloomy chapel which until now had been remarkably silent considering that the walls protecting it were about to give away. But now, as the first rays of early morning illumined its dark corners, they heard feet and desperate voices rapidly approaching. Irene gave a sign to everybody to get going.

– That's it! she exclaimed, – Those are the monks running back into the monastery. The town must have fallen. We gotta get out of here as quickly and unnoticed as we came.

She lit their last torch with the one about to go out, gave it to Felicia and told her to go ahead and lead the way. Meanwhile, she made sure the stone in the altar closed properly behind her and they all began the descent into the tunnel, so narrow it could only hold one person at a time. Felicia felt very uncomfortable having to be in the lead, but there was nothing she could do to change the situation, Irene and the children pressing her ahead.

– Let me know when you arrive at the fork in the tunnel, Irene said.

– What fork? Can't even see my own feet!

– I showed it to you when we came her, there is a place where the tunnel splits up in two directions. That's where you have to keep to the right, because that's the way to the water.

– I can't see anything!

– Just move until you do.

Sure enough. Some fifty steps below the entrance, Felicia stumbled on the stone marking the bifurcation. She dropped the torch while struggling not to tumble down the stairs. It fell to the ground, emitting an even thicker smoke than before.

– Get that damn' torch off the ground and hurry up! The invisible Irene commanded her. – Otherwise the smoke will fill this space in no time and the fire take away the air so we can't even breath in her. You simply gotta move it!

"Oh God!" Felicia thought, badly bruised and short of breath, "This is just horrible!"

She didn't even know how right she was. since worse was yet to come. Had the tunnel been precipitous before, it now slanted in a downward spiral that only got steeper. On several occasions Felicia was on the verge of falling into the void and had to admonish the children not to push her off the steps. The distance between the steps was increasing too, so that they were now almost climbing down the tunnel. The air kept getting worse, the children and Irene coughing behind her while she herself was gasping for air. Then came the water. The steps were leading right into water. Felicia stopped and shouted back to Irene,

– There's water here, we have to turn round, or we'll be drowning like mice.

– You gotta get in the water, came the answer.

– What!

– Go into the water, if the water level is normal we should be able to wade our way to the exit?

– And what if it isn't?

– Then we have to swim!

Instinctively Felicia reeled back from the cold and pitch black water merging indistinctly with the rough walls in front of her. There seemed to be no air left in the tunnel ahead. She would have done anything to turn back. But though on the verge of panic she also realised that ending up in Turkish hands wasn't a very pleasant alternative. Whatever other emotion she experienced it was cut short by the fact that the children, pushed ahead by a nearly suffocated Irene, forced her into the ice cold water. Overcome by the shock Felicia lost the torch. It fell sizzling into the water and was instantly extinguished. Frantically she tried to swim only to discover that the pitch black passage was too narrow to allow her arms and legs to move freely. At this point her feet hit the rock and she found she could actually walk. In fact the water only reached her up to the chest. That would still cause some problem for young Manuel, but the brave boy was now helped by his equally brave sister, tall enough to silently follow in Felicia's footsteps. Irene propped him up from behind too. They couldn't see a thing, though, and suddenly the stony ground below them gave away leaving all of them floating in the water. Felicia stretched out her hands to see if there was anything she could hold on to, only to feel the rough walls around her come alive with slimy crabs running over her arms and fingers. Not knowing what or how big these animals were, she screamed and nearly fainted from fear. But that wouldn't have helped them either, and so, forced by dire necessity, she pushed on, hoping that a gentle swell in the water, a whiff of fresher air and a faint but unmistakable sound of distant seabirds announced the end of the tunnel system. Then she began to be able to distinguish the wild gunshots from the banging sound of the waves hitting the walls of the grotto, and suddenly, at the very far end of the tunnel, she detected a bleak ray of light traverse the inside of the cave. – Look! she cried out to the others. There's the opening!

They moved towards that light as the water level again receded and left them standing on a piece of rock next to a small rowing boat kept in place by a chain running through an iron loop. It in turn was fastened to the living rock. Through an artful interlacing of branches and seaweed they glimpsed the sky beyond a hole in the cave wall. Below it was the seaside opening of the cave itself. What an incredible relief! The boat, kept above sea level thanks to Iannis's foresight, looked intact. Inside it were a pair of oars; the small mast with its sail lying next to them. Shivering of cold they gratefully kneeled down next to the boat, knowing that if only they could somehow get it out of there and into the open sea, there might just be a chance for them to escape.

Still, the boat wasn't all that easy to move. To their surprise they found out that the platform they had reached slanted towards the sea as though it had been a ramp built for the purpose. With joint forces they pushed the boat closer and closer into the lake of the cavern until it was afloat and they could verify with their own eyes that it stayed that way. Now they had to hold it tight so it wouldn't drift away. But before they could all get on board and dare to attempt a launch into the open sea, Manuel was sent over to peek through the lattice work to make sure no Turkish ships or soldiers were anywhere close. – Do you see anybody? Manuel shook his head. – Take a good look in all directions, you've got to make a small opening in the branches and then look out all around. Manuel did as he was told, wriggling half of his entire little body through the branches. – Careful! You can't let anybody discover you. – Do you see anyone? Again Manuel shook his head. – You're not making it up, are you? For the third time he shook his head. – So the coast is clear?

This time he nodded.

CHAPTER 67

Commander Giovanni Giustiniani Longo, exhausted by the fight and at long last overwhelmed by his wounds, lay on his back in a net swung between two props below deck in one of the Genoese merchant vessels and stared helplessly upwards. He could only follow the crew's swift manoeuvering with his ears, as he listened to orders given and executed, the heavy anchors being heaved, tackles and tarred ropes roll, oars dip into the water, sails flutter and the wooden floats of the Galata chain being attacked by axes. He also heard the high-pitched voices of dozens of fleeing soldiers who had taken to swimming out into the Horn in a desperate attempt to catch up with the still slowly moving ships. In the prevailing wind they would pick up speed as soon as they reached the waters beyond and opposite Galata, where a great many of them had already gathered ready to set course southward. Many of the men were fished out of the now seemingly boiling water with hooks, others rescued with ladders thrown off the railings on the hulls. The extensive rescue operation slowed down all the ships on the move. It wasn't until the enemy artillery positioned behind Galata once again opened fire on them that the over-charged vessels got under way for real, leaving some fellows still paddling too close to land to a very unhappy fate.

Otherwise the loading of panic stricken civilians onto the ships, the severing of the chain and the ships' subsequent dash for open water was surprisingly uncomplicated, and this, as mentioned, for the sole reason that the Turks now had only one thing in mind: the three full days of looting which Mehmet had promised them. Not before long oars were put to rest as sails unfurled in the north-eastern breeze and a flotilla of mostly Venetian and Genoese ships put more and more distance between themselves and the ravaged city. Over the Lycus valley and its still bleeding wound in the wall, in themselves invisible from the sea, stood an enormous dark cloud, like a pillar of destruction raging into the sky. The flocks of seagulls always circling the dome of Hagia Sophia, had been joined by hawks, vultures and other scavengers waiting for the dead soldiers in the field and on the walls to be left to their carnivorous administration. The knowledge of what was going on right now in the city was terrible for everyone, but most people on board the ships were too relieved to pay too much concern to the inevitable carnage happening back there. Some though had left family members behind, and they did feel the sting.

From the sound of the waves and the ship's steady pace, Giovanni concluded they had safely rounded the city's northeastern cape and unhindered set course due south. He closed his eyes and an immense fatigue almost got the better of his pains, working like a natural opium through his pumping veins. "I'd never forgive myself if I die before I get to see her again. God give that I shall not be dead before we reach Chios", he thought and clasped his hands over his soiled and injured chest as though preparing for it all the same.

On deck the commotion was great. Even though it might have been a natural thing for the age old Greek-Italian animosity to flare up again, it didn't. Many of the refugees were indeed Greeks, and some of the ships too. But all these people had seen each other fight so hard and so long for a common cause, that they knew themselves to have been baptised in fire and iron – together. And on this morning of late May, as the city behind them dropped below the horizon, everyone witnessed in tears and sadness a whole world slowly disappear into the sea, knowing that it would never rise out of it the same again.

Ahead of them lay the unbroken vista of the Marmara Sea, still safe for navigation while the trap in the Bosporus snapped behind them. The last city landmark to disappear was the once beautifully polished, now sadly damaged Marble Tower. Separated by a promontory from the juncture of land and sea walls by the Marmara shore, it had been seized by the Turks during the early days of the siege, but was now, like so many other Turkish posts, abandoned in the name of greed. Most terrifying of all though were the many corpses and decapitated heads which the strong northerly wind had carried far into the sea.

The refugees could only watch in silence how fish and birds consumed them piece by piece.

Wild outbursts of tears and wailing ensued as the Greeks had to bid the waning contours of their city a last farewell, but the voyage into the unknown had to continue, and soon even cannon-blasted marble was but a memory. Now there was only sea and more sea ahead – or was there? What in God's name was that single tiny sail doing so far out into the sea? The Genoese merchant who ended up being closest to it, changed its course and approached it. Getting nearer, its crew and astonished passengers discerned two women and three children, the apparently youngest of whom was at the rudder. A ladder was lowered and all five of its passengers, harassed but seemingly in otherwise good condition, were helped on board. The small boat, deemed useful, was taken in tow.

Chapter 68

– How are you feeling? She whispered softly, caressing his in between scars and blotches of coagulated blood, while he regained consciousness. Incredulously he looked at her, blinking and refocusing his gaze once, then again, and again, unable to figure out how she, unless he was still dreaming, could actually be seated next to him.

– How did *you* get here? He finally said, confused over whether, perhaps, he'd been unconscious for days and the ship had in fact reached Chios. But then he recognised the motion of the prow plowing steadily into the waves, and he concluded that although they were still at sea, Felicia, and not an apparition in her likeness, was with him.

– You never went with that boat, did you? He took his time before formulating the question, expecting the answer to make some sense of the situation. She shook her head, a tear watering her eye,

– I was inside the city to the very end.

– I suppose it doesn't matter now, but why?

– Because I wanted to be close to you.

– Close to me?

– Yes, I thought you were going to die, and… I don't know, I just couldn't leave without you.

– Hmmm ... good thing I didn't know you were still inside the city, because then I really would have died there. Now ... it's just going to take ... a little more time, he uttered falteringly, his cold sweat and wincing betraying the pain he endured.

– Oh my God, you really are badly hurt! Let me see. Oh that's some wound you've got there!

At this moment the Venetian doctor, Niccolo Barbaro, appeared behind Felicia, giving her a sign to come with him. At some distance from Giovanni, now battling his pain with closed eyes, he told her,

– We operated on him as soon as he reached the ship. That projectile was lodged inside his left arm. Luckily we managed to get all of the tissue out of the wound as well, since otherwise infection will most certainly be lethal, but it's too early to say whether or not he will make it over the next few days. We just have to pray and hope.

– Isn't there really anything more you can do for him?

– Only this, I'm afraid, Barbaro said, handing over a corked jar to her.

– What's that?

– Tsipouro.

– You want me to put that on his wound?

– No, just pour it down his throat. A smile, meant to be reassuring, shaded his lips.

Felicia returned to Giovanni's side.

– Have some of this, she said and opened the jar.

She managed to elevate his head so that he could sip some of the alcohol. It seemed to do him some good, then he leaned back saying,

– You must tell me how you managed to get onboard this ship, I didn't see you anywhere in port.

– Yes I will, my love, I'll tell you everything, everything. But for now you must rest as much as you can. When you feel better...

– No, tell me now, he mumbled, I want to hear it ... now... later... is... too late...

– Alright. In the middle of the night, just as the cannonade had begun, I was on my way towards the gate where I knew you would be fighting, when I was intercepted by a fisher woman and her two children. You see, they were on their way to escape the city and they forced me to come with them. At first I protested but then...

She looked at him trying to read his reaction. As none was forthcoming, she took his blood-stained hand and kissed it again, covering it in her hair. Eventually she put it back to rest. She would tell him the story later. As for now, Giovanni, mercifully taken over by utter exhaustion, alcohol and fever, had fallen asleep, deaf and blind to the outside world. Or at least that's what Felicia believed until she, still whispering, added the words,

– If you die, I will never forget you…

Upon which he muttered,

– What are you talking about… You haven't even started … *remembering* me.

Though still in tears, Felicia now smiled, seeing that her beloved would not give up his life without a fight.

Chapter 69

Among the last to reluctantly give up his fighting position was Bishop Leonard, stationed close to the Golden Horn at the far end of the land wall. Leonard had always had a tendency to belittle Greek bravery at the expense of Genoese mettle. He was quite shocked to receive the news that Commander Giustiniani Longo – the hero himself – according to preliminary Greek reports had abandoned his post for no good reason, thereby causing so much uncertainty among his men that they failed to stick together. Their dereliction, unimaginable in Leonard's view, had left the remaining defenders unable to prevent the Turks from pouring in over the breach in the Lycus valley. Seeing people fleeing in the thousands, he too finally gave the order to his force to retreat and run for the ships.

At the eastern extremity of the city, at the point where the Bosporus widens into the Marmara Sea, Cardinal Isidore likewise was forced to realise that the game was up when Turkish vessels without further ado were deliberately grounded on the beaches, spewing out their crews right beneath the walls. Alerted by his gatekeeper, Isidore, gazing to the north, beheld a plethora of Turkish flags. The only conclusion to draw was that the city had fallen with the result that their own situation had indeed become precarious. He signalled to the gatekeeper on the inner tower to open up a small gate, through which he began to send his men. While they withdrew, he heard the din of the Turks who were already inside the city and quickly sensed that if he happened to run in to some of them, his lavish ecclesiastical garments would certainly not be the best currency to appease them. Isidore well knew that the Sultan was particularly hostile to officials from the Holy See, and that he would like to see all of them publicly humiliated, perhaps executed, perhaps even impaled… Isidore trembled at the mere thought. But he couldn't just throw off his clothes and run naked, could he?

Desperately looking round for a solution, he detected the body of a dead Italian soldier left behind in the peribolos. Isidore, cut off from his military force and only surrounded by three members of his retinue, decided to make a bold move. Though in constant danger of being seen by Turks about to climb the outer wall, one of his servants helped him to quickly strip himself of his clothes. Meanwhile the two others had begun the painstaking procedure of undressing the dead man. It wasn't exactly easy, but eventually they managed to pull off his breast plate, his iron jacket and his pants. Isidore then got inside pants, jacket and armor, exchanging his own ornate weapon for the sword of the deceased. Isidore sufficiently dressed, his servants hurried to wrap the corpse in Episcopal regalia and left it that way for the Turks to discover. Still running among trees and bushes Isidore and his men heard the cry of joy of Turkish soldiers as they discovered what they believed to be a cardinal's body. Isidore froze in his tracks while looking over his shoulder to see what they would do with it. In the next instant they had severed the dead man's head from its body, triumphantly put in on a spear and carried it off as a trophy to be presented to the Sultan.

Isidore, at the moment failing to appreciate the high, albeit sinister, esteem in which he was held by the Turks, was encouraged to run again in order to catch up with the rest of the soldiers, but he was no longer the youngest, and it so happened that he got separated from his fleeing servants. Just before he reached the harbour seawalls he was spotted by Turks who rapidly closed in on him. Whether the God of Rome had such special plans for Isidore that he couldn't really do without him at this moment, or whether it was pure luck that the soldiers were so eager to get on their way to Hagia Sophia that they didn't even bother to strike him dead on the spot, is hard to say. Isidore, however, being close to end his days at the point of a crooked sword, played his last card. A psychologist and a diplomat, Isidore was coldblooded enough to realise that the soldiers wouldn't bother to take an old man prisoner since he'd be worth next to nothing on the slave market. Thus the alternative to death was to offer the Turks more money than they could possibly hope to make out him if traded. This Isidore did. But it's unlikely that he would have pulled off the trick had not the Turks also seen that many more Greek defenders were on their way towards the sea, and that these men would most certainly fight for their lives to get there. This could spell trouble for a small detachment of Turkish soldiers if surrounded.

Isidore saw the opportunity in the offing. Pretending his was simply an old Greek of some means, he pulled out a leather pouch full of coins and handed it over to the soldiers. Without even opening it they grabbed it, and to Isidore's surprise, just knocked him out of the way before taking off in the direction of Hagia Sophia, leaving him to continue to the port where he safely arrived well before the harbour captain, Alex Diedo, ordered the gates to be closed behind the ships to prevent the fleeing masses from sinking them in their desperate attempts to climb on board.

Simultaneously, in the northwestern corner of the city, Bishop Leonard had been fatally trapped in the maze of lanes surrounding the Blachernai area. From all directions Turks were approaching while Greeks and Italians ran for their lives. Many of them were killed or captured. Judging from the Turkish cries of triumph, growing louder from every direction of the city, it was now only a matter of seconds before Leonard himself would be cut down or apprehended. He kept close to the houses to see if he could possibly find an open door somewhere. He wasn't in luck. Utterly incapable of figuring out how to extricate himself from this predicament, he suddenly felt a hand grabbing his arm and vigorously pull him inside a house. Leonard, about to raise his sword in defence, then heard a familiar Greek voice reaching him from the obscurity of the narrow passage way inside the building. It was that of Francis.

– I know you think we Greeks are pretty useless, but let me at least offer you the advantage of knowing this city better than you, Francis said closing the thick door behind them and inviting Leonard to follow him deeper inside.

– Where are you taking me? Leonard asked,
– To the cisterns.
– Won't they discover us there?
– It's not the main cistern built by Justinian, but a small annex to the main system, specifically supplying the Blachernai palace. It's connected to the cisterns of the Forum though, but the canal is hard to

detect and it will probably take them a few days before they actually find us.

– And then they'll cut our heads off.

– I don't think there is reason to be that pessimistic. Today and tomorrow they will all be in a frenzy, but once they have divided up most of the things between them and the Sultan has entered the city things will calm down and we might at least stand a reasonable chance of surviving, perhaps even to buy ourselves out of captivity. Could you help me carry this?

– What's that?

– Oh, just some oil for the lamps, wine, bread, cheese and olives. I don't want us to starve while awaiting our destiny.

– How did you know I was coming?

– I didn't, but I feel greatly honoured having such a distinguished fellow escapee. Now would you please follow me?

They went down a flight of stairs and reached a cellar, the floor of which was covered with debris. Francis moved his hand through splinters of wood and gravel and pulled up a hatch hidden beneath it. From there a straight ladder went further down. Francis did his best to make sure the hatch was still covered and invisible from above while cautiously allowing it to close above their heads. When they reached the bottom, he lit an oil lamp and from its faint light Leonard could make out a large vaulted room supported by antique pillars surrounded by fresh water.

– I think we'll be safer here than anywhere else for the time being, Francis said urging Leonard to take a piece a bread and some olives while offering him wine from a large jug. Gratefully, Leonard received the provisions, still wondering what on earth had just happened to him.

An hour later that same morning, Gennadi was found as the Turks released the few remaining Turkish prisoners from their jail cells. He was found in one of them, but instead of being killed, or dragged to the Forum along with countless other victims, he was honorably dispatched directly to the Sultan. At the same time, the people who had gathered in the church of the Chora found reason, if not exactly to rejoice, to remain grateful. Though there had been neither Christ nor archangel to prevent the Turks from entering the city, the Sultan had nonetheless ordered the church to be guarded, under death penalty, by some of his most trusted Janissaries. As long as the looting of the city went on, no one was allowed to either enter or exit the church, and it was the Sultan himself, who, when riding by it, ordered the church to be opened, spared from any intrusion and its congregation to be brought to safety. Meanwhile, their spiritual leader, Gennadi, was nowhere to be seen as he was on his way to Adrianople, escorted by a contingent of Turkish soldiers, sent there to announce the Sultan's stunning victory and prepare for his triumphant return.

Chapter 70

In the Aegean sea, the evening of June 2, 1453 was warm and bright. On the western horizon there wasn't a single cloud, and the orange sun, majestically sinking into the sea, had an outer rim as clearly defined as that of the moon. As the galley carrying, among so many others, commander Longo, Felicia and the wife and children of Iannis Papanikolaou, approached the harbour of Chios, the hills embraced them in deep green while the fragrance of flowers in bloom quickened their spirits. On land, however, the news they brought was received with sadness and exasperation. Although members of the Genoese community were content to receive its prodigal son, many were outraged to learn that Venetian ships, which had not participated in the defence of Constantinople, but had merely been cruising around in the Aegean sea waiting for news, had dared to attack Genoese vessels on their way home.

The still weak and feverish Giustiniani confirmed that this had been so, but underlined that their safety in the last instance had depended on the decisive interaction on the part of Venetian gentlemen and captains, such as Alex Diedo, who in spite of being told that all Venetians had new orders from the Doge and the Council of Ten to intercept any ship carrying commander Giovanni Giustiniani Longo, refused to let them come close enough to force themselves on board. Instead, the hostile Venetians furiously realised that their mission would have to be postponed. So far as the Genoese knew, this new force of Venetians were merely biding their time, still infesting the waters around Chios. What they didn't know was that Diedo himself, threatened to be put on trial for high treason, maintained before the captains and officials of other Venetian ships, that he, as well as those other Venetians responsible for protecting Giustiniani, was not going to allow harm come to a man who had done everything in his might to defend thousands of people, including many Venetians, that Venice herself had left to a hellish fate without lifting a finger.

– You have done absolutely nothing, while this man, at the head of all of us, tried the impossible, Diedo stated in front of all the other captains. – And it was impossible precisely you weren't there! So take me to Venice, and I'll repeat to the Doge and the Council exactly what I have told you here today.

With a sardonic smile he added,

– And I can see that once again you're too cowardly to lift a finger. Isn't there anyone who will put me in chains, anyone who's got the nerve to arrest me? Anyone, anyone at all?

He looked around, but all he saw was embarrassed faces.

– In that case, get the hell off my ship and mind your own business. As for myself, I shall sail straight for Crete to report there according to *my* orders. And those orders specified my responsibility to defend our vital trading interests in Constantinople. Now, did you hear that?

The Mayor of Chios on the other hand, though playing to the galleries by also showing himself outraged by the attack, knew better. Two days after the event another Genoese ship arrived in port carrying a cargo which in spite of its physical insignificance was potentially worth more in gold than that of all of the Italian cities taken together. It had been handed over to Bishop Leonard – who on the morrow of the conquest had rather miraculously managed to reach Galata – and consisted of a thin vellum carefully folded in a roll protected in a leather tube. It was precisely this piece of parchment that the Venetians were looking for, and which they wouldn't have found had they boarded Giustiniani's ship. The ship responsible for its transportation had left Genoese Galata on May 30, on explicit orders of its mayor, only one day after Constantinople had been taken. But it arrived two days later than the other ships. Not because it moved so much slower, or had been subject to less favourable wind conditions, but because it carefully tried to avoid being spotted by the Venetian fleet in the Aegean, and therefore kept closer to the coast line. It had even been granted a letter of safe-conduct, bearing the elaborate signature of Mehmet himself, should the merchant, against all odds, be approached by Turkish ships.

In great secrecy, the much coveted document was handed over to the Mayor, who didn't dare to open it except in the presence of Giustiniani. The reason for this was that it was Giustiniani in person who had been entrusted with the secret task of bringing it with him back to Genoa. It was consequently kept sealed in its tube until it could be brought to the room where the wounded man lay in bed. The doors were closed and in the sole presence of Bishop Leonard, the Mayor and Giustiniani, it was cautiously unfolded and its content for the very first time scrutinised by Europeans.

The map unfolding under their curious eyes was made up of two circles, merging in such a way as to allow the left circle to slightly superimpose on the right one. The left circle, the content of which could thus be overlooked in its entirety, contained the not unfamiliar outlines of Europe, Africa and Asia as far east as China and Japan. The right hand circle, on the other hand, contained beyond the eastern ocean a detailed image of an entirely unknown continent, almost as comprehensive as the other three taken together. In addition there were contours of three unknown gigantic islands in the southern ocean. Like its left counterpart, the right hand map indicated rivers, mountains and lakes on the unknown continent, and was full of Chinese signs presumably providing further clarification.

– Why is the map inscribed in two circles, and not just in one? the Mayor was eager to know. – It doesn't really make sense does it? If you want to circumscribe the world with a horizon you only need one big circle. And besides, I don't really see the point of interest for us. China and Japan already are so far away that it would take a year to make a round trip, and that under the most favourable of circumstances. Then there is another enormous expanse of water before you even reach those far off lands that, I suppose, the Chinese claim they have found. Please, explain to me why our republic has been so eager to come into possession of this document. It seems unreasonable to me.

– It certainly does, Leonard said, – but only as long as you assume that the map reflects the topography of a flat surface.

– What else could it be representing?

– Well assume for a moment that the circles, illogical as they may seem, in reality depict the two halves of a spherical body taken to be the earth; then that new continent would probably be considerably closer to Spain than to China.

– But the earth is not spherical!

- How do you know it isn't?
- Simply because if it were, we would know that by know, wouldn't we? What do you say commander?

Giustiniani, having difficulties moving in order to take a closer look, was presented with the map above his head. He looked at it attentively before speaking,

- I'd say we'll be well advised to not let our curiosity get the better of us and just make sure it reaches its destination. I suggest you carefully roll it up again. I will make sure that whatever happens to me personally, it will be delivered as convened.

Leonard and the Mayor, seeing that Giustiniani was tired, respectfully withdrew, leaving the encased map next to his bed. He leaned back, still very much in the grip of fever and pains that were only tolerable as long as he didn't try to move. While the sunset's glow transformed to embers and darkness began to invade the room, Felicia silently entered and sat down beside him. Ever since their arrival in Chios she had taken care of him piously, assisted by members of his family. In a sense Giovanni really was at home there. An important branch of his large family had moved there in the early 14th century, and it was as firmly established as respected there. Still, Giovanni dreamed of being able to reach Genoa; now more than ever, since he knew it might not happen. And if that might not happen, there were things he would like to tell Felicia – before it was too late.

Chapter 71

- You have said you'd do anything for me. Would you stick to that even if I asked you to do me a very big favour?
- Of course my love. What is it that you want me to do?
- I need your assistance in a very urgent matter that I don't dare to entrust to anybody else. You see, I have here beside me an important document, a map in fact, which our Mayor in Galata succeeded to obtain from the Sultan in the aftermath of the conquest in exchange for a number of far reaching concessions. It can also be regarded as a token of gratitude to the population of Galata for not having interfered with the Sultan's plans and manoeuvres during the siege.

– You mean his thanking them for having betrayed you and the others fighting for creed and country?

– In a way, yes.

– Aha. And what is that you want me to do?

– I want you to go with the next available ship destined for Negroponte on the Greek mainland and from there get on a ship to Venice. I want you to carry this document all the way and once in Venice bring it to the attention of a certain Domenic Colombo, who's a Genoese friend of mine living there, and in all secrecy the finest cartographer the world has ever seen.

– If you're asking me to leave you again, I won't do it. I swear to God, it's the one and only thing I won't do!

– Listen my love. You just told me you'd do anything for me, and this is very, very important. Besides, it's only a matter of a temporary separation. I'm not yet fit to make a voyage to Italy and must stay here until my wounds have healed. But I need that map to reach Colombo safely before the Venetians, or anybody else for that matter, will be able to lay their hands on it. For this reason you must travel incognito. I'll make sure you get the papers and the necessary letters of introduction. My sister lives in Venice, and she'll take care of you and make sure signor Colombo is informed and brought to your house.

– Finally I begin to understand why those Venetians were chasing us all the way from Lesbos down here. There was simply nobody on board that could give me an explanation as to why they were so hostile. And you wouldn't tell me either. But please tell me now. If the Venetians are so intent on getting hold of this map, wouldn't it be plain madness to have me transporting it to Venice, on one of their own ships even?

– No, that's the whole point. Genoese vessels may be attacked anywhere from here to Italy, but the Venetians will never suspect a foreign woman, a refugee from Constantinople, to carry state secrets with her, especially not into the lion's den. You will be hiding the map among your personal belongings, preferably among your underwear, since it will be against republican regulations to look through those.

– But what is it really that makes everybody so desperate to get hold of this map. In the end, it's just another piece of parchment, isn't it?

– Of course. But it so happens that it's a Chinese piece of parchment containing a map not only suggesting the earth is spherical, as the ancients had well-founded reason to believe, but that there is on this sphere a whole unknown continent somewhere to the west of the remote Azores islands. With Genoese trading interests and revenues now dwindling in the Ottoman east, it will one day be of the utmost concern to find new prosperity to the west. Genoa itself is but a narrow stretch of land, little more than a promontory in the sea, surrounded by uncultivable mountains. It's just like a coin, and on this coin there are, for lack of space, buildings towering ten stories high over winding lanes no wider than six feet. Everything in Genoa has to strive for the sky. If we lose our strongholds in the eastern Mediterranean, as indeed we are about to do, we must consequently consider a *terra firma* expansion, first over jagged and useless land, and then onto fertile territories fought over by practically every kingdom and republic of Europe. Genoa at present is not strong enough to take on such a challenge single-handedly and will be even less so in the future. In fact, without new land to conquer, Genoa will very soon see its dominions reduced and its power once and for all broken. Luckily there are among the Genoese some highly intelligent and innovative people, money lenders willing to risk investments in new ventures, Jews and Catalans with connections to the Spanish crown, entrepreneurs, ship builders and seamen. It's my belief that an alliance with Spain could prove extremely promising in this regard. Signor Colombo, a naturalised Genoese subject, is both Catalan and Jewish by origin. He's been my mentor and the one who initiated me in the art and science of cartography. It's also from him I learned that a state not willing to expand will not even be able to retain their status quo, unless subjecting itself to a foreign suzerain. All his life he's advocated the idea of westward expansion, but nobody ever wanted to believe him because he lacked solid proof to back the claim that there must be land beyond the western seas. This map will prove him right, and with that in his hand he can reverse our decline and make Genoa the driving force in the discovery of a new world. According to the Chinese sources, there are incredible riches, yes, entire empires built from gold and jade, in this part of the world. Once this has been clearly understood, human greed will do the rest of the work.

– You wouldn't be one of those embarking upon a ship for the western ocean and disappear for years on end, perhaps forever, would you? Felicia said, suddenly realising that her life with this man might prove to be a series of unwanted ruptures and years of worry, loneliness and longing.

– Of course not my darling. Once this mission is accomplished, I will never allow us to be separated again. We shall live as husband and wife in Italy and raise our children together in love and respect of our venerable republic, our family, God and the church. But I owe my native country this one and last service. Just this one, I swear.

Felicia had the feeling he might just be talking to pacify her again, but her desire to believe him was stronger than any such thoughts. Seemingly in consonance with Destiny itself, playing its cards regardless of human will, she had made her choice long since, and she was not intent on letting go of him without a guarantee. For her to make the sacrifice he demanded she must ask him for a favour as well.

– I have been converted and baptised to your faith and I carry your child under my heart. Yet it's a child conceived in sin. Before I agree to what you're asking me to do, I have one request.

– And that is?

– That we get married before I leave.

– But I don't even know if I can stand up, let alone walk at this time.

– It doesn't matter. I can stand up while you lie down. I want us to get married in this very room, properly married, by an ordained Catholic priest and your family members as witnesses. Can you promise me that much?

– If that's the way you want it, so be it.

– No Giovanni, unfortunately that was the wrong answer. Please try again, just a little bit harder, will you?

Giovanni grinned.

– Since I can not bear the thought that you will embark alone on a perilous voyage on my behalf without knowing that we have pledged each other love and loyalty for the remainder of our days, I was just wondering if you would agree to marry me tomorrow?

– Oh, that's a great step to consider. I think I need a little time….

– Not too long, I hope. I might just be dead before you have made up your mind.

– You're right, it really would be awfully inconvenient to miss out on that opportunity. In fact, the only thing I have to add is this…

Giovanni waited for her to speak, but instead she bowed down next to him, allowing him to inhale the exotic fragrance of her bosom and feel the sweet moisture of her kiss.

Chapter 72

Early next day Bishop Leonard, learning that his services were in demand, entered Giovanni's room.

– Well, I hope I haven't been called upon to give you the extreme unction.

Even though it was meant as a joke, there was a slight but unmistakable tone of disdain in his voice. The relation between the two men, notwithstanding Giovanni's serious wounds and their joint efforts to secure Genoese possession of the Chinese map, was not the best. Leonard, having acted bravely on his – albeit less exposed – section of the wall, did indeed blame Giovanni for the Emperor's death and the city's downfall. Nor was there any doubt as to whom he considered guilty of conspiracy. Except for the obvious case of Gennadi, it was a woman. And not even one of noble Italian or Greek origin. No, a Turkish tramp, probably acting on direct orders from the Sultan! What a shame…

Weakened and humiliated, Giovanni seemed to hear the words that Leonard didn't utter better than the ones he actually spoke. He decided to take the bull by the horns,

– I know you think I should have left this world fighting. Perhaps you're right. Instead of standing in front of our Lord, knowing my soul to be saved by his grace, I now linger on, a mere shadow of a man, defeated, despised by all those who once trusted and admired me. I know you think I should have stayed and fought on, as I'm sure you would, had you been in my position. Alas, it's too late for me to die with honour. But although that might be true, I shall not add to evil by also withholding what I have also learned from the siege. Regardless of my personal shortcomings, I believe the governors of our republic would take great interest in the information I have to impart. I feel I should do this now, so that there will be no chance for my hard earned knowledge to disappear with me. To this end, however, I humbly ask you, monsignor, to assist me with pen and paper. No, no, I was actually wondering if you would be so kind as to write down my words as I dictate them to you. I promise that I will make my exposition as short and to the point as I possibly can.

Leonard, feeling strangely outwitted, walked across the room to fetch pen and ink from the escritoire placed in front of one of the two Gothic windows, through which the port of Chios, bathing in bright morning light, could be seen. Sitting down by it he calmly waited for Giovanni to begin his dictation. This is the letter Bishop Leonard wrote down to the governors of Genoa in Giustiniani's name:

"Most noble gentlemen,

This report does not seek to blame or to criticise those responsible for the defence of Constantinople in her hour of destiny, since its writer can clear his name by accusing others just as little as they can clear theirs by accusing him. In retrospect, all facts and circumstances duly considered, there was but one overwhelming cause to the Sultan's victory, and that cause can be spelled out in a single word: artillery.

It has perhaps come to your knowledge that the Sultan was in possession of a grand number of large guns. Among these the biggest was nick-named the bear, and the smaller ones the cubs. It would be natural to assume that it was the big gun which finally succeeded to bring down the walls and shatter our defence. But it wasn't primarily the impact of single, giant projectiles, but the steady bombardment from the smaller guns, diligently and skillfully used, that weakened the walls to the point where they could no longer withstand infantry attack. I happened to witness how this all came about, week by week, day by day, hour by hour. No matter what we did to strengthen ruined walls, the power of destruction was greater, and unless help would be forthcoming from our allies, it was only, and I repeat, only a matter of time before the city must surrender. The Sultan's army on the other hand, no matter how large, could only profit from its vast superiority in numbers once the wall had been breached.

It should be understood that at the time of the creation of the city walls, gunpowder had not yet been invented. The artillery of the time, as we all know, consisted of catapulted projectiles. Although we have since learned the art of casting cannons and to use gunpowder to fire them, there has to my knowledge never existed a range of guns comparable to those employed by the Sultan during the siege of Constantinople. At his disposition he also had a brilliant German engineer supervising the casting of barrels, carefully calculating their elevations and force of impact. The same man had previously offered his services to the Emperor, who in my opinion should have accepted them. If the towers and turrets of the city had been prepared to absorb the shock caused by its own guns, it could have successfully countered the enemy fire by aiming at the destruction of its artillery. In the event this was never possible, and the truth is, that not all of the destruction of the walls was caused by enemy fire; some of the damage, yes I'm talking about veritable cracks and fissures, resulted from the use of our guns as the towers proved to be too weak to withstand the force of their repercussions. The consequence was that we couldn't even use the little artillery we had to full effect.

The lesson here is that artillery of this magnitude, if allowed to unleash its full power of destruction, will in due course bring down any city in the world. And the reason why I point this out to you, gentlemen, is because I really want you to pay attention to the following categorical statement: Unless something is done to simultaneously better and reinforce the construction of town walls around Europe, every single town will be doomed provided that the enemy has the necessary fire power and a chance to apply it. I therefore urge you, governors of our noble republic, to immediately consider the reconstruction of our own city walls, vulnerable as they are to attacks from both land and sea. So far, the best idea I have heard of comes from none less than the venerable Archimedes of Syracuse. Almost two thousand years ago he suggested that a wall built in an exact 90 degree angle to the ground is considerably more likely to crumble under artillery than a wall with an outward declination of 10 to 20 degrees. Of course, apart from being more difficult to construct, such walls would also be easier to climb once one gets close enough, and for this reason the upper reaches of them should still be kept perpendicular to the ground. Projectiles launched at this kind of inclined lower wall, however, will have considerably less impact than projectiles fired onto traditional walls, and it is this reduction in the destructive power of enemy fire which any walled defence must henceforth consider its most vital concern. If such measures are not taken, and taken soon, I predict the imminent end of siege warfare except between contending powers of limited artillery capacity, such as our Italian republics and city states. Faced with an enemy equipped with the latest technology and quasi unlimited manpower, such as the Ottoman army at present, none of our cities will stand a chance. Our only hope will be that some other big enemy, closer to our borders, will find the prospect of governing our city interesting enough to overtake responsibility for its timely defence and meet the enemy army in open battle.

This said, I conclude my reflections by adding that it now seems imperative to me that Genoa turns its attention westward, in particular to the possibility of transatlantic exploration. From the east we have been hit with pestilence, a calamity now reinforced by the Turkish military and fiscal presence in practically all of the eastern Mediterranean as well as in the Black Sea. Once proud and independent Galata has seen itself being reduced to a defenceless community subject to exactly the same laws and restrictions as other Christian enclaves subjugated by the Turks. Thus, we are not about to loose our dominant position as a nation of maritime trade, we have already lost it. We must consequently turn our regards towards new horizons. Although we should build our walls strong and high, they must not be so high as to obscure the sun and block out the sea. Dear gentlemen, we have but one direction of expansion, and that is overseas. Let that be our guiding star for now and for the future.

May God protect our glorious city and republic, like a watchful eye in the wide sea.

Chief Commander Giovanni Giustiniani Longo"

Chapter 73

– Was that all?

Bishop Leonard, a mischievous smile on his lips, looked up from the paper and scrutinised Giovanni. The latter, exhausted by the effort, closed his eyes while hinting a nod.

– I'd say that was a fine plea, forcefully argued and certainly not without merit.

– But you don't believe in it, do you?

– It does make a strong case, and I wouldn't be surprised if the magistrates take kindly to your apology.

– Apology? It's above all a military argument. Ah, you didn't like the "just as little as they would be able to clear their names by accusing me", did you? And you're not going to endorse my opinion in your own report, are you?

– First of all. If ever I write anything on my experiences of the siege, it will be addressed to his holiness the Pope, as he happens to by my supreme authority. Secondly, I doubt that the city of Genoa will ever endeavor to find the means, nor the motivation, to undertake anything so risky as to navigate beyond the known confines of the Atlantic ocean.

– But we have Admiral Zheng He's own map to prove that there really is an unknown continent out there, and since you yourself said that the earth is spherical.

– Excuse me, I said nothing of the sort.

– But I heard you myself, you said…

– It was by way of hypothesis. As a man of the church I obviously can't risk advocating such an uncertain and potentially dangerous proposition.

– For God's sake, Leonard! Aristotle knew it, Eratosthenes calculated its circumference and Archimedes planned a fleet taking those calculations into consideration – and that was all more than two thousand years ago! How come we have grown so incredibly ignorant that we can't even admit what is apparent to the naked eye? If I climb the Ligurian mountains above Genoa I can see Corsica in clear weather, when I go down to the seashore it disappears. Why is that would you say?
– It's because the atmosphere is much denser at sea level.
– Nonsense, Leonard, and you know it!
– I'm afraid I can go no further in this discussion. Was there anything else you wanted from me before I leave? I shall travel to the north of the island tomorrow.
– As a matter of fact, there is one small thing. I was just wondering if you could help me get married this evening.
– Married? To whom?
– To whom do you think?
– Not to that Turkish woman, I hope.
– She has converted to our faith, Bishop, and I would much appreciate it if you, for want of something even more pejorative, abstained from calling her "that Turkish woman". Her Christian name is Felicia. I love her very much. As a matter of fact, you've got to help me to settle this with the church, or I'll be damned.

Giovanni urged Leonard to approach his bed and put his head next to his. Very softly he added,
– She's pregnant, you know…

Leonard rose, took a deep breath, adjusted his purple robe and prepared to leave the room.
– Alright, he said, – But let that make us square. As you have correctly inferred, I have little sympathy for the willful choices you seem to be making in your life, but I do admit that most of the time you've behaved like a man. And yes… she is a very beautiful woman. I'm sure you'll be able to make her happy. And I do hope your health will soon be restored. At what time did you say you wished the ceremony to take place?
– Thank you, Bishop. I won't forget it, and I do appreciate your honesty. Would you be able to come here after sunset to perform the sacred ritual? Excellent, see you then.

Leonard was already half way through the door when Giovanni made him turn round one last time.

– By the way, and please forgive me my curiosity, how did you ever manage to get out of the city a full day after it fell and apparently unseen reach Galata?
– That, my friend, will remain a secret between me and Francis.
– Francis, the secretary?
– The same, and perhaps the only true friend the Emperor ever had. Now, try to get some sleep signor Giustiniani. You look like you need some.
– I wish I could fall asleep for a hundred years, Giovanni mumbled.
– Yes, but don't. You'll be late for your wedding.

In the afternoon the two rings arrived which the goldsmith had ceaselessly been working on since the day before. Each took the form of an exquisitely braided gold band, inlaid between the slightly elevated rims, ended in a stylised representation of the two-headed eagle, the coat of arms of the house of Giustiniani, crowned with an amethyst. Giovanni weighed them in his hands, feeling a strange kind of power emanating from them. The two rings were wonderfully complimentary, Giovanni's stone being slightly bluish, hers more purple. While supervising the servants about to decorate the room, spreading table cloths, putting candelabras and chalices in place, he presented his compliments to the family jeweler Isaac and made sure he was handsomely rewarded. By sunset everything was prepared. It was suggested that Giovanni should be propped up in his bed, but instead he insisted on being dressed for the occasion and seated. Members of his family had gathered in the room, gossiping, laughing, whispering, until they were told to remain quiet and Felicia, dressed in an elaborately embroidered white gown, illumined by a hundred wax candles, entered the room accompanied by Lorenzo Giustiniani, an uncle of Giovanni's and the elderman of the Chios branch of the family. In her hair a spider-web-thin net with clustering gems reflected the lights of so many stars. Her profile nobler than that of Nefertiti, her eyes darker and more inscrutable than those of Cleopatra, her mouth more red than a ripe cherry, she was escorted to the altar, where Bishop Leonard, the central figure between two incense burners, had begun the incantations preceding the ceremony of holy matrimony.

Outside, in the streets and squares of the town of Chios, rumours spread that local boy Giovanni Giustiniani was finally marrying, hands pointing in the general direction of two gothic windows festively lit on the top floor of Palacio Giustiniani. And as people, filling their goblets with wine, began to celebrate the beautiful bride and her bridegroom, who no matter what church dignitaries and politicians had to say, remained a hero of the people; the sun, hidden behind the western horizon, fanned its waning rays like a peacock feather over the sky, spreading its Argus eyes in glittering swarms, fading like dying fireworks into the rapidly darkening eastern horizon.

– Do you, Felicia take this man's hand in marriage, promising to love and care for him until death do you part?

The moment was as intense as it was exalted, and after Giovanni Giustiniani Longo had been asked the same question, and given the identical answer, the windows were opened wide and the news joyfully propagated, first through the streets and taverns of the town, then along open country roads and winding hill paths, at the end of which it reached the fisherman's hut. The fisherman's wife, however, was not in residence. She was a special guest of honour, her daughter chief bridesmaid, while her son Manuel, seven years old, proudly escorted the hero to the altar.

Giovanni participated in the celebrations of his own wedding as much as he could, but although his fever had begun to abate he was still unsteady on his legs and soon had to return to bed. His wife was the last to leave the room, kissing him good night.

– Sweet dreams, my love she whispered as he was about to enter the shadow lands.

But it was almost as if destiny was mocking the joy and happiness of the evening. His dreams did not turn out sweet at all. For days he had suffered from anxiety and feverishly contorted visions. This night proved to be no exception. He dreamed that he was back on the walls inspecting one battalion after the other as they filed in front of him. While still on the approach, the soldiers seemed vigorous and eminently disciplined. But the closer they got to their commander, the weaker they became. When finally reporting for duty, Giovanni saw that they were all, without exception, horribly mutilated, lacking legs, arms, sometimes even heads, their entrails hanging out of their bellies, armours stained with blood and bile. Terrified Giovanni realised that all his men, many of whom were no longer clearly recognisable, were all dead and that he must order them to return whence they came, to the land of the dead. At that moment he looked out over the Lycus valley and saw thousands and thousands of mortally wounded soldiers marching into the darkness where they disappeared. Giovanni felt his heart gripped by a sadness beyond words as the Emperor himself walked up to him, his head under his own arm.

– I shall be the last to leave you, the blood stained head said, – But before I return to my loyal friends and warriors, I want you to understand that all these dead men, including myself, make up the price you choose to pay to get your freedom. Now go away, enjoy it, and don't ever bother us again.

– Your Majesty, – Giovanni stuttered, – I never meant for this to happen, I swear it was an accident, just an accident.

But Constantine's eyes, deep and melancholy, just stared at him, while the mouth of the severed head uttered the words,

– It's too late Giustiniani Longo, it's too late. Your regrets will never bring us back. You killed us, you killed us all. Now go, before I change my mind and have you killed too.

The Emperor, putting his staring head on the battlement, mounted his white, steaming horse and rode off into the darkness. At the same time Giovanni saw that the sky was full of stones raining down on the abandoned city. He ran for his life towards the harbour while a giant boulder came hurtling upon him from the sky.

Bathing in his own sweat and panting for air, Giovanni woke up in horror. So intense was the experience that it took him a while to even realise it had only been a dream. For the longest time he couldn't rid himself of the sensation that the walls and ceiling around him were in reality those of a tomb in which he had been buried alive. The images kept rolling through his head for hours after, but sometime before dawn he must have dozed off, because when he woke up his wife sat next to him.

– How are you? She said, – You seemed so worried in your sleep, moving your lips as though you were talking to someone, sighing, moaning. I just wanted to tell you to at least not worry about me. I'll be fine and I promise you I'll arrive safely in Venice – with the map.

– Thank you, love. I too believe you'll be fine, otherwise I would never allow you to go. It's just that I had such a bad dream… I don't really know… it just feels so terribly, terribly wrong somewhere, as though my conscience will never allow me a peaceful moment again.

– Would you like to tell me what it was all about?

– Oh, I don't think I should bother you… It's the same old thing.

– You mean you feel guilty because you didn't stay and give your life for the Emperor.

– You know, perhaps he was right. Perhaps we could still have pushed them back, perhaps the defeat was not inevitable. But when that second piece of metal entered my body, I suddenly had no command over myself any longer. I swear to you, it was the strangest thing, I simply had no force, I just… lost it, and then… I was carried away. Can't even remember if I ordered it myself or if someone else took that decision. Oh God, it's as if I don't want to remember, as if I'm refusing to accept… What am I to do, Felicia? How can I justify my actions, or lack of action, in the face of God… I just don't know any longer.

– I know how you must feel, Felicia said, – and I know you're accusing yourself of not having done everything you possibly could to prevent the catastrophe. But in reality, deep, deep down, you know none of you would have survived, and then, what would have become of you and me? You know, it isn't all that difficult to die like a man. It only takes a moment. The really difficult thing is to live like one.

There was a long silence in the room during which they just watched one another. Finally Giovanni broke it saying,

– That was really eloquent, Felicia. But although those words were perfectly true, they nonetheless were only just words. And you don't really have the right to pronounce them, because you neither know what it is to live like a man, nor what it is to die like one.

– I was up there a couple of times. I saw what it was like.

– Yes, and you did really fine. But that's not what I'm talking about. It's one thing is to visit a battlefield, another thing to endure the battle. And you simply don't know what it's like not getting any sleep for two months, to be constantly cold, wet and hungry, to have every bone in your body aching, to always expect the next projectile to hit you, to listen to men cry out in agony as their bodies are torn apart, to smell the putrefied odours of urine, of faeces, to wade through the entrails of dead and dying men, to see a wall of death and destruction come against you, and try hard not to lose control of your own bladder and bowels, to be surrounded by death and the dead every minute of your life, to mercilessly kill every single one of those bastards trying to scale your fortress, even and quite especially when their eyes beg you to spare them, to do all this, and still try to maintain some kind of respect for human dignity and value. Felicia, the truth is that you die out there, even if you survive. You can't do it and come back to your wife, your children, your country as if nothing ever happened. Something has changed; you're dead, on the inside. And even if only you know it, and nobody else will notice, and you still have some kindness in your heart, a sense of justice and charity perhaps, you have become dead to this world. In a sense then, it really doesn't matter if you die for real or linger on in one form or another. To live like a man, it all sounds so great. But the thing is that once you have become a man, you can no longer be proud of it. It was only when you were a still a boy that you would dream of becoming a hero. To actually be the hero, is to sacrifice yourself, is to die, one way or the other. And all heroes, eventually, have to die.

When Felicia saw the earnest and sorrow in Giovanni's eyes accompanying his words, she couldn't hold back her tears.

– I'm sorry, she said, – I didn't mean to sound as though I knew anything. I just don't want to lose you. Please, Giovanni, please, whatever you do, don't die on me. Please…

Chapter 74

Leaning on to the escritoire, gazing through the vaulted window, Giovanni saw the ship carrying Felicia and her precious cargo set sail and vanish into the fog. Towards noon the morning mist had dissipated, but then the ship was no longer visible on the horizon. Five days earlier a Genoese ship from Galata had arrived. In its hold it had more refugees from Constantinople. Among them were Irene's brother Zacynthos, who had the dolorous task of delivering the news that her husband Iannis had fallen in battle close to the palace of Blachernai while heroically defending one of its postern gates. Irene and the children were devastated. They had never given up hope that their ever resourceful father and husband must have found a way out of the city. Irene now believed he surely would have survived, had it not been for that religious extremist Gennadi, now apparently enjoying happy days in Edirne. She also knew that Iannis had not fallen in battle, because he had told them he would join them at the monastery before it was too late. There had never been a question of him taking up arms. So how on earth could it be that his dead body had been found in a place where there hadn't been one single further casualty on either side?

Luckily Irene and the children were not just abandoned. They were provisioned for by the Giustiniani family, which would always remain grateful for what they had done for them. They were given a pleasant house with a small garden to live in close to the port. In addition Irene was to receive a yearly pension of 30 ducats for the rest of her life. Furthermore, the children were to be provided with a private tutor, allowing them to make progress not only in all the arts and sciences, but in Latin and Italian as well. It was an exceptional opportunity for these Greek refugees of the common people, and one they would never have had in Constantinople regardless of who its ruler was. Irene would never grow tired of instilling in the children how lucky they should consider themselves. Along with the offerings to the soul of their departed father, they all prayed together and lit candles for aunt Felicia as they now called her, asking the Madonna to protect her, her husband, and her forthcoming child from all evil.

Standing opposite each other on the pier, hearing the ship bell sound departure, Irene and Felicia fell in each other's arms. Felicia then embraced the children, encouraging them to do well in school until the day she would come back to visit them. This they all promised, waving to her, gifts in hand, as Iannis' small boat which had served them so well took her out to the waiting brigantine. Then she was gone.

Back home, as they were lighting candles for her and their father, Manuel said,

– You know mother, you always say Father said things hard to believe. But that isn't so. Everything he said was true, except for one thing. He hadn't left the flying carpet in the boat.

Irene looked at her son and smiled inwardly,

– No Manuel, she said, embracing him and kissing him on his forehead, – The flyin' carpet was there alright. It was just – invisible. Because look, how else have we ever ended up here and got all our wishes fulfilled?

– An invisible carpet?

– But of course. The very finest, 'cause you hardly even notice you self flyin'. Suddenly you're just in a different place and you can't even tell what got you there.

– All I know is we came here with a boat and not on a carpet.

– Yes, but one day, many, many years from now you'll see your father again in a place you can only reach by magic. And then you'll know for sure you have actually been travellin' the air.

– Why do I have to wait that long?

– Because, because that's just the way it is, Irene replied wiping a tear from the corner of her eye. Now, would you like your favourite cake after dinner?

– Oh yes, mother, please let us have cake after dinner! the girls rejoiced.

Only Manuel had a hard time forgiving his father for having cheated him of his carpet ride. It was only many years later, when already a grown man, that Manuel too understood that his father had been right all along. But that's another story.

Meanwhile Giovanni was forced by the invisible enemy to return to bed. In his day Giovanni had seen many wounds of apparently harmless aspect turn into festering sores that would literally eat a man away from within. He consequently knew that the new wounds he had sustained might very well take a turn for the worse. As long as the fever held its sway the outcome was uncertain. It could go either way. He would have preferred Felicia to stay with him, nursing him back to health and vigour by her mere presence – as soon as that ship had left the bay he missed her intensely. Even though they had talked about a great many things, making extensive plans for the future, he still felt there was some important detail he had failed to convey in words. Truth was that the delivery of the Chinese map was a military assignment. It was the professional soldier in him that acted on its behalf and who couldn't tolerate procrastination, because he knew that a few days from now he might possibly be dead, where-after the map could easily fall into wrong hands. Although good old Luca, a man of unwavering loyalty, was still alive and installed at the local garrison, Giovanni didn't trust his judgment when it came to state secrets. And then there was the problem of Genoese ships being attacked by Venetian flotillas, doubtlessly searching for that map as well. No, it was a cunning plan to let her carry it into the lion's den. She was smart and she could do it. He felt sure of that. But then again he missed her in every fibre of his weakened body. Her eyes, her smell, her touch... And he loathed the idea of having to die. Especially at this point, since death now would be anything but heroic. He had Leonard's derogatory words ringing in his ears: if he were he to die here and now, his reputation would scarcely survive the calumny that he had let the personal interest of a foreign woman dictate the outcome of the entire battle of Constantinople. In short, Giovanni knew that at heart he had abandoned ship, and done so because of her. There were no two ways about it. Defection might be too strong a characterisation, but his word as a noble man and military commander had been compromised. That the only man who could recall the vow was now dead didn't make things better, since the unsolved dilemma had turned into a ruminating remorse, aggravated by Giovanni's present incapacity for action. There, in bed, he could no longer fight back sword in hand. The enemy he faced was nobody less than his own soul and conscience. He was vain enough to deplore the possibility that his family name, because of him, might for all time hence be stained. Glory and honour were not just empty words. They were the very backbone of his upbringing and training. At the same time he was well aware that his relation with the defunct empire from the standpoint of the Genoese republic would always be viewed in terms of commerce. Consequently the council would never openly accuse him for having failed in his mission as long as the Galatans survived and were allowed to continue their Black Sea trade. But again, it wasn't public opinion that bothered him. It was his own conscience and the ghastly presence of all these men who had given their lives in battle. In his feverish state the dream, in which Constantine appeared with his own head under one arm, was repeated *ad infinitum*. And he couldn't even ask Felicia to comfort him by holding his hand. Life was such a fragile thing, glory and honour transient, not to say ephemeral – his own life dangling in a thin thread that could be severed at any moment.

While brooding on the lugubrious prospects of his own imminent demise he dozed off. During his sleep the family's old midwife Agathe discreetly entered the room and put a letter on his blanket. He found it in the late afternoon, lit up by a sun which also illuminated the Gothic windows which were standing ajar, allowing the warm air and the capricious fragrances of early summer to stray freely in the room. He felt slightly less feverish and his heart jolted from sheer joy as he realised the letter must be from from Felicia. By opening it he had his happy suspicion confirmed. She must have written it just prior to departure, and although succinct in its wording, it was immensely melodious to his inner ear.

"My dearest and most beloved hero husband,

It is with a heavy heart that I part from you lying sick in bed. Until I hear from you again I will be sick myself from worrying about you. If only I were with you I know I could dissipate the clouds above your head. I would kiss you until you get well. I would also tell you, once again, that the choice we made was the right one, because it does not only concern us but the lives of beings still in God's mind. Constantine may be one of the ungrateful dead, but future generations will carry your name into history and you yourself, long after your time here on earth, will appear in legendary tales. We can not fight destiny, nor retrace our steps. There is no turning back and the dream we call life must continue with or without us. I pray the Almighty that our destiny is to live side by side for years to come. Moreover, I pray to God every hour to give you the courage to fight and win the battle for your own life. You must survive and be reunited with me! Do you hear me?

I love you, and I love you, and I love you!

Felicia

When Giovanni again closed his weary eyelids he no longer saw the nightmarish image of Constantine before him, but two deep brown almond-shaped eyes, a bird's nest of fluffy hair, full red lips and two divine breasts swelling in anticipation of the hungry human creature growing under her bosom. Before he again fell into a deep, dreamless sleep, the vaguely bemusing thought crossed his mind that she really must be in earnest, and that in the end God might forgive him for having been weak in the flesh, now that he was a married man, and she a respectable woman. At the same time he knew that as long as he would still be allowed to remain on earth, the horrors of the siege and the final battle would continue to haunt him. Quite especially the last words he had heard Constantine pronounce: "You boneless, slimy coward. Get on your feet so that your men can see you're still standing. For Christ's sake, get on your feet, you're bringing us all down!" From far away, as if gazing at the scene from the opposite end of a field glass, he then saw the emperor furiously throw his imperial regalia to the ground, grab a sword and throw himself into the boiling snake pit, where, moments later, he disappeared out of sight.

Later Giovanni was told, that in spite of Mehmet's subsequent promise of a huge reward for whomever could deliver to him the Emperor's corpse, it was never found. It was also said that his spectre kept showing up on the ramparts at night in the form of a headless rider on a white horse. That it had to be the ghost of the late Emperor was clear from the unanimous observation, that the stately mare was covered in a swathing blanket carrying the imperial emblem, and that the rider had a cut off head with the Palaeologi dynasty's imperial crown tucked under his left arm.

Giovanni could hardly remember what had in the final analysis compelled him to appear by the doomed man's side. Whatever the motives might have been, God's will to bring him into contact with Felicia now seemed to not only supersede the purpose of his mission to Constantinople, but that of his entire life. "If I were to die now", he concluded, "that too would have been in vain. Even though I might live on through my son, I will not be there to see him grow up and become a man. And forever will those rosebud lips be taken away from me. In truth, I wouldn't like to lose her now. I really wouldn't..."

Chapter 75

On the Venetian island of Crete, Alex Diedo hauled into port. After having made his report, he was exonerated – just as he had predicted – from all accusations of non-cooperation with other Venetian captains by referring to previous orders. He might have hoped to get a few days off to rest up, but he was instructed to immediately return to Venice. This time his mission was to bring Jacob Foscari, the Doge's only son held in custody in Crete, to stand trial before the Council of Ten on charges of conspiracy with enemies of the republic. Jacob, already once banned from Venice after having being accused of implication in the murder of a council member, knew this was going to be his last chance to clear his name. And so did his father.

Francesco Foscari, the ageing, appointed leader of the Venetian republic, sometimes seemed to take little interest in the republic's immediate affairs. Often absent from the council's deliberations, he preferred to remain an anonymous power, shaded by the stained glass windows of the ducal palace. In these days the thing that concerned him the most was the fate of his only son. Following a renewed investigation by the council, Peter Loredan and his party – who had been the sworn enemy of the Foscaris ever since Francesco's election to the ducal office thirty years earlier – had gained an important foothold by managing to have Jacob's case opened again. Peter Loredan, a maritime, richly decorated war hero and the foremost proponent of Venice's eastward expansion, never grew tired of criticising Foscari's *terra firma* policies. For three full decades, opinions in Venice had been divided over the question of whether the republic should primarily seek to reinforce and expand its dominions in the eastern Mediterranean, or strive to lay the foundations of a land empire by slowly, but relentlessly, bring the weaker cities of the Italian north into their fold. The goal, eventually, was to force Milan and Florence to their knees, and to create a pan-Italian state under Venetian sovereignty. But after thirty years of inconclusive fighting garnished with uneasy truces, the idea of *terra firma* expansion which had enthused so many followers of Foscari, had ground to a halt, leaving its instigator vulnerable and open for attack. For Loredan and his clan this was an opportunity not to be missed, all the more so since, in addition, the future of Venice's long standing sea empire looked more uncertain than ever after the deplorable fall of Constantinople. Somebody had to be blamed for Venice's inner discord, poor finances and uncertain prospects. Peter Loredan was determined it wasn't going to be him.

Ever since those mysterious tarot card from the Sforza court had first been presented to the Doge, he had, willy-nilly, grown more and more interested in them. Although he knew that potentially they represented a threat to his unbiased judgment and cool intellect, he could not quite resist the temptation to regard them as symbolic harbingers of events to come. Had they not been astonishingly accurate in predicting the fate of Constantinople? Foscari liked to think so and he was now seeking advice in arcane divination on behalf of his son and the continuation of his family line. His greatest frustration, however, was that his plan to force the Genoese to hand over the sensational Chinese map had utterly failed. It might otherwise very well have been Jacob's ticket to freedom, showing him as a glowing patriot, zealous in his quest for Venetian independence, prosperity and domination. Little did Francesco know how close at hand it actually was.

A steady stream of refugees, not only from Constantinople, but from all of Greece had prompted various legislative bodies of Venice to formulate clearer rules for the acceptance of those seeking asylum within the republic. People who could pay their way obviously were in a more favourable position, but Venetian authorities were also on the lookout for skilled workers, especially specialists in ship building, as well as men of learning who not only brought wisdom in general, but specifically incunabula containing the ideas and theories of Greek philosophers and mathematicians. In some cases such scholars, although financially destitute, were able to buy themselves Venetian citizenship by simply donating a precious manuscript to the city. As soon as it became generally known among refugees heading for Venice that a piece of writing that looked ancient enough could be turned into a passport to freedom, the number of alleged treatises by Aristotle and Pythagoras offered to the state increased to an almost alarming degree. The scholars already accepted soon found themselves hired by the authorities to scrutinise and determine the authenticity of every new document presented. But no matter what, all refugees, and there were no exceptions allowed, had to go through quarantine for two weeks before being allowed into the city proper.

One of the greatest fears of a densely populated town like Venice was the spread of pandemics. The plague which befell Europe a century earlier had left an indelible mark on Venice too, and there had been several new outbreaks, albeit less devastating, ever since. To this end the *lazarettos*, such as the Santa Maria di Nazareth, on the lagoon were now over crowded and in themselves breeding grounds for disease. Felicia was lucky to share a room together with a mere thirty other women, most of whom were Greek. Felicia's own documents presented her as a Greek from ancient Phrygia, but she was careful not to reveal that secret to the other inmates, who could easily have denounced her foreign origin on account of her slight Turkish accent. Felicia's fluency in Italian, although in principle a valuable asset, was also potentially dangerous as it now contained many traces of Genoese wording and dialect. In the end, it was the letter of recommendation on Felicia's behalf from the Mayor of Chios to the widow of the unfortunate captain Antonio Rizzi, which opened the gates for her. A bewildered Elenor Giustiniani Rizzi, who had no idea she had some important Greek relative, met Felicia on the Piazza di San Marco and escorted her to her house. Once inside Felicia could finally reveal her true identity and hand over the explanatory letter from her husband, Elenor's brother. At the bottom of her traveling chest, under what seemed little more than a mess of female paraphernalia, the map, wrapped in a purple scarf, was still intact and carefully put aside. The scarf also contained a letter from Giovanni to Elenor, obviously of much more immediate interest to them both.

– Oh God, he's still alive! You can't even imagine how much I have missed him. How is he?

– Elenor, I pray to God every hour of the day that he will survive and get well again! Why does he even have to do this to me? When I left Chios, on his insistence, he was still battling a fever, but the doctor, seeing that he was still alive after a week, said there was a good chance he'd make it. But infections are always dangerous; they can go away, seemingly, only to come back with renewed strength. I'm worried sick about him, and I didn't want to leave him. I hated the idea, but he literally forced me, and now he forces me upon you as well.

– It must be some document of unimaginable value, considering he was adamant about your leaving the day after you had just got married.

– I don't understand it either. But I hate to think he just wanted to get rid of me.

– No, never. He's not like that. If he says he will do something, he will do it and stick to his word. My brother is honesty itself. Now, you must tell me everything about how the two of you met.

Over the next hours Felicia gave Elenor a breathtaking account of how she was visited by a vision and in a near somnambulistic state set out to reach Constantinople. When she arrived at the point in her story where Giovanni admitted to her that he too had been deceived as to the underlying motives of his quest in Constantinople, Elenor suddenly moaned, objecting,

– No, no, he meant it. He wanted to see that beast dead just as much as I did, you must never think otherwise!

Felicia, who didn't know anything about Giovanni's sacred vow to his sister, and only now became acquainted with the cruel circumstances surrounding her husband's death, suddenly understood that she and Elenor had more in common than just being sisters in law. She also saw that Elenor was still fired up by hatred and a burning desire to see her dead husband avenged. But Felicia felt that unless there were divine intervention, Mehmet was likely to enjoy many years to come, and she tried to the best of her capacity to make some sense of that as well.

Eventually she even threw her child to be into the discussion, at which point Elenor suddenly stopped her tirades, exclaiming,

– That's it, that's going to be our child of revenge. *Ille fecit!*

– No dear Elenor, with all due respect. Not even Giovanni would like to have it that way. Believe me, this child will not avenge any of us, because is not a child born of hatred. It's a child of love.

Meanwhile, in the holy city of Rome, the bewitched Pope Nicholas stared into Raymond Lull's circular toy as though he had been staring into the blank of the eye of the devil himself. For hours he had been contemplating the apparent blasphemy inherent in the suggestion that love and hatred might be considered two sides of the same coin. As far as human affairs were concerned, it was of course not only conceivable but unavoidable. Nicholas recalled the doctrine of the pagan philosopher Empedocles of Sicily, then part of *Magna Grecia*, according to which the two fundamental forces of the universe were love and hatred inscribed in a circle flowing in and out of one another in endless opposition and union – *philia* and *neikos*. But that was the pagan idea before Christ arrived, and how could the love of the perfect man ever have anything whatsoever to do with hatred? It must be refuted, he thought, but then, as though illumined by divine dispensation, he came to think of a possibility. What if perfect love could be seen as the other face of divine wrath? It was apparent that God in his omnipotence had on numerous occasions throughout history showed himself merciless to those people who did not obey his commands. In acts of sudden vengeance he would then either destroy or visit terrible calamities upon them, and these acts had ever since unanimously been interpreted as signs of his love, at least where they concerned his chosen ones. Could the destruction of Constantinople thus be regarded as a sign of his love insofar as it was a *Mene Tekel*, such as it appeared written on the wall before the terrified Belshazzar, serving as a warning for the Catholic church not to get stuck in the same doctrinal intolerance as the eastern church? Was it possible then that the Catholic church, seized by divine rage, could actually inspire the western powers to mount another crusade against the infidels now desecrating his abode on earth?

For a moment Nicholas wanted to believe it, but his scholastic discipline finally came to his rescue. Furious at the failure of Venetians, Catalans, Genoese, Germans, Hungarians, Serbians, Albanians, Franks, Germans and Anglo-Saxons to give Byzantium a helping hand, furious at Ramon Lull and his diabolical instrument, he picked it up from the table and flung it against the wall where it shattered in pieces. In the same moment a lightning flash lit up the wall and a deafening thunder rolled through the room. There was violent rain to be expected, and Nicholas hurried down the stairs of his palace to rescue the lavish papal robe he had unsuspectingly left on a chair in his garden.

At the very same moment, in the chiaroscuro of the ducal palace of Venice, Doge Francesco Foscari could no longer resist the temptation to spread a celtic cross for himself and his son. It told the story in vivid detail. The penultimate card depicted a man standing outside a palace distributing money to the poor. Francesco saw in it the spitting image of himself, because all morning he had been signing petitions from needy citizens and institutions; in fact, a great part of his renown rested on his famous charity, in particular his concern for the less wealthy noble families of the city, for schools, monasteries and hospitals. The card immediately beneath it depicted a desolate young man pierced by swords. It was the image of Jacob, no doubt about it. Trembling, Francesco drew the last card, indicating the outcome of the event in question. It was The Tower. A younger and an older man had been ousted from a burning tower, helplessly falling to the ground. It was the very same card that weeks earlier had given Francesco the secret satisfaction of knowing the Byzantine Emperor to be in trouble, because if Constantinople fell, the blame, whether he deserved it or not, would fall on Peter Loredan, by public consensus considered responsible for upholding Venice's strongholds in the east. This time around Francesco had a most chilling sensation. The card indicated his and his son's downfall. Disgusted Francesco stared at it. Then he returned all the cards to the deck, shuffled them on the table, re-collected them and put them away in his cabinet, firmly determined never again to believe in such unabashed superstition.

Chapter 76

Felicia was received and welcomed like a true sister into Elenor's house. During the days that followed the two women got to know each other better. They felt a bond growing between them dictated by the love they both had for Giovanni. And the one did not infringe upon the other; existing side by side they only seemed to strengthen one another and confirm their hope for his return.

On the second day of Felicia's stay, Elenor, following Giovanni's instructions, sent for signor Colombo who promptly arrived. The two women were eager to see his reaction to the map which obviously was of such immense importance to so many men of this world. They were not going to be disappointed. A last letter from Giovanni explained how the Galatans had managed to buy it from the Sultan and pass it on to him to bring back to Genoa.

Domenic Colombo, having studied the map very carefully, finally looked up.

– I thank you ladies for giving me such extraordinary opportunity to be part of history in the making. This map will one day change the world in ways we can't even begin to dream of. If I have understood your brother's words correctly, I'm supposed to take it with me and without delay bring it to Genoa, where it will be presented to the Great Council.

Felicia nodded.

– That's exactly what he wants you to do. He also sent this money for you to cover your travel expenses. It is his wish, on behalf of the Genoese government, that you will set out for Genoa as soon as circumstances allow.

– Venerable ladies, we shall all hope for Giovanni's recovery and safe return. Meanwhile I'll make my preparations and shall be leaving Venice tomorrow. I thank you immensely for having safeguarded this map with your life, and I'm sure you will be rewarded according to the great service you have done for our republic. Farewell.

A week later, after a perilous journey through lands and towns torn apart by factional interests and family feuds, Domenic arrived in Genoa. Still a week later he was admitted to an extraordinary assembly of the Great Council, presided by Peter Campofregoso, appointed Doge of the republic. Asked what his opinions were concerning the authenticity and possible value of the map, Domenic Colombo answered, that,

– In my view, this is the most valuable map that has ever been produced in the entire world. It comes directly from the head quarters of the legendary Chinese admiral Zheng He, known to have made eight major sea voyages, the last of which brought him to a *terra australis*, hitherto unknown to both Europeans and Asians. There are numerous legends about his last voyage, but they all concur in describing the land he discovered to be rich beyond imagination in gold, silver, jade and other precious materials. I agree completely with Commodore Giustiniani Longo, who by the way is sending you his best regards, that this map could serve as the spring board from which Genoa can again acquire a status of *primus inter pares* among the states of the world fighting for supremacy. You will find Giustiniani's own reflections on the matter in this letter, sent from Chios where at present he's recovering from the many wounds he sustained as high commander during the ominous siege of Constantinople. Since his opinions in this matter completely coincide with mine, I shall not burden you gentlemen with redundant repetition.

Domenic Colombo was thanked for his valuable service to the republic, whereupon he was invited to excuse himself. After many hours of deliberations in the council it was decided that the map, though no doubt of extraordinary value, was of no immediate interest to the republic as the latter sadly lacked the funding necessary to prepare for an expedition destined to find out about the unknown. At the same time it was absolutely essential that none of Genoa's enemies should be given the chance to get hold of it. It was therefore sealed up in a box and carried deep down to the cellars and archives of the ducal palace, where it was stored away among thousands of other documents of various importance and value. Once down there it was soon forgotten, and even though Domenic did ask a few times about its destiny, he was always given the answer that it was in safe custody, and that the city of Genoa was still considering how to best act in relation to it. There were however no immediate plans. And so the years went by.

Chapter 77

Certainly, Mehmet's entry through the Gate of St Romanus on the afternoon of May 29, had been a triumph resounding throughout his empire. But as prisoners were rounded up, houses stripped of their interiors and churches plundered, there was a moment of sober realisation on Mehmet's part. After all, the city hadn't been so full of riches as he and his soldiers had imagined. In fact, most of its official buildings were in such a dilapidated state that Mehmet as early as the actual day of conquest had to put an end to the promised three days of looting for the sole reason that there was nothing more to take. That same afternoon he had found some soldiers hacking away at church mosaics in the desperate hope of gathering some gold dust and a splinter of lapis.

Another few days after his victory, when the days of drunken frenzy had given way to one of general hangover, Mehmet rode over to the palace of Blachernai, where he knew the Emperor had lived. He was surprised at how small it was, how few the commodities were, in short, how frugal his court must have been. "Was it really worth it?" he asked himself, realising that he had been so intent on cracking open a nutshell for so long that he had forgotten to ask himself if there really was any nut inside it. But then he also remembered that the value of Constantinople did not so much reside in her non-existent treasures. It was, above all, an investment for the future, for the future control of all trade between the two seas. That was of course the purpose. He did, however, have to remind himself of it.

He looked up at the dusty beams, saw the holes in the wall caused by his own artillery, and heard the wind, like a forlorn bell, intone its melancholy melody in cracks and empty windows. "Spiders", he thought: "Everywhere spiders weave their webs and seem to feed on nothing, while the owls call the watches in the empty towers of Afrasiab." Was that an old Persian poem? A Sufi proverb? He couldn't remember where he had heard it, but it was something he had carried with him, like a forlorn bell, such as those he associated with the Christians. There were no such bells in the realm of Islam, no such bitter-sweet, melancholy song to accompany sunset and vesper.

The spiders were a different story. It was through the help of one single spider, weaving its web from the centre outward, finally entangling the entire city, that he, Mehmet II, had been able to force himself over its walls. Had that spider not been there, the defence would probably have remained uncorrupted long enough to allow the decisive moment to slip away. But thanks to that one black spider, a moth, by the Creator himself destined to seek the flame, had flown straight into it, only waiting to be consumed in a deadly embrace.

"I'll make him the new Patriarch, I will. And I'll let them keep the Saviour in Chora for their services. I wonder though, what ever happened to their famous relic, the Hodegetria? Rumours tell of a secret passageway in Hagia Sophia, through which four priests allegedly fled when my men stormed it, bringing the icon with them. But no hidden opening in the wall was ever found, and no one seem to know if one should believe in this story or not. The Greeks believe that there shall be a day when Constantinople is Christian again. Then the four priests, carrying the Hodegetria, shall return through the same passage way in the wall, and re-assume their service exactly where it was interrupted. Well, let them wait. From now on Islam and the Ottoman dynasty will rule the world. And there is nothing, absolutely nothing, that will be able to prevent us from becoming the masters of the entire world.

– Praise to thee Allah, the one and only God! Thank you for letting me carry out your intentions in this world! Thank you for choosing me as your humble servant!

In a gesture of deep humility, Mehmet bowed down, picked up some dirt from the floor and sprinkled it on his turban. A sigh from the wind, blowing straight through the palace, reminded him of the transience of existence. From far away a lonely owl was heard calling, persistently, into the evening.

Chapter 78

– Father! Father! You must tell me if it's true or not. I keep hearing these rumours all around town, that a map showing unknown continents full of the strangest creatures and riches is kept deep down in the vaults of the ducal palace, and that you sixteen years ago gave it to them, and never since have been allowed to take a second look at it. Now tell me, how could you do such a thing? I mean, you're a cartographer, at least in your spare time, aren't you?

– Christopher, don't stand there yelling. Come inside, and close the door. So you came to hear about the map, eh?

– Yes and I keep asking myself how it's possible that you so easily gave it away. I mean, it must be something extraordinary, right? You know how passionate I am about these things, all I can think of are ships, maps and voyages. I'm burning with the desire to get out there. Father, are you listening at all?

An apparently absentminded Domenic Colombo turned around and said,

– Hmm?

– I said, I'm dying to get out there, and why did you give them the map when they are doing absolutely nothing with it?

– Christopher, how old are you now?

– I will be eighteen next month. Why?

– Good, then you're actually old enough to keep a secret. Can you keep a secret?

– Of course, what is it?

– Will you solemnly swear to me to keep a secret?

– Yes, I just told you. What's it all about?

– I never gave them the map.
– You never gave them it?
– No.
– So why is it that they, and everybody else, think they have it?
– It's a copy. I had it made for them. It's accurate, but it's not the original. The original is right – here!

Domenic pulled out one of his large folders and opened it. And there it was.

– You're pulling leg my leg.
– No, I only pulled the drawer! I'd like you to have it as a gift for your birthday, but you can keep it in here together with the other maps if you like. I want you to study it, compare it to other maps, calculate and think. Because one day, my son, this map will be reality, and of all the people in this whole world, you may be the one who makes a voyage that nobody has ever made before.
– Father, this is amazing, and you still haven't told me anything! Where does it come from?
– Originally from China, but it was traded off by the Sultan of Turkey in the aftermath of the conquest of Constantinople. This all happened many years ago, when you were still a little baby.
– But how come the Sultan didn't realise the potential of such a map?
– You're right, he more or less just gave it away. I believe he considered it a mere curiosity. You see, these people of Islam are not very curious to know about the unknown, or even the unknowable. They are content that God, in his infinite wisdom, has provided everything for them, and so they don't feel the need to know more than what tradition and scripture has already given them. Now, although we Italians and Spaniards too are immensely grateful for all the blessings God has given us, we have this curiosity in our blood. We want to find out what lies beyond the horizon, because we can see it's just a line, and a moving line at that. Where's the border? That's what we want to know. And we won't stop short of reaching it.

Today and tomorrow the Sultan might still be the mightiest person in the known world. But there will be a day when the Turks have to regret that, in spite of their professed tolerance of religious creeds based on what they call "The Book", they have not been sufficiently open to new ideas. You see, when Constantinople fell, a number of brilliant minds fled Greece since they all saw that the Sultan, because of the rigidity of the religious doctrine he embraces, would never be able to listen to all the new and wonderful things they were about to discover. Instead they are now settling here in Italy, and so far we have only begun to see the marvels they are paving the way for. You see, one of the worst things a human being can ever do is to boast of his ignorance. It's not conceivable that God wanted us all to be ignorant. Because if that is so, he would have made sure we would still be surrounded by obscurity and superstition. But he has given us the light of understanding so that we may learn and better ourselves as we go along. Ignorance is bliss? Maybe so, but it's a bliss bestowed upon us by the devil, and anybody who maintains that we shall all remain ignorant and just believe what we have always been told, he too is of the devil!

– Now, this is all very secret stuff, and you must never whisper about what I have told you. Those who have broken new ground in this world have often been ridiculed by their fellow men, if not downright persecuted and even killed. Knowledge is dangerous for the one unprepared for it. I believe you are properly prepared to take responsibility for this map, but you must handle it with caution and don't tell anybody about its existence until you're absolutely sure that it will further your interests insofar as it brings you closer to achieving your goal. Last but not least, I want you to remember, that when we are young, we think we already know everything worth knowing. But I tell you, and mark my words, that the owl of Minerva – the very emblem of wisdom – never leaves her nest before dark. Only then can she finally see her prey. I promise you my son, there will be times on that big, big ocean when you're all surrounded by darkness and nobody will be able to see clearly ahead. That's when you need to have the vision of an owl and never, ever, lose sight of your goal.

– But what if nobody will ever believe me or my map? Maybe they'll all say it's a falsification, and that there isn't anything to be found out there except water and more water.

– I told you the earth is not flat, it's round. This much people will eventually be able to agree on. Thus, to those weak in faith you might have to pretend that you're going to, say – India!

– And how can you be so sure that there really is land between here and China?

– Because I also have other maps in my collection supporting the theory. One of them was made by monks on the remote island of Ultima Thule, and depicts a vast stretch of coastline way out in the

Atlantic ocean. The map also contains texts in Latin that describe how the pagan ancestors of these monks found people, cities, crops, even wine, on this new territory. The sources concur, my boy, and although all existing descriptions of this *terra nova* are incomplete, they are sufficiently coherent to allow for the hypothesis that there must be some continent between the Azores and Japan. Now, that's all for you to verify the day you actually get there. For now, would you please do the dishes, as you promised!
 – Father.
 – What is it?
 – One last question.
 – Alright.
 – Sea captains never have to do the dishes, do they?

Epilogue[1]

Il primo o ultimo Trionfo, numero zero: Il Mondo

Idle though it seems to speculate how things might have been had circumstances been different, I sometimes find myself ruminating over the past. But perhaps I should consider it rather natural, in view of the fact that the better part of my life is now behind me while little lays ahead. In other words, I have today many more memories than I have

---

1 This text by George Francis, perhaps intended as a letter, an introduction or some kind of invocation, remains enigmatic as it seems to be a fragment taken out of a wider context. It was found in the monastic archives of the Agios Papa Nicholaous in Corfu by Heinrich Schliemann on his way to excavate Troy. Alerted to its possible existence by informers in Venice, he purchased the letter in calligraphic writing on vellum for 100 drakhmas. On his return to Germany, Schliemann deposited the letter with his old friend, count Arthur Leyendecker von Leyenstein, himself an avid collector of antiquities and old manuscripts. Following von Leyensteins' untimely death, the letter remained in the possession of his widow. Eventually it was auctioned together with other documents of uncertain provenance and authenticity, and it is now part of a collection of medieval manuscripts at the University of Uppsala, Sweden. I was able to obtain a copy of the text and subsequently presented it to my old friend and professor emeritus in Greek, Mårten T:son-Odenson, who happily obliged me by transcribing the text to Swedish. It is on that translation the present English version is based. For whatever it may be worth, I present the fragment to the reader, feeling that it contains essential hints as to why Constantinople fell, provided by the eye-witness who perhaps stood the emperor closest. The chronicle referred to in the text no doubt is the part of Francis' well known *chronicon maius* that specifically deals with the siege. The heading in Italian, referring to the Tarot, appears in Italian in original, but is surely a later addition by another hand. – *The author*

future plans, and some of those memories not only still haunt me, but seem to gain intensity over time. You see, almost twenty-three years have elapsed since the fall of God's city on earth. My wife and I, having lost our children to the Sultan – they both ended up and died in his seraglio – decided to take the monastic vow shortly after we arrived here on Corfu as refugees. It was a unanimous decision, since of the affection between us – may her memory be blessed – only altruistic love remained.

The island is ideal for the kind of meditation prescribed by our holy faith; because when Greek men or women of some standing reach a certain age, it's expected of them to spend less time in service of the public good, and more time in pursuit of the peace of mind which befits a human being preparing to meet with his creator and answer for his life. Socrates' appeal, 'Know thyself', has never lost its appeal to Greeks hungry for divine wisdom. Like so many others before me, I must scrutinise my soul, prepare for the inevitable and teach my heart to remain impervious to fear. But the antique saying perhaps even closer to my heart, is that which states that "the best thing that can ever happen to a human being, is never to have been born; the second best, to die young." I did neither. And indeed, much of my life has been wretched. I lost everything I ever hoped for. On top of it all, and although I always tried to serve my master dutifully and with insight, I have to admit that oftentimes I acted little wiser than a fool or a court jester. It's sad beyond words having to regret one's life. That's the reason why I would at least like to find some peace in my heart before it's too late. May God in his infinite wisdom and foresight forgive me my sins.

The monastery that, in spite, or perhaps because, of my many sins, adopted me, is situated on the edge of the westernmost cape of the island. On this day of slowly waning summer, the sky alternates patches of clear blue with clouds charged with rain and thunder. Across the glittering bay, full of playing dolphins, I see the silhouettes of the village of Afionas and its long peninsula, grazed by goats and donkeys, slowly descending towards the turquoise sea. Beyond the island's northern cusp some islets rise out of the waters like monsters of some ancient saga. Cloudlike, the massive Albanian mountains stretch from north to south as far as the eye can behold. Opposite, in the direction of the afternoon sun, the sea lies unperturbed by sails all the way to the horizon, beyond which the heel of Italy comes crushing down against the enemies of Rome.

It would be easy to feel forgiven by nature herself in a place like this. But I know God gave me a soul to allow me to peer beneath the brilliant surface of reality. So was there, everything considered and in spite of appearances to the contrary, anything I could have done differently to help the empire escape its ignoble destiny? Although I still like to imagine this destiny as an ordeal before we shall all be reunited in the heavenly Hagia Sophia, surrounded by floods of light and a sky broken down into a mosaic of infinite depth and splendour, I do hope to one day meet again with my friend and master, the brave Constantine, for another and more mundane reason. I would like to convincingly demonstrate to him that he was actually mistaken about the reason for Venice's defiance. Subsequent events in the republic have revealed that the real cause of Foscari's reluctance to send aid wasn't his vexation over a broken marriage proposal, but an attempt to forestall his arch-enemy Peter Loredan. Over centuries the Loredan family had secured the future of Venice, and thereby also that of their own, by maritime conquests in the eastern Mediterranean. At the time of the final siege, the old Doge had begun to feel his power slip away from him while the noose around his son's neck tightened. The prime cause of this was Loredan's scheming to undermine his ducal power to the point where Foscari would be forced to resign. Foscari – whose claim to fame and glory was inextricably linked to his life-long policy of *terra firma* expansion – knew only too well, that giving the by now legendary war hero an opportunity to wrest Constantinople from the Sultan's grip would spell disaster for Foscari personally, since public opinion was bound to be swayed by the eloquence of his victory. It would mean the end not only of his own career, but also of his dynastic ambition to see his son succeeding him on the ducal throne. Later events fully confirmed that through Loredan's machinations and careful plotting, the old man was indeed brought down and forced to abdicate. Simultaneously his son was exiled for the very last time, because he died soon after having arrived back in Crete.

Neither Constantine nor I knew enough of Venetian politics to clearly realise this at the time. Indeed, there was precious little we could have done had the underlying circumstances been revealed to us, except hoping that Loredan's party would make short history of Foscari's reign. Alas, the man tried every trick in the book before finding himself outmanoeuvered. When finally cornered, the city bearing my master's name was no longer. Nor was the Emperor's body ever found, so nobody knows if he was even properly buried.

With hindsight it's easy for me to forgive Constantine the harsh words and accusations he threw at me on the eve of his demise. They must be understood against the background of desperation and impending disaster. It nonetheless saddens me that I parted from him with my heart in uproar. I do hope that, God willing, we shall meet one day in heaven and embrace each other in brotherly love.

On the other hand, I was perhaps biased against Lucas Notaras, because no matter how arrogant and self-conceited that man was, his fate was an atrocious one. At first he was treated by the Sultan with some leniency. The catastrophe came when it turned out that two of the young boys whom Mehmet had selected for his harem, were in fact Lucas Notaras' own sons. The distraught father pleaded in vain for their release. Solidly drunk for the third day in a row, Mehmet had savoured his conquest to the dregs and began to run out of ideas as to how to best entertain his officers at the banquets. Dancers of both sexes, fire-eaters, jugglers, acrobats, trained wild animals and hunts staged in the ancient hippodrome had begun to lose their charm. Everyone was drunk, satiated and seemingly indifferent to any new sensation. At this moment the Sultan's eye fell on one of the Notaras boys among the illustrious captives he kept in a giant, bell-shaped iron cage on display for the visual enjoyment of his dinner guests. Lucas Notaras, also among the captives, vociferously protested as his son was brought out of the cage and presented to the Sultan. Mehmed eyed him from head to heel, had him turn around and show various parts of his well-shaped body. When Lucas Notaras began protesting, he too was brought out of the cage together with his youngest son. Notaras fell on his knees imploring Mehmet to take his life in exchange for their freedom. But something in Notaras' voice, his usual arrogance perhaps, must have angered Mehmet, easily bad-tempered under the influence of wine anyway.

I underline the role of wine and hasch-hisch here, because I doubt that Mehmet under more ordinary circumstances would have resorted to such atrocities as he now did. When the father, in spite of having been ordered to keep quiet, began yelling and cursing at Mehmet and his men, Mehmet had the two boys' hands tied behind their backs. They were then abused in various unspeakable ways and finally, crying for help and mercy so heart-rendingly that it could squeeze tears out of a stone, they were strangled. Every time the devastated father closed his eyes to escape the horror, he received whip lashes over his face, and not before his two sons lay dead on the floor was he beheaded. Hereafter the bodies were thrown to the dogs and the festivities resumed, invigorated.

I find it hard to believe that our merciful Lord in heaven ever meted out such a cruel punishment for Lucas Notaras. But his death came about in this way and in spite of the esteem in which the Sultan held him for his courage and valiant fighting spirit. It is probable that he and his sons would have got away alive had not the father had the temerity to openly criticise the Sultan in front of all his guests. By all means, for boys to end up in the Sultan's harem can sometimes be a career opportunity. I have heard of young men receiving the best possible education there and going on to hold high offices within the Ottoman administration. Not being one of the Sultan's own sons also considerably lowers the risk of being assassinated by the mothers of royal babies and their accomplices among the eunuchs.

Even though I must admit that there have been times when I wished to see the man dead, I thus refuse to believe that God almighty ever wanted him to meet an end like this. It would have been proper for him to die, sword in hand, while defending his native city. Ultimately it was his impetuous character which brought about the very unnecessary tragedy. May his soul, and those of his poor innocent sons, rest in peace.

As for the survivors from the siege and fall of Constantinople, I have lost track of most. I did hear that Cardinal Isidore was made Latin Archbishop to Constantinople by the Pope – surely one of the emptiest titles that has ever existed. He then died in Rome many years ago.

More recently Bishop Leonard died in Chios. Although I can't say I ever really made friends with him – he always thought we Greeks were unreliable – I did find his honesty and sense of irony refreshing. And I guess he, just as little as I, could never forget the spectacular manner in which I helped him to escape the city. Knowing that we would sooner or later be discovered in the Blachernai cisterns where we had taken refuge, we both went back up into the abandoned house situated right above it, where we found some clothes that had belonged to a widow. We then dressed up as two old women, hoping to be able to make it over to the church of Our Saviour of Chora, inside which Leonard claimed there were Greeks being protected by explicit orders from the Sultan himself. While I was apprehended and forced to give up my disguise, to the apparent amusement of the Turks taking me prisoner, Leonard, referring to some bizarre agreement with Mehmet, managed to get inside the church before my identity was revealed. I was taken away, but for some strange reason the soldiers didn't dare to go after Leonard inside the church even though they must have known by now that he too had been dressed up. From the Chora he then made it down to the Horn and from there managed to get over to Galata. I can't understand how that was even possible, but from what I have heard that really is the way it happened.

About the right hand of my master, commander Giustiniani Longo, who in the critical moment of the siege failed to act with dignity, valour and honour, there are several rumours. Apparently he turned up in Venice a couple of months after the city's fall. Later, so they say, he had a fall out with the Genoese Government, in spite of the services he had undoubtedly rendered his country. Then – perhaps partly due to the many injuries he had sustained during the siege – he decided to renounce his military career altogether, and went to southern Germany to financially help out a man by the name of Gutenberg to print books, notably the Bible. While still in Germany he had his own treatise on siege warfare published, dedicating it to "any contemporary or future prince intelligent enough to read it, to understand it and to act according to its precepts." The last thing I heard was that he moved to Barcelona, where he has become a librarian, trading in antique and modern books as well as maps from the entire world. His wife, a Turkish noble woman who most mysteriously appeared in Constantinople in the midst of the siege, has followed him on his travels and given birth to in all seven children, four of whom are supposedly still alive and well to this day. In the depth of my heart I can't blame the man for having surrendered, but the only reason why I do forgive him, is that I know myself to be imperfect. Because as our Lord Jesus says: "It's easy to see the speck in your brother's eye but fail to recognise the beam in your own".

God, you who reveal your might in the dead of night or in the dazzling light of high noon! Thank you for having chastised my heart and humiliated my spirit. Only now have I truly learned to change what I can possibly change, and to accept as inevitable the events unfolding beyond my control. Here, on the beautiful island of Corfu, I have learned to see your grace through the immense horror which life itself presents us with on so many occasions. I know, however, that the suffering you inflict upon us is only meant to show us the path to the inner light of your wisdom, buried in the darkest recesses of our own hearts.

I see your sea, your trees and mountains. I see your limpid, perfect sky, blue like the robe of the Virgin herself. I know I have come here to die, embraced by your creation. During the days that might still be reserved for me, I hope you will give me the strength and lucidity of mind necessary to bring to its successful conclusion the chronicle of the siege and fall of Constantinople which I have recently begun. It has, as you well know, not been undertaken with the intention of justifying my own mortal sins and human error. Instead it serves the purpose of saving from oblivion the extraordinary heroism displayed by so many men and women who are now dead. It's also a memoir of my dead friend and master, Constantine XI Dragases, who gave the city his life in its ultimate hour of existence.

To him and so many others I'm indebted beyond words. I'm indeed privileged to sit here, beneath the warm wall of the monastery of St Nicholas, and know that when the sun, in its relentless course through the heavens, reaches the farther end of the sea beyond the islands, Vespers shall call me to hymns and prayers. Later, guided by a few lamps, I shall share bread, soup and wine with my brothers. Tomorrow, before dawn, we shall pray again and thank you Lord for giving us everything we need to live and to rejoice in thy name. And there will be another day preparing hundreds of olive trees for the coming harvest. In the valley the grapes are slowly saturating to the core, and from countless cypresses and pines, like soldiers in dutiful lines, comes the resin that so graciously preserves our amber coloured wine.

Oh God, let me thank you for having given me my life! You have created all this beauty for anyone who can see, and sometimes I feel that the only reason we close our eyes to the marvels of your will, is that the light illuminating your truth is almost blinding.

Just as every day is a gift from You, Creator of the World, so, having lived through this day is a miracle revealed. Everyone whose lonely barque succeeds in crossing the dark waters of the night to safely reach the shores of dawn, should remind himself that by so doing, he's been given *another* second chance.

In your name and glory, may the deeds of those who bravely gave their lives in defence of our holy city never be forgotten. Like amber preserves an insect that lived centuries ago, let my writing seal my memory against the corrosive effect of time. I confess that although I did uphold the idea of the union of the two churches for political reasons, nothing now prevents me from finally conceding Father Gennadi, presently Patriarch to Istanbul, to be right, by openly embracing that true article of faith which says that the Holy Spirit does not proceed from the Father and the Son, but manifests itself spontaneously as one of three hypostases of divinity, sharing equally and simultaneously the same arcane substance.

Corfu, September 29, 1476

Principal Characters
A Presentation

The Emperor

Constantine XI Dragases (after his Serbian mother Helena *Dragas*) descends from a long line of imperial rulers of the Palaiologos dynasty that recovered Constantinople in the mid 13th century from alien Frankish lords, who had been ruling Constantinople for half a century after taking it during the Fourth Crusade. He's the eighth child of ten. Although he rules the city in the absence of his emperor brother John between 1440-43, he probably never imagines that he is one day going to be its officially appointed head. The death of John changes all that. Even so, Constantine can only, and in competition with another brother, claim the imperial title through arbitration by his arch enemy, the Turkish sultan Murad II.

Once emperor his political position is difficult to say the least. On the one hand he has to oblige the sultan in order to sustain the truce concluded after the latter's latest unsuccessful attempt in 1422 to conquer the city. On the other hand he has to take steps to protect it from simply being engulfed within the relentlessly expanding Ottoman empire. To do so, Constantine, in spite of the resistance among his people, must rely on the continued support of the Aragonese Kingdom of Catalonia, the City Republics of Genoa and Venice, as well as the Papal State, all of which have vested commercial and military interests in the eastern Mediterranean. Consequently, he has no choice but to uphold the union of the Orthodox and the Catholic churches agreed in writing at a Church council held in Florence a decade earlier. But this union is not only bitterly resented by the common people. Considered heresy and treason, it has its fierce opponents among the upper clergy, yes, even among Constantine's own generals and ministers.

With hindsight it's easy to see that Constantine and the people backing his views were right in considering the union an absolute political necessity. But what could he have done to win the others – still piously holding on to the millenarian Nicene creed – over to his side? His was a time when miracles authored by God were not only prophesied but fervently believed in. To the people everything seemed to indicate that the time of Christ's promised second coming was imminent.

In the historical documents Constantine comes across as an experienced military leader and a responsible monarch eager to secure a modicum of safety, prosperity and peace for his sadly reduced and war-ravaged people. But there is also something melancholy, even lonely about him. Two wives die young without securing him an heir – he had loved them both. As we enter the scene he has, aged fifty, been forced to relinquish the hope of finding a third wife. Like so many other people of his status in society, his personality at times has a tendency to disappear behind its official and ceremonial embodiment.

As a man of honour – obliged by the noble institution and tradition created by the first of the Constantines more than a thousand years earlier – he knows that in the last instance he will have no choice but to make the city's destiny his own. I thus envisage his imperial crown to also be a wreath of thorns. Not that he consciously tries to emulate our Lord and Saviour; as the plot thickens, though, he willy-nilly seems to grow into his sandals.

Old, dilapidated, a mere shadow of its former glory, Constantinople remains the city of God *par excellence*, the very pillar on which the Holy Trinity rests. Moreover it is precisely the definition of the Trinity that lays at the heart of the endless theological disputes between the two churches, at a time when not only Islamic fundamentalists, but many Christians too, found it worthwhile to sometimes die for their faith. I find one quote attributed to the emperor especially pertinent in this regard: "What would posterity think of us if we didn't even put up a fight to defend our holy churches?"

Legend has it that Constantine during the decisive great battle was petrified by an angel and laid to rest as a marble statue under the Golden Gate. Ever since he is abiding the time when Christians will again unite. He will then come alive, rise to the occasion and drive the Moslems out of Europe. Lord Byron and other prominent people of his day hoped the moment had come during the Greek war for independence – he gave his own life for the cause while trying to swim across the Bosporus.

To Byron and other romantic characters (to this very day) the last of the Constantines was an indisputable hero, the double-headed eagle incarnate. In truth, he did obey the dramaturgic rules incumbent upon a hero of a Greek tragedy and could subsequently see his maker eye to eye. Posterity too has exonerated him. What he himself felt deep at heart about the whole thing is, perhaps, an altogether different matter, parts of which might be glimpsed through the cracks of this story.

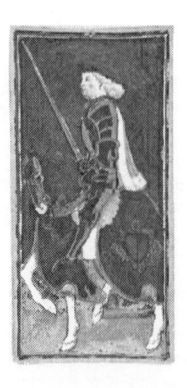

The Commander – Giovanni Giustiniani Longo
(all three names are alternately used in reference to him throughout the book)

A Genoese noble man, blond, blue-eyed, in his mid-thirties, of Norman descent on his mother's side. His influential family (its Coat of Arms carries an eagle similar to that of the empire) is represented both in the actual Republic of Genoa, and in the Aegean island of Chios, at this time under Genoese rule.

Charged with two, perhaps three, different missions – one of state, one of family obligation and one of entirely private character – he has above all been entrusted with the Herculean task of protecting the city's Genoese population and securing the Genoese trading town of Pera across the Golden Horn, a mere stone's throw from Constantinople itself. Giustiniani is the pivotal point in this account of the siege. Without him there simply wouldn't be any defence of Constantinople, and he is well aware of this. But although Pera is a point of utmost strategic interest to the Genoese by and large, Giustiniani's own position is ambiguous. True, he has, at his own expense, brought seven hundred mercenary fighters to reinforce the depleted domestic troops. But if this mission has indeed been sanctioned by the Grand Council back in Genoa, how come Pera itself has received orders (or has decided by its own volition) to remain neutral in the case of a military conflict with the Turks? It seems the Genoese are trying to simultaneously play at least two different hands. Doing so they also appear willing to sacrifice Giustiniani himself if need be.

His agenda is not obvious, and it's hard to guess in how many plots he is actually involved. One thing is for sure, though. The camaraderie which the ruthless siege forces upon the city's defenders brings him ever closer to the emperor, who's moral example in the midst of crisis makes a great impression upon him. An indivisible bond and a sense of mutual obligation between the two men is created. As time goes by Giustiniani finds himself more and more deeply involved in the "to be or not to be" of the celestial city. Tried to the utmost by the enemy and the wrath of God, maybe he too could in the end have been persuaded to become a tragic hero. But then we haven't taken that fair, foreign woman into account. She has a very different idea in her head, and the corresponding strength of heart to see things through.

State Secretary Francis

Is a childhood friend of Emperor Constantine and a key player behind the scenes. As a man of learning and, above all, diplomacy, he can be petty and scheming if he deems it necessary. But he can also exercise his reason and act accordingly. All his life he has striven to merit the respect and esteem he *a priori* enjoys with Constantine, and he does have the vanity of a courtier. Nonetheless, his loyalty to his friend and master is genuine. The empire to him, though presently reduced to a very small point in space, is an eternal truth which in the end must prevail. But even though this is his true feeling, his levelheadedness luckily gets the better of him and he clearly realises that wishes, dreams and the belief in miracles won't save the city from falling into the hands of the enemy.

As the drama opens Francis has been intensely preoccupied trying to rally the Christian powers to their aid. He has also tried to find his master a suitable new wife, but perhaps he has committed a major tactical error by single-handedly withdrawing the marriage proposal Constantine (then only a despot of Mistra in the Peloponnese) made to the only remaining daughter of the Duke of Venice. It doesn't take much imagination to realise that the old Doge doesn't exactly find it endearing to learn that the Byzantine Secretary of State suddenly, after Constantine has become crowned emperor, considers him, the head of the mighty Venetian Republic, too low in rank to come into question as a father-in-law.

Constantine has given Francis more or less carte blanche in finding him a suitable bride, but as time goes by, and the Venetians stubbornly refuse to show up at the scene of action, Constantine grows weary. It dawns on him that Doge Foscari – despite the Venetian Council of Ten meanwhile deciding in favour of a military intervention – probably does everything he can to delay the entire operation until it will be too late.

Constantine then begins to distrust his old friend and State Secretary's political judgment. Francis himself is devastated by what he feels to be his master's lack of appreciation for his unswerving loyalty to him and his family. This is also one of the reasons why he loathes their own local Grand Duke, Lucas Notaras. In Francis' eyes the emperor has been duped by this man, whom Francis considers deceitful, disloyal, and only simulating patriotism and noble bravery to the galleries, while in reality not giving a damn about the fate of the city and its population.

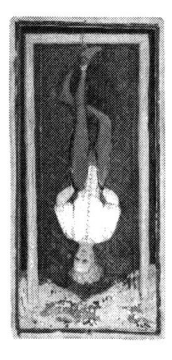

Lucas Notaras, Megadux

Is a member of a noble and influential family of long standing within the empire. He prides himself with the title Grand Duke. In this capacity he is also Prime Minister and Chief Admiral of the Fleet – a position of some consequence as Constantinople becomes exposed to a series of fierce naval attacks. Whether or not he is at heart set against the union of the two churches is not clear. Even though Francis regards him as a traitor to the unionist cause, Notaras' family has entertained privileged relations with the Catholic Republic of Venice for the better part of two centuries; he even has a second, Venetian, citizenship. In spite of this he has made himself rather popular among the sworn anti-unionists in the city, who are fond of attributing to him the saying: "I'd rather see the Sultan's turban than the Pope's mitre in Constantinople."

Neither the emperor, nor Francis, have ever heard him say so in person. It might just have been an emotional outburst, subsequently, and maliciously, quoted out of context, since Notaras is known to be temperamental, at times paying scant attention to the decorum of his position. But this lack of diplomatic caution certainly has not ingratiated him with Francis, who continues to consider him a menace to them all.

Francis' aversion on the other hand might be interpreted as his bad conscience for frivolously having waved a marriage proposal in the face of the Doge, only to pull it back when the latter readied himself to swallow the bait. It is possible that it is thanks to Lucas Notaras alone that so many Venetian galleys have in fact remained in the harbour, and that the Venetian population, fearing and loathing the Genoese both in the city and at Pera, and not really loving the Greeks either, could at all be persuaded to participate in the city's defence.

The Turkish Princess

Hadije, once wife to the late Sultan Murad II, is to this story what mercurial salt is to the hermetic process, the yeast to the dough, the fermentation to the grape: she is the secret agent that brings about the transformation of substances. Her provenance is shrouded in mystery. Where does she really come from? Who sent her? What is her purpose?

To Hadije herself, the outcome of certain key events have been obvious long before they actually occur. This is one reason why at first she must sound like a cry in the wilderness. Once brought within the ambit of the city she has to fight the incredulity of all those who see nothing but a devilishly seductive embodiment of the enemy, hence of evil, in her appearance. But even though, from the outset, she has the cards stacked against her (and although her bosom is stacked slightly more in her favour), she manages to drive home an overwhelmingly strong point, namely that the *memento mori* mustn't prevent us from realising that it is, above all, the exuberance of life we as human beings are meant to nourish and protect to the best of our capacity, and that dying for a lofty cause, however noble per se, may in the end prove to be an illusion without redemption.

With Hadije – or Felicia as her Christian name will be – the unforeseen factor enters the story, working as a catalyst, thus bringing the process to its last and perhaps inevitable consequence. I do charge her with *la forza del destino*, and she is the architect of treason, if you will. But in this capacity she is also a representation of the eternally feminine and that tenacious natural life which, no matter what, will always find a way.

The love story between her and the commander in chief is one of those that are simply bound to happen over and over again in the course of human history. In the semi-eternal light of archangels and apocalypses it is perhaps a banal story, meaning one we have heard many times before. But at the same time it is the symbol of an inner battle that bears the fatal hallmark of irresistible attraction combined with the determination of an indomitable soul. Whether or not she is in the end "right" in what she is doing is a moot point. It is not for nothing that the saying is so often repeated: "All is fair in love and war".

Doge Foscari

Francesco Foscari, descending from an ancient noble family, was elected Doge in Venice in 1423, thereby temporarily defeating a man destined to become his life-long political adversary, Peter Loredan, who ultimately brought him down. As our story begins to unfold, Foscari is already 80 years old and marked by a life of endless political intrigue.

During his long tenure Venice has been precipitated into numerous, and in the end very costly armed conflicts with the city state of Milan, first under the rule of Filippo Visconti, then by Francesco Sforza, a condottiere born in Venice who in 1447 became the implacable enemy of his native city by marrying Filippo Visconti's only remaining natural heir, Bianca Maria.

However, it wasn't just Foscari's obsession with *terra firma* domination on the plains of Po that made him reluctant to engage in overseas activities and send military aid to Constantinople. There was also his sense of hurt pride for having been rejected as an imperial father-in-law (see presentation of Secretary Francis above). In addition, his only son, accused of having conspired against the republic and, to this end, to have committed murder, was exiled from Venice to Crete. Foscari senior tries everything in his power to have his reputation restored and dreams of the day when the prodigal son will be able to return home to eventually – although the title as yet is not heritable – succeed him as Doge of Venice.

The dazzling last act of this real-life political drama inspired two prominent 19th century artists to dramatise the destinies of father and son. Lord Byron wrote a play on the theme of double and mutually exclusive loyalties – in this case the artful preservation of virtue and truth in a republic as opposed to the natural but potentially corrupt promotion of family interests – and Giuseppe Verdi composed a today all but forgotten opera named *I due Foscari*.

Around this time northern Italy witnessed the appearance of the first Tarot deck in western history, designed by an artist working for the court of Milan (still today this first deck bears the name of Visconti-Sforza, indicating that it was indeed produced in the late 1440s). Foscari – haphazardly coming into possession of these cards – becomes deeply puzzled by their enigmatic symbolism and he consults the humanists around him to elucidate him on the subject. Shortly after he is seen turning into something of a magus, dabbling in occult sciences in the hope of not only being able to foretell the future, but to actually change the course of destiny.

Pope Nicholaus V

Exhibits many of the paradoxes of the highly talented renaissance man. As a learned humanist he allegedly possesses a private library comprising over nine thousand books – one of his close friends even says: "What he does not know is outside the range of human knowledge". At the same time he can be a prelate of the most appalling bigotry, hurling intolerant decrees in all directions. One of his most infamous bulls, for example, gives the Portuguese the formal right to ruthlessly oppress, convert and then *enslave* all pagan populations they come across in their attempts to colonise the world. Simultaneously he envisages a morally irreproachable world of united Christians, but refuses to consider adjusting the dogmatic pillars of Catholicism even an inch. He advocates another crusade yet somehow fails to see what tremendous strategic importance the preservation of a Christian Constantinople, in the midst of a hostile Moslem world, would be to Rome itself. Although he eventually orders some ships to sail to the besieged city, it takes forever to get them under way since he refuses to pay his dues to his Venetian creditors.

As a man in constant self-contradiction it is no wonder he falls under the spell of Ramon Lull's magic wheel, inviting man to reflect on apparently irreconcilable opposites, such as: is it possible to be at the same time a good Catholic and a liar? In this spirit he also entertains a lengthy correspondence with Foscari, whom he suspects of not always being altogether sincere in his professed affirmation of the formal supremacy of the Papal State in matters mundane and religious.

It takes one to know one...

Mehmet the Sultan

To introduce to the reader the legendary Mehmet II, nemesis of Constantinople, I find no words better than the ones uttered by the awestruck State Secretary Francis at a state visit to the kingdom of Trebizond on the Black Sea coast:

> "– Your Majesty. With all due respect. We should perhaps do well in reminding ourselves that for every head cut off from the Lernian hydra two new ones emerged. The new Sultan is such a hydra. Although hardly twenty years of age he has developed several heads. One is belligerent, another deviously diplomatic.
>
> A third loves hunting, a fourth one speaks Persian, Hebrew, Greek and Latin fluently. A fifth knows the entire Islamic jurisprudence by heart, a sixth is accurately informed about the fathers of our church. A seventh drinks copious amounts of wine while the yet another studies maps, siege engines and weapons of mass destruction. The scope of his general intelligence and single-minded ambition is matched only by the fierceness of his many passions. He already has children but is said to prefer hardly mature boys to satisfy his lusts. He is, as you can understand, a perfect monster, but one to whom the designation of neither intelligence nor discipline can be denied. Above all, he's the most formidable, the most ruthless and implacable opponent to our Christian world since Tamerlane. And he will never give up the ambition to conquer every area within his reach still in Christian hands. Therefore, most venerable Majesty of the glorious House of the Comneni, I dare to disagree with the optimism expressed among our many friends around this table. Instead we should all concentrate on how to best unite and counter this formidable new threat to our peace and prosperity."

Bishop Leonard and Cardinal Isidore

Appear in this story as a couple of theological detectives. Leonard is born to Greek parents of what he himself refers to as "humble origins" on the island of Chios, at the time governed by the Genoese. Chios furthermore is the island on which the family of Giovanni Giustiniani – the right hand of the emperor during the siege – is in power. Leonard is consequently better informed than most others about the various motives that might have played a role in Giustiniani's decision to come to the rescue of the city.

As a young man Leonard becomes a Catholic and joins the Dominican order. Subsequent studies in Italy and contacts within the papal sphere make him eminently suited to mediate between the two churches, and a part of his mission to Constantinople is to make sure the Greeks are not in theory alone celebrating the *Laetentur Coeli* ("may the heavens rejoice"), which is the visible and audible liturgical expression of the unity of the two churches, concluded at the church Council in Ferrara and Florence in 1438.

Cardinal Isidorus, also Greek born and the former Metropolitan (Arch Bishop) of Kiev is the official papal legate to Constantinople and the highest ranking Catholic church official to be present during the siege. Both he and Cardinal Isidorus are forced to conclude that this new article of faith remains a paper construction as far as the divine worship by the people of Constantinople is concerned. At a high mass in Hagia Sophia on December 12, 1452, the hymn is recited, but the service is poorly attended. Lucas Notaras, the Megadux, is present but shows open hostility; the emperor himself seems listless.

The learned George Scholarius, also and better known under his monastic name Brother Gennadi, is conspicuously absent.

Brother Gennadi

Is the monk whom both Leonard and Isidorus suspect of conspiring against both the pope and the emperor. In spite of his erudition he is a very popular figure advocating blind faith in God and his capacity to work miracles when need be. For him to alter the millenarian creed in any way simply does not come into question. He is a typical example of the illuminated, inspired fanatic always to be found in communities held together by strong religious and traditional beliefs. It goes without saying that he is also an ascetic, carrying out countless daily prostrations and practising self-mortification by means of a knotted whip. In the eyes of the people he is the haggard prophet incarnate. That is one thing. But Isidore and Leonard from early on suspect his divine madness is not only simulated, but also that there is definite method to it. In the midst of the turmoil they do everything in their power to find out what he is, in reality, up to. When they finally do find out what is in the making, it has become too late to kill either him or the messenger.

Iannis Papanikolaou and his family

With the possible exception of the city itself, I believe Iannis and his family are the centre of gravity in this drama. In a way one could also say that they are the city. They are also the only members of the common people to detach themselves from the staffage in this account, and their role in so doing is crucial.

Iannis, the father, is a fisherman and it could well have stayed at that if he did not also possess a poet's soul. This soul in turn is linked to being a child at heart, which also could have been just fine had the circumstances been just a bit more favourable for poets and children. As it is he becomes entangled in a power-plot that his reason cannot fathom. Nonetheless he remains confident that he is participating in events that by far surpasses ordinary human understanding. To him this drama, no matter how fantastic, is real, and he is immensely proud to have been singled out to be the first to receive into the city of God our Lord and Saviour.

Iannis' wife and two children all carry names associated with imperial dynasties since times immemorial. There is the mother, Irene, who clearly sees that her husband's penchant for story-telling sometimes gets the better of his veracity. She herself struggles to keep family and home together under very trying circumstances while remaining calm and resourceful in critical moments. She has to her aid the clever eleven year old daughter Anna, whom she calls Princess and has promised a regal marriage in the fullness of time.

The eight year old Manuel, the namesake of so many legendary emperors, has inherited his father's psychic disposition. In addition he is from time to time afflicted with epileptic seizures. He too sees things hidden to the ordinary mortal eye, and his mother and older sister are not only worried about his physical health, but about his mental state too.

It would be fair to surmise that young Manuel, based on the evidence, is the one closest to God of all the men and women involved in this apocalyptic battle. It is through his eyes that I would finally like to view this story, namely as an instant in time and space where fact and fiction have temporarily been suspended in a higher union, not to say – reality.

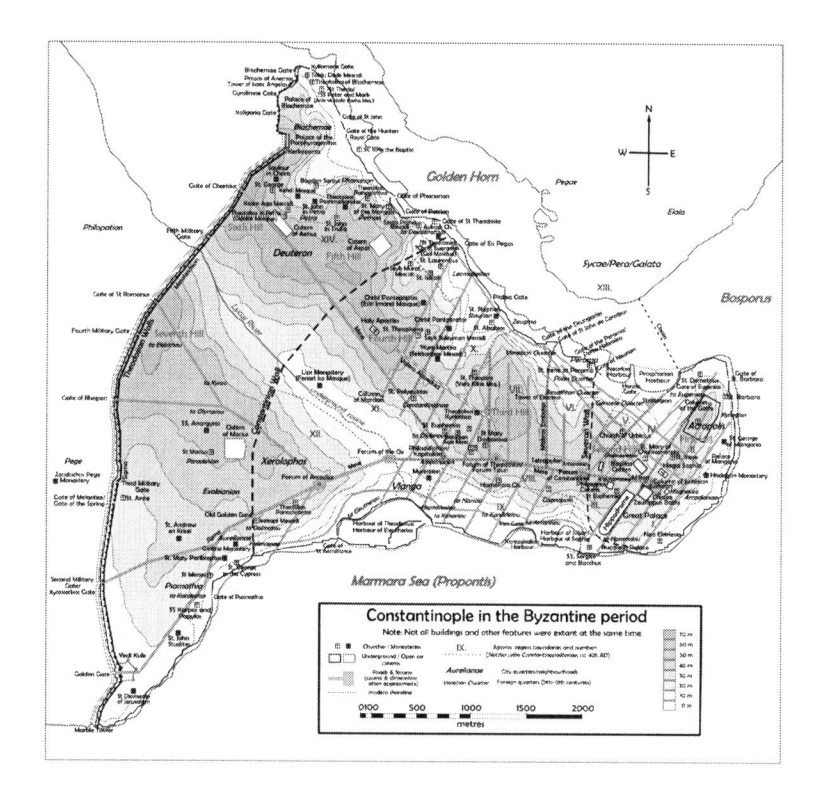

The City

Consecrated by Emperor Constantine I in AD 330 as the new capital of Rome, it subsequently became the capital of the Byzantine empire. It was to remain so through a checkered history of more than 1100 years until finally conquered by the Turkish Ottomans in 1453. The city, which ever since has remained in Turkish hands, was officially renamed Istanbul in 1950.

Through its famous basilica, the Hagia Sophia (Holy Wisdom), raised at a time when Rome lay in ruins after having been sacked and violated by one barbarian tribe after the other, Constantinople in the Middle Ages became known as the epitome of Christianity on Earth. Jerusalem would have been another candidate, but it was never on par with Constantinople in terms of architectural and artistic splendour. Secondly, it was never lastingly held by Christians.

Constantinople was able to withstand so many protracted sieges first and foremost because of its strategic and protected location – the Golden Horn is not only an excellent natural harbour; once the famous floating boom across its inlet was in place it could also be easily defended. The city itself, heavily fortified, is located at the southern end of the Bosporus which makes it both easily accessible and an excellent point for control and surveillance of all maritime traffic through the narrow straits that connect the Mediterranean with the Black Sea.

In the 5th century, during the reign of emperor Theodosius, the original city walls were declared obsolete and a magnificent new defence system, designed by master engineer Anthemius, was erected further to the west, along the line where its remnants now cut right through modern Istanbul.

Ironically the weakest link in that chain is still today an open wound in the cityscape. A multi-lane highway runs through the completely leveled walls in both directions. The remaining ramparts on both sides are used as outdoor toilets, aptly garnished with general rubbish, crushed bottles, cans and condoms. A part of the wall system a bit higher up on the eastern side serves as a refuge for male prostitution. A highway bridge runs perpendicularly to the wall. Under it, the gypsies have taken shelter and hang around in improvised lounges consisting of discarded furniture, as an alternative venue to occupying their make-shift shacks nearby. To be honest, it's not one of the more quaint places of the city, and it is not frequented by tourists.

Nonetheless it was right here that the destiny of Constantinople was decided. It was right here – on a rainy day in September, overwhelmed by the humdrum of the megapolis – that I was granted a secret glimpse of the city as she might have presented herself to a single witness during one foggy evening, full of strange omens, decay and despair, at the end of the month of May, 1453. And it was right here that the idea came to me to write the story of her fall as I see it.

This, strangely, was the image that opened the gate to the hidden chambers of imagination:

> "Fields, orchards, churches, monasteries, houses, villas, palaces, squares, streets and alleys – all enveloped in the same thick moisture, slowly depositing itself on every roof, dripping down, drop by drop, as though descending the insides of a gigantic watery time glass: tick, tock, tick, tock, like a clock still moving but showing no time. In once bustling loggias and open court yards made slippery by fungus and lichen, vast mosaic frescoes majestically sunk into a sea of no return. Neptunes, tritons, sirens and dolphins, dispossessed of their pagan innocence and exuberant gaiety, gaping empty-eyed at the forlorn silence over and around

as they disappear into the depths of oblivion. Neptune's horses, the very emblem of the Meltemmia at the height of summer, dragged out of sight by a giant octopus; the sirens dissolving into foam. Strewn all over the floors, flowers massacred in the prime of youth, left to wither and litter the cool marble turned sickly green and sulphurously yellow in a misplaced autumn. Red roses nipped in their bud and thrown to the ground by showers of hail, rain, pumice and sand. All exquisite art, all venerable tradition, covered in debris, disintegrating, rotting, sinking, and, most disheartening of them all, a magnificent statue of Nike, split in two by a falling beam infested with snails."

Illustrations above in part drawn from the Visconti-Sforza tarot deck.

KINGDOM OF HUNGARY
MOLDAVIA
Golden Horde
SEA OF AZOV
Kertch
Kaffa (Feodosia) To Genoa
Cherson
Save R.
Sirmium
Semlin
Temesvar
BOSNIA
Belgrade
Severin
Tergovist
WALLACHIA
Aluta R.
Danube R.
Dobrudsha
Silistria
Vidin
Spalato
Drina R.
KINGDOM OF SERVIA
Under Stephen Dushan)
1331-1355
Rasa
Ragusa
Rep. Ragusa
Cattaro
Dioclea
Prishtina
Nissa
Nicopolis (Nikopol)
Tirnova
KINGDOM OF BULGARIA
Varna
BLACK SEA
Sinope
EMPIRE OF TREBIZOND
Trebizond
Samsun
Scodra
Kroia
Scopia
Durazzo (To Naples)
Prilip
Ochrida
Kastoria
Philippopolis
Maritza R.
Adrianople
Amastris
Constantinople
Ismid (Nicomedia)
Boli
Thessalonica
Thasos
Gallipoli
Isnik (Nicaea)
Halys R.
Karahissar
Imbros
Brusa
Angora
Corfu
To Naples
Janina
Trikala
Lemnos
OTTOMAN TURKS (OSMANLI)
Arta
Larissa
Karasi
Karaman
R
K
S
Leucadia
IONIAN
Cephalonia
ISLANDS
Zante
Lamia (Zituni)
Lepanto
D. of Athens
Negropont
Lesbos
To Genoa
Chios
Sarukhan
Kermian
Smyrna
Philadelphia
Aidin
Ephesus
Maeander R.
Akserai
Patras
Achaia
Athens
Byz.
MOREA
Mistra
Prov. of Peloponnesus
Modon
Coron
Monemvasia
DUCHY OF NAXOS
Miletus
Mentesha
Halicarnassus
Hamid
Teke
Iconium (Konieh)
Adalia (Adalia)
KINGDOM OF ARMENIA
Tarsus
Euphrates R.
Aleppo
Antioch
Knights of St. John
Rhodes
Crete
Candia
KINGDOM OF CYPRUS
DOMINION OF THE MAMELUKES
Tripoli
G
H
I
J
K
L

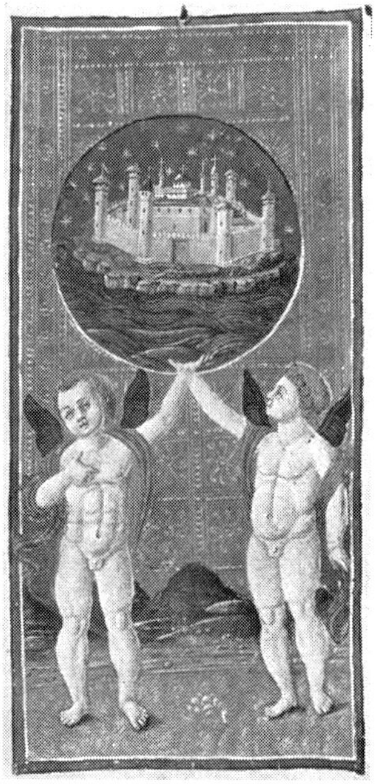

Other books in English by Lars Holger Holm available through Arktos:

Come Snow – A Psychic Thriller

Fawlty Towers – A Worshipper's Companion

Other books published by Arktos:

The WASP Question by Andrew Fraser

Why We Fight by Guillaume Faye

De Naturae Natura by Alexander Jacob

It Cannot Be Stormed by Ernst von Salomon

The Saga of the Aryan Race by Porus Homi Havewala

Against Democracy and Equality: The European New Right by Tomislav Sunic

The Problem of Democracy by Alain de Benoist

The Jedi in the Lotus by Steven J. Rosen

Archeofuturism by Guillaume Faye

A Handbook of Traditional Living

Tradition & Revolution by Troy Southgate

Can Life Prevail? A Revolutionary Approach to the Environmental Crisis by Pentti Linkola

Metaphysics of War: Battle, Victory & Death in the World of Tradition by Julius Evola

The Path of Cinnabar: An Intellectual Autobiography by Julius Evola

The Initiate: Journal of Traditional Studies